No Place Like Home

Tallenmere – Book 4

By

Mysti Parker

Published by
Melange Books, LLC
White Bear Lake, MN 55110
www.melange-books.com

Dedicated to my very own Tyger, who I love more every day.

Tyger Tyger, burning bright,
In the forests of the night;
What immortal hand or eye,
Could frame thy fearful symmetry?

~from "The Tyger" by William Blake

Prologue

A hidden lair...

They always scream.

Never once do they accept their place in the timeless dance of predator and prey. They cling to their mortality like a child clings to a tattered blanket, unwilling to let go. Yet, they *must* know their days are not without limit. Every creature on Tallenmere serves one purpose or another. These young things, so tender and precious, are serving the noblest purpose of all.

They are food.

Tonight's prey has gone from screaming to pleading when she's brought to my chamber. It's piteous, really—the whimpers, the big round eyes full of desperation and fear.

She's on her knees, quivering as violently as her voice. "Please let me go. I just want to go home."

I close my eyes and inhale deeply. Her terror is rich and musky. Fear, for those who have not yet acquired its taste, is a delicacy. To be the one inspiring fear, a privilege.

With utmost respect for the impending sacrifice, I kneel before the girl. She's fifteen, maybe. Or perhaps twenty-five? Human aging perplexes me. In any case, she's fully developed. Her life force—some may call it a soul—ebbs and wanes just at the surface, flaring bright with hopes and dreams. The old are no good to me. Their energy is buried too deep, rooted fast with stubbornness and routine. They do not fill me as the young ones do.

Yet, fear encases this one's life force in an impervious shell.

Extracting it in this state would take too much of *my* energy, leaving me hungry again too soon.

"Shh, darling. I won't hurt you." I skim my knuckles across her smooth cheek, smearing the tracks of her tears. "Don't be afraid."

She gives a slight nod, but her eyes remain skeptical. At least she's quiet now. They all turn quiet when I smile and speak sweetly. It's perhaps my greatest weapon of all, this beauty. I have my father to thank for the likeness, my mother to thank for nurturing it.

The longer I kneel, stroking her cheek, smoothing her thick brown hair, the more she relaxes. Fear subsides, gradually releasing its grip on her life force.

"What is your name, child?"

"M-M-Mavelle."

"A beautiful name for a beautiful girl."

"Who are you? What do you want with me?"

My smile widens, and I rub the round top of her ear—another human trait that mystifies me. "I need you, Mavelle."

"Please, my lady, my husband will be worried for me. Just tell me what I can do for you, and I will do it. Then, let me go. I won't tell anyone about you."

"Oh, how sweet. You are married?"

She swallows hard and nods. "Yes, we had just finished the ceremony when your...when they took me."

"Did he kiss you?"

Brow furrowed, she nods again, slowly.

"I'd wager he's never kissed you like this."

Hands on her shoulders, I pull her to me, so close I can smell the bread and honey on her breath. Her eyes widen. I press my lips to hers, and she whimpers. Still and patient as a tyger, I wait, kneading her knotted muscles beneath my fingers. And, it doesn't take long for her to exhale with a sigh, for *her* lips to part.

I know the battle raging inside her—how wrong it feels—woman kissing woman. Yet, when the moment dawns, it feels anything *but* wrong. It's warm. Gentle. Plump lips against plump lips. I slide my tongue inside to meet the barricade of her teeth, but soon they open to me, too. And she flicks with her own tongue, testing the waters of our

2

uncommon union.

Her hands have moved of their own accord now, tentatively seeking a refuge on my waist. Desire aches between my legs, pulls my nipples into painful peaks, but it is a rare night that I give into complete temptation during a feed. The hollow emptiness at my core must be filled.

Hunger wins the battle once again.

I deepen the kiss and lock my arms around her. She tenses briefly, but responds in kind until she feels it. Feels me drawing on her energy. And she plants her palms flat against my shoulders, tries to push me away, but it's too late. Already, she's wilting in my embrace, her mouth still molded to mine, plump lips growing cold.

By Tyr, it's pure pleasure—energizing, enervating, unexplainable pleasure! I direct part of her energy into the hollow chamber of the amulet that I must fill, but the rest will nourish me. I do not release her until every last flicker of her essence is inside me.

Then, I simply let go. Her body slumps to the stone floor—as inanimate and inhuman as any object in this chamber. I stand and dab her saliva from my mouth with a handkerchief, thankful to not have to rely on blood like my weaker creations.

Her escort, a necessity I'd rather do without, is standing quietly in the shadows, watching.

"You want me to give her to the vamps?" His voice is raspy, eyes gleaming.

I glance at the bulge in his trousers. Aroused, as usual. "No, deliver her to her husband. He has been searching for her. Let's not disappoint him."

He's staring at the girl, one fist clenched tight at his side, the other stroking his thigh, skimming the outskirts of his erection. He'll botch everything if I don't allow him a release.

I lean over the back of a dining chair and pull my robe up to my waist. His response is swift, and as he plunges into me time and again, I smile, knowing I'm one step closer to having everything that was taken from me.

Chapter One

~ Mirabelle ~

Port Valor, Capital of Hezral, ten years earlier...

Every spring when the star serpents returned from the southern skies, Lysander and I began our late-night fishing for the season. The ice covering the water around the wharf had all but melted, so we could cast our lines with ease. With all the boats tucked in their berths for the evening, the fish grew brave enough to venture out among their keels and rudders.

This time of night, we could also be out alone together without everyone asking why we hadn't gotten married already. We were sixteen, adults by Hezrali standards, and expected to contribute to the population.

But tonight, I was running late *and* we had company.

Marlow, the Wharfmaster's son, had Lysander by the collar in one bulky fist. Poor Lysander dangled out over the water just off the dock.

Darkness hid my presence as I crept behind some shipping crates to watch. The fishy aroma from the day's haul and Marlow's body odor burned my nose. I had to pull up my collar and breathe through my shirt so I didn't suffocate.

"I told you," Marlow said, "I get what I wants, and I wants that Hearton girl of yours."

"She's spoken for. Leave her alone already." Lysander held to Marlow's arm with both hands, looking anxiously to the frigid water below. He could swim, but only enough to not drown within minutes.

4

The cold would take his breath before he even had a chance to drown.

"Spoken for don't mean anything. Not when the Wharfmaster speaks, and he says I can have her if I wants."

"No, she's mine. Leave her alone or I'll—"

"You'll what?"

Lysander hauled back one bony leg and kicked Marlow's shin, but the ugly brute didn't even flinch. Like his father, the Wharfmaster, Marlow was tall and solid as an ebonwood.

"Was that supposed to hurt?" Marlow said, laughing.

I'd let Lysander suffer long enough, so I sneaked up behind Marlow, silently drawing one of my silver daggers from its sheath on my belt. Lysander saw me, eyes growing wide.

"No," I said, startling Marlow enough to make him spin in my direction. "But I bet this will."

I drew back my boot and kicked it hard right into Marlow's groin. He made a strangled sound and let Lysander go with a splash right into the water. *Not good.* Marlow hunched over, both hands cupping his man parts, and groaned.

"You bitch, I'll—"

I poked the tip of my dagger beneath his chin. "You'll what? What sort of dreadful things will you do to me? Take a hint—you'll never get me in your bed. Is that understood?"

With Lysander splashing and sputtering like a dying seal, it was hard to concentrate, but I had to hold my ground.

Marlow started to nod, but the tip of the blade pierced his skin. Blood dripped onto my hand. If I hurt him too bad, we could be in really big trouble. No one wanted to incur the Wharfmaster's wrath. Four hundred pounds of brute strength was no match for my skinny frame, nor Lysander's.

Lucky for me, the moon peeked out from behind a cloud so he could see my eyes. Holding my dagger steady, but still grazing his skin, I took my chance and brought my face within inches of his. His eyes locked onto mine, and he went slack-jawed as I made the connection. Good—I had him.

You will leave Lysander and me alone from now on. In fact, you won't be pushing anyone around anymore. You'll be—I almost suggested perfect, but people would suspect witchcraft or something equally superstitious—*a decent man, kind to the ladies and fair to the men. Got it?*

"Yes, I'll be decent," he said in a slow monotone.

Lovely. Now run home and tell your father you don't want that Hearton girl after all.

Stepping back, I broke the connection, keeping my dagger out just in case. I wasn't sure if my 'gift' was all that effective. Marlow shook his head like he had water in one ear and stumbled back down the dock. He finally steadied his steps and kept walking into town until I lost sight of him. At least I'd convinced him to leave us alone for now.

"Lysander!" Hurrying to the edge of the dock, I feared he would be frozen solid. Instead, he had pulled himself from the frigid sea and was climbing up the steep, washed out shoreline. I ran to meet a very wet, shivering Lysander, who hugged himself while his teeth chattered.

"Is he g-g-gone?"

"Yes, he's gone." I took off my cloak and draped it around him; then I gave him a quick kiss. "Oh my, you're freezing. Let's go get you thawed out."

"I'm s-s-sorry," he said, as I pulled him toward his parents' house.

"Why?"

"I sh-sh-should have f-f-fought him off."

I knew what he meant—that he should have *been able* to fight Marlow, but Lysander really wasn't fighting material. Whereas Marlow was built like a huge tree, Lysander would be more of a sapling.

"Don't worry about it," I said.

"It's m-my job to p-protect you."

Sliding my dagger back into its sheath, I said, "I don't need protecting. I need my best friend."

"More than that, r-right?"

"Right."

I still hadn't gotten used to the fact that we'd be married next week, under the light of the full moon in the Grove. Lysander and I were both singletons. Our parents were best friends. It was only natural that we marry, though most of our lives we'd been more like siblings who argued a lot. His parents were hosting a party for us tomorrow so our neighbors could bring gifts to bless our fertility. Lysander was a good kisser, but beyond that, it felt a little weird. He still seemed more like brother than lover to me. I worried that marriage would change us, and maybe not for the better.

An hour later, a much warmer and dryer Lysander sat a foot away, dipping his fishing rod casually while his cork bobber hopped over the dark water. As usual, the conversation migrated to marriage. And as usual, my frown deepened the more he dwelled on it.

"I think one wife is plenty," he said, drawing his untouched bait in and casting the line out again. "Even if a man is rich, how can he satisfy more than one woman?"

"Maybe *you* can't," I answered with a laugh. "But look at Wharfmaster Shruck. There's plenty of him to go around. Marlow's not far behind."

He shrugged. "I don't know. Maybe I should make an offer for the Bearden sisters. Lana and Jeena have some really nice—"

"Lysander!" I plucked at the shirt covering my flat chest. The three Bearden sisters belonged to Darvis Bearden, owner of Bearden's Fishhouse, the largest inn and tavern in Port Valor. Every boy in the city drooled over their curves and money.

He laughed. "What? It's true. Mavelle's really cute, too. Maybe I can get Darvis to throw her in if my offer's good enough."

"Oh really? Like those Fishhouse girls would want to marry you. They're almost as rich as the Wharfmaster. Besides, Mavelle's ten!"

"I'd have to wait a while, but she's cute."

"She comes over to play almost every afternoon. Stays in my room for hours, like the annoying little sister I never had."

Lysander was right. Mavelle really was cute. And sweet. Not at all like her stepmothers. We got along well, and I had to admit, I enjoyed her visits.

"You can't really blame her for not wanting to go home," he said, "with those mean wives of her dad's. All the more reason someone should rescue her from her plight."

"What are you, a paladin?" Something tugged at my line. I sat up straighter on the dock, tugging back just a little in the hopes I could get it to take the whole scaleworm *and* the hook. "Don't you ever think about

7

leaving Port Valor? Don't you want to see what's out there beyond the valley? We could visit Leogard, try some of that famous draeberry wine."

He looked at me, mouth agape, as though I had tentacles coming out of my head. I couldn't pretend I hadn't thought about going elsewhere. Port Valor was the largest city in the Hezrali province. But, our lives revolved around the unglamorous world of fishing and root vegetables. The streets were muddy ruts, the people hairy and odorous. When the men weren't fishing, they were getting drunk or bedding a woman. The most fun to be had for the younger sort was watching the rare elven traveler become a walking icicle in our perpetually cold climate.

We did have the honor of King Damien living within our city border. He and his family, which included a few wives, several children and his heir, Prince Halcyon, only made rare public appearances. They were so reclusive, I probably wouldn't recognize them if I saw them in common clothing. His castle sat at the southern edge, away from the fishy aroma and at the northern side of the Cavitel Valley where he could watch for any threats from Leogard. But, I didn't see other places as a threat. I saw them as an opportunity.

Lysander was still giving me the evil eye. "Why should I want to leave? I have everything I need right here, including you."

"Just to see the world..." There was his you've-got-tentacles stare again. "Oh, come on. If you had any brothers, you'd probably have to leave anyway."

"Why, because I'm so scrawny?" He sat up tall and stiff like one of the lone pilings from the broken pier beside us.

He was so touchy about his size. We were both tall and bony and unlikely to grow much more. After Marlow's assault, Lysander would be sensitive about it for weeks.

"You want me to leave?" he asked, his question ending in a high-pitched hysterical tone.

"No, Lysander, relax. I meant that you're lucky you don't have to compete with any brothers for an eligible girl. And if you left, you'd have to take me with you anyway. After next week, you won't be able to get rid of me."

He leaned close and kissed my cheek. "Good, because I don't want to. Besides, I'd have to work myself to death to make an offer for the Bearden sisters. We don't have enough obtainable girls to go around with all the rich, bear-sized men snatching up multiple wives."

"Yeah, well be glad you're not a girl, worrying every day that the Wharfmaster or Marlow, or some other bear-man will come calling to add you to his harem."

"Well, you won't have to worry about that, will you?"

"I suppose not, but what's to keep you from taking on another wife or two when you're tired of me?"

"Money, for one thing. But, it would never happen anyway, no matter how much money I have. I love you. Only you. Forever."

He'd told me this several times before, but it still made me uneasy. I wasn't sure why, except that I didn't feel worthy of him somehow. He was good and sweet and kind, and me—I wasn't really any of that. Another solid tug on the line. I yanked it back. The empty hook leapt from the water and dangled sadly in front me.

He sat silently for a moment, then scooted closer and put his arm around me. "Why don't you ever say it?"

"Say what?"

"That you love me. You do, don't you?"

"Why do you love *me* anyway? You used to find more joy in putting crayfish in my boots than kissing me."

He shrugged. "Do I need a reason? I just do. Is that so bad?"

All this talk of love plus a night of water rescues and stolen bait, and I was done with fishing. I stood and secured the line to my rod. Of course, Lysander had better luck. "Hey, Mr. Sentimental—you caught something."

"What? Oh!" Lysander jerked his rod and out came a fish from the water, scales glittering in the moonlight. It arched over his head and landed with a flappy thud behind him on the dock. "Hey, it's a copji!"

"Aw—Mom makes the best fishcakes with those."

"I know." He hurried to his feet, grabbed the line and held up his foot-long prize. It flopped at the end of the hook. "Well too bad," he said, waggling his eyebrows. "I bet Lana and Jeena would appreciate it more."

I got to my feet, grabbed his collar and attacked his lips with mine,

9

meaning to smack him a good one and go on my way. But, he responded eagerly, wrapping an arm around my waist, drawing me closer. The kiss softened, and I warmed in places where I'd been cold all night. It felt wonderful.

Pushing him away gently, I took his fishing line with one hand. With the other, I slid out one of my daggers. One quick swipe, and Lysander's copji was mine.

"Thanks for the fish," I said and hurried right home. My mouth watered from thoughts of fishcakes and Lysander's kiss.

My mother Evetta met me at the door. "Oh, you caught a copji!"

"Lysander did."

She smiled. "I see. He'll be a good fisherman and a good provider."

"We don't even have a house yet."

"It's coming along. Until then, you'll have plenty of room in the Devlin's home."

"Right…spending our wedding night in my in-laws' house. How romantic!"

"Be content with what you have, Mirabelle. Your father and I…"

"Yes, I know—you lived in a one room shack with my grandparents. I don't even want to imagine *your* wedding night."

Mom laughed while she tied her healer's apron and fetched her birthing supplies. "Tannah Lurck's in labor. Would you like to assist me?"

"Really? You really want me to?"

As one of the town's midwives and herbal healers, Mom had tended to many births and ailments. But she'd not let me come along for any of it. After an emotional fishing excursion with Lysander, I was more than happy to have a distraction.

"I wouldn't ask if I didn't. Let's go."

Ten minutes later, I wished I had gone to bed instead.

Mom and I sat in front of Tannah, who sat upon a worn, stained birthing chair. Sweat poured from her forehead. She wouldn't stop screaming. Her wails sounded like an amateur violinist practicing an inch from my ear.

"You must push with the contractions, rest and breathe in between," Mom said.

She didn't listen. Her husband Silas Lurck was a hunchbacked, scrawny old leather worker with a sparse gray beard. He sat nearby, whittling a piece of wood. The more Tannah screamed, the more wood chips flew. I think he'd meant it to be a rattle for the baby, but the end had started coming to a point like a spear.

Silas's other wife Flora—a woman past her child-bearing years—left her unfinished stew on the stove and came to stand beside Tannah. "You must calm down. The Shaman is on his way to offer his blessing, so concentrate and bring this new life into the world."

Mom glanced at me. "Perhaps you should go home, Mira."

"I'm fine," I said, though my head ached terribly from all the noise.

She always acted nervous when it came to the Shaman. He was Port Valor's spiritual leader and King Damien's most trusted advisor. Truth be told, he probably held more power than our reclusive king, so getting a blessing from him must have been quite an honor.

Tannah quieted for a moment, and Flora took her hand. That was a mistake. Tannah applied a death grip that made Flora cry out then resumed screeching.

Poor Silas wobbled in his chair. He had turned pale as lamb's wool. I thought he might faint. He'd had two other wives besides Flora, and both had died young. None of them had given him children. He'd been ecstatic when Tannah, a young lady barely in her twenties, had finally gotten pregnant.

I let my eyes relax, directing them to Tannah's periphery so I could detect her aura, yet another gift I'd had for a while. The energy flashed bright red with puffs of black, ebbing and waning like a fog being sucked up and spit out again. She was anxious, terrified, on the verge of panic. My eyes watered. If she didn't be still and get the baby out, they could both die.

Mom knelt in front of Tannah, trying to pry her legs apart so she wouldn't squish the baby that was *right there*. Why couldn't she just push it out and get it over with? Another shrill scream flared her aura into a blinding red light and a sharp pain sliced through my head.

Death by noise wasn't the way I wanted to go. I crowded in by Mom and slapped both my hands onto Tannah's cheeks, holding her face still. She stopped screaming, shut her mouth and opened her tear-reddened eyes. Her lips twisted in anger, she thrashed her head, but I held tight. She opened her mouth to scream again, but I made her look at me. Her eyes widened. I had her.

"Mira..." Mom whispered. Her warning was clear, though left unsaid.

Calm down. My thoughts projected through our shared connection, through her eyes, the pathway into her conscious mind. *Relax your body until the next contraction, then push. Let your body do the work. Ignore the pain.*

Tannah nodded, her face relaxed, and I let her go. Her head rested on the back of the birthing chair, and she took a deep breath. Mom gently guided Tannah's legs apart. She glanced at Flora, who was staring at me with wide, unblinking eyes, her mouth twitching as though she was shocked, disgusted, or maybe both. Mom looked at me, and I knew I'd done something really stupid, something she'd warned me about time and again.

But, another contraction came, and in two calm, but focused pushes, the baby's head emerged. Silas stood, sticking his miniature spear-toy into his goat-hide vest pocket. Color had returned to his cheeks, and a wary smile played beneath his mustache.

Another push, and the baby was out.

"It's a boy!" Mom said then wiped the baby clean and cut his umbilical cord.

Silas hooted with joy and grabbed Flora, spinning her around in an impromptu dance.

Flora smacked at his chest. "Let me go, you silly man!" But she laughed right along with him. Though many older wives would have shown at least a measure of jealousy, Flora loved Tannah like a sister, so any children the younger woman produced would be loved just as much.

Tannah watched them with a tired smile, while I let myself imagine what it would be like to bear Lysander's children. Would they have his jet-black hair or my full lips? Would it hurt this much, and if so, who would calm me down when I screamed like a willowhoot?

Turning back to Mom, I froze. Her smile had faded. She held the baby there on her lap and just stared at it.

"What's wrong?" Tannah asked, righting herself as much as she could so she could see her child.

"The baby," Mom whispered. "His legs are malformed."

Silas and Flora stopped dancing. Their joyous expressions turned to horror. Tannah shook her head, reaching for the infant. "No, you're wrong. He's fine. Give me my baby!"

Mom handed the child over, and I got a glimpse of his deformity. One leg was very short, ending at the knee with a tiny foot with only two toes. His other leg was the proper length, but ended in a clubfoot. Tannah's lip quivered as she took in the sight of her crippled son. She wept silently, but looked down at him with so much love, it brought tears to my eyes. And why not? He was beautiful, pink, and healthy. Perfect just the way he was. He'd have extra challenges in life, but who didn't? If anything, he could become stronger by it.

Someone pounded on the door, breaking the spell. Tannah held the baby tight to her chest. Silas hurried to the door, opening it just a crack. Muffled voices followed, then Silas said, "Everything's fine. He and Tannah are sleeping sound, my lord. Tomorrow would be a better time for the blessing."

The baby didn't cooperate, and let out a hungry cry.

"Ah, sounds like he's awake. We will come in, bless the child, and be out of your way."

Mom whispered, "The Shaman's here."

She grabbed my hand and pulled me past the curtain separating the great room from the kitchen. She ran to the back door and swung it open, waving for me to come. "Mira, hurry—we must get you home."

"Wait," I whispered, peeking through the curtain to the great room.

Silas was still trying to reason with them. "But, Tannah is tired, my lord…"

One of the Shaman's guards pushed his way in, almost knocking Silas off his feet. The Shaman entered next, his black-feathered cloak whipping in the wind behind him. Black kohl striped his face. It surrounded his eyes, making the whites glaringly bright. He wore his hair shaved close on each side of his head, with one thick strip of finger-long hair down the middle, made stiff with beeswax. I used to have nightmares about him, though I'd never seen him this close. Parents all over Port Valor used to scare their children into staying in at night with scary stories about the Shaman taking them away to turn them into a pack of snow wolves.

Maybe the stories weren't just tall tales after all. His dark eyes, the smirk on his lips—behind the makeup and weird hairdo was a man who reveled in power and who would do anything to hold onto it.

He strode straight over to Tannah, while one of the guards blocked Silas with a large two-handed axe. The other guard did the same with Flora.

"Let's see the new arrival," the Shaman said.

Tannah had wrapped him up tightly in his blanket, but she still hesitated.

The Shaman bent down, leveling his cold, dark eyes with hers. "Well?"

"Please, please, I beg of you!" Silas cried. "He'll not be a burden, I promise."

Tannah and Flora both snapped their gazes to Silas. He closed his eyes and hung his head, knowing he'd given their secret away, but it was inevitable. The Shaman would see the baby, one way or another.

He held his hands out to Tannah, palms up. She started crying hard, which only made the baby cry harder. My heart thudded, fueled by fear. I wanted to run in there and help—to look the Shaman in the eyes and tell him to go jump off a cliff. But, how was I supposed to do that with two armed guards watching?

He narrowed his eyes until it looked like they'd disappeared within his black mask. Without a word, he reached out and snatched the baby from his mother's arms. A few quick flips of the blanket, and he nodded at the deformity.

"You know the will of King Damien. Only the able-bodied are a benefit to Hezral."

"We'll take him to Leogard or north to the barbarian lands." Tears glistened off Silas's grizzled face and graying beard. He sounded desperate. "He won't burden Hezral. Please, have mercy!"

Flora went to Tannah, and the two clung to each other, weeping bitterly.

The Shaman said nothing, just wrapped the baby up, turned around and walked out the door.

Silas fell to his knees, weeping uncontrollably. "My son…my son!"

Tears rolled from my eyes. It wasn't fair. What could be so wrong with the baby to take him away like that? The guards lowered their axes and followed like good minions. Mom grabbed my hand and tried to pull me away, but then Silas staggered to his feet and pulled the spear-like piece of whittling wood from his vest. He charged at the last guard, plunging the sharpened point into the man's right shoulder, close to his neck. The guard cried out, spinning around and knocking Silas to the floor.

Flora and Tannah screamed. The other guard ran back inside, took one look at his partner then hoisted his axe above his head.

I drew a dagger and started to pull the curtain back so I could throw it. If I missed, I could rush in and slash his throat before he knew what was happening. Dad had trained me very well.

But, Mom grabbed my wrist and held tight. She jerked me away from the curtain with a harsh whisper. "No, Mira!"

The Shaman's voice handed down the sentence. "Kill him."

There was a thud from the great room that reminded me of Dad butchering a goat—the sound the axe made when it severed the neck. A second of silence followed, then horrific screams from Tannah and Flora. I wanted to throw up, but Mom didn't give me time for that. She dragged me so hard I could barely stay on my feet. I stumbled after her. We ran through the Lurck's kitchen garden. My foot sank into a muddy rut, twisting my ankle. I cried out in pain, but Mom kept pulling, and I kept limping along behind her until we were safely at our back door.

Mom screamed, "Abbott!" and pounded on the door with her fist.

Dad flung it open, took one look at her face, and ushered me into the house in a panic. They whispered back and forth for the longest time, saying things about escaping with me, keeping me indoors, and every other fear-inducing scenario they could think of. I sat at the kitchen table rubbing my ankle while they argued by the hearth.

My gifts—or curses, if I'm honest about my feelings on the subject—had been a source of worry ever since I turned ten and started seeing auras. Mom and Dad convinced me to never tell anyone about it, warning about 'terrible consequences'. I didn't understand what those could be, but I kept quiet. The mind-bending had come about a year ago, on a normal day of tending our livestock. We had a nanny goat that wouldn't nurse her kid. The aura around her underside was discolored—a sickly brown instead of a healthy red. I checked her udder and as I guessed, it was red and hot, sure signs of a blockage. After some heat, gentle massage, and a poultice Mom concocted, she produced milk again, but the stubborn old nag still wouldn't feed her baby. She kicked the poor thing every time it tried to suckle, leaving it bleating and growing weaker by the hour. Holding her horns to keep her head still, I looked into the nanny goat's eyes. I didn't say anything out loud, but my mind conjured up the image of her standing calmly while the kid nursed and had its fill. She did exactly what I pictured.

Dad had watched the brown in my eyes swirling as I did this. He and Mom had been terrified ever since. "Be responsible with this power, Mira," Dad had said. "Don't use it for your own gain, and never use it here in the city if you can help it."

Well, I'd broken that rule, and now they were convinced I'd be taken away.

Mom sat beside me at the table, crying her eyes out.

"What are you so worried about?" I yelled. "Why would anyone come after me? I've never told anyone about what I can do, not even Lysander. You shouldn't be worried about me. Silas is dead, and the baby..."

"Quiet!" Being a lowly fisherman with an inexhaustible supply of optimism, Dad rarely used his dead-serious tone. So, I knew to be quiet and lower my eyes in solemn respect. "Before you were born, the Shaman delivered a ridiculous prophecy to King Damien. He told the king that a child would be born, an unnatural child, who would throw his kingdom into chaos. Since then, Damien has ordered the execution of anyone deemed different, newborn or not. He's even ordered the deaths of those who are not able-bodied, be it with age or crippling injury. He keeps a watchful eye on Leogard as well, fearing the elves are unnatural enough to warrant a threat."

His story scared me, as I'm certain the Shaman had intended. But it made sense. How many blind, lame, or very old people had I known? None. That realization sobered my smart-ass spirit. The fate of Hezral balanced on a vague paranoia-induced prophecy that most likely came about for the sole purpose of giving the Shaman a guaranteed position of power for the rest of his life. But, how could anyone be scared of a tiny baby?

"The baby..." I pointed limply toward the front door and the madness happening to our neighbors. "What is the Shaman going to do with him?"

Mom started to wipe her eyes with her apron, but used a towel instead. Most of her apron was stained with blood and amniotic fluid.

Dad reached for my hand, took it, and knelt beside me. He spoke barely above a whisper. "He'll be tossed into the sea, Mira. That's why you have to be careful. That's why we worry so much. If they find out..."

"She bent Tannah's mind," Mom whispered, her eyes avoiding mine. Was she frightened of me?

"By the Great Sea Serpent, Mira, what have you done?"

"I helped! I thought it was the right thing to do. Tannah was acting like a lunatic. Her aura was all over the place—she and the baby would have died."

"It would have been better to let that happen."

"What?" I jerked my hand from his. "You can't be serious!"

But he was serious all right. And just like Mom, he averted his eyes just enough to keep me from making a connection. "We told you to keep this to yourself, and now what's happened? Silas is dead as well as his son."

"So losing his wife and son would have been better? Who are you to judge whose lives are worth saving? Am I that much of a disgrace that you can't even bear to look at me? You're afraid of me. Is that it?"

"That's enough, Mira!" He shot to his feet and pounded the table. Mom started crying again.

If he wanted to behave like a savage, I would too. I slapped my hand hard on the table beside his. It stung, bringing tears to my eyes. "You can't just let a baby die because his legs aren't normal! I can stop the Shaman. I'll go right now and *make* him leave the baby alone."

My ankle hurt like crazy, but I ran limping to the front door.

Dad caught me in a crushing hold and held tight. "No, Mira!"

"Let me go! I can help him, please, Dad!" My words melted into choking sobs. "Please."

"No—if the Shaman discovers what you are, he will do the same to you."

"Not if I get to him first." I struggled against him, but I was no match for his six foot, seven inch fisherman's bulk.

"There are his guards to think of—you can't bend their wills *and* his at the same time."

"Then help me subdue them."

"And then what, Mira? Will you bend the wills of everyone in Port Valor who believe in the law? Will you bend King Damien's will after that? You would need an army to even come close."

I stopped struggling, but Dad held tight.

"What good is this 'gift' if I can't help people with it? What good am I?"

"You're our daughter. That's good enough. You're *our* gift, and someday maybe you'll find a way to use your abilities. Until then, you must hide it—for your sake, for ours, even Lysander's."

Fear shivered its way through me. We were to be married next week. But if Dad was right, and the Shaman found out about me, I could be killed. Lysander could be, too. Any children we may have—if they were the least bit different, they could be tossed in the sea just like Silas's son.

The room spun, and if Dad hadn't been holding me, I would have fallen. In a matter of minutes, my life had changed. The future I'd planned with my best friend, with the only man I'd ever loved besides my father, was slipping away from me.

All night, I dreamed of frigid, dark water and a little bundle in a blanket sinking into the depths. I woke up well before dawn, sweating, heart beating erratically. I couldn't let Lysander be hurt because of me. There was only one thing I could do to make sure that didn't happen.

Chapter Two

~ Lysander ~

The next day…

The clock said five past one. Mira was late.

"Maybe she changed her mind," I muttered.

"No she didn't," Mama answered. "She'll be here any minute now."

A kitchen full of neighbors mingled about, snacking on cabbage rolls and onion tarts. Even Wharfmaster Shruck, all four hundred pounds of him, along with his three wives and the youngest four of his nine children were roaming about and eating us out of house and home.

"Well met there, lad." He smacked me on the back and knocked the breath from my lungs. "Mirabelle's a fine lass. I'd have snatched her up myself if you hadn't beat me to it."

His wives stopped chasing the children and gave him dirty looks.

The minutes ticked away. One of the babies started crying. Sympathetic frowns and whispers multiplied.

Mama frosted the cake, using her tarnished spatula to add decorative swirls in the pale yellow buttercream. "Will you hand me that jar of candied talaberries?"

"Sure."

I picked up the jar and tried to open the lid. It didn't budge. I gave it another try, gritting my teeth and twisting until my palm hurt.

Papa walked into the kitchen. "Here, let me." I handed him the jar.

With one quick turn of his wrist, the weathered fisherman removed the lid. I couldn't help but notice the pity in Mama's eyes for her weakling son. She took the jar from Papa and concentrated on the cake again, adding a layer of dark red berries over the frosting.

I sighed and plucked at a hole in the stained linen tablecloth. Papa had begun slouching when we were in the same room, but he couldn't hide his size. His muscular frame still filled out his plaid tunics and long wool sleeves. My father, Tyberius Devlin, was second only to the Wharfmaster in terms of build. But, his son—me—was a bony disappointment. I sat back in the chair and crossed my arms, fingers easily encircling barely-there biceps.

I checked the clock again. Ten minutes past one o'clock. "You think I should go see about her?"

Papa smiled. "It's your blessing party, Lysander. She's probably putting the extra touches on her hair or whatever it is you women do." He swatted Mama on the rear, and she feigned an attack with the icing-covered spatula.

Finally, a knock echoed through our crowded kitchen.

"Shh, everyone quiet!" Papa said, holding his fist above his head. "On my signal, we yell 'Surprise!'"

I rolled my eyes. Mirabelle knew about the whole thing. The only thing she wasn't expecting were the added neighbors. But, she liked parties, and I wanted to marry her more than anything, though we'd been like brother and sister most of our lives. Lately, she occupied my every thought and waltzed about in my dreams, wearing nothing and making me hungry to have her to myself.

Papa yanked open the door and lowered his fist.

Everyone yelled, "Surprise!"

Mira's father, Abbott, stood at the threshold, his eyes wide and darting between all our guests in the kitchen. Cries of joy withered to silence like the confetti that floated to a stop on my hair. I peered around Papa and anxiously waited for Mira to step out from behind Abbott.

But she didn't. Instead, Abbott held a piece of paper in his hands. The crisp edges snapped with the cold tidal winds that blew in from the Draekkan Sea.

"I think this might be best done in private," Abbott said, nodding to both me and Papa.

"Yes, of course." Papa gestured toward the bedroom.

My stomach felt like I'd swallowed a stone, but I stood from the chair on wobbly twig-thin legs. I kept my head down and followed them. Whispers from our guests burned my ears, and their stares weighed down every step. *Poor boy, she's done tossed him off the dock. Probably took off with one of those Opera men—they're so burly.*

Once inside, with the door curtain drawn, Abbott cupped one of my bony shoulders in his wide hand. "Lysander," he began in a gentle tone, "I'm sorry. Mira's not coming. She's gone."

"Gone?" I repeated dumbly, eyeing the paper in Abbott's hand. "But where did she go?"

"Leogard. She left this note for you, son. I'm so sorry."

"May I?" I reached for the note with a trembling hand. Abbott handed it over, and I read the words, written in Mira's firm, steady script.

Dearest Lysander,

I'm sorry, but I cannot marry you. It wouldn't be fair to you. I can't tell you why, but it's for the best. I am going to Leogard to surrender my life to the Temple, to help those in need. I hope you will not hate me, because in my heart, we will forever be friends, and maybe one day you will find someone worthy of your love.

With deepest regret,
Mirabelle Hearton

I sank to the floor like a toddler and hugged my knees. "I need to be alone, please."

Papa and Abbott exchanged a sorrowful look and left the room. I read that note over and over. The outcome was still the same. Mira was gone, and I didn't know why, and I couldn't do anything about it. I waited until the footsteps and farewells of our guests quieted, grabbed my cloak, and stepped into the kitchen.

Mama approached, her eyes red and swollen. "Sweetheart, are you all right?"

"I'm fine. I'm going for a walk."

I stepped out the door. Sleet stung my nose and froze on my eyelashes. Pulling my hood over my head, I cocooned myself within the gray wool. My legs were numb by the time I passed the last dock at the edge of town where Mira and I once fished and laughed and dreamed. We were the best of friends. We knew everything about each other. We'd even kissed. I thought she loved me.

But, she didn't want me. I wasn't enough. Port Valor wasn't enough. Mira wanted more. I should have seen it, from the way she'd talked about traveling. I kept walking. Straight out of town, into the forest where the bare, moonlit trees cast eerie shadows across the snow.

I walked forever.

Dawn's first rays peeked over the horizon. My legs, my arms— numb. So tired. Dragging my feet through snow that grew deeper by the minute, I lifted my heavy stump of a leg for one more step. But my body gave up. I dropped mid-stride, crumpling to a heap on the rutted road.

* * * *

Ice-cold liquid smacked my face.

A man's raspy voice said from somewhere nearby. "Wake up, boy."

I opened my eyes to sticky brown goo. Not water. Sitting up, I wiped my cheeks with numb fingers. "What…?"

"It can speak. What are you doing out here?"

The gooey liquid still coated my hands, so I slung my fingers around, then wiped them on my pants. They tingled. Hopefully they weren't frostbitten. My eyes focused past the brown film and onto a snowbear. I crab-crawled backwards and fell onto hard, dry dirt.

"Shit!" My heart thudded in my chest. Weapon—I needed a weapon, but all I saw were stacks of furs and a cot.

The bear peered over the top of the cot. Only it wasn't a bear, but a thin man with a long nose and sharp cheekbones wearing a bear's head cloak. "I asked you a question, boy. What are you doing out here?"

"Walking."

"In this weather? You must be stupider than you look."

"What did you pour on me?"

"A little herbal concoction I made. Woke you up, didn't it?"

"Yeah." The stuff had started to dry, feeling like a thin layer of mud on my cheeks.

Wind howled through the branches of nearby trees, carrying stinging snowflakes to my face. The late afternoon sun filtered through hazy clouds. Snow circled the dirt perimeter of a shoddy campsite.

I pulled my cloak around me and smelled wood smoke. Getting to my feet, I migrated to a nice fire and stretched my numb fingers into the heat. A pot of something bubbled over the flames—the heady aroma made my stomach clench with hunger. While my circulation returned, I realized I hadn't seen this part of the wilderness before. The man with the bear head sat on the cot where I had been lying. His light gray fur cloak covered him from head to toe, complete with the dangling skin from the snowbear's arms and legs. He stared at me with dark brown, elongated eyes, slit from corners of the eyes to the temples, like the barbarians from the islands to our north.

We had feared them for centuries. Horrific bedtime stories of their murderous plundering used to keep me awake long into the night. Did he mean to kill me? Make me a slave? Add my entrails to his stew? I could feel my legs, so I could probably run. But the campsite was in the dead center of a wide open clearing. The trees around it were too far apart and lacked any shrubs in which I could hide. The man didn't seem very old or infirm, though, and considering how I'd been half-frozen, he could probably catch me easily enough. Or shoot me with an arrow or impale me with a spear. Neither idea made me feel any better.

"Where are we?" I asked, trying to hide the tremble in my voice. Maybe he'd offer me some answers before he had me for dinner. "How long was I asleep?"

"We're in the forest. You were asleep a long time." He pulled out a knife with a curved blade from inside his fur boot. Out came some potatoes from a sack at his feet. He placed them on a rock and chopped them with rapid, fierce strokes.

I stepped to the far side of the fire, keeping an eye on his knife. "Who are you?"

"Stone," he replied with a few more vicious chops. "Harker Stone."

"Why did you – why are you out here?"

"I live here."

"Seems a rather exposed place to live."

"Bet I'm warmer than you are." He stood, came to the stewpot and dumped in the chopped potatoes.

I backed up farther until cold licked my ears. The fire's warmth beckoned me to linger. But he had that knife, holding up the blade like he was considering whether to gut me or slit my throat. I was on the verge of turning to run when he slid it back into his boot and went back to sit on the cot, which was nothing more than a pile of evergreen branches covered with furs.

He didn't kill me, maim me, or even threaten to do so. I hesitated at the border of warm and freezing, no idea how far I was from home, but with no real desire to return either. Somehow, the threat of being murdered or freezing to death was easier to accept than going back home to a world without Mira and the humiliation of her leaving me.

With no clear answers, I sat on the hard ground, still keeping the fire between him and me. But I was able to see him over the dancing flames, and from here the smell of the stew flooded my nose with the promise of a good meal. If he wasn't going to kill me, maybe he'd at least offer some food. A little stew in my gut might help me think straight and give me the energy I needed to make a run for it. Or leave. I wasn't sure whether the man even cared what I did.

"So, Mr. Stone," I said, watching him stuff a long, skinny pipe with some dried leaves from a pouch on his belt, "which way is Port Valor?"

"It's a ways off."

His vague answers were getting tiresome. If he wanted me as a hostage or slave, or what have you, he could at least admit it so I would know whether spending energy on an escape would be worth it. "Understood, but which way might that be? I have family who will be looking for me."

"Haven't seen anyone about." He picked up a piece of kindling, held it in the flames until it caught fire, and lit his pipe with it.

This nonsense was getting me nowhere. Time to be candid. "If it's ransom you're looking for, you'll be disappointed. I'm the son of a common fisherman, not a prince. If it's a slave you want, I'm scrawny and weak."

"I don't want any of that."

"Then what do you want? Do you want to kill me?"

"If I wanted that, I'd have done it when you were lying on the road half-frozen. I'd have put any animal out of its misery had I found it in such condition."

"Then why rescue me? Why bring me back if you don't want to kill or enslave me and won't tell me how to get home?"

He stood, went to a wooden crate, and pulled out a couple of bowls. "Hungry?"

I wanted to yell, *Fuck you! I'm leaving.* But he ladled out some steaming stew into a bowl, and damn if my stomach didn't almost gnaw itself in two. My mouth watered so much I had to swallow twice to keep from choking on my spit.

"Yes," I muttered, "I'm hungry."

Instead of handing me a bowl, he set it just out of my reach a few feet from the cot, then sat himself down. With loud slurps, he ate his stew, while I stared at my potential dinner. He paid no mind to me, just kept slurping, chewing, slurping, chewing. Perhaps he was afraid I'd attack him if he got too close, so he set it where he did to be safe. All I had to do was retrieve it. Simple enough.

Standing slowly, I kept my eyes on him as I crept closer. Every second that passed, the steam died a little more. The stew would get cold if I didn't hurry. A quick pause showed me Harker was still eating, his eyes focused on the fire and not me. Hunger spurred me to close the last few feet of the distance until the stew was at my feet. I bent, picked up the bowl with both hands and tilted it toward my mouth.

Steam warmed my face; the warm, savory goodness of a satisfying meal touched my lips. And then...*whack*! The bowl went flying. The precious food splattered on the frozen earth and sizzled in the fire. The old man laughed, pointing a walking stick at me. To add more insult, he poked me in the ribs with it.

"What...why did you do that?"

"Do what?"

"You knocked the bowl from my hands! Didn't you invite me to eat?"

"I did."

"Then why did you knock it out of my hands?"

He yawned, stretching out hairy, lanky arms from beneath his bear cloak and thick wool garments. Lying down on the cot, he muttered, "Get another bowl. Don't drop it this time."

I started toward the empty bowl turned upside down on the dirt, but hesitated. Harker Stone, I gathered, was nothing more than a crazy old hermit. If I got another bowl, he'd try to knock it away again.

"No, I'll just warm up here for a while. Maybe later."

"Suit yourself."

I'd wait for him to fall asleep; then I'd have my fill and regain the strength I needed to find my way home. I sat cross-legged by the fire, holding my hands toward the warmth. The soup made me drool.

In the course of a few minutes, Harker snored softly, his chest rising and falling with the deep, heavy breaths of sleep. The sun was already sinking below the horizon, so I had very little time to find my way out of here. Easing up to all fours, I kept my eyes on him while my hands found the upturned bowl. The painful gnawing of my stomach made it difficult to move slowly, but I forced myself to creep forward to the fire. The stew was almost gone. Surely, it would be enough for a decent meal. I wiped drool from my mouth, and with a shaky hand, reached for the ladle.

Gently, carefully, I scooped up the last remnants of stew and poured it into my bowl. It didn't look that appetizing, being only a thin, greasy broth with leathery-looking strips of meat and bruised potatoes. But I was too hungry to care. I dropped the ladle a little too hard. It clanked against the pot.

Not wasting another moment, I put the bowl to my lips. A splash of hot stew poured into my mouth and then…*whack!* The bowl somersaulted out of my hands again and landed in the fire. Stew boiled and splattered on the rocks.

The old man jabbed his walking stick into my chest and shoved me down to the ground. He pinned me there, laughing.

"Are you crazy?" I screamed. "What's the matter with you? You want to watch me starve to death?"

"No reason to starve to death, boy. Get some food."

I tried scooting away, but he pressed the tip of his cane into my breastbone, forcing me to wheeze. "You're making it very difficult."

"Am I? You're the one that can't find a meal."

Wrapping both hands around his stick, I gritted my teeth and tried to push it off me, but couldn't budge it. Why did I have to be so weak?

"What do you want, boy?"

26

My arms quaked, veins protruded beneath my skin as I tried, but failed, to remove Harker's cane from my chest. "I want you to let…me…go," I said, pushing the words through clenched teeth.

"No, what do you want right now? More than anything?"

Mira's face flashed through my mind's eye, the feel of her arms around me, her soft lips on mine. But I didn't say her name. I couldn't. It hurt too much to even try. Right now, I couldn't have her. Right now, I had to focus on staying alive and getting home.

He leaned over me, pressing his weight into the cane. My sternum cracked and popped—he'd crush my chest any second. "What do you want, boy?" he demanded. Spit flew from his thin lips. "Tell me!"

Using what little air was left in my lungs, I screeched, "Food! I want food!"

He lifted the cane; I sucked in a merciful breath of fresh air. The last of the sun's muted orange light disappeared beyond the horizon.

"Good," he said. "Be honest. Trust your instincts. Take life's trappings away, and we all want the same thing—air, shelter, and food. Everything beyond that is the cream in your berries."

He took two steps back and leaned on his stick, squinting at me.

Afraid he'd come at me again, I eased myself up on my elbows, ready to roll away and run as far as I could make it.

"Well?" he asked, shrugging innocently.

"Well, what? I've already told you I'm hungry. You brought me out here to who knows where, for who knows what, and keep telling me to eat, but then you won't let me eat. What am I supposed to do?"

"Find food."

"There *is* no food!"

He gestured to the sparse forest. "You mean to tell me that this forest has no food in it? I wonder how the snowbear eats. Does someone make his food for him?"

"I'm not a bear. I'm just a fisherman's son. I've never gone hunting."

"Good time to learn, then eh?"

Horrible growls came from my stomach, which hurt so bad, I had trouble standing. Perhaps I'd been asleep for much longer than he claimed. One day's fast shouldn't be so torturous. My parents had to be worried sick. I still had no idea what Harker Stone wanted from me, but he seemed to be pushing me to go out alone. He could still have some sick game in mind, waiting for me to get out of sight before hunting me himself. Or perhaps he worshipped a barbarian bear god, and I was his sacrifice.

Unable to stand up straight, I remained hunched over. My chest ached from the prodding of his cane, and my stomach felt like it was trying to sink in on itself.

"Well, what are you waiting for? Go," he demanded.

"It's getting dark. Which way should I go?"

"Whichever way leads you to food. I'll wait here, and if you're not back by dawn, I'll pack up and move on."

"Don't you have a lantern or anything so I can see?"

He lifted the furs on the cot, and pulled one out. "No, but here's a tyger skin. Wrap yourself up in it."

He tossed it to me. For a moment, I studied the heavy pelt. The fur was dense and black as night, with lighter black stripes that were only visible when I held them at certain angles. I'd heard about tygers many times, how fishermen would catch an occasional glimpse of one along the craggy cliffs that made up much of Hezral's shoreline. No one I knew had ever caught one. They were supposedly solitary and could take on the colors of any hunting ground.

I ran my fingers along the soft, thick fur, but other than the odd stripes, it didn't blend in with anything. I guess it had to be attached to a tyger to do that. The thought made me a little sad, but we all relied on animal furs to stay warm. At one end of the pelt was the tyger's head, but not the skull, just the skin and fur that made up its face and ears. Draping the pelt over my shoulders, I let the skin of the front legs drape over my chest. The head fell naturally over mine like a hood. It took a minute to get used to the added weight, but it did keep the bitter cold wind from biting into my skin.

"Thanks," I muttered, but he wasn't there. He wasn't anywhere in the camp that I could see. The fire, spit, pot, and fur-cushioned cot were still there. A couple of grass sacks lay on the ground. After another quick scan to make sure he wasn't about to pounce at me, I rushed over and swooped up a sack. If he had just one morsel of food, just a wrinkled up potato or withered turnip, it might be enough to ease my hunger a little.

But, there was nothing except a few old rags. I dropped that sack and picked up the other, dumping out the contents on the cot. A pair of ragged linen pants, a tunic, and some cloth shoes tumbled out, but that was it. No food, no weapon, nothing useful at all.

I stuffed the rags and clothes into one of the sacks, and tied it onto my belt. Harker still wasn't anywhere to be seen. A strange prickling sensation crawled along my back. Perhaps he was watching from somewhere in the shadows. I almost expected a spear or arrow to zip through the night and impale me, but nothing happened. The moon had risen and shone its silvery light through the hazy forest. That's where I headed. I'd travel that direction. If I was lucky, I'd stumble upon something familiar or a small village. Or I'd starve or get eaten by a snowbear. Either way, ruminating on what could happen wasn't getting me anywhere.

Night creatures hooted and chattered as I headed toward the moon's birthplace on the horizon. The farther I got from the camp and the fire, the colder it was. My eyes fought to sort out a reasonable path. The moon's scant light wasn't enough to let me discern bushes from rocks until I came right up on them. But I kept going, picking my way along the frozen ground, crunching through leaves and snow drifts. Though spring had arrived, it took a long time to convince winter to leave.

My legs grew so weak, I had to stop and rest. It felt like I'd gone miles, but I could still see the faint orange light of the campfire behind me. Hunger doubled me over.

I hugged my stomach. "Please," I whispered, praying to the Great Sea Serpent or whoever would listen, "let me find something to eat. Anything."

The tyger pelt felt heavier, tighter, like it was hugging my skin. Comforting me.

Not a second later, I smelled something. I wasn't even sure what it was, but I knew it was food. Meat. My ears picked up a sound—gentle, light steps— hooves against frozen ground. My eyes watered and burned. I rubbed them, then blinked and saw an entirely different landscape.

"What the…?" It wasn't different at all. I was simply seeing things more clearly. Where trees and vegetation had been shadowy objects upon an almost invisible ground, they were now vivid, cast in a greenish tint bright as midday. I could see every tree limb, the ridges in the bark, rocks jutting from the ground, round owl eyes shining down at me from the top of an ebonwood.

A few yards ahead, a stag nibbled moss from a boulder. He was an impressive specimen—huge, branching antlers, well-muscled, a gray coat specked with black. I salivated. Breath steamed from his large muzzle. Food. I didn't know how, but I knew he would be my next meal.

I moved forward, but stopped mid-step. The loose front legs of the tyger pelt ripped through my sleeves and wrapped themselves around my arms. The skin of the paws stretched over my hands and fingers like gloves. The rest of the pelt ripped through the body of my shirt and my pants, wrapping around my shoulders and back, my buttocks and thighs, until my garments lay in a pitiful heap at my feet. I tried to pull it off, but the skin of the tyger's head wrapped around my face. It adhered to my skin with sharp stabbing pains, like a thousand needles being jabbed into my cheeks.

What sort of dark magic was this? I cried out, falling to my knees in agony, hoping it was all a nightmare. Yet, in a moment, it was all over. The pain was gone…and so was the stag.

I couldn't let him get away. I had to eat or die. Following the smell of his hide and mossy breath, I ran after him. Unable to see him just yet, I kept following the scent and the sounds of him crashing through the forest. He darted right, then left. Somehow, I was able to mimic his every evasive move without stumbling or falling. Rocks, fallen logs, brush—none of it proved an obstacle. Like the stag, I leapt over everything in graceful bounds. It didn't take long for me to catch up with him, and when I did, I pounced.

Wind whistled past my face as I propelled through the air right at the stag. A moment before impact, I reached out, ready to claim the prize. But my arms weren't human. They were the arms of a tyger—black, almost imperceptibly striped, with curved claws that could slice through the deer's thick hide.

I landed on its back, claws dug into its shoulders. The stag let out a bleating cry as I flipped him onto his side. And then my jaws, a tyger's jaws, clamped down on his throat. I could taste his warm blood and the mossy breath from his windpipe. The pulse from his jugular vein vibrated against my tongue. Hooves and long, slender legs flailed in vain against the fallen leaves. Minutes passed, until he stopped breathing and went still. I tore into his rear flank, ripping through the hide to reach the hot, bloody flesh. With teeth and claws, I stripped meat from bone, gnawing and swallowing until finally my hunger subsided.

From above, laughter echoed through the forest, followed by Harker's voice. "Now that's how you find food."

Jumping to my feet, I stumbled back, falling against a tree trunk. From head to toe, the fur that covered my body rippled like an illusion before disappearing into my skin. Standing naked, without the tyger pelt or anything else, I lost my breath when a gust of frigid wind swept over me. I sank to the ground, shrinking up into a trembling ball of scrawny boy. I still tasted blood and flesh, still wanted more, but didn't dare move.

"W-what have you done to me?" I asked, staring at the dead stag's body, its steaming entrails spilled upon the ground.

Harker jumped from the tree, landing in a crouch beside me. In his hand, he held the same cane as before, only the end of it glowed bright yellow like a torch with no flame. His mouth twisted upward in an evil grin. "I'm simply fulfilling a prophecy, boy." He had the sack I had taken with me—he must have picked it up before finding me like this. He dug out the clothes and shoes, and a couple of rags. "Time to clean up and get dressed. We have work to do."

Chapter Three

~ Mirabelle ~

After two days of traveling, I was already homesick. My old gray gelding, Donovan, ambled as fast as he could southwest along the windy road that cut across Cavitel Valley. I'd been all over the northern coast of Hezral, sailing with my parents and Lysander's to help with their joint fishing business, but this was the farthest I'd ever been alone. I didn't miss the seasickness, but horseback riding wasn't easy on my backside. Skin wasn't supposed to chafe like this.

Squirming in my saddle, I consulted the worn map, which showed a river ahead, though its name was an unreadable smudge. I squinted into the distance, where a dark outline that could pass as a body of water stretched as far as I could see along the misty valley floor. Crossing it posed a challenge, and I really wished Dad was here to assist. But, he wasn't, so I folded up the map, put it away, and kicked at Donovan's sides again. He sped up to a slow walk.

"You know," I said, and Donovan ticked an ear toward me in response, "Leogard is a bustling city, full of people and things to do. If the Priestess finds me acceptable, I'll be so busy, I won't even miss Port Valor. It'll take some time, but I'll make friends, and I'll have a good life there."

Donovan just snorted.

My mind, on the other hand, had plenty of objections.

You'll miss your goats.

"Leogard must have plenty of animals, maybe even a pet shop," I answered. "I'll get something exotic, like a...drake! Yeah, a fire-breathing little drake. And I'll train him to walk on a leash."

Right...good luck with that. Your parents will be worried sick, you know.

"I left them a letter, and I'll send them another when I get there. I'll keep up a correspondence, and they'll see that I'm doing fine. Leogard must be teeming with magic, so my measly powers won't even raise an eyebrow."

You broke Lysander's heart.

At this, I swallowed past a stubborn lump in my throat. "Lysander will be fine. He'll be a fisherman like his dad. In time, he'll forget me and move on."

A tear splashed onto my cheek. I smacked it away. Stupid tears.

Still, I tried to convince myself that I hadn't made a mistake. "I did the right thing. Lysander's just a normal boy; he belongs with other normal people. Being with me would ruin his life."

It did no good, all these justifications. I missed him so much it hurt, and I doubted that hurt would ever go away.

Behind me, the rattle of tambourines and whistling of flutes drifted into the valley. I turned in the saddle to get a look at the commotion. The red and orange flags of the Port Valor Traveling Opera bobbed along the skyline. Soon, the flag-bearers themselves topped the rise, and the caravan proceeded into the valley. I groaned, unsure whether to try coaxing Donovan into a trot or wait for them to catch up. At the rate the procession wound along the valley road, they would pass me in a few minutes anyway. Besides, two days of nothing but slugfish jerky and brawbean paste had left a twang in my mouth I thought might never go away. They might at least have some decent food I could buy.

I halted Donovan and got off to stretch my legs, landing on the soft brown grass and green moss that carpeted the valley. The line of wagons and riders drew nearer. I recognized the ringmaster, the acrobats, the bearded lady, and conjoined twins. Behind those familiar faces came the star performers' carriage, glittering with shiny ribbons and fake gems. The curtains were closed, but inside, I imagined the lovely singers—the "opera" portion of this traveling circus—reposing on fluffy pillows and eating fancy delicacies.

My mouth watered.

A rider I didn't recognize approached and tipped his floppy red hat. "Good day, young lass, might we assist you?"

I knew that voice. The lanky man with the hooked nose was one of the clowns. When the Opera performed in Port Valor, Lysander and I would make extra noise when he and the others passed by, so they'd toss us candy. They often had unique delights from other provinces. Dragon nips were the best—you could only get those in Leogard. They were clear on the outside with colored dragon candy in the middle. That was one thing I could look forward to at least.

The off-duty clown finally reached me and rode alongside. I opened my mouth to greet him, but a bug flew down my throat. I coughed and spat, covering my mouth with my sleeve to ward off more bugs. How embarrassing.

"So many gnats!" The man removed his hat and swatted at the swarm. Once they moved on to annoy the rest of the caravan, he asked, "As I was saying, do you require assistance, young lass?"

I blushed. "Oh…yes…I'm traveling to Leogard, and if you have any extra food…"

"I'm Randell," he said, "and you're in luck! We're heading that way ourselves to escape the bitter winter cold and bask in Leogard's milder, and richer, climate." He laughed. "If the weather holds out, we'll be there in ten days or so. Travel with us, my dear. You won't go hungry, I promise."

"Mirabelle Hearton," I said, "and thank you. I admit I was getting a bit lonely."

He reached into a saddlebag and tossed something to me. I caught the small object, pulled back the handkerchief it was wrapped in, and found a golden brown roll inside. It smelled heavenly, so I bit into it— draeberry jam surrounded by flaky, buttery bread. It was gone in two more bites.

Randell laughed. "Glad you like it. I make them myself. Now, hop on that old horse of yours and come along with me. Nella here won't win any races either."

The rest of the trip was pleasant. Luckily, the river crossing was easy thanks to a new barge. In two more days, we finally reached the other side of the valley and the northern border of Leogard. Up ahead, the towering ebonwoods and oaks of Wildewood Forest cast their shadows on the ground. The air was considerably warmer there than it was back home. Winter still hung on by its chilly fingernails, puffing chilly breezes across my face at irregular intervals. But, I had to strip down to one layer of wool so I didn't sweat constantly. My feet alone were enough to repel any living thing within a five-mile radius. The warm climate would take some getting used to for a girl who'd grown up in a land of perpetual cold.

We rode under those big trees, and I was mesmerized. Such giants! The tallest trees in Hezral were not half this tall. Most were scrubby bushes. How lucky I was to be among such splendor.

But after five more days of nothing but forest, the trees were much less fascinating.

At least my companions were interesting. Randell introduced me to his wife, Laalu, whom he claimed was a real mermaid. She spent most of her time rolling behind the clown carriage in a blue cylindrical tank of water that had "Ladyfish" painted in bright white on the side. In there, she indeed appeared to have a tail, complete with shimmering scales. Her face was fishlike, kind of squished up at the midline so her eyes were situated more on the sides of her head than in front. She even had what looked like gills on her neck. But when she did come out on dry land, her tail split into two legs with feet. Was she really a mermaid or just a freak of nature? I'd grown up thinking mermaids were just fisherman myth, stories told over steins of beer to charm the ladies and entertain the children.

Laalu did have beautiful blonde hair, twisted into thick ropes, interlaced with shells and ribbons. She took great interest in me, going so far as to arrange my hair when we camped at night. She spoke in a strange language that included several sounds that were a lot like bubbles popping in a pot of boiling water. Randell did the interpreting.

"Where are you from?" I asked her.

"Ustamer," she answered.

"It means Under the Sea," Randell added. "That's what they call their city."

Careful not to imply any deception on Laalu's part, I smiled and looked appropriately naïve. "So, how did you two end up together? Did you go there, Randell?"

"No," he laughed. "Humans can't breathe down there. I caught her quite by accident in my fishing net. It was love at first sight, once I freed her."

"Ee did nut et me," she said with a bubbly giggle. "Randeel gud mon. Ree gud man. Me lay menee eggs fur hem sum day."

Randell blushed, caressing her slender arm. "She says I didn't eat her, so that makes me a good man, and she…wants to have many children with me."

I leaned in close and whispered, "Is that even possible?"

He shrugged. "Doesn't matter. We love one another. That's all we really need."

My eyes watered, wishing that were true.

"So, why did you come all this way?" he asked gently. "I bet it wasn't to become a circus recruit."

"No, I'm heading to Leogard to join the Temple."

The road brightened up ahead, signaling the end of the forest. He frowned, eyes sad as though he felt sorry for me. "My dear, from what I've heard, life in Leogard's Temple is difficult. The Priestess accepts nothing less than perfection. What could have been so terrible in Port Valor to make you wish for such a life?

"I didn't want to get married," I answered, deciding Randell was trustworthy enough to tell him part of the truth.

He fanned himself with his floppy hat, and flashed a wicked grin. "Was the man that terrible? Did he have one wife too many or did he look like a toad?"

We emerged from the trees, and I took in a breath at the scene ahead. A vast plain of rolling green hills stretched westward to the coast of the Hansom Sea. On the highest hill sat a shining city surrounded by white walls. Leogard at last. A new life waited for me. A chance to right my wrongs and do something good for society. But, why did I keep looking at the road behind, wondering if I'd made a big mistake?

The caravan stopped so everyone could get their bearings. Randell's stare made me realize I hadn't answered his previous questions. "Well," he said, "was he so terrible you'd rather live out your years behind those white walls?"

Those walls did look imposing, like a fortress...or a prison. I shivered. "Lysander wasn't terrible at all," I said. "He was my best friend."

"Then why not marry him and have babies and spend the rest of your life with your best friend?"

"I...he's better off without me."

"If you say so, lass. But it's not too late to change your mind."

We approached the yawning white doors of the North Gate, each one engraved with gold V's, wrapped in the wings of an eagle—the Vaelorian crest. The symbol of King Leopold, king of the elves. A symbol of ancient superiority. As we passed under the arch, my confidence faded to mere crumbs of doubt. The guards at the gate, the passersby, the fancy homes and plants and trees—they were all so immaculate, so perfect. So unlike me.

I couldn't go back to Port Valor, but I knew that I didn't belong in Leogard.

* * * *

~ Lysander ~

Harker said I needed training, for what I didn't know. It involved a lot of exercise—running at full speed in the dark, leaping over fallen logs, climbing trees, and attempting to catch prey. My second kill was a bush quail that didn't get away fast enough when I frightened the flock into a flying, squawking panic.

I had just bitten off a leg when Harker whacked me over the head. The pain switched me from tyger to boy in an instant.

I dropped the bird and stepped back, rubbing the lump on my head. "What the hell? Can't you let me eat for once?"

"If you remember nothing else, remember this—only through pain does one become strong. Hunger feeds the tyger in you."

It must have been true, because it took only a growl or two in my empty stomach to bring out the fur, claws, and teeth of a predatory cat.

"But...it just seems wrong, killing things like this, when we could go into town and—"

"No more talk of town, boy. Not yet. Not until you're properly trained. You have too much remorse as a human. Predators can't survive if they have remorse. Do you feel sorry for a turnip when you eat it?"

"But what am I training for?"

"To kill. Plain and simple. King Damien needs a good assassin."

"What? You want me to kill people?" My voice had risen to a rumbling shout, the tyger starting to emerge.

"Calm down!"

He struck me across the knee with his staff, sending me to the ground and making me howl in pain. But it kept the tyger at bay.

"An assassin kills enemies of the kingdom, boy. You'll be doing Hezral a favor. You won't be killing innocents. You'll be keeping our citizens safe, like your mother and father. You want to keep them safe, don't you?"

Rubbing my knee as I sat on the ground, I begrudgingly answered, "Yes, I want to keep them safe. But why me?"

"Why *not* you? I'm not cut out for it. You see, King Damien took me in as an orphan, found me stranded on the Hezrali shore after a shipwreck took my family. Imagine me, a poor barbarian boy, alone and in enemy territory. He could have killed me on the spot. But he didn't. He let me work for my keep, so I owe him for showing me such mercy. He said he wanted me to find an assassin, so that's what I did. You're young and taking to it well, so now you'll be the king's assassin."

"But what about my family? They must be worried sick."

"You'll see them in due time, boy." He got right into my face. "You will be paid well, and it doesn't hurt, does it? Think about it, you'll be keeping your family safe, and will be able to buy them anything they want. You can even take a few wives with the kind of money you'll earn."

Wives, no, but I did want to take care of my parents, especially after I'd put them through so much worry. Harker was right about the transformation, too. It didn't hurt. It felt like nothing I'd ever experienced before—like an itchy tingle. Each time I shifted, it was as though the real me had been sent to my room to observe everything from afar. I certainly impressed myself.

I wasn't an all-fours creature like a tyger you might find on the craggy bluffs near the coast, but more of a human cat. I still had arms, hands, feet and legs like a man and stood like a man. But the rest of me—from bifurcated lip, to whiskers, to a long tail that sprouted out through the back of my trousers—was all cat.

Days, maybe weeks, passed. No one came for me. Harker wouldn't allow me to go home, not that I knew where home was, but he kept reassuring me it would happen, once I'd been 'trained'. My parents would think I was dead by now, but I still had no clue which direction to go. Though I hated to admit it, I was afraid that I might hurt them if I did return. And I didn't know if I could hunt well enough to survive on my own. Once I felt confident in myself, I'd escape. That's what I kept telling myself anyway.

When I wasn't chasing something and sinking my teeth into it, I learned to walk silently, rolling my feet from heel to toe. He'd venture off into the forest, leaving me at the campsite for an hour or more. Then, I had to track him. He didn't make it easy. The man knew how to cover his tracks. Even his scent trail was erratic, ending at one location, then picking up again several yards behind.

When I finally found him, the trick was to make sure he didn't detect my presence before I sprang on him. That involved the art of learning to be still. *Really* still. Like a tyger waiting to ambush their prey. So still you don't blink, you don't twitch, not one muscle moves except your diaphragm to keep moving air through your lungs. You breathe through your mouth because air whistles through your nose too much.

"Be more than still," Harker said. "Be the tree, be the rock, be the cold, dead object that hides you. You are the master of every muscle in your body. Will it to be unmoving until you say so."

Before I realized it, I had actually learned to camouflage. Like a real tyger, my fur shifted colors and patterns until it blended in with whatever was around me. The most aggravating part was ruining boots with my strong, large feet and claws that tore through the leather. So I began removing them before I went on the hunt.

Once I found Harker during each seek and find session, I had to pounce before he became aware of me. Or he would cry, "Lost your supper!" which meant I wouldn't eat that night. Hunger, I learned, is a great motivator for success.

Chapter Four

~ Lysander ~

Fog crept along the forest floor, hugging the ragged bark of evergreens and filtering through thorny shrubs. It crawled over our backs, crinkling the fur on my neck. We crouched in the shadows, observing what appeared to be a dilapidated cottage in the middle of nowhere. Harker called this 'stalking', though I didn't see how or why anyone would stalk an empty house. We were upwind from the structure, which he said was bad since I couldn't smell anything but wet dirt, mold, and a curious snow wolf who'd been following us for some time. The fog, however, was more valuable, as it provided the cover we needed in a mostly open forest.

Tonight's stalking was the first in which I wasn't hunting down Harker or a hapless creature. We hid inside the hollowed-out carcass of a dead tree. A thick beard of sawtooth vines concealed our hiding place. Serrated leaves, sharp as talons, kept most sane people from ever touching it, and the vines themselves contained a milky liquid that could kill ten men in a single drop.

Harker had pushed them aside with his cane like they were mere weeds, and now he was piercing the sharp points of darts into the vines. Milky poison made rivulets along the stems and dripped off the leaves, splattering on the ground and on my feet and legs. It smelled like rotten cabbage.

"Watch it!" I whispered.

"It's only lethal if you ingest it or if it gets inside your skin," he whispered back, "like in this dart." He jabbed one of them at me, and I shrunk back against the termite-eaten walls of our tiny hiding spot.

He chuckled quietly. "Don't be a kitten. Pay attention."

We were watching a dark, tiny cottage that lay in a small clearing. Its shutters were falling off and paint peeling like sunburned skin. What little thatch remained on the roof had rotted. The rest of the roof had gaping holes so the interior had to be rotten and mildewed from decades of rain, sleet, and snow. Hezrali weather wasn't kind.

I was about to ask Harker why we were here again when the wind shifted, bringing with it the smell of flesh. An odd mixture of both rotten and fresh meat hooked its bait into my nose, and I started forward.

Harker held me back. "Not yet, boy."

Door hinges squeaked. Two figures emerged, much to my surprise. Perhaps they were ghosts, as I couldn't imagine anyone who would want to live in such a place. Turns out even Harker had a place he called home—a well-insulated, dry cave with plenty of room for the both of us—a far cry nicer than this shack.

The people walked a little ways in front of the house—one was a head taller than the other. A mother and child, perhaps? They both wore thick cloaks with hoods. The taller one's hood fell back, revealing a blonde woman with pale skin and a coy smile. She tucked some hair behind a pointed ear. A high elf? Out here? The shorter one's hood fell back too, and I held my breath. This one had blue hair streaked with white. Her skin was a deep indigo. She also had pointed ears.

"A dark elf?" I whispered, looking to Harker, but he stared at them with narrowed eyes and twisted his hands around his cane like he was imagining how it would feel to crush their necks under his fingers.

"Who are they?"

"Lovers. She promised to save the lightie for me. Lying whore."

"But how do you know the dark elf?"

"How do you think I learned all this magic? She's been coming here for years, experimenting on…various things. I found her out here as a boy about your age. She taught me things in exchange for favors."

"What favors?"

"You're too nosy for your own good, but then again, that might be useful. Let's just say she enjoyed a good fucking, and she needed someone like me who could bring her specimens. Dark elves don't exactly blend in around here."

Harker Stone never failed to perplex me. Who was he really? I doubted I'd ever truly know. "And the high elf? How do you know her?"

"I don't yet. Enough questions."

I turned my attention back to the women and almost lost my balance. They were locked in an intimate embrace, kissing passionately, the dark elf having to tiptoe to meet the taller high elf's lips. My fur bristled, partly because I felt like a voyeur, intruding where I most certainly didn't belong, but also because it aroused me. The erection in my trousers grew uncomfortable, yet I couldn't look away. Most men fantasize about two women fucking, and some men get that and more if they marry multiple wives. I'd never have the latter, so why not enjoy the show?

The blonde elf pulled back, trailing her hand along her lover's cheek. They spoke in hushed tones, but the wind carried their voices to my sensitive ears.

"You're closer than ever to fully reviving Queen Ellyse," the dark elf said. "Leopold will be putty in your hands."

"Perhaps, but not if my sister has anything to do with it."

"Then get rid of her. Better yet, bring her here. Let me deal with her."

The blonde elf hung her head and bit her lip.

"Your compassion is a hindrance."

Her sentiments reminded me of Harker. Don't care about anything. Just do what you must. Perhaps it wasn't such bad advice. I'd cared more than anything about Mira, and look where that got me.

"Come now," the dark elf cooed, sliding her hands down the blonde elf's face, neck, and her cloak-covered bosom. "Don't worry so much. I have it on good authority that you will be welcomed with open arms in Ironhaven if our plans fail."

Interesting. Ironhaven was the capital of a savage land in the Southern Sea, led by an unnaturally long-lived human, Emperor Sarvonn, arch nemesis of King Leopold, the high elf King of Leogard. As far as I knew, our King Damien had not allied with either side, preferring instead to maintain the delicate balance between the rowdy citizens within Hezral's borders.

My back had grown stiff, hunkering down in our hollowed out shelter. I shifted my weight, which rustled some of the detritus beneath my feet. The dark elf suddenly tensed, then turned her head in our direction.

She waved her hands, making invisible circles in the air. Soon, a tiny puff of black smoke appeared, and within seconds, grew to a man-sized swirling oval. "Hurry," she said, pushing her lover into the smoke. "We've been discovered."

"Wait," the blonde said, "come with me, Sirynna...or let me help you."

"No. We'll meet again tomorrow."

The smoky oval—a portal, perhaps?—swirled faster, shrinking down on the blonde elf, as though swallowing her whole. "Be careful! I lo—"

She disappeared into a black, smoky whirlpool that unraveled like a ball of thread and slithered faster than the wind into the night. I wondered where she would end up. But the bristling hairs on my neck told me we had much bigger things to worry about. The dark elf drew a skeletal hand from inside her cloak and cast it on the ground. With a few waves of her hand, the bony appendage rattled around on the leaves and dirt until the fingers dug into the earth. The ground itself mounded up like a gopher escaping its burrow, and then *BOOM!* The dirt exploded into a shower while an entire skeleton clawed its way from the depths.

Tattered skin hung from the bones. Blood-red eyes bulged from their sockets, and in its hands were a sword and shield, both shimmering in a translucent, ghostly blue.

"Shit," I whispered, feeling like I just might lose control of my bowels before this was over.

"It's been a long time since you've been this close, Harker," the dark elf said, looking right in our direction.

Harker didn't seem surprised at all. He pulled back the ivy curtain with his cane and answered her call. "You've let down your guard with your new distraction."

"She's a hungry lightie. Very addicting and much better in bed than you!"

Harker's nostrils flared. One eye twitched—sure signs he was about to erupt. I'd felt his cane across my skull too many times. "I've had my own distraction as of late." He pulled back the vine curtain enough to reveal me—a shaking all over, puffy-furred cat boy—and said, "Kill her."

My eyes flicked between these two former lovers or enemies or whatever they were to each other. "W-what?" This had to be some test, part of the training he thought I needed. She must be in on it. But then again, he said I was to be an assassin...

"Are you deaf? I said kill her!"

He grabbed my arm and shoved me out past the vines. A serrated leaf sliced my ear, and I roared. The dark elf's eyes grew wide, standing out like ice blue gems against her indigo skin and the dark of night. She didn't expect this. And neither did I.

Her skeletal guardian crouched into a fighting stance. I couldn't tell whether one swipe of my claws would send him tumbling into a pile of bones or if he'd be stronger than any living fighter. He certainly looked intimidating enough, with his glowing red eyes and gaping toothy mouth.

"You've made a little tyger, I see." She laughed, her momentary shock apparently gone. "I really expected more from you, Harker. Sending a cub to fight a necromancer."

"A necromancer!" I shrieked, looking back at Harker. "What the— have you gone completely insane?" Whatever arousal I had felt minutes earlier had long since gone and instead my dick felt like it was trying to crawl up inside me. Necromancers outdid barbarians in our sordid bedtime stories. They infected you with horrendous diseases, tore your body apart and stuffed your bits in jars to use in strange rituals. They could turn you into a vampire, a zombie, or some other undead creation depending on their mood.

I'd gone from killing deer and rabbits to necromancers? This was too big a jump in the training sequence. I shifted my weight to break into a run—to hell with Harker and eating tonight—but something stabbed my shoulder. Fire streaked through my back, down my arms, and exploded across my chest.

I fell to my knees screaming and slapped around my shoulder until I felt the cause of my torment. A dart. When I pulled it out, Harker lowered the shooter from his mouth.

"This is p-poison." My voice turned raspy, hardly intelligible. I'd be dead in seconds. Had he been aiming for the necromancer and missed?

Harker knelt down as the skeletal minion charged. "No," he whispered to me, "Not poison to you. Just feeding the beast. Remember boy, only through pain does one become strong."

I shot to my feet. Energy surged through every muscle, expanding them in waves of aching agony. Like growing pains times ten-thousand. A roar loud enough to shake the forest rumbled from my throat. In a flurry of rattling bones, the skeleton warrior was upon me, raising his ghostly sword.

My hand shot out and caught his wrist as he brought it down. The force jarred me from head to toe—this abomination wielded unnatural strength. I should be dead, my head split open like a cleaver to a melon. Yet I still stood, unwavering, with not one tremor in my arm muscles to indicate weakness. Whatever poison Harker had infected me with, it made me stronger.

The minion, brainless as it was, had gone still in a moment of shock. Recovering from the surprise, he swung his bare-boned leg at me, hoping to knock me off my feet. His shin collided with my thigh. Though it hurt, I didn't budge. Every bone in his meatless frame rattled as though he might fall apart with very little force.

The necromancer waved her hands again, summoning the beginnings of another portal like the one into which her lover had fled. Harker shot her with a dart. The portal shrank to nothing. Her shrill cry penetrated my ears. She dropped her cloak and fled into the rundown shack. Rage scorched its way through my veins—she would not leave here alive, nor would her summoned warrior.

I grabbed the skeleton by the ankle and yanked him off his feet. His conjured sword hit the ground and dissipated into a puff of blue smoke. In one powerful, slingshot-style circle, I hurled him around my head. Imagining the horrors this thing could wreak upon Port Valor, I pounded him into the ground. His bones scattered everywhere in a clacking thunder that echoed through the forest.

"Kill her!" Harker screamed, though it was a needless order. I was already in pursuit, covering an incredible distance with each springing stride.

Bursting through the pitiful excuse for a door, I stopped. Splintered wood clinked off jars that lined shelves along the walls and into bowls on a rickety table that held pestles filled with herbs and powders. The interior didn't match the dilapidated appearance of the exterior. In here, the roof was intact, the wooden floor dry, the walls plastered. A fire burned in a large stone hearth. Steam rolled from a large pot that hung above the flames, burning my nose with an acrid, rotten-flesh odor. At the rear of the room was a small nook containing a dresser, mirror, and good-sized bed with crumpled sheets.

Perhaps the exterior had been a cloaking spell, designed to deter thieves, who wouldn't expect such a trashed pile of sticks to contain anything valuable.

The necromancer hunkered in a corner against the bed. She held her shoulder, wincing as though in tremendous pain. Had Harker shot her with the same poison he'd given me? Would she transform into some super necromancer? From the looks of the foam bubbling out of the corners of her mouth, I'd say she didn't take it as well as I had.

Harker came in behind me, his voice ominous. "Go on, finish her."

A growl rumbled from my chest. *Finish her.* I sniffed the air, smelling her sweat, saliva, and the perfumed silk dressing gown she wore, so transparent, her dark nipples showed through it. My mouth watered at the promise of fresh, hot blood and meat. Yet, I hesitated. She may have been a disgusting lover of all things dead, but in this state, she provided no challenge. She'd likely be dead in a minute or two.

"She doesn't deserve your empathy," Harker said. "Look in the jars."

Reluctantly, I withdrew my eyes from the dying necromancer and scanned the shelves. Animals, parts of animals, organs, a hand. My eyes lingered on a few large jars with fetuses of various sizes and ages. One had clubbed feet and twisted legs. But all of them were in various states of experimentation, filleted open like fish, organs and brains exposed. They floated in lifeless slumber. One opened its eyes. Growling, I flinched from the sudden shock. Tiny red eyes locked onto mine. The baby opened its mouth, baring two sharp fangs. It clawed at the side of the jar with nail-less pink fingers, unable to escape its prison or to satisfy the bloodlust that was much too great for such a tiny creature.

What had this woman done—had she stolen babies for this? Did she plan to turn them into an undead army of infants? Directly under the babies were jars of faces. Young, old, men, women, submerged in their liquid tombs like sheets of thick fabric. These had no eyes or teeth, just empty sockets and gray, gaping lips. One of them, though one-dimensional and inhuman, looked familiar. Bushy eyebrows mottled with gray and a beard to match. A scar from a wayward fishing hook on his left cheek.

"Dad..." I whispered, and not a moment later, noticed the jar beside him. A lovely woman who had given me her jet-black hair. "Mom?"

"Yes," Harker said, his accusing voice hot and horrible against my ear. "Sirynna killed them. She's gone too far this time. Make her pay."

Sirynna slumped against the footboard of her bed, her body convulsing. Bloody foam dripped from her mouth. Did a necromancer enjoy death when it came upon them? She didn't seem to be enjoying it. Fear danced in the glistening whites of her eyes.

"Liar," she moaned. "Liar!"

I couldn't stop staring at their faces. My parents—hardworking, honest, loving. They'd given me all they could and loved each other like mad. They'd had what I had wanted with Mira. But, she was gone, and now they were too. All because of this monstrous woman. But she'd called Harker a liar. Why? My mind couldn't penetrate the fog of what I'd become and the death of everything I'd ever known.

"She's the liar, Lysander. She found them when they were out looking for you, when they came too close to this godforsaken hovel. Necromancers will say anything to weaken you enough to destroy you. They'll take everything you love and corrupt it, like she corrupted me. Don't let her do it again. Don't let her hurt more people you love...like Mira."

Mira. She could have just as easily been in one of those jars. Drool slavered from my jaws. I'd kill this bitch before the poison did. With a thunderous roar, I leapt onto the table. My posture shifted forward. On all fours, my hands became paws, and I was more tyger than I'd ever been. I ran the table's length, knocking concoctions, mortars and pestles away as I went. Like tiny cannons, they exploded onto the floor below, shattering into jagged pieces and heralding my descent into murder.

My paws met the table's rough edge, my mouth opened wide. I sprang, sinking my teeth into the neck of my first kill as an assassin. I wouldn't go hungry tonight.

* * * *

~ Lysander ~

North Leogard, five years later

"This one's got a strong back," the little man said, nudging the child forward. Phlegm rippled his voice. He smoked too much, obviously. An ebonwood pipe dangled from his fat lips, filled with expensive curweed-laced tobacco from the smell of it. "He'll make a good gardener."

Lady Lisanna Arrochet arched a brow, eyeing the boy with the sneering skepticism typical of upper-class high elves. "I don't know. He looks scrawny to me." She picked up the boy's wrist, holding it between her finger and thumb like he was a dirty handkerchief. "His arms are like twigs. How is he supposed to tend our roses and prune them properly? I doubt he can even lift the shears."

"Oh, he's stronger than he looks. Give him a month or two of some good meat and milk, and he'll put on more weight. Poor lad can't help it if he's been half-starved. His folks were poor as willowhoots, Omri rest their souls. If you'll take him on, I'll give you a good deal, even throw in his little sister for free."

She dropped the boy's arm and wiped her fingers with a lacy handkerchief. "I don't know..."

He leaned closer to her, glancing at the little girl huddled up under her brother's protective arm. "Come now, my lady, your husband will enjoy her when she gets a little bigger and starts to sprout."

She shrugged and gave a tired sigh. "I suppose they will do. Jariel will appreciate the gift, I'm sure. He likes the ones with dark complexions like that."

Disgusting prick. Preying on little girls must have been the side effect of living a thousand years and becoming bored of centuries with the same cold woman. Damn elves.

I breathed deeply, doing my best to stay focused and not turn tyger just yet. I'd get my chance soon enough and couldn't blow my cover until I had enough evidence stored on the tracker beetle's memory stone. Not that anyone would miss this bastard. He and that "lady's" husband deserved castration with a rusty knife. Better yet, a set of tyger claws ripping their dicks off at the root.

We had been tracking the whereabouts of these "orphans" from Hezral for some time now. Truth was, the ringleader of this illegal adoption ring hired highway bandits to kill the parents and snatch the kids. This little minion wasn't the ringleader. He was just a dealer. The ringleader, we believed, was right here in Leogard, likely one of the nobles who resided in one of these fine manor houses. So long as King Leopold turned a blind eye to the dealings of his nobility, this disgusting practice would continue. I was about to send him a clear message that the children of Hezral were not for elven consumption.

The tracker beetle—a wondrous device Harker and I had engineered from dwarven clockwork bits—had a clear view of their exchange in the sitting room of this pristine manor. The images and sound carried perfectly into my headset, which was fitted with clear lenses and round metal earpieces. Being the size of a real beetle, the little tracker could fit into chinks in mortar or gaps under doors as in this case, allowing me to spy easily and to confirm my targets.

Not everyone deserved to die. This guy, though…let's just say I couldn't wait to get my claws into him. I'd become reliable enough to handle solo missions and had quite the following back home. When I returned, I'd have all the ladies mesmerized, gathered around my table at the Fishhouse when I told them about this adventure. Mavelle Bearden would scoot up close, and I'd get to admire her figure while she would accidentally-on-purpose touch my arm or thigh. At fifteen, she was still a bit young for me, but it wouldn't be long before I'd be able to do more than look.

Money changed hands, and the kids were ushered off into another room with a servant.

Wiggling my fingers like a pretend bug, I guided the tracker beetle back out under the door and up the wall to where I perched upon the roof over a side entrance.

The man emerged, tossing his bag of gold into the air, triumphant with himself. He turned right into the dark alley between the house and high-walled garden. I dropped to the ground right in front of him, staring him down with feline eyes.

The terror on his face was oh so satisfying.

"Who do you work for?" I asked.

His pipe fell from his lips with a clatter on the brick walk. Embers cast an eerie orange glow upon his trembling jaw. "W-Who are you?"

"Answer my question first, and maybe I'll tell you."

He took a step back, but froze when I growled. "Fine. His surname's Sivenya, owns some bakeries in the city where all the adoptions are arranged. I'm just the delivery man, don't know nothing about the rest of it. I'll take you right to him, eh, in exchange for letting me go. Gotta make ends meet, you understand."

"Oh, I understand. But I don't need help to find your boss. I've got enough information to do the job myself."

"I'll give you all this gold," he said, jutting the bag at me with a trembling hand. The coins inside clinked like little bells.

I took it from him, ripped it open, and poured the coins onto the dirt by the walk.

He stepped back again, arms out in front of him, like he could really ward me off with those pudgy fingers. "I'll give you whatever you want. Who are you?"

"I'm the Tyger, and you've sold your last child." With a hard and fast jab, my claws speared his neck, puncturing his windpipe. He couldn't scream. I wrapped my fingers around his cervical vertebrae and lifted him off the ground. He kicked and wheezed, scratched at my arm, but only managed to ruffle my fur.

With a firm squeeze and a solid shake, his bones snapped in my fist. My ears picked up soft steps behind me. I recognized her smell.

"Don't move a muscle," a woman's harsh whisper grazed my ear. Her invisible blade sat against my jugular. I'd seen her in action a few times during my travels. Caliphany Trudeaux, niece of King Leopold, leader of the Leogard Intelligence Organization, and one hell of a ranger. Not to mention a deadly fire mage. She wasn't one to take lightly.

I chuckled. "Hello, Lady Trudeaux. You're a little late to the party."

"Drop him."

"Gladly." I flung the bastard off my fist. He landed in a heap on the brick walk. "But I'm not your enemy."

"A cat shifter ripping out people's throats in my city is not what I'd call an ally." She came out of concealment, rippling to solid form as she circled around me. One hand aimed a wicked-looking sword at my throat, while the other held a swirling blue flame. "You have five seconds to explain yourself."

"I'm merely stemming the tide of a festering disease, one that is harming innocent children from Hezral. Your uncle should spend less time crusading in foreign lands and more time babysitting his nobles." In my hand, the one not covered in my target's blood, I held the memory stone from the tracker beetle. "I know you don't know me, but I know you to be an intelligent and just leader of the L.I.O. Look into the dealings of a nobleman named Sivenya. There are two stolen children in this house that need your help. And take this…"

I tossed her the memory gem. The fire in her palm disappeared as she caught it, but she had taken her eyes off me for a second. Which was all I needed to bound straight up and flip in a backwards somersault to the roof. In a few long strides, I ran to the roof's edge on the opposite side of the house. One giant leap carried me over the gap between the manor and the Temple.

Caliphany didn't follow. She may not have trusted me, but she must have known I was more than just a rogue killer. In the future, perhaps we would become true allies, but for now, she had the proof needed to bring down this black market adoption ring. I had no doubt she would see to it that these children were freed and well cared for.

I hid in the shadows of a small private balcony on the Temple's top floor and washed the gore from my hand with a watering can. The bloody mess soaked into the soil of a big potted plant. The window, dimly lit from the other side, was cracked open. I caught another very familiar smell, and soon heard a voice I knew just as well, coming from inside.

Mira.

"Can I come in?" she asked. "I know it's late."

"To what do I owe the honor of your visit?" That was Ivy

Munroviel's voice. Middle daughter of the Priestess, dick-hardening beautiful, but a complete and total bitch.

"I'm not here for a chat," Mira said. "I-I need help."

"Perhaps you should ask Loralee for that. You and she are so very close after all."

"She can't help me with this. I'm…pregnant."

All the blood escaped my head in a whoosh. I had to hold to the balcony's railing so I wouldn't lose my balance. Mira, pregnant? I'd spied on her before, of course. She did cozy up to some of the paladins like Sir Francis. Whether she had bedded them or not didn't concern me. It wasn't like I was celibate either, but the thought of her carrying another man's child hit me a lot harder than I would have imagined.

"Oh," Ivy said, nonchalantly. "Is that all? And I suppose you want to get rid of it."

"Y-yes. Can you do that?"

"Of course I can. But it will cost you."

"How much?"

"Don't worry about that now. But someday, I just may need *your* assistance, and I will expect you to heed my call then. Do we have a deal?"

There was a long pause, then Mira answered, "Yes, we have a deal."

I'd had all I could take. It was one thing for her to cavort with elves, but having one's baby was apparently too inconvenient for her. Just like I had been.

"Fuck you," I whispered, then dropped silently to the ground and disappeared into the night.

Chapter Five

~ Lysander ~

Hezral, the Cavitel River, five years later…

Stars hung from the black sky over the Cavitel Valley and the rushing river that ran along it. Tonight's targets were smugglers from Port Valor meeting the ferryman at midnight. They were picking up curweed, an old Leogardian herb responsible for creating new addicts in Port Valor. It could kill in larger doses. King Damien had already survived one poisoning attempt and suspected Leogard of seeking his demise. My job was to dispatch them quickly and destroy the curweed before anyone ever took the first nibble.

Harker's voice crackled through the ear cuff. "Ten minutes 'til interception."

"Understood."

I crouched in a tall tree out of sight, just above the road near the ferryman's shack, letting my eyes soak up what little light I could. With a new moon, I had to make do with the starlight, but my vision still lit up ten times brighter than your average assassin. Superb night vision was just one of the perks of being half-cat. The others—speed, strength, agility, quick healing and camouflage—I had wholeheartedly embraced. The super sense of smell also had its advantages, unless I found myself in a sewer system like the catacombs under Leogard or the fishmonger's shop in Port Valor.

The past ten years had been a blur of training and missions. Harker had his eccentricities, choosing to live mostly outdoors rather than his quarters in the castle. But he was bright, and he taught me more than I would ever learn on a fishing boat. We didn't kill for sport. We eliminated threats. It kept Hezral safe and paid well. I'd bought the nicest home in Port Valor and added some inventive gadgets to make it unique. Mavelle loved it, and I couldn't wait to climb into bed with her tonight. I only wished my parents had lived long enough for me to spoil them.

Wagon wheels crunched on the pebbled road. Seconds later, a horse came into view, pulling a cart. Two people were in the seat, both wearing fur-lined cloaks with hoods. They kept their heads down, so I couldn't see their faces. One looked smaller in stature—either young or female. The wind blew the wrong way, so I couldn't pick up their scent.

In the back of the cart were bales of straw and sacks, open just enough to show their contents of beets, turnips, and potatoes. A little too obvious with their cargo, I thought. The only people who kept everything out in the open were the ones who wanted to hide something. A little more focus, eye muscles straining, pupils stretching into full circumference, and there it was—a small chest just under the straw.

I adjusted the headset and spoke into the clear gem on my ring. "They're definitely ready to make an exchange."

This gadget was made of a flexible copper wire, coiled to adapt around changing ears like mine. Both ends were fitted with gems that synced to my ring and were shaped to fit inside my ear canal. The ring transmitted my voice to Harker's and his back to me. His set worked the same way. I readied myself for the leap down.

"Watch for the signal," Harker said. "Wait for the pickup."

"They could be simple merchants, selling prized beets to the elves."

Harker chuckled. "No one likes beets, especially elves."

The cuff hurt a bit. It still needed some adjustments. I didn't have anyone else like me to experiment with. But that was my second job—Lysander the tinkerer. Not cut out for fishing or farming. Just killing and tinkering. Wouldn't Mira be surprised if she knew? She didn't think I'd amount to anything.

As expected, the travelers lifted a lantern and blocked the light with their hands in a code-like series of flashes. Long, short, short, long, short, then off. I stored that in my memory for future curweed smuggler takedowns. An identical signal flashed from the ferryman's shack. A door squeaked, the ferryman shuffled out, and the cart pulled up to meet him.

The trio gathered at the back of the wagon. Some rummaging through the sacks almost hid the retrieval of the box, but not quite. The larger of the two handed a sack of beets to the ferryman, who handed a very small box over in return. Some hand shaking occurred, followed by whispered farewells, and in went the curweed into the smuggler box in the guise of readjusting the cargo.

The ferryman shuffled back inside while the two smugglers climbed into the cart, turned around, and headed back down the road. I readied myself to ambush them from the tree. It wouldn't take much. All I had to do was drop into the back of their cart, break their necks, and they'd never know what happened. I'd leave the bodies as a warning to other drug smugglers. I'd burn the curweed at Harker's latest campsite, breathe a bit of the smoke and enjoy the ride until it turned to ash.

I was about to let myself fall when the smaller of the two broke into a violent coughing fit. The driver slowed the horse to a stop and patted his companion's back, but it didn't help. His hooded head scanned the area before he pulled off his hood and that of the other smuggler.

"Now!" Harker yelled through the earpiece.

I froze, not even daring to breathe. I knew those faces well. Almost as well as my own family. They were Mira's mom and dad, more wrinkled and gray than they should be for their age. But, I loved them dearly.

Abbott Hearton retrieved a water skein for Evetta. "Here, drink."

Evetta stopped coughing long enough to do as he asked. She coughed again, expelling some of it.

"More," Abbott said. "I've added some absinthe. It will help."

Harker came through again, so loud, it scraped my eardrum. "Now! Kill them now!"

"Wait," I whispered.

She drank again, then covered her mouth and breathed deeply. Poor Evetta had been ill for some time.

"Thank you, love," she said. "We must hurry. Mirabelle is counting on us."

Mira? What did she have to do with this? The fur on the back of my neck and back bristled into a stiff, nervous ridge.

"What are you waiting for?" Harker screamed in my ear. "Kill them!"

"No," I answered. "I can't. They're family."

"I don't care who they are. You have orders. Do your job!"

Abbott picked up the reins and snapped them. The horse started up, and the cart pulled away from me.

"I will not hurt them," I said. "You're wrong about them. They're not smugglers."

"You won't do it? Fine. I will."

Shit. We had stolen teleportation secrets from Leogardian mages, and Harker knew how to use them. He appeared in a puff of smoke just a few feet in front of the cart. The horse whinnied and reared. Evetta screamed.

I'd die before I ever let anyone hurt them. I sprang from the tree, landed in the back of the cart, and leapt over the horse. Harker had his staff pointed right at them. The tip glowed bright red, sparking and whistling like a teapot. I tackled him just as he set off the charge. Red lightning struck just a few feet from the cart. The horse whinnied and bolted, while I rolled around on the ground with Harker, trying to knock the staff from his hands.

A quick glance told me Abbott had gotten the horse under control. They were well out of harm's way.

Harker got his staff between him and me and swiped me in the jaw. I roared, tasting blood. He'd knocked a tooth loose. We wrestled like that, rolling and punching until both of us were bloodied, but I couldn't let him point the deadly end of his staff at me. I had no idea how much power he might actually possess. If there was anything I'd learned about Harker, it was that I only knew what he let me know. He was a walking enigma.

We kept rolling, our momentum gaining down the mossy slope toward the steep cliff above the river. "Stop! What are you doing?"

"I should have let you die."

"Why did you want to hurt them? They're innocent."

"They have something valuable. Now get off me so I can kill you properly."

56

He opened his mouth like his jaws were unhinged and let out an ungodly screech. I grabbed a scrubby plant, pulled myself away from him and tore off my headpiece. Blood poured from my right ear.

He kept rolling and came within feet of the cliff's edge, using the hooked end of his staff to catch a rock and stop his fall. An incessant ringing filled my right ear, while the river's roar drowned out everything else. Harker clawed at the rock until he could pull his legs beneath him, then got on his knees. He leaned on his staff, trying to push himself up to his feet.

Damn him, and damn his lies. I'd never kill for Harker again. I'd make him pay for how close I had come to killing Abbott and Evetta. Baring my teeth, I let the tyger take over, announcing its arrival in a full-fledged growl.

In two bounds, I reached him. He got to his feet and lifted that cursed staff to fry me like the seal blubber he once insisted on feeding me to add bulk to my frame. My hands smashed into his chest, my claws sank into his skin. We both fell over the edge.

The ground disappeared. The river roared far below, throwing mist into our faces.

Shit. I couldn't just let him die, even now that I hated him to the core. The bastard wasn't exactly a father figure, but he was the closest thing to family I had left. I caught Harker's arm with one hand, and with the other, grabbed for a tough root that stuck out from the muddy cliff where the rain had washed away the soil. Digging in with my claws, I slid down the root until it finally stopped my fall. It anchored me, but the force from Harker's falling weight pulled it loose from the bank. Pain shot through my shoulder. I felt the pop when it pulled from the socket.

But the root didn't hold. It kept ripping from the soil on the bank the farther we fell. I held tight while we swung out over the water. Harker screamed and cursed, but he might as well have been whispering, the river was so loud. Claws and fur receded. I needed skin to skin grip. I clung to his forearm, and he clung to mine. We had about two seconds before the hungry river swallowed us.

Looking frantically at the bank, I tried to find another root or rock to grab hold of as we spiraled to our death. There—just out of reach—a rope, and above it, the lantern-lit face of the ferryman. He'd come to save the poor souls who had almost murdered two innocent people. He must have not witnessed that part. One fierce kick at the air in the opposite direction gave me the boost I needed to reach the rope. I let go of the root, caught the rope, looped it quickly around my hand and wrist, and looked back down at Harker.

Instead of his terrified face, I stared into the glowing red end of his staff. With a wide swing of my foot, I kicked it aside. Red lightning cracked through the air and grazed the rope. It began to unravel. It wouldn't hold us both. One of us would have to die…and it wouldn't be me.

I let go of his arm.

He fell with a river-silenced scream and hit the water. Rushing waves devoured him. The end of his staff bobbed for a second, casting a bright red beacon. But the river gulped it down, too. I hit the muddy cliff with a squishy splat, but the rope held.

"Goodbye, old friend…and good riddance." I climbed back up the rope and paid the ferryman more than he would make in one lifetime for his silence.

Chapter Six

~ Mirabelle ~

Leogard, The Temple, present day...

Charred skin and incense perfumed the air in High Priestess Arianne's inner sanctum. I slipped as far into my mind as I could, while red-hot branding irons burned a curse into my forearm. I'd read in one of our medical journals: *Under the duress of torture, it is not uncommon for the subject to drift from his or her own mind, either to create alternate realities or to recall more pleasant memories from the past.*

But, I could not force my mind to create a happy make-believe world where there was none to be had. My screams echoed into the ivy-covered rafters where an errant dove flew frantically. It collided with a closed window and fell to the floor at my feet, loose feathers drifting down a second later. The screams died into morbid silence.

I shivered so hard my teeth clacked together. My tongue swelled from where I'd bitten down on it, drawing hot, iron-flavored blood that I desperately wanted to spit out. I swallowed it instead, staring at my forearm. The marks stared back at me, blackened and bloodied, the same symbols as those on the priestesses' foreheads. They represented the five tenets—loyalty, honesty, purity, wisdom, and devotion. They'd gotten theirs when they were newborn babes, and every time they broke a tenet, the symbols responded with a jolt of pain from mild to severe, depending on the severity of the sin. But mine were meant as a death sentence, not moral reminders.

My ten-year stint as an acolyte in Leogard's Temple now seemed

59

like a distant dream. Like all the good things in my life, it wasn't meant to last. Because of me, the Priestess's oldest daughter, my best friend Loralee, had been forced into exile, and I'd never forgive myself for that.

I had but one thing I could do for Loralee now—something she had entrusted to me, and I would guard that secret with my life. The key to her lab, a pretty lavender stone called an opening gem, should be in my parents' hands by now. It wasn't safe with me. I just hoped Sir Francis was truly trustworthy enough to deliver it to them instead of going to the king. He'd been betrothed to Loralee, cared deeply for her, and was the best friend of the man she truly loved. Surely, he would have her best interests at heart.

One of the two city guards who had held me down stood behind my chair with one hand on my shoulder. He groaned like he was about to throw up.

"Now," the Priestess said, "tell me where Loralee kept her specimens."

My throat burned from all the screaming. I coughed and tried to still my trembling jaw. "I t-told you I know n-nothing about that."

"Liar! You and she were an inseparable pair," she said, with more than a little sarcasm. "Little did she know how you would betray her, but that is beyond our control now, isn't it? Tell me where to find those specimens. I know she hid them somewhere, probably in the catacombs. Her knowledge couldn't have been granted by the goddess."

"Maybe it was," I said, drawing from the courage of knowing I had not fully betrayed my dear friend. "Loralee committed herself to healing. Doesn't the goddess bless those who help others? *Blessed is she whose hands come to aid and not to harm.*"

"Preaching to the Priestess, are you? Perhaps I should have the guards gouge your eyes out so they, too, can cause no harm."

Blood rushed from my head, making me dizzy. She wouldn't think twice about blinding me under normal circumstances, but I would never tell her where to find Loralee's secret lab. She had already branded me with a curse, which she wouldn't want to waste. I'd need my eyes to carry out her plans.

She never cracked a smile, but still chuckled. "Is that fear I see on your blanched face? Fine, let's return to your punishment. You will go back to Port Valor and find the assassin known as the Tyger. He is rumored to have stolen valuable artifacts and spells from me and those in the Mage Academy. He is alleged to have killed people within our city walls, but no one has been able or willing to put an end to it. You have two months to locate, capture and deliver him to me, dead or alive. Is that understood?"

All five of her tenet symbols were lit up like pyrogems on her forehead. They must have been burning like the Abysmal Sea, but she never flinched. The only hint of her discomfort showed in her green eyes, cold and intimidating as ever, but they glistened with tears. I'd never seen the Priestess's symbols lit—they were only supposed to do if she had broken her tenets. I guess forcing me to endure branding with an enchanted, hot iron and asking me to hunt down an assassin had broken them all.

I couldn't take my eyes off the orange lights flashing against her alabaster skin. "How do you expect me to do that?"

"I don't care. Stab him, poison him, seduce him into submission. Better yet, bend his mind to your will like you did with my daughter."

The persistent lump in my throat broke my voice. "I'm s-sorry. I've told you time and again that if I could have prevented it, I w-would have."

"Yes, yes, quite the timeless tale for all mortalkind, especially you short-lived humans. Sorry for this. Sorry for that. You are never truly sorry unless you face consequences. You could have very easily sacrificed yourself for my daughter as she would no doubt have done for you, yet you chose to save your own skin instead. Now you must accept the consequences. King Leopold will not grant me the pleasure of your execution. He wants to simply export you back to your cold and filthy Hezrali homeland, but I am not satisfied with such an easy punishment. Bring me the Tyger."

"And if I cannot? He may not even be in Port Valor or even in Hezral by the time I arrive."

"That's your problem, not mine. Embedded in each symbol on your arm is a bloodgem filled with Hezrali basilisk venom." A smile crawled across her lips. "Ah, you know exactly what that will do, don't you? Loralee taught you well."

Oh, I knew what Hezrali basilisk venom did, all right. It dissolved you from the inside out. When we were kids, we heard horror stories about people found in the form of shapeless puddles after an unfortunate encounter with one of those big lizards. My own father lost half a herd of goats to one of them. Combined with bloodgems, which broke down completely at normal human body temperature after a convenient two months, mine would be a slow, tortuous death. Loralee and I had successfully used them with patients here in the Temple to deliver gradual doses of medicine. That meant I'd start to feel the effects earlier than the expiration date. How nice.

"Should you attempt to remove them before your time is up," she continued, "they will release the venom—I've assured that. And do not think of pleading your case to the Mage Academy or the king. They know better than to cross me."

The Priestess avoided direct eye contact, and for good reason, so I focused my defiance at her peripheral vision and read her aura. It flashed orange and yellow like the scared, insecure woman I knew she was deep down inside. "Let me get this straight. If I find the Tyger and bring him back here, you'll remove these things and let me go. But, should I fail, I'll die a horrible death. Are you really so desperate to capture an assassin that may not even exist?"

She walked to one of the long, narrow windows near her crystal collection and peeked around the curtain as though someone might be eavesdropping. Highly unlikely, unless they'd learned to fly. We were three stories up. "Leopold denies the existence of this assassin. Yet, you claim to have betrayed Loralee because you believed the Tyger was threatening the lives of your parents. Either you are right, and he does exist, or he's simply a rumor, as the king believes. I'm giving you the chance to prove you are right."

During any normal day in the Temple, I would have never argued with Priestess Arianne Munroviel. But, this was no normal day, and I was going to die one way or another. She would see to that. Might as well put up a good fight first.

"Why not just kill me and get it over with?" I covered my seared arm with the sleeve of my light blue acolyte robe. The silk fabric brushed over the wound. The sudden sting made me suck in a breath through my teeth. "You could say it was an accident. I'm sure the king would believe you, considering how…close you've been over the centuries."

That got her rankled. The symbols on her forehead flared. She must have been in agony. With a soft groan, she gritted her teeth and turned away. Her immaculate white robe caught on the corner of her desk and ripped as she rushed to her personal fountain of blessed water. She yanked her hood off, and I gasped. Where a full head of coppery red hair once grew, was a stubbly scalp. The points on her ears were exaggerated against her bare skin, like fleshy daggers. She must have shaved her head—whether in mourning, repentance, or perhaps both, I didn't know. She leaned over, cupped some of the sparkling water in her hands, and splashed it on her face. There was a sizzling sound, followed by steam.

"You are an abomination. You should have been killed the moment you were born." After patting her face with a towel, she leaned on the edge of the fountain, her shoulders rising and falling with each labored breath. "Yet, I've still given you the chance to redeem yourself."

"Why don't you ask Ivy where he is? She's the one who claimed to have hired the Tyger to hurt my family. She would have killed me had I not done as she wanted, and she threatened to have my parents murdered. It's Ivy you should be torturing, not me!"

"You dare lay blame on her? Had it not been for you, she would have never turned against us."

"Keep telling yourself that."

"Silence!" She took a deep breath as though calming herself. "You leave at dawn."

"You know I won't be able to find him."

"Of course you won't. But, if this phantom assassin hasn't yet killed your family, you have the chance to see them before you die. You should thank the goddess for my mercy."

"What good will any of this do?"

"Nothing!" Her voice ricocheted off the high, white-domed ceiling. "Absolutely nothing but making sure someone pays for what has transpired within this Temple."

"This will only lead to more death. Aren't you supposed to be a healer? A defender of life?"

"I never asked for this life!" The Priestess turned her head to not-quite-look at me over her shoulder. "Vengeance is mine..." Her tenet symbols flared. Her eyes watered. "...and I will have it despite the king or the goddess."

I lowered my head like a reverent dog. "Your will be done, Priestess."

"Take her away."

As though I was a toddler of twenty pounds, the guards easily picked me up by my armpits and swooped me from the chair. They escorted me to my room, where I would spend one final, sleepless night in the Temple of Leogard. The one place I'd called home for ten years. The place I'd wanted to make a difference, where my...talents...were an asset, not a liability.

No, I had to muck it all up. Loralee, the best friend I had in Leogard—exiled because of me, because I feared for my parents' lives. I would never forget her green eyes staring into mine, how willingly she had done as I commanded, how she had told me she loved me like any good friend would before she boarded that ship. And for that crime, now I had to capture or kill a man I had no idea how to find. A man who may have never existed at all.

Even if a miracle occurred, and I did manage to capture him and bring him to Leogard, I'd still probably die. If I didn't find him, I would most certainly die.

As if this whole situation wasn't nightmarish enough, it wasn't capturing a possibly fictitious assassin or dying that had me truly terrified. It was knowing that I'd see Lysander again, the boy I would have married if I hadn't left home for Leogard all those years ago.

But he would be a man now, wouldn't he? And sometimes men aren't quick to forgive.

Chapter Seven

~ Mirabelle ~

Port Valor, two weeks later...

Spring in Port Valor—cold, damp, foggy and incredibly muddy. Like winter with less snow. I hadn't had the pleasure of coming back home with the Port Valor Traveling Opera and their toe-tapping ditties. Instead, I had to cram myself into hired coaches with a changing assortment of passengers as they rolled from stop to stop on the road north. Most of the elven sort were amicable enough, in awe of a Temple escapee. But others—humans and halflings—were ill-tempered, rude, and reeked with sweat. They were none too fond of elves or Leogard's Temple. And I could have sworn a couple of them stole my sweet talaberry rolls. My mouth still watered from the thoughts of enjoying them with a hot cup of coffee. Of course, I could get my fill in Bearden's Fishhouse. But there was one problem—who would be there? Mom and Dad or maybe Lysander, the man I was in no way ready to face yet?

I had come to appreciate the lack of body hair and meticulous cleanliness of my pointy-eared neighbors, but the farther north I went, the hairier and smellier the passengers were. Two weeks of traveling hell. Then, there were the auras. Thanks to Loralee, I'd learned to make sense of the colored hazes I saw around people. I'd learned to pinpoint diseases and other afflictions with them. My fellow passengers had a variety of ailments, from chronic headaches, to liver rot, to bunions. I treated a few of them on the way, earning a farebit or two for my efforts. At least I could still make a living, not that I had much time left to live.

The final coach dropped me at the corner of Port Valor's largest butcher shop, across the street from Bearden's Fishhouse & Tavern. My father and Lysander's had sold their catch at the tavern for years, and our mothers had worked in the kitchens. Out at the harbor, I could see the fishing boats coming in, which meant Mom and Dad would most likely be there at this hour. My first instinct was to travel home and wait for them so we could have quiet and privacy, but surely people wouldn't recognize me right away. Then again, I wore my acolyte robe, and it didn't exactly blend in with the dull browns, blacks and grays of Hezrali clothing. Hunger gnawed at my gut, and I could really use a nice drink, so I decided to risk a visit to the Fishhouse.

"Can't you drive right across the street there?" I yelled to the driver as he held open the door for everyone to exit the coach. "That's where I need to go."

"That'll be two farebits," he said.

"Two farebits? Just to...? Oh, never mind. I'll walk."

"Suit yourself."

As soon as I stepped onto the boardwalk, the footman tossed me my bag. I caught it, but lost my balance and toppled off the walk and onto the street, taking a sloshy seat in the mud.

Ugh. I'd be nasty when I met my parents, not to mention cold and wet. "A little help here?"

Both men laughed. The driver walked into the butcher shop. I finally got to my feet and locked eyes with the footman. Once I'd connected with his mind, I said, "You will carry me and my bag to Bearden's."

"Yes, miss," the footman answered, nodding slowly. He hoisted the strap of my bag over his shoulder, then picked me up in his arms. Every squelching step he took toward the tavern made me grimace. Once again, I'd proven the Priestess right. I couldn't be trusted with my abilities. Good thing I wouldn't be alive long enough to cause much trouble. Should I be caught using my powers before then, I'd likely be executed. Being different wasn't tolerated in Port Valor. If you weren't stock human, you were better off dead or elsewhere. That's one reason why I'd chosen elsewhere ten years ago.

Finally, the footman set me down gently on the boardwalk and dropped my bag at my feet. He stood there staring at my eyes until I said,

"You may go."

"As you wish, miss." He bowed stiffly and turned to leave, but I caught his hand and pressed two farebits into it. "For your trouble," I said. "You never saw me."

He pocketed the money, shook his head like he was shaking himself from a daze and squelched back across the street to the coach.

I started toward the Fishhouse when someone ran by, sideswiping me so hard I almost lost my balance. "Hey!"

The young man didn't stop. He had a big bouquet of flowers in one hand and what looked like a coin purse in the other.

Down the boardwalk from where he had come, an old woman scurried toward me. "Come back here, you thief!"

Really? Five minutes in Port Valor and I had to witness a robbery. No one else had noticed yet or cared enough to. A stack of crates on the boardwalk blocked the thief's escape route. He'd dodge around those and get away with what might be her life savings if I didn't do something.

Fine.

I drew a dagger from its sheath on my belt and held it by the tip of the double-edged blade. With one foot behind the other, I kept my arm straight and drew it back over my head. My weight shifted forward. My arm came down with a whoosh of speed and blade. The dagger spun in a perfect, blurred arc and sank into the coin purse, impaling it on one of the crates.

The boy skidded to a stop and spun around, meeting my gaze with terrified eyes. When I drew my other dagger, he dropped the bouquet and sprinted away across the muddy street.

I walked to the crates, retrieved my dagger and the coin purse. The old woman caught up to me, breathing hard. I recognized her now—she'd been selling flowers on the streets of Port Valor for ages, but I couldn't remember her name. I handed her the money and picked up her bouquet. Long white petals from the snowflowers fell around my feet. A few of the stems were broken, leaving the blooms drooping sadly toward the ground.

"I'm afraid some are a little worse for wear," I said, then offered them to her.

She hugged the coin purse to her chest and shook her head. "Keep them—the good ones, that is. I can't thank you enough for stopping that dirty little thief. He's a curweed addict, and this is the second time he's robbed me."

"That's terrible. Are you hurt?"

"Nothing but my pride, dear. I'm Nadene."

"Mirabelle."

Her eyebrows arched in surprise, disappearing under the black kerchief on her head. "Oh, the Hearton's girl. Well, don't let me keep you. Your mother talks about you all the time."

I smiled and glanced down the boardwalk at the swinging sign above the Bearden's Fishhouse door. Nervous jitters made me shiver.

"Take care, Nadene. Maybe you should invest in a weapon of your own."

"Maybe you're right." She chuckled and shuffled back to her flower stand.

Let's try this again. I walked back to the Fishhouse and tried to scrape the muck from my boots on the edge of the doorstep. Then again, mud and all things nasty were part of life in Port Valor. I'd fit right in.

I reached for the door handle. Glass shattered on the other side. Typical bar fight. Smiling, I paused and waited for another crash, but instead there was a roar of laughter. They'd made amends, or someone had been knocked out. Either way, I knew it was now safe to enter, so I pulled open the door.

* * * *

~ Lysander ~

Flexing my fingers, I yelled over the roar of drunken laughter. "Who's next?" That last fellow had quite the squeeze.

"I'll have a go!" Darvis stood up from the back of the bar. Still in his work clothing, the tavern owner swaggered to my table. He reeked of the eel guts smeared across his apron. The crowd of ladies who had gathered round to watch parted to let him pass and wrinkled their noses. "Twenty farebits says I'll take you. Might even break that arm of yours in two."

I whistled. "Are those melons or biceps?"

He slammed his mug on the table and dropped ungracefully into the chair opposite me. "I don't want to hurt you, but twenty farebits'll get my wives in the mood for a good romp. Both of 'em together if I'm lucky."

The ladies gathered around close again. One of them massaged my shoulders. Another brought me a full mug of beer. They were certainly easy on the eyes, but there was only one woman I'd be taking home tonight, and she was waiting tables, smiling sweetly at me as she passed. She'd never been the jealous sort and had no reason to be.

"Well, it's a risk I'll have to take," I said, winking at Mavelle. "My future bride will appreciate the money."

"Marriage ain't for the weak." He propped his elbow on the table, his huge hand open and ready. With the other hand, he slapped twenty farebits down. "Mavelle, you watchin' this?"

Mavelle came over with her tray, picking up my empty mug. "Try not to hurt him, Dad. I need all his parts working for our wedding night."

I caught her hand and kissed it. "You needn't worry about that, dove. You can test all my parts tonight if you ask nicely."

She giggled, and I pinched her backside. Squealing and swatting at me with a bar towel, she retreated just out of reach. "All right, boys. Ready?"

Darvis bared his teeth. I slapped my hand into his.

"On my count," she said. "One, two..."

A hush fell across the entire tavern.

But, they weren't quiet because of our arm-wrestling match. I caught a whiff of cloves and Leogardian soap. Everyone stopped to stare at the person who'd just stepped through the door. Some poor elven traveler with mud on his boots? Or a rare visit from King Damien or Prince Halcyon?

I peered around Mavelle to see who could be important enough to interrupt our game. The traveler wore a cloak and a light blue flowy garment beneath it. She carried a bouquet of crushed flowers and set them on a table by the door. Then she lowered her hood, revealing a messy head of hair, thick and brown like a rich stout beer. She had warm caramel skin, full red lips, and black coffee eyes that glanced around nervously before she made her way to the bar. Though she'd grown a bit taller and had lost the youthful roundness in her cheeks in favor of more mature, chiseled features, I knew this woman.

Mirabelle had returned.

* * * *

~ Mirabelle ~

Everyone went quiet. A sea of eyes shifted my way. Someone dropped a mug.

"Mirabelle?" Dad's voice rang out over the sudden quiet; he got up from a barstool, and in two strides, had me engulfed in a bear hug.

With my face pressed into his prickly horsehair tunic, I managed a muffled, "Hewwo, Dod."

Finally, he released me and held me at arms' length. "My girl! Home at last! You didn't tell us you were coming. Evetta! Evetta!"

Mom's voice shrieked from the kitchen. "What?"

"It's Mirabelle! She's come home!"

Clang! A pan clattered to the floor, along with several utensils. I winced. Mom came flying through the curtain between the bar and kitchen, almost ripping it from the rod. She slapped a hand to her mouth and instantly broke into sobs.

"Mom..." Tears stung my eyes. She came around the bar and hugged me tight. Had it really been ten years? We'd written to each other often, but it wasn't the same as seeing them in person. Time had scattered gray through my mother's hair and father's beard. Their faces had deeper wrinkles from age, sun, and probably worrying about me while we'd been apart.

"My baby," she cried, "Oh, Mira, we've missed you so much!"

All those years apart squeezed my chest until it hurt and sent tears rolling down my cheeks. "I missed you too, Mom."

She kissed my cheeks and forehead, stepped back, and grabbed a tray from the bar.

"Mom, I—" Before I could utter another word, she stuffed a piece of fried slugfish in my mouth.

"You look like you've not eaten in months! Are you well? Let me feel your forehead."

Maneuvering the hot, chewy meat into one cheek, I reassured her. "I'm fine, Mom. What about you? You look pale."

"Don't you be worrying about me." She snapped a towel at a man on a barstool nearby. "Shoo! Go sit somewhere else. Mira needs to rest."

The man snatched up his mug, gave me a dirty look, and lumbered to a table.

"Mom, I'm fi—"

Dad planted me on the barstool. "What's happened? Are you hurt?"

"No…not…" Both their faces were puckered with worry and about an inch from mine. What was I supposed to tell them? That I would die in a few weeks? "It's a long story." Lowering my voice to a whisper, I asked, "Did you get the gem?"

"Yes," Dad said. "It's safe."

"Good." One less thing to worry about. I wouldn't ask about its location. Ignorance was usually the safest route.

I chewed the fish into a lumpy surrender and swallowed it down. Mom force-fed me pickled okra next, then made me coax it down with sickeningly sweet talaberry wine.

"Lysander's getting married," she said as matter-of-factly as if she were making a passing comment about the weather.

My windpipe decided at that moment to suck up wine and okra bits. Dad hammered my back with his palm while I tried to cough up a lung.

"I told you she was sick," Mom said, fetching the water pitcher.

Dad kept pounding my back. "It's that damn Leogard air. Too dry."

I finally caught my breath and wheezed, "I'm fine!" Mom shoved a cup of water in my hands, and I took a few sips. "You said Lysander is…"

"Getting married."

"Oh."

"To Mavelle Bearden," Dad added.

Mavelle, youngest daughter of the Fishhouse owner. They weren't as wealthy as the Wharfmaster, but Mavelle and her sisters were not so rich as to be unobtainable. All the other boys had aspired to wed them when we were growing up. All of them but Lysander. He only had eyes for me. But that was then. This was now.

Dad inclined his head toward the tables. "He's right over there if you're wantin' to talk to him."

I wobbled on the barstool, heart thudding in my ears. I knew I'd have to face him at some point, but I'd just reunited with my parents and almost choked to death on okra. No—I wasn't ready. Yet, it didn't stop my eyes from wandering to where Dad had pointed. People were scattered about the tavern—a fat drunk man was passed out by the hearth. There was the Wharfmaster's son Marlow with four women whom I assumed were his wives, two of whom were twins. I recognized him from his curly red hair and bulbous nose. One of the twin wives leaned over his lap, and soon her head bobbed up and down behind the table.

Ugh—I squeezed my eyes shut, reminding myself that this was not Leogard, where such things remained behind closed doors. In Port Valor, having money meant you did what you wanted when you wanted, so long as it didn't involve murder.

At a table near the bar, a small crowd of people, mostly young ladies, gathered around an arm-wrestling match. One of them was Mavelle's dad Darvis. I recognized him by his spiky, so-silver-it-was-almost-white hair. He squared off with a younger, and very handsome black-haired man I didn't recognize.

Darvis wore his standard beige working tunic, covered with a dirty apron. The stranger wore fine clothes—a black short-sleeved shirt with peg-shaped whalebone buttons and a snug fit, along with black trousers tucked into gray seal-leather boots. He had a wide, heavy looking wrist cuff covered in gold and silver gears. On each hand, he wore rings with large gems like diamonds. Etched into the skin on his right bicep was a pattern of stripes with words between each one, but I was too far away to read them.

Fists locked together, the fight was on. Each man's arm muscles bulged, their veins protruded and healthy green auras flared. The harder they grit their teeth, the redder their faces became.

The crowd chanted, "Go, go, go!" In one sudden move, the younger man slammed Darvis's hand down on the table. Coins and mugs rattled, and the crowd cheered.

But I didn't see Lysander anywhere.

"I don't see him," I said to Dad, but a second later, I watched a young lady lean in and give the younger man a deep kiss. "That's not...is that...?"

"Yeah, that's him," Dad said with a grin. "He's grown up a bit."

"A bit?" There was no way in the Great Void that stack of muscles in a tight black shirt could be Lysander Devlin. But then again, he had Lysander's dimpled chin and thick black hair that never obeyed a comb. "Mavelle's really grown up, too."

"Yes, she has. Go on, go talk to them," Mom whispered. "They've missed you."

"I doubt it."

Mavelle had jumped onto his lap and wrapped her arms about his neck. Several young ladies surrounded him, giggling. They ruffled his hair and rubbed his shoulders, like some sort of mating display. Disgusting, but who could blame them?

"Just how many wives *does* he have?" I asked.

"None yet," Dad said, looking from Lysander to me. "Much to many a lady's dismay."

Surprising—he was clearly doing well for himself and had Mavelle, but what had held him back from marrying years ago? If men didn't marry before twenty, that usually meant they were not worthy of a wife or preferred the company of men. With me in Leogard, he had nothing to keep him from settling down.

"He traveled a lot, saved his money until he could buy that nice graystone across the street. But I think he's like me," Dad said, smiling at Mom. "A one-woman kind of man." Mom kissed his cheek, and they both turned expectant eyes on me.

"All right, fine." I had to face him at some point. Swallowing another bite of pickled okra—it was really quite good—I stood and approached Lysander's table.

The crowd dispersed, including Darvis, who stood from his chair, grumbling, "Guess I'll be sleeping alone tonight."

All the ladies gave me a choke-on-an-eel-and-die look before going back to their tables. Everyone knew our history. They probably assumed I had come back for Lysander. A sudden burn in my arm stopped me in my tracks. I rubbed my death sentence through my sleeve and stood

73

there, waiting.

Lysander kept his arms around Mavelle, who was still on his lap, nuzzling his neck. He finally looked at me. I looked away, not trusting myself enough to keep eye contact.

"Hello, Lysander."

"Why, look what the Great Sea Serpent dragged in," he exclaimed. "If it isn't Mirabelle Hearton! If you're wanting a go, you'll have to put down twenty farebits." His voice had gotten deeper and rumbled with the confidence of a dominant male. Goosebumps prickled across my skin.

"No thanks." I hugged myself and stared at the beer-stained floorboards. "How have you been?"

"I've been well. Very well, eh Mave?" He kissed Mavelle on the lips and set her on her feet. She picked up two empty mugs and, smiling shyly, walked up next to me. She'd always been pretty—with waist-length, dark brown hair that had just a hint of red. And she was curvy in all the places that counted. Unlike me. Her black peasant-style dress had a drawstring at the top, joined with a whalebone button like the ones on Lysander's shirt. A tight leather corset cinched her waist in beautifully, while displaying her feminine assets well. She caught every man's eye. Also unlike me.

"Welcome home," she said. "Can I get you a drink?"

"No, thank you."

"Suit yourself." There was no malice in her sweet, girlish tone as she set down the mugs and gave me an unexpected hug. She whispered, "I've missed you so much. I hope you're here to stay."

"I...thank you. I've missed you, too." My mind flicked through memories of her and me in my room, giggling, painting, sharing our girlish secrets. She'd been the sister I never had, and until this moment, I didn't realize how much I had really missed her.

"I hope you won't be angry with me," she said, glancing at Lysander.

"No, of course not." I tried to conjure up a smile, but it felt weird and fake on my lips.

"Good. Maybe you'll come to our wedding?"

"Maybe."

With that, she nodded and continued on to the bar, while I resumed my study of the floor and slumped under the heaviness of guilt. Mavelle, despite how much I envied her, had always been kind to me. If anyone deserved Lysander's love, it was her.

With nonchalant grace, Lysander draped an elbow over the back of his chair. His legs were spread wide. "That Darvis," he said, gesturing for me to take the man's vacant seat. "He's a better sport when he's sober, but he's giving me his daughter to marry, so he's got good taste."

Obeying his wordless command, I scooted up Darvis's chair and sat, allowing myself a peek at his tattoo. It looked like a pattern of cat stripes, from his elbow, over his bicep, then disappearing under his shirtsleeve. I could read part of the words etched there: ...*through pain does one...* It wasn't anything unusual—Hezrali men often tattooed themselves with animal patterns or shapes that represented their occupations. Maybe Lysander was a fur trader.

Silence reigned, and everyone stared, perhaps waiting to see if I'd fall at Lysander's feet and beg his forgiveness. Or maybe they'd rather see him toss me out the door. With one sweeping look from Lysander, however, everyone withdrew their prying eyes, and the dull roar of conversation started up again.

Lysander flashed a flawless white smile. "Did you come all the way back to Port Valor for a good meal? Looks like you could use one."

Ten years hadn't changed my thin figure. Almost everything I wore had to be taken in, though I hadn't done so with my acolyte robes, which hung from my skinny frame in sad defeat. I hadn't given it much thought back in the Temple with its complete lack of vanity. But, Lysander's remark struck an unexpected nerve. My cheeks burned in response.

"Mom stuffed me full already," I said.

"So, why *are* you back, Mira? Ten years with no word from you—I assumed you were devoted to the Temple or dead."

"I'm sorry," I said, paying undue attention to a dried spot of blood on the table. "Didn't you get my letters?"

"Yes, and they were very well-written." He huffed out a laugh. "Both of them were so vivid, I hardly knew you were gone."

"I guess you're still angry with me."

He cocked an eyebrow. "Angry? Whatever for? I've had a lovely life, as I'm sure you've had in Leogard. You heard I'm getting married?"

75

"Yes," I said, my mouth suddenly dry, but I forced a raspy, "Congratulations."

"Why, thank you. The moon will be perfect for the ceremony tomorrow night. Full and bright. Of course, you're welcome to attend."

What was I supposed to say to that, having been on the brink of marrying him myself? I settled on, "That's very kind of you."

Narrowing his eyes, he leaned in and propped his elbow on the table. "Well...you still haven't told me why you've returned. My parents' death wasn't deemed important enough, though your note was sympathetic. It must be some official Temple business."

I really wished he'd stop trying to make eye contact. Being reminded of his parents' death cut me deep—they were like a second set of parents to me, even called me their daughter. I wiped a tear from the corner of my eye. The dull roar around us had grown louder. Another fight had begun in the back corner. One of Marlow's twin wives broke a bottle over her sister's head, and soon they were rolling on the floor, throwing punches and pulling hair. Marlow ran over, doing his best to pull them apart. Everyone else turned their attention to the latest brawl, cheering on one wife or the other.

But, Lysander kept his eyes on me, waiting. With everyone distracted, I decided to tell him part of the truth. If there was any chance the Tyger actually existed, he might have heard something about him. "I'm looking for someone called the Tyger."

"Really? Is he another jilted lover of yours?"

"No." I crossed my arms, knowing I should have been prepared for resentment. "He's supposedly an outlaw who may pose a danger to Leogard and my own family. But I suspect he's just a rumor."

"You didn't come all this way to confirm a rumor, did you? What are your plans for this Tyger, should you be so fortunate as to find him?"

He'd laugh at me, but I'd already told him this much and had only a few weeks to live. Might as well surrender the last of my pride. "I'm supposed to capture him and bring him back to the Priestess."

"So, you're a bounty hunter now? An odd assignment for a Temple acolyte. But, I do have it on good authority that the Tyger isn't just a rumor."

My eyes widened, and I sat up straight, daring to look him in the eye. Could he actually exist, or was Lysander punishing me by leading me to believe in a phantom, only to crush my hopes for a good laugh?

"Let me guess," I said, "he was here earlier, but I just missed him, right?"

"Not exactly."

"Fine, I'll bite. Then where is he?"

He smiled wickedly. "You're looking at him."

Chapter Eight

~ Lysander ~

Mira's dark complexion turned paler than the northern moon.

I put the last of the farebits I'd won into my pocket. "Why, Mira, you look like you might faint. You really should eat something."

"You can't be the Tyger. You're lying," she said. "This isn't funny."

"Not funny at all. Everyone here knows I'm the Tyger. I'm an assassin for King Damien. But you think I'd actually hurt your parents? They're like family to me—they've been here for me ever since…" Now was not the time to look weak. Mira had come for the Tyger, not the weakling she'd left behind ten years ago. "…since my real family died."

"There must be some mistake."

"Unless someone's impersonating me, there's no mistake. I'm the Tyger."

"You've killed people?"

"That *is* the definition of an assassin, isn't it?"

"But…you're called the Tyger?"

"For the quick and efficient way I hunt my prey, yes." *Not for my furry alter ego*, I wanted to add, but only one other person knew about that part of me, and he was dead.

Poor Mira held to the seat of her chair, eyes fixed on the floor. She really did look like she might faint. I recalled the day she left me, how I'd succumbed to the cold and fallen unconscious. Since then, I'd learned the law of reciprocation was an unforgiving teacher. *Only through pain does one become strong.* It was time she learned that lesson as well.

"I guess it's time to bring me to justice." I held my fists toward her, waiting for the shackles I knew she didn't have. "Well…what are you waiting for? You have a job to do, don't you?"

By then, Marlow's twin wives had stopped fighting. With one on each arm, he escorted them downstairs, no doubt to give them both a good fucking among the kegs of beer and wine. He never could wait until they got home, the sorry dog. With that show over, people turned their attention to me and Mira again. Mavelle returned from the kitchen to stand at my side, her face full of worry and questions.

Mira stared at my fists while I held them steady a foot from her face. One of her hands slid down her thigh to the leather sheath where she kept her dagger.

"There's no need for that," I said with a smile and a shake of my head. "I'm making your job easy."

Mavelle gripped my elbow. "Lysander…?"

"It's all right," I said, keeping my eyes on Mira's hands. She had once been exceptional with dagger throwing, and I suspected she still was. "Mirabelle came here to find the Tyger and bring him back to justice in Leogard, so I'm offering him to her."

With a tense jaw, pulse throbbing on her neck, Mira sat up straight. She scanned the room, shrinking as she realized how much of an audience we had. Her eyes finally rested on her parents. Evetta had her mouth covered with both hands, like she might burst into tears at any moment.

"Lysander, please…" Mavelle said, trying to pull me away.

I stood firm. "No. Come on, Mira, do your job! Take me in if you think it will help. Maybe it will make you feel better, redeem a few sins. Go ahead, take me."

Her head snapped toward me, eyes wide and intense, the deep brown of her irises swirling like rich coffee stirred in a cup. Round and round, mesmerizing, drawing me into their depths. Amazing…

"No, Mira!" Abbott yelled.

She squeezed her eyes shut. Then she sprang from the chair and bolted out the door. Abbott and Evetta quickly followed.

Mavelle wrapped her arms around my waist, holding me tight. "Don't you do that to me again! What's wrong with Mira? Did she really

79

come to take you? Were you actually going to go with her?"

I held her close and kissed her hair. "No, dove. I'm not going anywhere."

* * * *

~ Mirabelle ~

I'd just reached the top of the ladder that opened into the loft when Dad came thundering through the front door. "Mirabelle! Are you here?"

Closing my eyes, I held to the rung and answered, "Yes, I'm here."

He came through the kitchen to the bottom of the ladder. "What were you thinking, young lady?"

"Abbott, not now," Mom scolded as she hurried to Dad's side. "Mira, baby, are you all right?"

"I'm fine, Mom." I hung there for a bit, looking down over my shoulder, and didn't know whether to continue up to my old room or go back down to the kitchen. But, Mom would likely try to stuff me with something pickled or fried, and I had no appetite for anything but feeling sorry for myself. "I'm going to get some sleep," I said.

"Do you want some sour leek soup?"

"No, Mom." I climbed into the loft, expecting things to be covered with sheets, but instead, my room was just as I'd left it. No dust, no cobwebs; the bed was made and turned down like I'd simply been gone for the day and would be coming home the same night.

"How about some warm goat's milk?"

"No, Mom, I'm not hungry."

My room, same as it was the day I set out for Leogard. Same books on the shelves, along with a few choice collectibles—a whale tooth necklace, a moonreaver's iridescent blue tail feather, and a pink ribbon Lysander had bought me to wear in my hair for our wedding. He'd saved up for weeks to buy it—silk was a rare commodity in Port Valor.

I picked up the ribbon, sliding the smooth fabric between my thumb and forefinger. Mom climbed up into the loft, standing in reverent silence while I reunited with memories of another life.

"You left it all here," I said. "Why not sell it?"

She walked up to me and gently wrapped one arm around my

shoulders. "Because I knew you'd eventually find your way back home."

"Oh, Mom…" I couldn't hold it back anymore. I held to her and cried, comforted in her familiar smell of Fishhouse grease and wood smoke.

She patted my back and stroked my hair. "Shh, baby, it's going to be all right."

"No, it's not."

"Because of Lysander?"

"I made a huge mistake. I should have never gone to Leogard."

"What's done is done. You can't change the past. But, you're here now. You can start over."

"It's not that simple." I sniffed up the last of my tears and sat on the edge of my bed.

Mom sat beside me and took my hand in hers. "What happened in Leogard, Mira? Why did Lysander think you were supposed to take him back there? Why did you try to…bend him?"

They'd known what I was for a long time, but never thought I could be dangerous. They were wrong. I really wanted to tell her everything, just like when I was little and we lay on my bed, watching the stars outside my window while we shared secrets and dreams. "Because the Priestess…" The bloodgems produced a sharp pain as intense as a hornet's sting. I cringed in agony as I cradled my arm against my chest. Could they be triggered by a mention of the Priestess? Over the past two weeks, I'd felt increasing discomfort but nothing this intense before. One of them must have begun to leak.

"Mira?" Mom grabbed my hand again and yanked up my shirtsleeve. She gasped, eyes wide, shaking her head. "What did she do to you?"

"It's nothing…"

Mom's usually soft-spoken voice turned hysterical, full of rage. "Mirabelle Hearton, what did she do to your arm?"

Dad's head popped up above the ladder. "What's wrong with her arm?"

"Horrible burns," Mom said. "That despicable priestess mutilated our daughter!"

Dad launched himself up into my room, and in two strides, he had my wrist in his hand and examined my arm for himself. Under his beard, his face flamed red. Had High Priestess Arianne Munroviel been standing in front of him, I had no doubt he would have strangled her.

"Is this what you've had to live with in Leogard?" Dad thundered. "What other tortures did those elves inflict on you?"

I shook my head and stood, gently covering my arm again. "No, it wasn't like that. There's so much to tell you, so much to say..." Tears spilled down my cheeks again and pain squeezed my chest, knowing that for their sakes, I had to tell them everything.

Mom placed a gentle hand on my cheek. "Mira, it's all right. You can tell us."

I looked to her and Dad in turn, hating myself for having to break their hearts all over again. "I'm dying."

After a moment of silence, Mom wilted into sobs, and Dad held her while I told them everything. It was after midnight before I finished, and we'd all shed enough tears by then to fill the Draekkan Sea two times over. We sat at the kitchen table, quiet and exhausted.

Dad finished off his mug of ale. "You have to ask Lysander to help you. He's not the monster that elven witch has made him out to be. King Damien has paid him well to hunt down criminals. He's stopped assassination attempts. He's become a local legend. The Tyger—good name, if you ask me."

"That's all well and lovely," I said, slumping on the table. "But he'll never go with me willingly after tonight. Even if he did, there's no guarantee the Priestess will keep her word, and Lysander could die for crimes he never committed."

Mom slid a plate of cold fish cakes toward me. "Here, eat. Lysander could get you past all the guards so you can make her remove the curse."

"But if everything went wrong, we could both die. And he's getting married tomorrow. I can't take that away from him."

Mom took my hand and opened her mouth to say something.

But, I shook my head. "No, Mom. Someone's bound to die at the end of this nightmare, so it might as well be me."

"No!" Dad slammed his fist on the table. "I'll kill that elven witch before I let her take my daughter from me."

His outburst startled me.

"I'm sorry," he said. "Anger won't solve anything. Let's get some sleep and see what the morning brings." Dad retreated to his bedroom, shoulders slumped, and feet dragging as though his body and spirit were exhausted. Mom, however, climbed up to the loft and lay with me on my bed. There in the dark, we studied the stars outside my window.

She held my hand against her cheek. "You don't deserve such punishment. Please ask Lysander to help you."

"It's all right. I've done some terrible things. I've used my abilities against others, like you always warned me not to do. I deserve to die for my sins. The longer I'm here in Port Valor, the more I'll put everyone in danger."

"You can't help how you were born, Mirabelle. And I know you would never have hurt anyone had you not been forced. The old Shaman is gone, and the new one isn't so heartless. He's calmed the king's fears about that silly prophecy, and he's not had anyone killed but thieves and murderers. You won't be in danger from him."

"I suppose Lysander does his bidding."

"Lysander could help you," she said. "He knows important people. Tell him what happened, and ask him to take you to Leogard. He could get you inside the city so you can bend the Priestess's will and make her take those things out of you."

"You really want me to do that?"

"No, but I can't bear to lose you again."

"I know, Mom."

We lay back down, and before long, she drifted off to sleep. There in the silence, I listened to her steady breaths. I should have never left. I had to do something.

Mom was right. Lysander *could* probably help me if he was the legendary Tyger. But he was getting married tomorrow night. He'd take Mavelle away for a lovely trip and forget all about me. He hated me, and even after his dramatic display in the tavern, I knew he'd never go willingly.

He'd let me die first.

And maybe I should have just accepted that, being an abomination and all. But, my parents' hearts were breaking from the thought of losing me again, I couldn't just give up and die. Not without a fight.

Quietly, I eased off the bed, slid my daggers into their sheaths on my thighs, and put on my boots. In my belt pouch, I placed a vial of paralytic powder Loralee had taught me to make. Luckily, I'd managed to snatch a few nice substances before I left Leogard. Lysander already hated me. What could delaying his wedding hurt? The Priestess likely had spies watching for me to return so they could ensure I never reached her in time. If he was as talented as he claimed, I could bend his mind so he could get me into Leogard and help me subdue the Priestess so I could make her remove this curse. Then, we could both escape back to Port Valor and pretend we never knew each other.

I could ensure that for *him* anyway.

With one last look at my mother, I eased down the ladder and out the door. I had a tyger to catch.

Chapter Nine

~ Lysander ~

Mavelle came up behind me as I watched Port Valor sleep from the parlor window. *Our* window—everything I had would also be hers after tomorrow night. I could give her an even better life than her father could, and for that I was glad. She wrapped her arms around my waist, and rested her cheek against my back. So warm against my skin. I pulled her around and held her tight against my chest.

"I'm glad we didn't wait," she said. Drawing my hand to her lips, she kissed my knuckles and sighed with pleasure. "I'd rather know whether my man is good in bed before I commit my life to him."

I laughed. "And have I met your expectations, dove?"

"If you were any better, I'd be fucking a god." She quickly covered her mouth. "Oh, I'm sorry."

"You don't have to apologize for the truth."

She playfully smacked my chest. "Don't think so highly of yourself, Mr. Devlin. I may have grown up in a Fishhouse, but I know a good lady isn't supposed to speak so crudely. My mother taught me that."

She resented her father's two younger wives. He'd married them both when Mavelle's mother was ill, and they'd treated Mavelle badly after she died. I couldn't blame her for hating them. They were both as ugly inside as they were in appearance.

"Your dad made a mistake, but he did what he thought was right," I said. "He never meant to hurt you."

"I know Dad means well, and he hoped I'd get along with Shanna and Taylen, but I'll never forgive him for letting them be so cruel to me."

With a gentle hand, I tipped her chin up to look at me. "Well, you'll never have to worry about another woman sharing my bed. I'm all yours."

We kissed, and though I was tempted to swoop her up and take her back to bed, I didn't. We needed to save our energy for tomorrow night, after all. Mavelle and I had shared a bed on occasion ever since I asked her to marry me. I had been willing to wait. She hadn't.

She pulled away, breathing hard. "I have a secret, Lysander."

"What is it?"

"I never thought I'd be married at all."

"Why ever not? You're a tygress under the sheets."

Smiling, she cupped my face in her hands. "What I didn't tell you is that I never thought you'd want me, when I saw how much you grieved after Mira left. I know how much you wanted a big family with her, and…I can't give you that."

Sweet Mavelle, born with a defect that had become more common over the years in Hezrali women—no womb. A few decades ago, women had a good chance of being killed for it, since their value was measured in how many children they could produce. As time passed, though, killing them meant fewer hands to help feed the masses. So they filled the gaps, working as servants or as spare wives or whores.

Mavelle, thankfully, had a safe role in her father's tavern. Her defect hadn't marred her looks or her heart, and I didn't relish the idea of fathering children. Especially if they might inherit what I'd become.

"A woman is more than a womb, dove." I traced my finger along her collarbone and followed the cleft between her breasts, slipping beneath her blouse to gently squeeze one of them.

Her nipple hardened against my palm; she pressed closer against me. "Do you think Mira will be all right? She seemed so upset. That horrid priestess couldn't have made life easy for her in Leogard. I really missed her, too. She was like my big sister."

As much as I'd hated Mira over the years, Mavelle's concern about her left me at a loss for words for a moment. "You never fail to amaze me."

"Why?"

"Most women would be frothing at the mouth with jealousy, but not my Mavelle."

"Mira and I were good friends. I can't exactly hate her for leaving, since that led me to you. Besides, jealousy is a fruitless emotion." Ducking her head shamefully, she added, "Rather like me."

"No more fertility talk. There are always orphans who need a good home."

Her eyes glistened with tears. "Really? You'd do that?"

"Of course I would."

"Oh, Lysander, I love you so much!"

I captured her lips with mine, kissing her, picking her up around the waist until her feet dangled a foot off the floor. She pushed against my chest and leapt away, giggling. I started for her, and she held her hand up to ward me off, picking up her cloak and shoes as she backed toward the door.

"Oh, no you don't! You and I both need a good night's sleep before we wear each other out tomorrow night."

"Then, you better sleep very well, dove. You'll need endurance for our marathon."

"I'll be ready. More than ready." She opened the door and winked at me. "Not many women can boast that they've tamed a tyger."

"Rawr!" I bared my human teeth and growled. Mavelle knew nothing of my feline side. I'd feared how she would respond and how well I could control shifting in front of her. Soon I would tell her, perhaps on our wedding night. I wanted no secrets between us.

She giggled and left. Standing in the doorway, I watched until she had safely crossed the street and had entered her father's tavern, where she'd spend one last night in her room on the top floor. Tomorrow night, she would be mine for good. We'd live in this fine home with ten rooms, eight hearths, and plenty of storage. She could tend a large garden out back, or I could hire someone to do it for her. The choice was hers, and I could give her that. I could give her anything she wanted, though Mavelle was content with much less.

She wanted me to retire, afraid I'd be hurt or killed. I could do that now, and I would, as a wedding present. We had but one problem.

Mirabelle.

I couldn't say I was surprised at her "mission". Of course she didn't come back *for* me, but to *take* me. She'd likely been threatened with some nasty curse that would leave her bald or deaf. Such were the methods of elves. Mirabelle cared about one thing above all others— herself. So, she wouldn't think twice about turning me in if it meant not being cursed with warts or toe fungus.

Yet, her assumptions disturbed me. If I was really considered a threat in Leogard, one of the L.I.O.'s secret agents like Lady Trudeaux might attempt to kill or capture me if Mira didn't do the job. I had plenty of secrets, but my name and occupation were public knowledge. That could put Mavelle in danger. I had no choice but to take her away from here where no one could find us. She would understand, and we'd leave right after our wedding.

I started up the stairs to my room and paused on the fifth step. Sniffing the air, I caught a hint of cloves.

Mira. She must have sneaked behind the house and climbed up the trellis to my window. Served me right for leaving it open. Mavelle and I had needed cooling from our romp in the bed.

I crept up the stairs and stuck close to the wall, carefully avoiding the creaky spots on each knotted wooden step. Reaching the top, I heard the gentle thump where she must have landed on the floor beneath the window.

Down the hall I moved silently, shifting my weight evenly from toe to heel with every step. Mira was doing it all wrong, trying to tiptoe, but straight onto the balls of her feet. In a noiseless environment, she might as well have been clunking about on peg legs. Back pressed against the hallway wall, I reached the bedroom door and peeked around the frame. Mira crept to my bed, pulling a small vial from her pouch.

I had to hold back a laugh—she thought the rumpled covers and pillows were me. She hadn't given her eyes enough time to adjust to the dark before moving in for the kill.

Time to pounce.

In the span of a heartbeat, I closed the distance and sprang. Capturing both her wrists, I spun her around and pinned her to my bed. It took her mind a second to catch up to her eyes, which widened more the longer they looked into mine.

"Why hello, Mira!" Lowering my nose to her neck, I took a good long sniff and felt her shiver as I let my breath out upon her ear. "I always dreamed of having you in my bed. Just not quite like this."

She struggled beneath me. The hard lumps of her sheathed daggers rubbed against my thighs. I picked up her wrist and inspected the vial she still held in a death grip. Some sort of powder.

"Were you going to drug me before you slit my throat?"

"I wasn't going to hurt you," she said, still struggling and bucking like a wild Hezrali filly.

"Pardon me if I don't believe a word you say." She bucked harder, her thigh bumping against my groin. Of course, my cock had to betray me. Damn it, I really wanted to not enjoy this.

"Let me go."

"I will, but first..." I kissed her lips, hard. No tongue, but enough pressure that she wouldn't soon forget it. She froze, lying stiff and still as death. Her body began to shudder, and her lips parted, then moved with mine for one brief moment. Like the one kiss we'd shared on the dock before she left, the kiss I'd thought about a million times since then...

Releasing her wrists, I leapt off her. Her chest rose and fell as she caught her breath.

"Your methods are sloppy and predictable," I said. "If you want to catch your enemy off guard, you have to watch him from a distance, know when he comes and goes. If you'd done that, you would know that Mavelle left here not a moment before you climbed through my window. You'd know that we had just fucked there on the bed where you're lying. And you'd have waited until you knew I was sound asleep instead of assuming I was."

Mira raised up on her elbows, sticking her failed poison back into her bag. She stared at me, the dim light of the moon on her face. Too dark for her to get a lock on me with her crazy eyes. "I was trained as a healer, not a bounty hunter."

"I know what you are. We both have nicknames, don't we, Mind Bender?"

She sat up slowly and averted her eyes. "How did you know that?"

Circling around to the window beside the bed, I said, "I know lots of things. I've traveled extensively, spent a lot of time in Leogard, and you never even knew."

She got to her feet and backed toward the door. "You were watching me?"

"Don't flatter yourself. I only watched you when I was bored. You were quite chummy with Sir Francis and the Priestess's daughter at one time. What happened, Mira? What happened in Leogard to make you so desperate to capture me?"

"You—you spied on me?" Her voice had risen to near-hysteria.

"Oh, don't worry, I didn't tell anyone your secret. I didn't want to disturb you, not with all that important work you were doing. Besides, I was working, too. Can't mix business and pleasure, you know. Spying and stealing arcane items isn't an easy job."

"So you did steal from the Priestess? And the Mage Academy?" Mira crept backwards, closer to the door.

"Of course. King Damien pays me well for it. I'm not the only one doing sneaky work, am I? What was it you sent for your parents to collect from the ferryman?"

"The bandits on the road," she gasped. "They told me they barely escaped that night." Her other hand slid down her thigh. Going for a dagger, no doubt. "It was you? Damien hired you to kill my parents?"

Shit. I'd let my anger and tongue get away from me and said too much.

"I told you I'd never hurt them. All you need to know is that I kept them from getting killed that night."

She shook her head. "Liar."

"Believe me or not, I don't care. Must be all that elven wine muddling up your thoughts."

In the blink of an eye, she flung her hand. I dodged. A dagger whooshed past me with a swift wind across my skin. Glass shattered, raining shards on my back and floor. Apparently she *did* still know how to use them. In the old days, she'd have sunk it right into my eye. Either the darkness had thrown off her aim or she hadn't been aiming to kill. She took off through my bedroom door. I sprinted after her, shot my arm out, and grabbed her hood before she could make it even two steps down.

She gave a little scream, teetering on the edge of the stair, her arms flailing for balance. True to her talents, she had the other dagger out in a flash, but I captured her wrist before she could jab it behind her and stick it between my ribs. I let go of her hood with the other hand and lassoed my elbow around her neck, holding her in a headlock. To disarm her, I hammered her dagger hand against the banister. She cried out in pain, and the dagger fell, clattering from the stairs to the first floor. Damn thing was sure to leave marks on the hardwood—another small reason to hate her, but a reason nonetheless.

Still restraining her like a snake ready to swallow a rat, I held her in a crushing hug. She tried to thrash, but the more she fought, the tighter I squeezed. When her breath started coming in short gasps, I stopped constricting and put my mouth against her ear.

"Impressive display, but not good enough." Sweat dampened her skin—I licked just below the earlobe, tasted the salt. My nose inhaled a mix of spices, sulfur, and something indescribable that was pure Mirabelle. I'd never forget her smell, no matter how much I wanted to. "If I was a killer, you'd be lying in my bedroom where I found you with your neck at a very unnatural angle, and you would have never known what happened."

"Please…let me go…" she whispered, trying desperately to wiggle out of my claustrophobic embrace. She'd always hated cramped spaces.

"You know," I said, licking her earlobe this time. She whimpered and slumped, knees trying to buckle beneath her. "I could kill you right now if I wanted. Toss you right over the side there where your dagger fell."

With a sudden shift of my weight, I feinted toward the banister.

"No!" Her voice rang out that time, lungs overcoming the assault from my death hold.

I shifted back to center. "No? Too messy—yes, you're right. That means I'll have to come up with something better." Working my arm up her body enough for her to see my hand clearly, I produced her vial from within my fist. Her sharp intake of breath told me that move had been completely unexpected. Oh, how little she knew about me.

"I'll paralyze you with this first, and then what? What should I do with you, Mira? Do you want me to kill you or fuck you, then kill you? That's what despicable assassins like me do, right?"

I loosened my hold just enough to allow her to burst free. She lost her balance and started to tumble down the stairs. She caught herself on the banister, holding to it like she once held to the side of her father's fishing boat when seasickness hit.

She looked over her shoulder, jaw quivering. "I'm sorry. I thought you were—"

"Evil incarnate, I know. You've never thought I was worth anything, so I'm not going to try to convince you otherwise."

"Please, I..." She took a few shaky breaths. "I've always cared about you, Lysander."

"If that's so, then why did you leave? And why all the theatrics in trying to capture me now? The Priestess must have cursed you with baldness, is that it? Or will she turn you into a toad or a grub? Go back to Leogard, Mira, and repent your sins. Bow before the great Priestess like a good little acolyte, and maybe she'll have mercy so you can resume your happy—"

"I'm dying!"

Still leaning against the banister, she raised her arm and pulled up her sleeve. Smoke, sulfur, charred skin—all hit my nose, stronger than ever. And there on her forearm, burned into her skin, were the symbols of the five tenets. A dim, red glow pulsed inside them, under Mira's skin.

Dying? No, it had to be some desperate attempt to get me on her side, but the old Mira would have never lied about something like that. Instinct compelled me to comfort her, but I pulled back. Harker had warned me about letting compassion sway my choices.

"I have about six weeks before these bloodgems release basilisk venom into me." She stood there, straighter now, more like the proud Mira I once knew, but her voice was flat and tired. "I know I deserve to die. And I would have been content to do so, but I can't hurt my family again. All I'm asking is for you to get me into Leogard undetected and help me subdue the Priestess. I'll bend her mind and make her take these things out of me. Then..." She drew in one shuddering breath. "...we can come back to Port Valor, and I can make it so you'll forget me...and everything between us."

Mira being gone had torn me apart once. But, the thought of Mira being dead drew fresh blood from that old wound. My jaw tightened painfully. I gripped the banister until my palm hurt. "You think it's that easy, do you? Why didn't you erase my memories before you left? It would have been the humane thing to do, like putting down a crippled old dog. No, you let me suffer for ten years and only now have decided to extend your mercy. You're no better than the Priestess."

"You won't help me, then, not even for Mom and Dad?"

Not fair, this game she was playing. She knew how much I cared about her parents. But, I would not let her guilt me into submission. "I'm sorry, Mira. You cast your net, now deal with what you've caught. Enjoy the time you have left with them."

She gave an almost imperceptible nod, continued her stiff descent to the first floor, and picked up her dagger. With one last look up to where I stood, she opened the door and disappeared into the night.

"Damn her!" Rage funneled its way into my fist and drove a solid punch through the wall. The board imploded into a gaping, jagged hole. I sucked on one burning knuckle. Blood flowed into my mouth. I spit out a splinter.

Fuck it all—I couldn't let Mira die like that. But I'd marry Mavelle first, and let Mira feel the same abandonment I did for a while. She deserved at least that.

Chapter Ten

~ Mirabelle ~

"Won't you go with us, Mira? Mavelle would love you to be there." Mom stood on the loft stairs, with just her head and shoulders visible. She'd fixed her hair into a pretty bun, with ribbons woven through the coils.

I lay on my bed, flat on my back, and hid the pink ribbon Lysander had given me years ago under my pillow. "I can't. They deserve a nice wedding. If I go, it'll make Lysander uncomfortable and everyone will be whispering when they should be watching the happy couple."

Mom sighed and came all the way up to my room. She walked over, leaned in, and kissed my forehead. "Will you be all right here alone? I can stay if you need me to."

I sat up, forcing a smile, and hugged her tightly. "I'll be fine. You better hurry, or you'll be late."

She nodded against my shoulder. "We'll come right back."

"And miss the big after-wedding party at Bearden's?"

"I spend enough time in there working as it is. I'd rather spend the rest of the night with my beautiful daughter."

That time, my smile came on its own. "All right. I'll see you later."

Mom walked back to the ladder and started to climb down.

"Oh...Mom?"

"Yes, baby?"

"I love you."

She smiled sadly, wiping a tear from her cheek. "I love you too, Mira. More than you'll ever know."

94

A minute later, she and Dad left, the door clunking shut behind them. I pulled out the ribbon and rubbed it against my cheek, remembering how Lysander's lips had felt against mine last night. It wasn't a romantic kiss by any means, but it opened up a neglected storehouse of emotions I hadn't been prepared to face. And though I'm sure I had only imagined it, Lysander had lingered a second too long. The forceful pressure, for just a moment, had become soft and tender. Like the kisses we had shared so long ago.

But, what did it matter? He loved someone else, and they'd be married within the hour. Wind rattled the windows. A full silver moon winked between the clouds. Perfect for a wedding.

I sat up and looked at the delicate pink silk of the ribbon, remembering Lysander's shy and boyish grin when he'd given it to me for our wedding. *"I hope you like it,"* he'd said. *"It'll be pretty in your hair."* He'd whispered to me right after that, *"And I can't wait to take it out and watch that hair falling over your bare shoulders."*

With a few quick twists, I coiled my hair up in a messy bun and tied the ribbon around it. Maybe the silk, memories, and cherished kisses worked together to change my mind. Before I could talk myself out of it again, I was out the door and headed just east of the town toward the Moon Grove. The last time I'd been there was right after Lysander had proposed, when I had stood under the bower, imagining—and fearing— what it would be like to be married to my best friend. All those doubts now seemed so childish. What had I been afraid of? Time had changed so many things.

The Moon Grove, however, looked just as it had a decade ago, with a smooth stone path that wound lazily up a hill, ending in a tall stone archway. Talaberry bushes grew in a ring from the arch, surrounding the grove. Leaves and flower buds sprouted along their branches. Avoiding the main path, I sneaked around to the cemetery that adjoined the grove. I'd hide here and watch through a gap in the bushes, and at least in my heart, I'd be there to support two of the people I loved most in the world.

Lysander's name lingered in my thoughts as the wedding party arrived. Soft flute music accompanied lantern light up the path. Pulling my cloak tight around me, I sat next to a tall granite gravestone, knees hugged to my chest. The cloud cover didn't allow enough moonlight to let me read the name of my long-dead wedding date. I couldn't feel anything carved in it either. Whoever this grave belonged to, I hoped he didn't mind me spying on people while I sat six feet above his sleeping bones.

At least I wouldn't be spotted by the living. They were several yards away, far enough that their lanterns didn't reveal my presence. From where I sat in the shadows, I'd look like just another gravestone in the cemetery. Familiar voices sang, growing louder the closer they came.

Come to the Moon Grove;
There we'll find true love.
She'll have a good life;
Gods bless the first wife.

Lysander and Mavelle came into view, arm in arm, leading a parade of wedding-goers. They wore matching white robes. His had a sea blue sash, while Mavelle's had a dark green one. They symbolized water and earth, the building blocks of life, the perfect marriage. Each robe had intertwining patterns of star serpent scales—those celestial creatures that never touched the earth unless they died and fell from the sky. Someone long ago had found one and used their scales for these ceremonial wedding robes. The scales soaked up every bit of star, moon, and man-made light, reflecting it back with twinkling splendor.

Yet, the glimmering scales were no rival for the light in Lysander's eyes. The way he looked at Mavelle with such devotion and love, I knew he would have only one wife. I'd seen that look before in Dad's eyes for Mom and in Lysander's eyes for me so long ago. Mavelle's expression reflected all that and more. Regret squeezed my chest. Mom and Dad's voices announced their arrival behind the happy couple, in the spot usually reserved for the husband's family. It did seem as though he loved them. I had been stupid to doubt him. Yet another strike on my record of hurting Lysander.

The couple went to the center of the grove, where a stone bower stood some eight feet high, green along the height of its columns from generations of moss growth. Releasing one another as though it was the hardest thing they'd ever done, they took their places under the straight arch, she near one column, and he at the other. Tradition would keep them separated until the simple ceremony was over.

All the guests spread out in a circle at the edge of the grove. Wharfmaster Marlow, as the most prominent member of our neighborhood, stepped forward. He had inherited his father's title a few years ago, and like his dear dad, was working on an equally wide girth. Tradition had everyone waiting anxiously to see what he would offer the groom to tempt him into handing over his bride. I always thought it a ridiculous practice, like some sort of livestock auction. Highest bidder gets the girl—no wonder so many of us dreaded marriage. Thankfully, the groom didn't usually accept the offer, though it had happened a few times before. That's how Marlow got his fourth wife—the twin sister to his second wife. Neither sister was happy with the situation. I guess that explained all the fighting.

Marlow scanned the crowd, scratching the rust-colored beard along his plump jaw. "Now I know you may be asking, 'What would ol' Marlow want with a wombless wife?' I'll tell you—ol' Marlow has enough litluns running around his legs. I'd love to have a new young lass who won't be ruined by childbirth!"

He rocked his pelvis back and forth, while everyone laughed and cheered. Mavelle crossed her arms and ducked her head. Vulgar as Marlow's speech was, it was all huff and no glory. It was simply custom, though one I didn't find funny, and I'm sure Mavelle didn't. I didn't envy her either, not with the way the twin wives were looking at her, as though they could rip her apart at any moment.

Marlow continued, "So, now Lysander Devlin, I'll offer you a treasure you will surely want over that lass."

Lysander nodded his consent. "Impress me," he said.

"Very well—to you I offer my biggest, finest, fishing boat—The Sea Serpent's Nightmare."

Gasps filled the grove. I had to admit, that was quite the offer. Other men would have been tempted, for that boat was bigger than our childhood homes, more finely furnished, with gear big enough to haul in a whale *and* a ton of slugfish.

But, I knew what Lysander would say before he uttered a word.

"Your offer is certainly tempting..." Lysander tapped his chin, looking from Mavelle to the Wharfmaster.

Marlow's hopeful smile warred with Mavelle's fear-widened eyes.

"But," Lysander said with a shake of his head, "I'm afraid I must decline your offer. May a better man be worthy of it."

Bowing graciously to Lysander, Marlow gave a nod that suggested he knew exactly what the answer would be and wasn't really bothered by it. I thought as much. The Wharfmasters respected those who didn't bow down to their every whim.

"Let them be wed!" Marlow exclaimed.

Lysander and Mavelle joined hands, Mom started crying, and I stopped breathing. The moon made a timely appearance from behind a cloud, shining its blessing upon the lovers below. Together, they recited the vows countless Hezrali couples had invoked before them.

By the light of the moon
And a cool kiss of dew,
I take you as mine
To start life anew.

Mavelle threw her arms around his neck, and they kissed to the cheers of the wedding party. I rolled to my knees. I had to get out of there. Lysander had moved on. He'd be happy with Mavelle. Good. Perfect. Now I could die in peace, but instead of standing up to march away in resigned dignity, I fell to all fours and wept. A chilly wind evaporated my tears.

I looked up toward the main path. A thick fog crawled toward the grove like a cloudy, skeletal hand. Misty fingers crept along the ground, headed for the wedding party. No one else seemed to have noticed it yet. But, the weather in Port Valor was unpredictable and strange. During one surprise cyclone when I was little, the storm swept up a school of squid and rained them down all over the town. Being a people who considered waste to be a sin, we collected as many as we could and ate squid for a month. I had never eaten it again; I'd gotten so sick of it.

Thankfully, there was no sign of a squid storm tonight. But those foggy fingers kept coming. They fanned out, surrounding the Grove like a hand preparing to capture an unsuspecting mouse. The core of each mist pulsed from dense to sparse, in a rhythm like a heartbeat. Surely they were seeing this by now. But, no one paid any mind. They all clapped for Lysander and Mavelle, who had finally let loose of each other long enough to acknowledge they had an audience.

And that's when I realized why no one saw it—it wasn't a fog. Those fingers, now reaching upright and growing more solid, were auras. Living energy. But these auras…were different, not glowing with the bright colors of normal life forces, but rather a sickly gray.

A voice as airy as the breeze whispered, *"Find her…"*

"Find who?" I whispered back, ducking behind my dead wedding date's gravestone.

These auras—I'd never seen them before. But memories sparked to life, bringing flashes of the day Sir Robert Everlyn, captain of Leogard's Holy Paladins, clung to life after an ambush, and how Loralee had almost been overcome with the unnatural energy when she healed him. I had pulled her mind free of the influence. The paladins told me later what to look for, as they could also read and feel auras. These auras matched their descriptions of nasty, undead, blood-sucking…

Vampires! And where there were vampires, a necromancer wasn't far behind. They hadn't detected me yet. It was pitch black in this area where I hid outside the Grove, and I had never had an aura. Strange, but true, nonetheless. They probably hadn't caught my scent either, since I was downwind. Their auras kept advancing on the wedding party.

I scrambled to my feet, whipping my daggers from their sheaths. Lysander jerked his head up just as the fog exploded with a thunderclap around us. Thick, noxious, decayed-meat odor filled my nose. Gagging, I coughed and tried to wave away the dense, putrid fog, but it lingered. I couldn't see.

But I could hear everyone else choking, coughing…and then the screaming began.

"No!" If they had hurt Mom and Dad…or Lysander, I didn't know what I would do.

One dagger held ready, I plowed through the bushes and into the Grove, turning the other dagger sideways to protect my face. Thorns clawed the skin on my good arm. Holding back a groan, I pushed onward until I couldn't feel anymore branches or thorns.

Growls and more screams cut through the nastiness. A guttural roar from somewhere in the fog vibrated in my head.

Ahead, I caught movement. Dark figures flashed through the fog. A gust of wind cleared a section of the Grove. Dad, holding daggers of his own, slashed out at a male vampire. Black blood sprayed from its neck, and it went down, turning to ash seconds later. Mom cringed behind Dad. Another vampire careened straight for her. I flipped a dagger from hilt to blade, holding the sharp silver firmly between thumb and forefinger. Just like Dad taught me. Lined the vampire in my sights, gauging for velocity. Reeling back my arm, I flung the dagger. Blurred like a fast-turning wheel, it flew, finding its mark in the vampire's neck.

Mom screamed as the creature tore the sleeve from her dress and fell to the ground, writhing and wailing until it, too, had turned to ash. Dad saw me, grinned and nodded. I'd finally done something to make him proud. I ran toward them, but another wall of rancid fog collided with me. Bile rose up my throat, and I held my breath to keep from gagging.

"Mira!" Dad called. "Here! Hur—"

His words were cut off with a cry of agony and Mom screaming.

"Dad!" I ran blindly. *Not Dad. Please, goddess, no.*

Something knocked me to the ground, driving the wind from my lungs. I lost hold of my dagger, and it fell to the ground. A rough hand yanked my hair back so hard, I thought it might be ripped out at the roots. Right at my cheek, with reeking breath and red eyes, a vampire bared its fangs, but stopped an inch from my neck.

I held my breath and clamped my eyes shut, waiting for the bite. If it didn't kill me straight away, I'd slit my own throat before becoming one of these things.

"You," it said, the voice so raspy I couldn't tell if it was male or female, "you're the one."

The one? What on Tallenmere did that mean? The earlier voice that said, *Find her*...did that mean find *me*?

It yanked me by my hair completely off the ground, leaving my feet dangling. With one swift toss, it had me tucked under its arm and took off at a blazingly fast run, parting the fog as it went. I struggled and screamed, but it held tight until another dark figure sideswiped us, knocking us both to the ground. My wrist cracked from the impact.

But, I was free. I lay on my stomach, wrist throbbing and too stunned to move. Too scared. This was beyond my abilities. I couldn't see well enough to use my daggers effectively. I'd also never bent a vampire's mind, and from what I'd seen it do to Loralee, I knew it would be bad if I tried. And in this fog, it would be near-impossible to get a lock on one's eyes anyway.

Bone-chilling growls and shrieks came from the fog to my left. Then the sound of bones snapping, splintering, and tearing of flesh. A head bounced through the fog. It landed an inch from my nose. I screamed and belly-crawled backwards. Red eyes stared lifelessly at me from a deathly pale face. It was the vampire who had captured me, but who…?

Holding my broken wrist, I scrambled to my knees. "Dad?"

I still could see nothing beyond a couple feet around me. The rotting-flesh fog sat thick in my mouth. Not able to hold it back anymore, I bent over and wretched until I could gag no more. Wiping my mouth with my sleeve, I sat up on my knees again and listened. Moans, people calling for each other.

Lysander screamed, "Mavelle!" Footsteps pounded on the ground, heading away from the Grove.

A bitter, hollow voice surrounded the Grove like it came from everywhere. "Come find her, if you dare!" The voice sounded female, powerful, the voice of a necromancer.

Wind whipped the fog into a nasty whirlwind. I covered my face to keep the leaves and dust from my eyes, and in a moment it was gone.

Slowly, I lowered my arms and dared to look around me. Marlow's body lay a few feet away, his neck shredded into a bloody pulp. Three of his wives hunched over him, wailing in grief. One of the twins was missing. Every few feet, scattered and torn apart like slain sheep, lay people from the wedding party. Cries grew louder, more frantic. Some people ran wildly to and fro, screaming the names of their loved ones. Finally, I could see the spot where I knew Mom and Dad had been fighting for their lives.

One body lay in a crumpled heap by the wedding bower.

"Mom," I whispered, stumbling to my feet. The pain in my wrist was horrendous, but not as bad as the pain in my chest the longer I watched for a sign of life. Just a twitch, a breath, a sound, a hint of an aura—but there was nothing. She laid completely still, her back facing me. Blood pooled on the ground by her head. My feet felt heavy as an anchor, but I dragged myself forward, serenaded by cries of despair. It wasn't right, not here in the Grove where silver moonlight had sparkled on the dewy grass. The only place in Port Valor where peace and love had reigned for centuries.

I stopped inches from my mother's body and leaned over just enough to see her face. Her eyes were open, staring blankly at nothing, her skin paler than the snow atop the bower.

Dropping to my knees, I grabbed her shoulder and shook it hard. "Mom! No," I commanded, forcing the words past my clenched teeth, "you can't be...no, please. Mom!"

Her limp body rolled to and fro with every shake, until finally I shook too hard, and she rolled from her side to her back. I knew what I would see before my eyes even registered the sight. Mangled neck, drenched in blood, her pretty blue dress torn and forever stained red.

I let my forehead fall on her shoulder. "I'm sorry! Goddess, I'm so sorry!" Like everyone else who still breathed in the Grove, I cried loud and long, until my lungs begged for mercy and my throat produced no more sound. The scent of blood, metallic and thick, polluted the air, but I took a few breaths to regain some sense of reality.

Finally, I sat up on my knees and searched as far as my eyes could see. "Dad?"

No answer. I got to my feet and called out, though my voice was feeble, scratching my grief-weakened throat. "Dad!"

Feet trudging numbly all around the Grove, I went from one body to the next. They were all the same—throats ripped apart, blood drained. A pile of ash here and there where a few of the vampires had met their final death. Dad wasn't among them. Neither were Lysander or Mavelle. I remembered him screaming her name, and that malicious voice taunting him to come find her. Maybe he was out there now, searching. Maybe he was still alive.

Oh goddess, please let him be all right.

Anguished cries grew quieter, replaced with questions and plans of action.

"Why?"

"Who would do this?"

"Let's get back to town, organize a search party. They've taken some of us—we might find them alive if we hurry."

I asked a man whose face I knew but whose name my mind could not exhume, "Have you seen Abbott Hearton?"

His eyes held the same grief and helplessness that I felt. "No. My wife is gone, too. Why her? Who would do this?" He covered his eyes and walked away, sobbing.

A few men had gone searching beyond the Grove. Their lantern light bobbed around in the darkness. I stumbled to meet them, carefully avoiding the bodies and blood on the ground. One of them ran up, blocking me from going any further.

"No, miss, you don't want to be goin' out there."

"Dad...Abbott Hearton...have you seen him? Or Lysander and Mavelle?"

Another man joined us from their search party. Clothes hung from his hands. One was a horsehair tunic, ripped near the neck and covered with blood. Dad had worn that thing since before I could remember. The other was part of a wedding robe with a sea blue sash, equally torn and bloodied.

"No, they can't be dead!" I shook my head, tiptoeing to peer into the darkness beyond the men, praying that Dad, Lysander, and Mavelle would come walking back into the light. I tried to scoot around them, but they held me back. "Dad! Let me go, I'll find them."

The first man grabbed my upper arms and held firm. His aura flashed yellow, red, and indigo—he was as scared, anxious and grief-stricken as the rest of us. "No, miss. They're gone. It's not safe for you to go out there alone. We'll retrieve the bodies and bring 'em home to you soon as we can. I'm sorry. Head home and get someone to take a look at that wrist."

He turned me around, and I walked numbly back through the Grove. Past those who grieved loved ones, comforted the survivors, and cared for the injured. Dad, Mom, Lysander and Mavelle—all dead. Wounded and exhausted, I couldn't conjure up the energy to be useful or to even remember my training. The only thing I had accomplished was losing everyone I ever loved.

Snow fell in soft flurries, melting on my tear-soaked cheeks as I returned down the path that led to home. Once inside, I fell into a chair at the kitchen table. Everything looked and smelled the same—glowing embers in the hearth, earthy dried herbs and smoke-cured meat hanging from the rafters, Mom's embroidery in the seat of her rocking chair. She'd been stitching a gift for me, with the words: *Welcome home Mi—* in green thread. It would never be finished. Without them here, the house was dark, quiet. Dead. Not like home at all. I had wanted to live in order to spare my parents any more heartbreak. All for nothing. Some necromancer with a horde of hungry vampires had taken them from me within the span of a minute. Lysander and Mavelle, too. Gone. Forever.

I slid my remaining dagger from its sheath on my thigh and clicked my thumbnail across the blade's edge. Silver daggers—a cherished gift from Dad. We'd spent countless hours practicing offense and defense, throwing at targets, learning proper sharpening. Oh, what fun we had—I loved every minute of it. But those happy memories had faded into a distant reality I could never get back.

Holding the dagger straight up in front of me, I caught a sliver of my reflection—a brown eye, cursed with an ability I couldn't trust, reddened from tears I couldn't bear to shed any longer. I wouldn't wait here alone until the poison took me, and my life wasn't worth traveling back to Leogard in an attempt to save myself. Placing the blade against the skin on my broken wrist, I closed my eyes and drew a shaky breath.

The sharp silver edge sliced through my flesh like butter. It barely stung, numbed from the swelling. I let my arm fall down and hang limp by my chair. Hot blood coursed down my palm and dripped from my fingers, soaking into the floorboards.

Laying my head down on the table, I closed my eyes and pushed the night's horror from my mind. I thought instead of Mom and Dad's joyous smiles when we were reunited…and Lysander. I'd tried so hard to tell myself I had done the right thing in leaving him behind. But it was all a lie. My entire life had been one lie after another.

All my weight rested on the table. Vertigo spun the world. In my mind, I said what I should have said a long time ago. *I love you, Lysander. I'm so sorry I hurt you. I should have never left home. Please forgive me.*

Sounds, sights, smells were all suffocating into utter silence and numbness. *Come quickly, death...don't tarry.* Everything faded to black.

Chapter Eleven

~ Lysander ~

No trace. Mavelle was gone. For an hour, I had circled the perimeter of the grove, fanning out wider with each pass and found nothing but tracks that ended abruptly for no reason. Plenty of blood streaked and dripped along the various trails, but none of it smelled of Mavelle. I found no pieces of her wedding robe, no distant screams, no anything. She and the vampires must have been sucked up into the ether of wherever that voice originated. It had to be a necromancer. As a young assassin, I'd killed one under Harker's command. Could this be revenge? I doubted it—necromancers weren't known to be sentimental to one another, and it had been nearly a decade. Why wait so long?

All I could think about was how frightened she must be. My poor Mavelle. She'd be praying that I would come, expecting me to swoop in at any moment and save her. But how could I? How could I help my wife if I couldn't even find one trace of her? We had just finished our vows when the vampires appeared out of nowhere. If they had wanted to kill her, they would have done it then. There had to be more to it than a bloodsuckers' feast. Whoever this necromancer was, she wanted me to come looking for her, and I would not disappoint.

I snatched up a rock and hurled it into the night. "I'm coming for you, bitch, and I won't be bringing you back alive!"

The only answer was a rustling in the bushes from whatever I had frightened with my stone throwing. Weeping sounds from the Grove drew me back there. I had to calm myself, gather my thoughts, form a plan. Stumbling along, not from clumsiness, but from strength-sapping grief, I concentrated on transforming back to my human self. The Tyger in me demanded to emerge again like I had allowed it to in the fog-shrouded chaos. It pulsed against my skin, wanting to take advantage of all this rage and desperation, ready to rip a few more vampires apart. Or anyone else who got in my way.

I relented with my eyes, letting them retain their feline properties for a while longer. At least I'd be more likely to notice any visible signs I might have missed in my frantic search. However, the nocturnal scenery, clear and bright as it appeared in my superior sight, still didn't lend any evidence as to the whereabouts of my wife.

Walking slowly through the dark, I breathed deeply and relaxed, letting my good side suppress the wild part of me, which craved bloody vengeance. To my neighbors in Port Valor, I was Lysander the Tyger. Lysander the hero. Protector of king and kingdom. They'd expect me to have killed the villain, returning in triumph with Mavelle at my side. They'd lynch me if they saw my alter ego. I had no choice but to return empty-handed and fully human, covered in vampire blood and ash. Part of my robe had been torn away during the fight and the rest when I fully shifted to tyger form. My tattered trousers were the only thing keeping me from being naked.

Once I stepped foot into the Grove, a few men with lanterns ran to greet me. The bouncing lights overwhelmed my eyes, glaring like miniature suns.

"Lysander? We thought you were dead! Are you hurt?"

I squeezed my eyes shut against the brightness before they noticed anything odd. "No, I'm fine."

Once the stinging that accompanied my tyger sight had subsided, I opened my eyes and blinked into the now dimmer light. They shared a look of sympathy, but also disappointment. For once, I had no clue where to find and capture my prey. Their eyes settled on my chest. I followed their gaze to thick black vampire blood splattered over my skin and some black tufts of fur stuck to the mess. My jaw tightened, waiting for their questions.

One of them lifted his lantern. "We're getting a search party together. Join us?"

"Oh…" I relaxed a little, glad their suspicions weren't raised.

I was about to say yes, but then again, if *I* couldn't pick up on their trail, these men had no chance in the Great Void of doing it. And there were still dead and wounded to tend to…and Mira. Why had she even been there? Her parents had said she was holed up in her room, refusing to emerge. What if she had arranged the whole thing? No, I couldn't think that way. She'd been terrified when I caught up with the vampire who tried to run away with her. She wouldn't have put herself and her parents in harm's way if she'd had anything to do with it.

"The Heartons?" I asked. "Are they all right?"

"You don't know?" Their faces darkened with the subdued frowns of those who dread delivering bad news. "Evetta's dead, and Abbott's…well, we thought he was dead out there with you. We found his tunic and part of your wedding robe all covered in blood. But he must have been taken elsewhere, along with several others."

He handed me Abbott's tunic and what was left of my robe. A sinking feeling washed over me. "Mira?"

"Headed back into town."

"Thank you." Why would she return to town instead of remaining to grieve over Evetta? Perhaps she went back, hoping to find Abbott. At least she was still alive. I ran to the Grove, but dreaded what I would see there. I was right—my worst nightmares could not have fathomed the destruction. Mangled bodies, weeping wives, mothers, and children. And Evetta, just a few feet from our bower. My second mother, so happy for us just a little while ago, smiling with love and pride at Mavelle and me as though we were her own children. I broke down and wept while I partially covered her body with her husband's tunic.

Wiping my face, I ran again toward town, into a scene of sheer confusion. People gathered on the boardwalks—survivors with unblinking, panicked eyes and those who were just hearing the news, covering their mouths or breaking into sobs. Some wilted to their knees in shocked silence. I didn't see Mira among them. Mavelle's father Darvis ran up to me, lantern in one hand, harpoon in the other.

"Thank the gods you're still alive! Where's Mavelle?" His desperate eyes studied mine, and it took all my will to hold his gaze.

"There's no trace of her."

His jaw trembled, and he swiped at his eyes. "Others are missing, too. I'm going to find them. Come with me."

"No matter how much I want to, our efforts will be futile."

He butted the harpoon against my chest, the grief on his face igniting into red-cheeked anger. "You're just giving up?"

"Of course not!" My voice roared along the street. Everyone went quiet and still. I took his harpoon in both hands and gently pushed him back. Rage was building, and I had to keep it subdued before things got out of hand. "But searching blindly through the dark when there's not even a trace will be a waste of time. Necromancers use powerful magic. They can open portals. Mavelle and the others could be anywhere. We have to regroup and form a plan."

Darvis yanked the harpoon away from me. "Fine, then what's the plan, Great Thinker?"

"I have to find Mira."

His fists clenched, and the harpoon shook. I thought he might spear me with it. "Mira? You want to find the bitch that left you before you look for your own wife?"

"Watch your tongue!" Turning away, I tried to breathe and keep the rumble from my voice. "You don't understand. She may have seen something that we missed that will help us find Mavelle."

"Like she would help her rival."

"Mavelle's not her rival. Mira only came back because…she missed her family." Lying about Mira's motives weighed upon my already heavy guilt, but I had to settle for the lesser of two evils. "She and Mavelle were once good friends. I know she wouldn't wish her any harm."

"Right. Meanwhile, the rest of us will be out there doing what you should be."

I closed my eyes, breathing hard, fists clenched to keep from doing or saying something I'd regret. He brushed past me, and I gave him a few seconds to put some distance between us. Opening my eyes, I looked down the street toward Mira's house and broke into a run. With every stride, I prayed she would prove my doubts wrong. But, she'd fooled me before.

I didn't bother knocking on the Heartons' door, but burst into the dark house like a mad man. "Mira!" My eyes immediately adjusted to

109

Mysti Parker

the darkness, and then I saw her, slumped in the kitchen chair. Blood
puddled on the floor beneath the table. Its fresh metallic odor wafted up
as I ran to her. "Oh, Mira, what have you done?"

I pressed my fingers to her neck. Her pulse was weak, but thankfully
still there for now. But time was not on her side. Another minute and
she'd be gone. I tore the sleeve from her shirt. She let out a faint groan
when I wrapped the fabric tightly around her wrist. Bones shifted
beneath the swollen joint. She must have broken her wrist. Noise from
outside reminded me I hadn't shut the door. I couldn't let anyone else see
her like this. Gently, I slid one arm under her shoulders, and one under
her knees, scooping up her slight frame. Voices grew louder, and lantern
light flickered, getting closer to the front door.

Under the welcoming cover of darkness, I ran through family
gardens, leapt over waist-high fences and across yard-wide drainage
ditches until I reached my home on Main Street. She was so light, I had
no trouble at all.

The back door was locked as always, so I shifted Mira's weight and
placed my palm on the hand-shaped indention right above the knob. An
orange glow and a slight vibration greeted my skin. Gears inside the lock
clicked to life, spinning until the mechanism disengaged with a solid
clank.

As the door opened, Mira lifted her head from my shoulder.
"Lysander...don't...go..."

"Shh." I carried her inside. The door shut and locked itself behind
us. "I'm not going anywhere."

Chapter Twelve

~ Mirabelle ~

Potato soup with smoked ham. I'd know that aroma anywhere. It was one of the few things Mom made that wasn't fried. My stomach growled mercilessly. Something tickled my arm. Probably a fly or spider. Eyes still closed, I reached across by body to swat it off.

Lysander's voice froze me mid-swat. "No, Mira, be still."

I hadn't gotten used to how deep and grown up he sounded. He shouldn't have been there—he should have been gone with Mavelle to start their lives together. I tried to wake up fully, but my eyelids felt like they were anchored to my face. My body molded to whatever I lay on. I couldn't even will myself to roll over.

"I said be still," Lysander commanded again.

Eyes and body useless for now, I tried my mouth, which was dry as cotton. Moving my jaw to speak was harder than forcing rusted hinges apart. But I managed a hoarse whisper. "What are you doing here?"

"Bringing you back to life."

"But, you're married."

A long silence passed—at least it felt long—awareness drifted between reality and dreams.

His voice sounded shaky when he finally spoke again. "Rest now, Mira."

* * * *

Bzzz, bzzz, bzzz. My eyes popped open, expecting to see a bee or a fly buzzing around my face, but instead an unfamiliar wall rose above

111

me. Strange weapons and armor hung over a hearth that blazed with a hot fire. My fingers scratched across the surface of whatever I was lying on—it felt like a silky cloth. Every few inches were indentations with fabric-covered buttons. An ottoman? Why would I be on an ottoman? Was I in a new part of the Temple?

My arm felt heavy. I lifted it up and froze. A strange metallic device was attached to it. Copper bands held it in place on my forearm and across my hand. The bands were connected to four metal support rods that ran parallel to my arm, and at my wrist...I sat up, eyes wide, panic setting in with shallow breaths. What looked like a silver beetle was partially embedded in my skin, buzzing and clicking. I could feel its vibration all the way through my fingers, which tingled like blood rushing back in after the circulation had been cut off.

Tentatively, I reached for it, when a voice startled me. "Don't touch that!"

My head whipped around, and there was Lysander, coming around a big kitchen table with a bowl of something. He wore a loose white shirt, the drawstring at the top left untied, revealing a muscular chest with fine, dark hair. He really wasn't a boy anymore. This was grown-up Lysander, the one I'd met at Bearden's Fishhouse, the one who had gotten married...

"Oh goddess!" Memories hit me all at once. The vampires, the blood...

Lysander rushed over and knelt beside me. He set the bowl on the floor and took my unencumbered hand.

"Mom?" I cried, searching his face, imploring him to tell me this had all been a nightmare.

But instead, he shook his head. "I'm sorry, Mira."

He caught me before I hit the floor, too overcome with grief to even stay upright. Somehow, he managed to keep my broken wrist and the device from hitting anything. He gently lifted me back onto the ottoman and kept his arms around me until I stopped crying.

"I saw them coming," I whispered.

He stiffened. "What do you mean?"

"The vampires. I saw their auras stretching across the Grove like a foggy hand."

His body trembled, as did his voice. "You…saw them coming, and you didn't bother to warn anyone?"

Shame squeezed my throat, and though my brain told me admitting this would only hurt him more, I did my best to choke out the words. "I didn't know what it was. I'd never seen vampire auras before."

Sitting up straighter, he leaned away from me, putting a few inches of distance between us. "Yet, you didn't find it odd or menacing enough to say anything?"

"I…" How could I tell him that my heart had been breaking at the time, knowing he loved someone else? Then there was that voice—*Find her*—but I didn't know what it meant or even if it had been real. "I didn't know what to think."

He sprang from the cot, leaving me wobbly and off balance. With his back to me, he faced the fire in the hearth. His silhouette was that of a man on the verge of attack, legs wide in a slight crouch. His voice deepened, turning it into a menacing growl. "But you hid in the shadows and didn't bother to warn anyone. Why is that, Mira? Did you want Mavelle dead? Or me?"

"No! I didn't want that. I didn't want any of this." I looked at both my wrists—one that held my death sentence and the other, my attempted suicide.

Fists clenched and trembling, he roared, "Then why didn't you say something?"

"I didn't…I couldn't…I didn't think anyone would listen."

"I would have! Why were you there anyway? Was breaking me once not enough for you?"

"No, Lysander, I never wanted to—"

"Did you arrange this?"

"No!" My heart beat erratically. The room spun. He might as well have slapped me across the face with such an accusation.

"Anything. Just a shout—a few seconds of warning. She'd still be here!" He grabbed a poker and swung it. I cowered, afraid he'd take off my head with it. Instead, he struck a mosaic vase on the table next to me. It flew off and shattered. Colorful glass squares scattered across the floor.

He threw the poker down. It bounced off the floorboards and hit the hearth, knocking pieces of brick onto the rug below. Before I could say anything, he stormed out the door, slamming it behind him. A lock spun and clicked, engaging fully with a loud click.

Had he locked me up? Was I his prisoner now? I felt too weak to get up and try the door. When he might come back, I had no idea, but I had to let him go. He was right. I could have warned them, but I didn't. The room spun, and my eyesight blurred. Hungry, tired, and weak, but not worth saving. I lay back down, willing the goddess to take me.

Instead, I woke to someone shaking me gently. Slowly opening one eye, then the other, I saw Lysander looking back at me. He knelt by the cot. His eyes were bloodshot, his hair a mess. His face was flushed and sweaty as though he'd been running for a long time.

"I'm sorry," he said. "I had to get out of here for a little while, so I wouldn't..."

"It's all right," I whispered. "Did you find Dad? Or Mavelle?"

"No, not yet. But, I helped bury some of the victims."

'Victims' included Mom. My jaw trembled as I fought back tears.

"I have some soup here. You should eat and build up your blood."

He handed me a steaming bowl of stew with big chunks of ham and potatoes. My mouth instantly watered, not realizing how much I had missed the heartiness of Hezrali food. I tried to pick up the spoon with my uninjured hand, but the bloodgems under the tattoos flashed red, sending an instant streak of fire up my arm. Dropping the spoon, I cried out, drawing my trembling wrist to my chest. Another one of them must have sprung a tiny leak. Before long, I'd turn to a puddle of liquid me. Hopefully outdoors so I wouldn't become a mess on Lysander's floor.

Wordlessly, Lysander took the bowl, spooned up a bite of stew, and held it to my lips. Embarrassed, I hesitated for a moment before taking the bite. He watched me as I ate it. Some of the resentment had left his eyes, replaced with genuine concern.

"Thank you," I said. He offered another bite, and I took it. So good—I felt better already, but it didn't ease my worry. "They're dead, aren't they? They must be by now."

"No, I don't think so. I've never known vampires to take prisoners." He stood up and went to the hearth, picked up the poker and jabbed it at the logs. "I think this necromancer wants me to come looking for them.

That's why she wanted Mavelle. She wants me, not her."

"But why?"

"Who knows? I killed one once. Maybe it was her sister or something. Most likely, she's bored and wants to play."

I let him feed me another bite, then took a drink of the cool water he offered from a pretty ceramic cup. It was painted with roses and butterflies—not exactly a masculine design. Had Mavelle painted it?

"You really think they're still alive?" I asked.

His shoulders rose and fell. "I have to." He had so much pain in his eyes, it brought tears to mine again.

Clearing my throat, I decided to change the subject. "What is this thing on my arm?" The metal beetle buzzed and clacked as though it took offense to my question.

"It's a binder bug," Lysander said tiredly as though I should know what it was. "A rather ingenious clockwork device I got from a dwarven physician in Minzck."

"Clockwork?"

"All metal—gears and springs and an enchantment of some sort. You never used them in the Temple?"

I shook my head, eyeing the silver beetle as it worked beneath my skin.

"It sealed up your blood vessels and is now working to repair your broken bones. If you'd be still, it would work a lot faster."

I felt my thigh, where a dagger should be. Lysander took my hand and shook his head.

"I have them," he said. "They're safe, where you can't harm yourself or anyone else for now. Here, take one more bite."

He stuck the spoon in my mouth a little abruptly. I chewed and swallowed fast then gulped the water he practically poured down my throat. Placing the cup in the empty bowl, he carried them both to the kitchen.

"You found me...like that?" I wanted to shrink away, knowing what he must have seen—me in the lowest point of my existence.

"Yes, and I brought you here to my house so you could heal."

"But, I..."

"You what? Wanted to die?"

Biting my lip, I blinked back another onslaught of tears.

"Well, sorry," he said, taking his place in the chair beside me again. "We can't always have what we want, can we? The Mira I knew ten years ago would have never tried to kill herself."

"The Mira you knew doesn't exist anymore."

He sat quietly for a moment. "You're wrong. I think she's still here, buried under a mountain of regret. But we don't have time for that right now. We have a lot to discuss."

"Like what?" My original quest to find the Tyger and bring him back to Leogard had been trumped by the wedding-turned-nightmare, so I had no idea where to go from here.

"I'm going to find Mavelle, your father, and the rest of the people who were taken. And you're going to help me."

Chapter Thirteen

~ Lysander ~

The knowledge that Mira could have warned us still made my blood run cold, though if she was telling the truth, we would have had only a few seconds to react. Even with my talents, I probably couldn't have saved Mavelle. But, that uncertainty lingered in the air like the necromancer's thick, rancid aura.

It was time to act, not dwell, so I fixed us both a cup of coffee, carried it to the great room, and sat by Mira. She looked a little more rested now.

"Think you can hold this?" I held the cup out to her, handle first.

She nodded and took it carefully. The bloodgems on her arm glowed faintly. My tattoo had been somewhat painful, but I could only imagine how badly those things must have hurt. And the poison inside them—how much had already dissolved into her bloodstream? I held out hope that we could track down Mavelle and the others quickly enough that I could take her back to Leogard and do whatever we needed to do to get them out of her.

But we had to stay focused on the task at hand. "Let's get down to business. What do you know about necromancers?"

"Not a lot. Just that they're not the kind of people you want to invite to a party."

I cleared the tightness from my throat.

"Sorry," Mira answered, giving her coffee a long sniff as though appreciating the aroma. "I'm not sure what I can tell you. I've only seen one, and only briefly."

"Tell me what you know."

"The Priestess's daughter, Ivy, stole the necromancer's work, or had it stolen, I should say."

"Stolen? From where?"

"I don't know." She shrugged. "She was a dark elf, so maybe Ironhaven? That's where most of the dark elves are."

Mira's information sparked a few memories. A long voyage, an even longer hunt in enemy territory. But that had been a job Harker had gotten from King Damien. Not a priestess's daughter. So he had claimed, anyway.

I sipped my coffee, wishing I'd remembered sugar. "And the encounter? What happened?"

"According to Loralee and the paladins, vampires kind of dropped from the sky. I didn't see that part. I was down in the storage room. All I saw was the necromancer dragging Loralee through the basement. I sneaked up behind the dark elf and stabbed her with one of my daggers. But it wasn't the actual necromancer. It was what they called her shade—a semi-solid form of the real thing. Anyway, she went poof and disappeared. Loralee then rushed upstairs to heal Sir Robert from being bitten. It was terrible. Vampire sickness had already started to work on him, and when she used her Spark to heal him, it came through her. It would have festered inside her had I not been able to mind-bend it out of her."

"Amazing."

"What?" She lifted her coffee cup to take a sip.

"I've never heard of anyone being healed from vampire sickness. You really did some good with your gifts in Leogard."

She lowered the cup again, resting it on her lap. "It hadn't manifested completely. I don't think anyone can cure a fully transformed vampire." She scanned the walls as though looking for something and then directed her attention to the front windows. "How long was I asleep?"

"You were out all night and all day, a full twenty-four."

"Where are Darvis and the others?"

"Out searching."

"Then why didn't you go with them?" She flicked her gaze to mine, then focused on her full coffee cup.

"Isn't it obvious?" I swallowed the last of my coffee. "It's going to get cold if you don't drink it."

Her eyes never quite met mine, stopping at the outer edge of my face. Was that hope I saw in there? Not that it mattered now. She finally lifted her cup and took a sip.

"Don't misunderstand," I said. "I need you to help me find Mavelle. They're searching in vain until we figure out exactly where this bitch is."

Mira closed her eyes and lowered her head. She gave a small nod. "Fine, but I don't see how I can help you."

"Did you hear or see anything else before or during the attack in the Grove?"

"I'm not sure."

"Not sure?"

"It all happened so fast, and then afterwards, I…I don't know if it was real or not."

"Just tell me what you remember."

"Before the vampires manifested, I thought I heard a voice whisper, '*Find her.*' Then, when the one vampire caught me, I think it said, '*You're the one.*'"

Dear gods, why hadn't I thought of that before? I laughed—not from amusement, but from the bitter irony and injustice of it all. "It was you."

"What?"

"They came for you. Had you remained home and sulked, they'd have taken you and left the rest of us alone."

Mira's jaw dropped. A defiant glint lit up her sad eyes. "I had no idea a necromancer was after me! And how do you know she wasn't after you, too? She took Mavelle and taunted you to come find her. What's that got to do with me? You said you killed one. You've killed a lot of people, from the sounds of it. Anyone could be after you at any given time."

"Well now, there's the smart-ass Mira I once knew."

She closed her eyes and sighed. "What do you want from me?"

"The vampire attack you witnessed in Leogard—that was a bold move for a necromancer, invading the Temple itself—did you know her name?"

Mira shuddered. "Mortynna or something like that. The paladins found her several miles away in Cavitel Valley and killed her."

A damp, musty crypt flashed through my memories. The name *Mortynna* etched into the skin-bound tome that I took while she slept. But, Harker had claimed King Damien wanted it, not Ivy. There could be some secret alliance between Damien and Leogard's Temple. No royal family was without scandal. And of course, Harker could have been lying. But how did all this connect, and more importantly, how much could I trust Mira?

I stood to take my cup back to the kitchen. "That necromancer was a fair distance away from the attack, then. So, this bitch wouldn't be close to town. She'll be hiding somewhere isolated, where she can keep watch."

"Then how are we supposed to find her, and more importantly, how are we supposed to sneak up on her?" Mira handed me her barely drunk coffee. Maybe she'd wanted cream. She had always liked it like that.

"Leave that to me."

"First..." She lifted one arm, after another, grimacing at her sleeves, where dried blood and dirt covered much of the fine light blue fabric. I didn't want to tell her that her face and hair looked just as bad. "Can I clean up somewhere?"

"Certainly. Let me show you the washroom."

* * * *

~ Mirabelle ~

We took a break from rescue planning so I could visit Lysander's indoor facilities. The bathroom had a beautiful, polished red brick floor with a marble washbasin and recessed tub. The toilet existed in a similar recessed fashion, tucked away in its own little nook with a curtain for added privacy. Brass fixtures glinted in the lamplight. It was more like a luxurious Leogardian bathroom than the harsh practicality of most Hezrali rooms.

A bath area in Port Valor homes usually consisted of a curtained-off corner of the room, a pitcher of water, and a washbasin. Relieving yourself meant you used the outdoor facility, which was nothing more than a shack built above a drainage ditch. In warm weather, you had to contend with spiders, splinters, and horrendous odor if it had been a dry summer. At the coldest part of winter, you'd relieve yourself in a ceramic chamber pot and toss it out back. Sometimes the urine would freeze in midair, falling to the snow in yellow icicles. That was the high point of our days in the shameless cold of a Hezrali winter.

Sitting on the brick-lined edge of the tub, I turned on the faucet, and oh my! I'd gotten spoiled with the sophisticated water system in Leogard. Running water was practically unheard of here in Hezral. As the tub filled, I peeled off my clothes, carefully avoiding the beetle-healer thing on my arm. My robe was stained with dried blood, mud, and who knew what else. It had soaked through my undergarments too. I left them on the floor in a dirty pile and stepped into the steaming water. Easing myself down so the heat wouldn't shock my skin too much, I finally hit bottom and started to let myself sink.

Lysander yelled from the other side of the door, "Be sure to not get the binder bug wet!"

"Oh." I yanked my arm up just before it sank into the water. The binder bug still clicked and clacked under my skin, oblivious to its near-drowning. "All right."

He spoke again, softer this time, as though he were pressed against the door. "There are soap and bath oils next to you on a shelf. Along with towels. Pull that string with the red bead on it if you need anything."

"String?" Sure enough, a thick silk cord with a glossy red bead hung out of the wall under the shelf of fancy bottles and towels. I pulled it. A bell went da-ding somewhere in the house.

From the other side of the door, Lysander laughed. "Not now, unless you need something, that is."

I smiled for the first time in a couple days. "No, I'm fine."

"Good, I'll leave you to it."

After inspecting the contents of a few oil bottles—some of them were masculine and musky, some a more floral feminine scent—I chose one that smelled like rosemary and ginger. I added a few drops to the water and breathed in the steamy herbal aroma. Leaning back, I propped my broken arm on the side of the tub and closed my eyes, letting the majority of my body soak in the silky warm water.

My eyes snapped open. The water had become lukewarm, almost cold. Luckily my binder-bug arm was still safely on the side of the tub. The fingers on my other hand were wrinkled like dried talaberries. I must have fallen asleep, but for how long? A half hour? An hour? Quickly, I grabbed a bar of goat's milk soap and washed, though washing my hair with one hand proved a bit of a challenge. Finally, the task completed and my energy spent, I climbed out of the tub, dried myself, and realized I had no clean clothes. I could wash the dirty ones in the tub maybe, but I'd have to keep a towel around me until they dried.

I reached down to where I had dropped the nasty garments, but they weren't there. In their place was a neatly-folded, gray linen robe. Was it Mavelle's? It didn't seem right, wearing Lysander's...wife's clothes.

And then an odd realization hit me. He must have come in as I was asleep in the tub. That thought sent a warm shiver into places it shouldn't have gone. Too many of our loved ones were dead or missing. It wasn't the time to imagine him in the water with me. But there he was in my mind's eye, all wet and dripping, smiling while I rubbed soap onto his muscled chest, down his ripped abdomen, and lower, until...

Stop it, stop it, stop it! I yanked up the robe and slipped it on. It dragged the floor and swallowed me whole, so it couldn't have been Mavelle's. She was very petite. It must have been Lysander's robe.

I ventured outside the bathroom, where Lysander sat in a chair by the fire. He had a clear glass of something amber-colored. A drink that I'm sure would have been forbidden in the Temple.

I hadn't taken two steps when he asked, "How much do you trust your aura-reading abilities?"

"Um, it's good. Where are my clothes?"

"I washed them," he answered, as though I should have known. "They're hanging right there." He pointed to a line strung up just to the right of the hearth, where my wet clothes were draped. They appeared clean from where I stood. Was there anything he couldn't do?

"So you...came in there?" I stammered, my language skills suddenly hindered by more thoughts of what a bath with him might entail.

"I didn't look, except to check that your arm wasn't submerged, if that's what you're wondering."

My heart skipped a beat, but at the same time sank a little—he could have very easily seen me completely naked, asleep in the tub, but he said he didn't. Did that mean he didn't want to?

He swirled his drink and gestured for me to sit. I made my way toward the fire and sat on the edge of the ottoman. It really was a nice piece of furniture, upholstered with pale green silk, firm but comfortable filling in the seat and wooden ends carved into elaborate spirals.

"So, can you read me right now?" he asked.

Lysander's outer aura fluctuated between a hopeful yellow to a melancholy gray. A dull green aura throbbed on his knee.

"How long has your knee been bothering you?" I asked.

A sly grin split his face in two. "Long enough. That's pretty impressive. I think it might come in handy so we can find our prey and flush them out."

"I'm not a fighter, Lysander."

"Sure you are. You survived this long, and you know how to wield a dagger better than anyone I've seen."

"Maybe, but I don't want anyone else to get hurt."

"Leave that to me." He leaned in and checked the beetle weaver thing on my arm. "Almost done. How does it feel?"

Slowly, I wiggled my fingers, curled them into a fist, and flexed them again. "It only hurts a little." The beetle was fully topside now, tickling its metal pincers along the final half inch of the cut on my wrist. It fluttered metal wings, clicking as though it was happy to hear my compliment. "So, now what? Where do we go?"

"Tomorrow at first light, we head to the islands past the Cragstone Fjord."

"To the barbarian lands? Are you crazy?"

"Probably. But I searched the Grove while we were tending to the bodies. I think those vampires were once barbarians. There's a good chance our target is hiding somewhere among them."

"There are hundreds of islands there. How would you know where to start?"

"Ah yes, good question. However, each and every island is home to a different clan. And each of those clans carries specific charms that relate to their patron gods and goddesses. I found two of the same charm. There are only a couple of clans who wear those."

"I think I'm going to be sick." The only dealings I'd had with those rejects of the human race were unpleasant to say the least. "I don't think I can do this."

"Yes you can, and you will. They're just simple people."

"No, they're not."

"Why do you say that?"

I had no intention of dredging up the memories again. "Never mind. We should get going then."

"No, you're far too weak for that. Besides, it's the middle of the night. We'll set sail at dawn. That will give me time to gather my maps and some supplies."

I started to lie back on the ottoman when Lysander put a hand on my shoulder. "No, I think you're ready for a big girl bed." My jaw dropped as blood flowed to all the wrong places. After everything that had happened, why was my body responding like this to him?

He arched an eyebrow. "Not *my* bed, woman. You lost that chance a long time ago. This is a big house. I'll show you to one of the guest rooms."

"Oh…" He must have thought I was completely cracked to even think such a thing. But wearing his robe that channeled his musky scent to my nose every time I moved…well, it was a bit hard to remember I no longer had a place in his life.

I followed him up the stairs, past portraits of Lysander and his parents, him with King Damien, and Mavelle smiling prettily with a winter orchid by her cheek. We exited onto a landing, and turned right down a hallway with dark paneled walls and lit with the dull orange glow from pyrogems in iron sconces. My bare feet padded across a cool, polished wood floor. It seemed a lot more welcoming now than it did on the night I had tried and failed to capture him.

He showed me into a guest room at the opposite end of the hall from his room. "You'll sleep well in here. It's at the rear of the house, away from the street noise. Remember, I need you rested and *whole* if we are going to get through this."

"I understand." He was warning me to not attempt suicide again.

Not that he cared in the end, but he couldn't let me die before I helped him find Mavelle.

"Let's see your arm. I think the binder's done." I held it out to him. The beetle had finished piecing my skin back together. It crawled to one of the metal braces and fit itself into a beetle-sized slot. With a few twists and clanks from Lysander's strong, sure fingers, the contraption was off. "How does it feel?"

"Just a little sore, that's all."

"Good."

The bands had left indentations on my wrist and forearm, but other than that, it felt almost normal. His ingenuity amazed me. What else could he do? I had the sudden urge to sit up all night and talk like we once did, to catch up on ten years of all the things we had missed in each other's lives. But, we were different people now, in a situation where reminiscing with my best friend wasn't appropriate. Not with dead and missing loved ones to think about.

"Goodnight, Mira."

"Goodnight." He started to walk away, but I called out, perhaps a little too eagerly, "Thank you, Lysander, for…your kindness."

"You're welcome." The corners of his mouth lifted into a sad, gentle smile. His aura flared with a compassionate pink, before turning to sorrowful violet again. "Get some sleep."

A warm fire in the small hearth cast a comforting glow over the silver seal hide blanket on the bed. On the floor sat a crag bear rug, complete with gaping mouth and shaggy gray fur, each hair tipped with black so they'd blend into the rocky hillsides near the coast. Perhaps he'd hunted it himself.

I climbed into bed and settled under the deliciously warm covers, marveling at the brass warming pan in the middle of the mattress. I'd only seen them used on the chilliest of nights in the Temple, though they were a staple item here in Port Valor. He must have put it in there for me while I dozed in the tub. Mavelle was such a lucky woman to have him. Though I did envy her place in his life, I wished with all my heart that we would find her alive and well. She had done nothing to deserve such horror.

Low flames flickered sleepily from the hearth. I lay staring at it for a while. Lysander had done really well for himself, and I couldn't help but be proud of him. I owed him my help after what I'd put him and my parents through. A pinch of pain in my tattooed arm reminded me that even if we did find Mavelle, I probably wouldn't live long enough to even have a chance of lifting my curse. I'd pay for my sins with my life, just like the Priestess wanted.

So be it.

Chapter Fourteen

~ Lysander ~

We left the house just before daybreak, heading to the dock. I carried a large bag of essentials and had my cloak draped across my shoulder. Mira wore two thick cloaks and still looked like she was freezing. Only a few fishermen were up and about, striding quickly to the water. It was odd to see the streets so quiet. Usually by now, wives were stoking fires for the day's meals, children were milking goats and gathering eggs, and street merchants were vying for the choice spots. Instead of the usual laughter, gossip, and squeaky cart wheels, the wind carried rushed footsteps and impatient seagulls keening at the wharf.

"It's so quiet," Mira whispered as we reached the dock where my boat waited. It looked like any other fishing boat, though I wasn't a fisherman…not of fish, anyway.

"They're afraid of another attack," I said, "and who can blame them? As far as I know, there have never been vampires or necromancers this far north. If we can kill her, we'll cut off the source."

"But can't vampires make other vampires?"

"Yes, but that's rare. In the attack you described, where Sir Robert almost turned, he'd have most likely been killed if the other paladins had not intervened. Vampires don't care about reproducing. All they want is blood."

Soon as we boarded, a woman's voice called from the dock. "Wait! Lysander, wait!"

I gestured for Mira to go ahead and enter the cabin where she would be warmer. Then I focused on the woman who stood on the dock, holding a baby. It was Shanna, one of Mavelle's father's young wives.

"Is Darvis with you?" she asked. Her eyes were wide and frantic.

"No, he went out with a search party yesterday morning."

"He's not come back, nor have any of the others. Not even a message…and his boat's gone."

I peered through the near-darkness to where Darvis's boat usually berthed three docks over. Sure enough, there was just an empty space. *Damn him.* I'd told him my plan to search out the Barbarian islands last night, but I'd had to wait until Mira was strong enough to travel before we left. He called me a fool and a traitor, believing I'd chosen Mira over his daughter. Of course I couldn't tell him why I needed Mira's help. He didn't need more reason to impale her with his harpoon.

Trying to apply my most reassuring look, I turned back to Shanna. "I'll find him. He can't have gone far. Get the baby inside before she catches cold."

"Thank you, Lysander." Shanna glanced toward the cabin, where Mira peered out the window. Both of them frowned. No love lost there. I was certain Shanna suspected I had betrayed Mavelle as well, though considering the history with her 'stepdaughter', she shouldn't have cared. Most likely she was upset with anyone who might threaten her place in the Bearden household.

Shanna left, and all I could think about was Mavelle. How frightened she must be. If they'd hurt her…

I hauled up the anchor, unfurled the sails, and held to the rail as the wind caught the billowing black fabric and pushed us from the dock. Cold wind whistled in my ears, so I entered the cabin to check on Mira. Slight panic arose when I didn't see her right away. Then I heard her gagging.

There she was, her head hanging over a bucket by the bed.

"Already, Mira? We've just set out."

"Tell my stomach that." Her shoulders rolled with more heaving.

"I thought you would have grown out of that by now."

She sat back on her heels. "Yeah, well, I didn't."

I handed her a towel from above the washbasin. "Here. Would you like some lichen cakes to nibble on?"

"No thanks," she answered, wiping her mouth.

"It'll be several hours. You need something to settle your stomach. Lichen cakes and gingerroot. Best cure there is."

She gave me a sideways glance. "All right, fine."

"Smart girl."

I unlatched the pantry and took out the canister of lichen wafers, plus a hunk of gingerroot from the shelf. Fetching a knife from the drawer, I placed the food on the table. Gingery spiciness filled the air as I sliced thin slivers of the root and layered them on top of the green, crispy lichen cake.

Plopping them onto a small wooden plate, I handed it to Mira. "Here. Eat."

She looked at the food like I'd asked her to eat a rotten eel. Completely understandable. Lichen cakes neither looked, nor tasted appetizing, but were a necessity on long voyages. They provided all the sustenance one needed, while acting with the ginger to calm the stomach. But, it was most certainly an acquired taste.

Mira settled on the floor, resting her back on the side of the bed. She took a tentative nibble as I went to the controls cabinet carved with seafaring scenes of whale hunters and varnished like a fine captain's wardrobe. I applied my palm to the lock pad. It shimmered and shifted; clanking gears opened the doors. Inside, at the center of the control panel, was a series of levers.

"What is all that?" Mira asked, peering curiously around me.

"Ship's controls," I said with a smile.

"For what?"

"For sailing, what else?"

"Whatever." She let out an annoyed breath and nibbled more lichen cake. "Won't it be nightfall when we get there?"

"Not quite, but close."

"Prime playtime for vampires and necromancers."

"Precisely."

"Don't you think that's foolish?"

"Probably. For someone who doesn't know what they're doing."

"And I suppose *you* do."

"You better have a seat and hang on, perhaps to the bedpost there. We're starting up."

She scooted along the floor to the head of the bed where it met the wall and hooked her elbow around the bedpost. She didn't bother to ask what I meant by that, though I could tell she was dying to. Maybe it was ill-natured of me, but I enjoyed leaving her in a state of confusion. I'd lived in that state for ten years, thanks to her.

With a firm crank downward, I flipped the green lever. The ship gave a little shudder, which startled Mira. She hugged the bedpost tighter. It leveled off to a dull roar and pleasant vibration.

Peering out the window, she crinkled her brow in utter perplexity. "Are we...did you...is the ship moving faster?"

"Yes, it is."

She ate a little more and nodded toward the ship's controls. "More Dwarven magic, I assume?"

"You might say that. There's a propeller just behind the rudder that gives an extra boost when the sails aren't catching much wind. Or when you're in a hurry."

Mira set the cake back on her plate and stared sadly down at it. "Lysander, I know you are worried about Mavelle, and I'm worried for Dad, but how are just the two of us supposed to find and bring down a necromancer? The one who breeched the Temple required a whole unit of paladins to do that. I mean, even if they *are* on one of the islands, what's to keep them there? This witch may just want to toy with you. Who knows—"

"Quiet!" High-toned singing, like dreamlike flute music, floated across the sea. A song meant to entrance, to draw in their prey...I knew it well.

"Look, I'm sorry, but—"

"Do you hear that?" I wasn't in the mood for Mira's pessimism, but even less so for what I suspected was coming for us.

"What?"

"The singing. Damn it."

Mira set her plate on the bed and tilted her head toward the window. "It's faint, but I hear it now. What is it?"

"Bad news, that's what."

I rushed to the control cabinet and cranked the wheel beneath the propeller lever to speed us up. The propeller's roar amplified. Dishes

130

rattled in the cupboard.

Ka-thump!

"What was *that*?" Mira screeched, grabbing onto the bedpost again for dear life.

"Fuck!" They'd made it onto the deck. I rushed for the door to lower the bar. But it flew open, leaving me nose to nose with a poison-tipped trident.

* * * *

~ Mirabelle ~

"Walla too too oowee," said the creature who held a trident to Lysander's face. The language sounded familiar to me. Where had I heard it before?

This thing looked mostly like a man, but also like a fish. He was a head shorter than Lysander and had smooth white skin, mottled with opaque patches of green. The skin on each side of his neck was filleted open with gills. They pulsated as though gasping for water, showing hints of blood-rich red underneath. His facial features were human enough, but there was a long line cresting from forehead to chin as though someone had just begun to fold his face in half. This forced his eyes to appear situated slightly on the sides of his head, like a true fish. He had legs, but each of his calves had impressive fins like those of a lesser swordfish.

Then it hit me! This fishy fellow resembled Ladyfish, the mermaid I'd met during my migration to Leogard with the Port Valor Traveling Opera.

He wore no clothes, and I couldn't help but look for his male parts. But, he didn't have anything to look at. Not that I could tell without a closer inspection, and that wasn't happening while he wielded that trident.

I slid my hand down my thigh and touched the hilt of my dagger. Lysander waved a hand at me, but kept his eyes on the merman.

"I don't have time for this, Nautilon," Lysander said. "I haven't forgotten my tit-tat. Just give me a month or so."

"Ah ka no tit-tat. Oowee na too me." Fish Man shook his head, gills pulsating frantically. He grabbed Lysander's collar, dragged him out the door, and leapt off the boat with him in one single bound. I couldn't throw a dagger at the merman with Lysander between him and me.

Running to the deck's railing, I watched in horror as Lysander struggled with Nautilon, kicking the water up into an angry froth. Two more mermen joined the fight. They grabbed Lysander's arms and legs, pulling him under. I leaned way over, stretching my hand toward him. But, he was several yards away. Might as well have been miles.

He surfaced briefly and yelled, "Pull the blue le—"

And he was gone, dragged beneath the ocean waves. Three mertails with shimmering scales breached the surface as they plunged into the depths, and in an instant they were gone, too.

"No! Lysander! Oh goddess, no, please!" I stood there in shock, still reaching out, holding a useless dagger, alone on a boat I didn't know how to sail, heading to a place I'd never been.

I was tempted to jump in after them, but I wasn't accustomed to the cold like I used to be. Black, frigid water stared back at me, laughing in mirthful splashes of gentle waves. I'd freeze to death within minutes.

Wait…Lysander had said to pull the blue le— before he went under. He must have meant a blue lever. I sprang to my feet, ran to the control cabinet and saw it right away. There with the red, green, and black levers was a blue one.

I reached for it, but hesitated. What did it do?

Enough stalling—it didn't matter what the lever did. Lysander told me to pull it, so I had to trust him. At least it would be a valiant death if I died at sea rather than melting into a shapeless puddle from the basilisk venom.

I yanked down on the blue lever and scurried to the bed. Squeezing my eyes shut, I held on to the bedpost with one hand, the dagger in the other, and waited.

At first, nothing happened. The gentle hum of the propeller below didn't change. The ship kept its steady course toward the islands. I cracked one eye open, then the other. The lever must have been broken. Whatever Lysander thought it did no longer functioned. I started to get up when the whole ship began to shake.

Back down to the bed, hugging the bedpost, my teeth clacked harder as the vibration intensified. Wood creaked and popped. Metal clanged. The ship gave a great shudder, and outside the window, large brass plates emerged from the wooden frame. They were perpendicular to the ship, but angled back like a fish's side fins.

The clanging and creaking grew louder, almost deafening. One by one, each brass plate folded back, flush against the ship—*kabang, kabang, kabang*—until they'd swallowed up all the daylight. All was still for a moment. In the pitch-black silence, my heart tried to beat its way out of my chest. Then, the propeller sped up, the ship shuddered, and the world tilted.

Screaming at the top of my lungs, I hugged the bedpost with both arms and both legs to keep from falling. The noise became muffled, pressure built up in my ears until they popped. The blue lever must have made the ship dive underwater like a big metal whale.

I sure hoped Lysander knew what he was doing. I'd either be meeting him and the mermen soon or be crushed by a mass of deep water, whichever came first.

Chapter Fifteen

~ Mirabelle ~

Minutes passed, my ears popped the deeper the ship dove. It must have been a hundred or more feet under the Draekkan Sea. But it held. And not a drop of water had fallen on me. In fact, the ship seemed to have leveled out. The propeller had slowed to the same quick, but calm pace as it had topside.

Carefully, in case of another sudden shift in speed or direction, I extracted myself from the death hold I had on the bedpost. It was still pitch dark, but at least I was still alive. The bloodgems glowed faintly beneath my shirtsleeve. I took a few steps to where I thought the cabin door was and whacked my forehead on something solid.

"Ow...oh." I reached up with both hands to feel whatever I'd collided with. It was smooth, cool and oddly shaped, like a figure eight lying on its side. I hadn't seen anything like this before the ship turned into a metal whale.

Pulling up my sleeve, I angled my forearm toward the thing and used the dim red bloodgems' light to see. Some kind of metal composed it—most likely brass—with two stick-like protrusions on either side like handles. Two small glass lenses filled the figure eight's holes. The only things that had glass like this were spy glasses, so maybe...

Tiptoeing, I pressed my eyes to the lenses and held to the handles. Everything looked black and out-of-focus. I was about to pull away when faint lights in the distance shone through the darkness.

"What in the...?" A school of startled fish swam past the lens, followed by a squid. It squirted out a cloud of ink and darted away. Once

134

it cleared, the lights were brighter. The ship approached a city of sorts. The mer-people's home, maybe? Tall spires made of giant coral jutted from the sea floor. Holes like windows spilled light all around.

The entire city seemed to be surrounded by a white coral wall— much like Leogard. The ship nosed downward toward a large solid gate, guarded by two mermen with the same nasty-looking tridents. Their large round eyes glared my way. Their tails flicked as they turned to pull levers on either side.

Great, more levers.

The solid gate rose smoothly. My spyglasses suddenly retracted back into the ceiling of the cabin. I tried to hang on to them, but my weight did nothing, so I was left dangling a few inches off the floor in the pitch darkness. Letting go, I landed with a thud. The ship suddenly screeched to a stop, throwing me off balance and down to the rug.

My recently broken wrist hurt again, along with my knees and elbows. Another loud bang came next, followed by squeaks and clanks, and then a sliver of light hit my eyes. The light brightened as the ship's bronze panels that covered the cabin door slid back into their holding places. I squinted into the brightness, holding my breath to prepare for the crushing blow of water rushing in. But it didn't.

Instead, the cabin door opened, and the same guards I'd seen before stood there with tridents pointed at me. Blinking past the blinding light, I crab-crawled away, until I hit the bed and could go no further. The bloodgems wouldn't take me down. I'd be fish food instead.

Thanks a lot, Lysander.

"Too too oowee put wum," one of them said, and gestured behind him with his trident.

"You want me to go with you? Where? To your kitchen? You don't like raw meat, I guess."

He blinked at me with these strange third eyelids like a lizard. This one was better looking than the one who kidnapped Lysander, however. He had very light blond hair, hanging in braids along his shoulders, with tiny seashells woven along the length.

Both of them stood aside, jabbing their tridents at the city that lay behind them. But where was the water? Didn't they need water to breathe?

"Too too oowie!"

"Yes, fine, I'm coming." I got to my feet on wobbly legs and stepped tentatively to the door. "Do you have Lysander? Is he all right?"

"Too too oowee!"

"Yeah, yeah, too too oowee. I heard you the first time."

His greenish fingers clamped around my arm, and his companion did the same on the other side. They dragged me along, down the ship's gangplank and onto a shell-cobbled dock of sorts. Behind me, a portion of the ship's brass hull was pressed flush against the rim of the city gate. How was there not water coming in everywhere? Whatever seal had formed between the gate and ship must have been watertight.

"How is this possible?" I asked, not knowing whether these two aquatic men would understand me or not.

They didn't answer me, but I became too distracted with this magnificent city to even care. Every street, including the main thoroughfare along which these two escorted me, was paved with intricate patterns of shells. There were swirls and dashes, odd shapes like symbols or words. Iridescent mother-of-pearl lined the street's edges and sparkled as we passed. The buildings were all made of hard coral—some white, some orange, some brown. Others were red or yellow. Buildings of the same color were the same size and style. Lamps on tall posts stood at equidistant intervals all along the middle of the street. They were dim at first, but brightened as we walked by. They weren't fueled by oil and fire—these lights were alive—spiky-looking anemones with glowing appendages.

The same lights graced the doorways of each building, where curious mer-people peered at me from their doors and windows. Potted kelp sat by the entrances of many buildings. The strange thing was, it was wavy and fluid-like as though it was still in water. Some of the city folk, too, swam instead of walking along the road and around the buildings. Those who swam had tails, yet those on the ground had legs like my escorts. I slowed, both confused and amazed, but my hosts yanked me back into position.

"Sorry." I tested the air with a tentative sniff. Smelled a little fishy and salty, but at least I could breathe. With that miracle came another potential one—Lysander might still be alive and well.

Up ahead rose the tallest building I'd ever seen, built of black coral with dozens of narrow spires, their tips sharp as a trident's. Some of the crude round windows were lit, as was the arched passage leading into it.

"Is this a castle?" I asked. "You have a king?"

"King na tooee ill es."

It would seem they understood at least some of my language, and I recalled Lysander speaking to them in the common tongue before they kidnapped him. Maybe I could get something out of them before they brought me to their king or roasted me on a spit.

"Is Lysander here? Is he all right?" They both looked straight ahead, pulling me onward, so I raised my voice a bit. "I said, is he all right? Please tell me!"

Again nothing but our straightforward march to the castle. Since their eyes were slightly angled toward the sides of their heads, I caught one's gaze and made a connection. If he wouldn't tell me where Lysander was, I'd mind-bend him into doing so.

He paused, tilted his head toward me, and blinked his third eyelid. The one on my other side kept pulling, but stopped when he realized his companion wasn't walking.

"Oo na oowee?" he asked.

I focused on the other one's green fishy eye. *Is Lysander all right?*

Fish Man nodded.

Good. Take me to him. Now.

He nodded again, walking fast, which led to him dragging me and his companion along, wagon-train style. We marched past two large mermen clad in giant clamshell armor, and straight into the open doorway of the castle. Inside, we were in a gigantic corridor, supported with pillars of thin coral. The same sea urchin lights I'd seen before were stuck to the pillars, waving happily in the invisible currents. Their motion made for a startlingly beautiful effect of light dancing throughout the chamber. A wide strip of sea worms covered the floor along the distance from door to throne, waving their red heads as though yielding to deep ocean currents. I still didn't feel or see any water, though everything around us behaved as though we were submerged. As we approached the sea worms, they quickly retreated into their holes, with a *fwoop* and some bubbles, forming a red carpet beneath our feet.

The throne at the end of the cavernous corridor sat empty, with not even an attendant about. We veered suddenly left, past the last pillar before the throne, and straight for a wall of solid silver. I knew my power enough to know it had worked, but there was still the possibility that Fish Man didn't understand my command and was instead intent on giving me a concussion, then delivering me as a sacrifice to the Great Sea Serpent. I'd never believed it actually existed, but now...why not?

Instead of smacking into the wall, however, the surface came alive with a school of glowing fish, swirling like a cyclone. They moved as one unit down a descending tunnel in front of us. Fish Man and his friend pulled me along it without a word or a glance in my direction.

"Where are we going?" I asked, now doubting my abilities *and* my sanity. Maybe I was actually dead, and this was my version of the Great Void, where I'd be dragged for eternity through endless fishy tunnels by over-zealous mermen.

As suddenly as the fish had appeared, they dispersed, bursting away from the tunnel in a flash, leaving us in a warm-lit, smaller chamber. A few figures stood around someone lying on a bed. One of them turned.

"Lysander!" I broke away from the mermen. He ran to meet me and caught me in his embrace. I'd never been so happy to see him in all my life.

"You pulled the blue lever, didn't you?" he asked.

"Obviously." He felt so strong and warm against me, I wanted to melt into him for a while longer, but all the fish eyes were staring. Heat rose in my cheeks, and I pulled back. "Are you all right? No water in the lungs, no brain damage?"

He chuckled, giving me a full-fledged smile of perfect white teeth. "Why don't you tell me?"

A quick assessment of his aura showed mostly healthy green energy, with outlines of orange and violet. Worry and sadness. It was only natural that he would feel those things. Nothing physical looked off-kilter except his inflamed knee.

"Looks fine to me," I said.

He tucked my hair behind my ear and brushed my cheek with his thumb. "I'm just glad you're all right."

My breath lodged in what would have been my gills had I been a mermaid. He'd looked at me like this a decade ago, the day he dropped to his knees and offered me a wedding goat. But, it felt different this time, like a warm bed on a cold morning, when the thought of getting up was torture. Then, my mind dredged up the night of Lysander's wedding to Mavelle. That look in his eyes was for her alone. He couldn't switch that feeling from her to me that quickly. He must have swallowed too much seawater.

I broke eye contact and cleared my throat. "Um, what's going on in here?"

We turned to the others gathered around the bed, which was really more of a hammock woven from kelp. The one lying there was a mermaid with blue-green hair. She wore a gauzy garment of white, leaving nothing to the imagination, including very human-like breasts. The mermaid wasn't moving, and she had no discernable aura. All her kin had what I'd call very healthy auras, not that I knew anything about mermaid physiology.

She had to be dead.

"This is King Sturgeos, Mira." Lysander patted his lips and made a couple of popping sounds. The king returned the gesture, which I equated to a wave in human language.

He looked much like the other mermen, except he had pointed, fleshy growths jutting from the top of his head like a crown. White hair, braided and adorned with shells like that of my escorts, grew in a semicircle around his 'crown'. He wore the same giant clamshell armor as the guards at the front gate.

"Pleasure to meet you." For added charm, I attempted the mouth-slap-pop thing, but only hurt my lips instead of making any discernable sound.

"Playzure all min," said the king.

He did know our language, even if he couldn't speak it very well. It reminded me of Ladyfish, from the Traveling Opera.

"Who is this?" I asked, gesturing to the mermaid.

"Ma dawder Loola," the king answered. "Lyzendar goon hap her."

"Help her?"

Lysander nodded in affirmation.

I leaned close to whisper, "She's dead. No aura."

He shook his head. "She's not dead. Look closer."

Moving toward the mermaid princess, I paused to wait for the king's approval. He nodded and made a popping noise with his lips. Taking that as a 'go ahead', I placed two fingers to her neck before realizing she had gills there. They were bright red on the underside, indicating a good flow of blood. The pulse on her wrist was weak, but steady. Leaning close to her nose, I could feel her steady breaths on my cheek, though I had to look long and hard to see her chest rising and falling.

Turning to Lysander, I asked, "Could you bring me a lamp, please? Or a light? Something bright?"

He nodded and retrieved a lock pick from his pocket. Then he pried a glowing sea urchin from the wall above her bed. He handed it to me bottom first and sat it on the base on my palm, where it immediately latched onto my hand with a sucker-like foot. I shook my hand to loosen it, but it held tight.

"It's pinchy," I said.

Lysander chuckled. "I'll get it off, don't worry. Do what you need to do."

To test Loola's signs of life a bit further, I lifted one of her eyelids, but the third eyelid was still in the way—opaque with tiny red blood vessels traversing it. Gently pulling that back, I held the urchin light close to observe her large, black pupil. It should have constricted, but didn't. Maybe I could reach her consciousness somehow.

Fixing my eyes on her pupil, I focused inward, probing with my mind through a foggy emptiness. Then came the quick buzz at my temples, the sign of a connection made.

Speaking through telepathy, I said, *"Loola, can you hear me?"*

No one answered, but the fog cleared, and in its place came quick flashes of images. Bright smiles, laughter, swimming with her sisters among the coral beds. Loola had been a happy, vibrant mermaid, loving life and family as any young girl should. And then the vision shifted above, through sun-flecked water. A boat's shadow drifted above. She motioned to her sisters to stay behind and swam toward it. Red eyes zoomed straight for me before everything fogged over again.

Quickly, I broke the connection. Had Loola also seen those red eyes before this happened to her? Standing up straight again, I held my hand toward Lysander. He gently wiggled his lock pick under the urchin's foot. It gradually released my skin then adhered to the metal stick.

"How many locks have you picked with that thing?" I asked.

He responded with a none-too-apologetic shrug and a wink.

"So," he asked, gently depositing the luminescent creature back on the wall, "what's the diagnosis?"

Warily glancing at the king, who stared at me intently, I delivered the bad news. "She's functionally alive, but her higher brain functions are gone. I've seen similar cases in the Temple, but..."

"But?" asked the king, gently stroking his daughter's hair.

"She has no aura. I've never seen anyone even barely alive without an aura, except for me. Even the undead have a certain aura, though not everyone can see them."

Lysander's shoulders tensed, reminded no doubt, of my failure to warn him when the vampires and necromancer arrived at the wedding.

"Wot oorah?" He blinked his third eyelids a few times, as though trying to understand.

"Auras are like our life energy. Some call it a soul. When we die, it fades away, gone to the goddess or the Great Void, or wherever it will. But, I've never seen someone this *alive* without one."

"Mira, back to the point, please," Lysander said.

"Sorry." I turned to the king. "Can you tell me what happened to her?"

"Wooman white har, red eyes. Tuk Loola up top an kiz her. Loola seesters scar woman. She drop Loola back in sea."

Hopefully Lysander could confirm what I thought he said. "Did he say a woman with white hair and red eyes kissed her?"

"Yes, that's exactly what he said. And sounds like her sisters interrupted the attack. That may be the reason Loola is still alive in body, if not spirit."

"That makes sense. I saw those eyes in her memories. I think they were the last thing she saw."

Lysander frowned. "Kee Sturgus, ma ootee ta Mira bo parlee, ik et?"

The king gave a slow, sad mouth-pop and sat at his daughter's side.

Lysander led me into another room filled with shelves of colorful shells and objects that resembled toys. There were even a few tattered dolls. Maybe she had collected flotsam as a hobby. It reminded me of my old room back in Port Valor. That thought wedged a hard lump in my throat.

We sat on a small bench made of whalebone and kelp. "I think it's the work of our common enemy," Lysander said.

"The necromancer?"

He nodded. "We already guessed she was based in the barbarian islands, just north of here. I think she happened upon Loola, who was probably sunbathing or gathering flotsam, stole most of her aura, and threw her back in when the sisters intervened."

"So that's why they kidnapped you? To see if you can help the princess."

"Yes."

"You realize that's impossible, right? She can't recover from this—she's too far gone."

"But what if...?" He stood and paced the room. "What if we were able to get it back? What if the necromancer stole Loola's soul, storing it in such a way that we could take it from her and return it to the princess?"

"That's risky and outlandish."

"Why? Is it any more outlandish for the Priestess and your former friend Loralee to heal in the way they do? They absorb illness and injury into themselves, then transfer it to the blessed water beneath the Temple, right?"

"Yes, but they don't handle auras, and they can't store those ailments anywhere. It doesn't work that way."

"But what if it does? What if this necromancer is collecting souls to use for something else? That may be why she didn't kill Mavelle and the others outright. She could be saving them for later."

"Lysander..." I knew he wanted to find Mavelle—it's why we were here in the first place—but his hope seemed misplaced. I didn't want him to be crushed if worse came to worst.

"We still have a chance to save her. And your dad. They might be lying in this necromancer's lair somewhere, as unresponsive as Loola. Have you given up on him already?"

"No, of course not, but...even if we did get their auras back, how would we return them to their bodies?"

He stopped pacing, his dark eyes growing impossibly darker, like black storm clouds gathering in the wake of a typhoon. "I don't know, but I mean to find out."

His wide stance, his voice, and that fierce look reminded me of a predator stalking his prey. It made me shift in my seat; my leg muscles tensed, ready to flee. I'd never known anyone to have that much power in their gaze, except me.

The Tyger wanted blood, and I had no doubt he would get it.

Chapter Sixteen

~ Lysander ~

"They call it Ustamer—or 'under the sea'," I explained to Mira as we gathered food and supplies we might need from the castle's huge larder.

"How did you ever find it?" she asked, ducking as two of the king's young daughters swam overhead, chasing each other and giggling. "And you have to tell me how they do that."

"Do what?"

"How do they swim in air? I mean, it feels like air to me. I haven't felt a single drop of water on me anywhere."

"I don't know exactly. I can never get a straight answer from them. Some say it's magic or a blessing from the Great Sea Serpent."

"And how did you find them?"

"I didn't. They found me. I was fishing from our dock one night—you do remember our dock, don't you?"

She lifted her gaze to my chin for a moment, before she nodded and turned her attention back to the shelves. I'd taken for granted how nice it was to make eye contact with someone until now. If I could have reassured her that she had nothing to fear, I would have. But, she wasn't the only one leery of her powers.

I gave up hunting Mira's direct gaze and pondered some abalones—delicious stuff, but on a ship, they weren't easy to cook. "So there I was, fishing on the dock, when two of the guards—Nautilon and Cuda—popped up out of the water one night and pointed their tridents at me."

"Seems to be a habit with those guys."

I chuckled. "They demanded that I find one of the princesses who was sold to the Traveling Opera as a side show."

"Oh…so Ladyfish *was* a real mermaid."

"Very real."

"I came to know her when I traveled with them to Leogard." Mira picked up a jar of candied seahorses and took a cautious sniff. "She spent most of the time in a small tank and only came out at night. But, I thought it was all show at the time. She never mentioned being kidnapped, though. Actually, she seemed quite happy. Randell, the head clown, said they were married."

"That's right. She had fallen in love with Randell, and she had no intention of leaving him." Temptation won—I gathered a half dozen abalones, grateful that King Sturgeos allowed me unlimited food shopping. "I had to deliver the news to her father. You can imagine how that went. I found his princess, but wasn't able to bring her back, so he demanded tit-for-tat from me for three years."

"What's that?"

"It's a cycle of favor-mongering. I do something for them, they do something for me, and so on."

"What did they do for you?" Mira took a small bite of a candied seahorse and grimaced.

"They're an acquired taste. Anyway, they overhauled my ship and put a homing beacon on it so they could track me and so it could dive straight down to Ustamer. I'm glad it worked."

Her eyebrows knitted together as she frowned. "What do you mean you're glad it worked?"

"I'd never tried diving with it before."

Her jaw dropped. "So I was your test subject?"

"Let's call you a test-*captain.* Sounds more dignified."

She laughed. I hadn't heard that since we were sixteen. Her face looked so much softer, her cheeks plumper and her eyes bright. Like the Mira I once knew…and loved.

I must have been looking at her for too long, because she bent suddenly to pick up a roll of kelp twine. Bracing herself like she might be picking up a boulder, her arms encircled it, and she stood too quickly. Of course, it didn't weigh much more than a hen, and BAM! The top of her head collided with the shelf above. She dropped the twine. The jar of candied seahorses wobbled and fell, cracking open against her skull like an egg. Sweet, dead seahorses bounced down her body in an awkward race and landed at her feet.

"Lys—" She stumbled. Her eyes rolled back, and she went limp.

Not good. I caught her before she hit the floor. "Mira, can you hear me?"

No response. Hopefully she'd be all right. I had once hoped she'd be eaten by the Great Sea Serpent for leaving me, but now…I didn't want to think about what would happen if I lost her again.

* * * *

The youngest princesses, all ten of them, followed me to one of the parlors. They zipped back and forth overhead, chattering so excitedly, I couldn't understand what they were saying. Though I'm pretty sure I heard *mate, marry,* and *skinny* somewhere in all the gabbing. Ever since their sister had married the Opera clown, they were obsessed with who would marry the next land-dweller, otherwise known as me. I laid Mira down on a soft cloud-coral ottoman and checked her injury. The girls kept crowding in.

I shooed them back. "Give her some air, girls."

They shared confused looks.

"Sorry, give her some space. She's hit her head. Squilla, could you bring me some conch gel?"

Her sisters scowled, but Squilla beamed, nodded quickly, and shot away to fetch the treatment. She was back in less than a minute. I dipped my fingers into the jar and applied the gel to the sizable lump on the crown of Mira's head. She stirred and groaned, but didn't wake. Thankfully, she was breathing fine. I took her hand in mine and put two fingers on her wrist—strong pulse, too.

Instead of the silky skin I expected, however, hers was rough. I turned her hand over and touched the callouses on her palm. She must have done a lot of manual labor at the Temple. Funny, I'd imagined her sitting cross-legged and meditating all day. I studied the embedded bloodgems on her forearm, glowing dimly under her scorched skin. How badly that must have hurt. To think that in just a few weeks, those things could kill her. She didn't have to come with me to find Mavelle. She could have gone back, bent the Priestess's mind and saved her own skin, but she didn't. Mira had come with me, and she hadn't even made me promise to help her in return.

The long scar on her other wrist reminded me why. She *wanted* to die. With her mother dead and father kidnapped, her only friend in Leogard in exile, she must have felt like she had no one left. I'd spent so long trying to hate her for leaving, but now…I still wanted to find Mavelle so badly it hurt, and I still wanted to make a life with her. But, I didn't want this for Mira. She'd made mistakes, but she deserved a fate better than this.

Clearing the knot from my throat, I placed her hands gently across her belly and checked her head. The gel was working—instead of a chicken egg-sized lump, it had shrunk to a much-more-acceptable acorn.

She stirred again, mumbling something. "…baby…can't help…"

"Shh, don't talk. Let the swelling go down."

After a few seconds, her eyes blinked lazily until she opened them and focused somewhere near my ear. "Hurts."

"You have a nasty lump, but you'll be all right."

"Why do I always end up unconscious around you?"

"Perhaps I'm bad luck."

"I think you better carry the twine," she whispered with a groggy smile.

"I think you're right."

"We should get going." Mira started to get up.

I gently pushed her back down. "Not yet. Rest a little while longer."

Sighing, she nodded.

"May I ask you something?"

Another nod.

"You were talking in your sleep and saying something about a baby. What were you talking about?"

Mira lay still and didn't answer. She stared up at the rough coral ceiling.

"I'm sorry. You don't have to talk about it." She must have seen a lot of death at the Temple, including babies. There was also the abortion she didn't think anyone knew about. Would she confess it to me?

"I was dreaming about our last night on the dock," she said, barely above a whisper.

An involuntary shiver shook through me. Leaning close to hear her better, I nodded for her to continue.

"After I...kissed you, I went home, but saw something terrible."

"What was it?"

"I went with Mom to Silas Lurck's house to help deliver a baby. His wife Tannah gave birth to a little boy, but his legs were malformed. The Shaman came. I hid behind the kitchen curtain and watched. His guards killed Silas, and then he took the baby away."

"Oh." That secret came as a surprise to me. I didn't realize I was holding her hand until I hung my head and saw my fingers entwined with hers. "What happened then?"

"Dad said the Shaman was going to throw the baby into the sea." She closed her eyes for a second, pinching tears onto her cheeks. "I begged him to let me try to bend the Shaman's mind, but he held me back and said it was too dangerous. He said I could be killed if they found out what I am."

"Yes, you could have been. Why didn't you tell me about your abilities back then?"

"My powers had only manifested about a year before that. Mom and Dad were terrified and begged me to not tell anyone. Not even you."

"We all have our secrets," I said with a shrug.

"I felt so useless, Lysander. What's the use of having these..." She tapped her forehead. "...gifts if I can't use them for good?"

"Is that why you left, Mira? So you could use your powers for good?"

She swallowed hard and pulled her hand from mine. Her voice sounded ragged and tired. "I'm feeling better now. Let's go. We need to find Mavelle and Dad and bring them back home."

I tried to help her up, but she waved me off. The princesses helped us carry everything to the boat. King Sturgeos followed, and we bid him farewell on the dock.

"Oo hap Loola, ya?" He looked worn and tired, his face crisscrossed with worry lines.

"We'll do all we can. Thank you for the supplies." I popped my lips, and he popped back.

Mira tried it, but still made more of a smacking sound than a pop. She winced, and I tried not to laugh.

She gave me a dirty look before bowing slightly to the king. "Thank you for your hospitality, your highness." She hesitated before placing her hand on his cheek and raised her eyes to his. The king's gaze widened as her coffee-brown irises swirled. A guard stepped close, trident ready. I held up a hand, hoping—no, knowing that Mira wouldn't hurt King Sturgeos.

She said nothing out loud while holding his gaze for a few seconds. Then, she slowly lowered her hand and took a step back. The king nodded, his face relaxed, worry lines easing from his forehead. Even the tension in his shoulders left, as though she'd lifted his burdens.

"Ere, tak dis," he said, unfastening a pendant from around his neck. He held out his hands toward Mira. She lifted her hair and leaned forward so he could fasten it around her neck. It was made of a kelp cord, with tiny shells strung along it. The centerpiece of the necklace looked like a piece of whalebone, carved into the shape of a flat fish. A hole had been carved into the end of its tail. I knew what it was. Receiving one from the mer-people didn't happen often, especially from King Sturgeos himself.

"Thank you," she said and turned the fish medallion over in her hand, studying it. "What is it? A whistle?"

"It hap oo haf air ween seeming."

"He says it will help you breathe when you're swimming."

Mira's eyes widened. "Oh, really? That's amazing. Thank you, your highness." She gave him a bow, which he returned.

We left the way Mira came, in my ship turned sub-sea vessel. I held to her during our ascent; we braced ourselves against the foot of the bed. In the pitch dark, I couldn't help a smile. She snuggled up against my chest, trembling, like she actually needed me. By the time we breached the surface, she was sound asleep, her face peaceful and relaxed, as the mer-king's had been after she ministered to him.

But, I couldn't let her sleep for long. Outside, a gray, jagged rock arch loomed above us. We had emerged right between the Barbarian islands. It was time to find Mavelle, if it wasn't already too late.

Chapter Seventeen

~ Mirabelle ~

"Mira, wake up." Lysander gently shook me. I popped up, feeling a bit dizzy and more than a little embarrassed that I'd fallen asleep on his shoulder. Though honestly, I wished I could have stayed there for an eternity. But I was here to help him find his wife. Lysander was a married man now, and I had to remember that.

"Where are we?"

He stood, then helped me to my feet, pointing out the window. "Look up there."

Above us were gray arches of stone, equidistant apart, that formed bridges between two islands across the narrow waterway. Between them was open air. As we passed under each one, their shadows briefly blacked out the light, and a bright blue sky blinked at us.

"Are you feeling well?" Lysander asked. "You should eat."

"Why does everyone keep trying to feed me?" Then I realized 'everyone' included Mom. My throat tightened, and my eyes watered, but now wasn't the time for a cry fest.

He went to the controls cabinet and adjusted a few levers. The propeller's dull roar went quiet. "I'll steer us in manually. Less noise."

He stepped out of the cabin and took his place at the wheel.

I followed him, but stood by the rail on the port side to get a quick dose of mind-numbing fresh air. Cold mist nipped at my face. It didn't take long for the Draekkan Sea winds to freeze a person to the bone. I'd left my cloak inside. But, I didn't want to keep bawling like a baby every time I thought of Mom. So I hugged myself tight and let my teeth chatter a rhythm in my head, hoping the frigid temperature would soon outweigh my emotions.

At least we sailed on a sturdy ship that had remained in one piece during our submarine adventure. All the metal plates had receded inside the hull, leaving it looking like any other Hezrali fishing vessel.

After a couple minutes, my eyeballs felt like frozen talaberries. I'd had enough of the deep freeze, so I was about to retreat to the cabin when something touched my shoulders. I jumped.

"Thought you might need this," Lysander said, draping my thick cloak over my shoulders. His hands lingered on me for a moment, warming me from the inside out.

He went back to the wheel, leaving me cold again. The cloak blocked the frigid wind, but I craved his touch like a hunter craves a warm campfire. Wrapping the thick wool around me, I came to stand beside him, admiring the way he casually gripped the handles as though he had been sailing ships his whole life. And maybe he had—I'd missed so much. He glanced my way and smiled.

"Thanks for the cloak," I said. "It's pretty out here."

Now that freezing to death wasn't a worry, I was able to take in the view. The indigo sea sparkled in a cloudless, sunny sky. Bright green lichens and moss blanketed the rock walls on both sides of the passageway.

"Yes, it can be, except for that." He tilted his eyes upward.

I followed his gaze and studied the arches again, wondering if the barbarians had carved them. Spikes jutted out from the points where they connected to the islands. Dried and skeletal heads, with wispy hair and mouths open in silent screams, decorated the end of each spike. My stomach turned. Ugh—sightseeing over.

"It's just a scare tactic," Lysander said as though reading my mind. "Partly for outsiders like us, but mostly for their neighbors, to remind each clan what can happen when one of them becomes raid-happy."

"Well it works." I pressed the hood against my numb ears, teeth chattering less from cold now and more from fear. Would our heads wind up on those if we stumbled upon unfriendly natives? Lysander didn't seem the least bit perturbed. He also wore nothing over his clothes but hadn't become a human icicle yet. "Where's your cloak?"

He shrugged. "Forgot it."

"You'll freeze."

"I'll be fine."

"If you say so. So what's with the arches?"

"They form natural connections between the islands."

"Do people walk across those?" I stared up at the arch we were passing under. It couldn't have been more than a foot wide at the narrowest points.

"Only if they have to," he said, lips stretching into a secretive grin. "We'll be landing at the dock on Tugla Island soon. That's the first island to our left. See any auras about?"

Clutching my cloak under my chin, I scanned the rock walls of our passageway. A green aura, outlined with an aggressive red, moved across a small ledge, but I couldn't see anything solid that it belonged to. "There," I said pointing. "Something on the rock, but it's not a vampire or necromancer. Pretty sure, anyway. I just can't see what it is."

"Oh, that," Lysander said, looking in the direction of the invisible creature. "That's a tyger. Blends perfectly into any background. Lucky for him, that crag deer doesn't read auras."

Squinting, I watched the little gray deer and its healthy green aura exit from a wide fissure in the rock. The hidden tyger's aura leapt from the ledge, landing on its prey. Its image suddenly wobbled into view, revealing a stocky large cat, well-muscled and covered in sleek black fur with subtle stripes a shade lighter. The deer bleated. Tiny hooves kicked at the air. Fangs sank into its delicate neck, cutting off the prey's cries and its breath. In a matter of seconds, the deer's green aura dissipated, its life extinguished to feed the stealthy hunter.

"Poor little thing," I whispered.

"Such is the natural world. Should a crag bear come by, the tyger could be the next thing on the menu."

He watched the carnage impassively. I halfway expected his lips and fingers to be blue, considering the cold, but the wind whipped through his black hair and didn't even leave goosebumps on his skin. He stood at the wheel with exposed forearms draped casually across the wheel like he was on a holiday voyage on the Southern Sea.

"How are you not cold?" I asked.

"I didn't spend a decade in the pleasant weather of Leogard," he answered with a hint of accusation in his voice. "We Hezrali are tough enough to handle a little chill."

"A little chill? It's absolutely frigid." Shivering under my cloak more from his continued resentment than the weather, I added, "I never did like the cold."

One corner of his mouth slanted upward like a sarcastic checkmark. "So, is *that* why you left? Port Valor too cold for you?"

I didn't offer him an answer, and he didn't look at me like he was expecting one. Maybe he no longer cared to know my reasons for leaving. Good, since I never intended to tell him, but that lack of interest only thickened the wall between us.

Up ahead, the rocky passageway opened up to a quiet harbor. A few more islands appeared in the distance as dark dots on the horizon. An endless blue sky stretched above us, and a small dock poked out from a sandy beach at the nearest island to our west. Lysander steered the ship toward it. A few crude barbarian boats—not much more than the hollowed-out trunks of huge ebonwood trees—bobbed in the water. Yet, the closer we came, the more I could see…no one. Not one fisherman, traveler, ferryman, or merchant. Not one solitary soul. Scanning more closely, I didn't see any auras either, other than those surrounding the gulls atop the pier pilings and faint green fish-shaped auras just beneath the water's surface. I didn't know a lot about Barbarian culture, but judging from Port Valor's round-the-clock busy docks, this couldn't be normal. Especially in the middle of the day.

Lysander flipped a lever by the wheel. With a few clicks and clanks, the rigging folded in on itself, completely dousing the sails in a few seconds' time. A few yards from the dock, he flipped another lever. There was a thump then the sound of wood sliding back. I went to the rail and leaned over to watch. An anchor dropped with a *clank, clank, clank* of its chain, followed by a splash when it hit the water. In less than a minute, the boat slowed to a stop right at the edge of a dock. Lysander flipped a lever next to the cabin door. Metal plates emerged from beneath the railing in a quiet succession of clicks. They scaled over each other like roof tiles until they formed a gangplank.

"Status?" he asked, waiting by the gate on the railing.

"Nothing but fish and birds. It's odd, isn't it?"

"Very." He tightened the sword harness he wore around his waist and offered me his hand.

My heart skipped a few beats at the prospect of touching him again. I put my icicle hand in his, which was warm as a mitten dried by a fire. He led me down the gangplank, which rattled and shook as we walked. Soon as we stepped onto the dock, it quietly cling-clanged back upon itself, receding into an open gap in the hull, where a wooden slat slid shut behind it. It was flush with the surrounding wood as though it had never been there at all.

"Well, where do we start?" Finding our loved ones seemed about as likely as finding a sea-star with six legs in an ocean full of five-legged ones.

"In the villages. This island is really small, so there's only one village here."

From the dock, a worn dirt path inclined upward through a scattering of boulders that were stuck in the mossy ground as though the gods had randomly dropped them from the heavens. We made our way up the path to the top of the rise. I thought the entire island would be one big rock after another, but instead what waited below was a beautiful cove covered with grass as green as a fresh painting. Puffs of white dotted the pastures. Probably sheep.

The path was nothing more than a well-worn rut of bare dirt from years of foot traffic. It sloped gently downward, taking us farther into the cove and closer to the village. We reached the outskirts of the settlement, where brambles vined across wooden trellises. Homes hewn of thick logs sat in a circular pattern around a central cobbled courtyard. Animal pens and tidy, square gardens formed a colorful patchwork behind the houses. Barbarians all seemed so savage, I thought they would live in caves or mud huts instead of a pretty village.

In the very center of the courtyard stood a tall wooden sculpture. Ugly, leering faces were carved into it on the top half. The bottom half looked to be covered with naked people in varied sexual poses.

"Oh…" I said, "it's, um…"

"A Fertility Shaft. Those trying to conceive will do so in front of the shaft so the gods might bless them with a child."

"Right there in the open?" My cheeks burned as my imagination ventured to an unholy place.

"While the whole village watches." He laughed. "I never thought you'd be embarrassed. Haven't you seen all sorts of body parts?"

"Yeah, but not...*that.*"

"I thought you would have taken on a few elven lovers in Leogard."

I didn't have to look him in the eye to feel his accusing stare. "No. I was an acolyte. We were expected to remain pure."

"What's more pure than a man loving a woman like that?"

He was testing me, teasing me with suggestive words that teased a rush of blood to the juncture of my thighs. He wanted me to long for what I'd missed when I left him behind. But a dark memory invaded, one I had tried to suppress for years, but never did.

Clearing my throat, I focused on the neutral tones of the rough cobblestones. "It's not always pure."

"What do you mean by that?" He sounded half curious, half annoyed. He probably thought I'd whored around all over Leogard.

"Never mind."

"Come on, we'll take the grand tour later." Lysander took my hand rather forcefully, sending another warm shiver of pleasure through me, but it didn't last long. Pain streaked up my arm and into my shoulder—pure agony as though someone had poured acid into my bloodstream. Jerking from his grasp, I screamed and sank to the ground, cradling my arm against my chest. Another bloodgem must have started breaking down.

Lysander dropped to his knees beside me and placed a gentle hand on my shoulder. He angled his head to try and make eye contact. "I'm sorry. We'll go back."

Pain squeezed tears through my tightly closed eyes. "No, we have to find them."

"But you're not well. I can't keep making you do this."

"I have to!" My voice echoed against the rock walls surrounding the cove. All the people I'd failed tore at my conscience. "Stop trying to make me look at you."

"Fine." He shifted away from me. I cracked one eye open and spied Lysander's aura. Yellow worry, red anger, and a pink flare of something

155

deeper I never imagined I'd see bloomed around him.

He focused on my curse and brushed his fingers over the charred symbols with a feather-light touch. His voice was ragged and rough. "I don't want…you don't have much time."

"I know." Closing my eyes, I breathed deeply and savored his touch for a moment. "But I want to die knowing I did something to help instead of hurting everyone. Help me up. Let's go find Dad and Mavelle."

~ Lysander ~

Mira was deteriorating; it killed me to see her in this much pain. Guilt tightened my chest from having wished even worse upon her for the last ten years. I didn't know exactly why she left, but whatever the reason, I knew she hadn't done it out of selfishness.

She held to my arm for a few steps before letting go and walking on her own. The rancid odor of blood and entrails drifted from the pasture, so strong, I was sure Mira could smell it too. The sheep didn't move. Mira peered across the fields, her face creasing with worry the longer she looked.

"No auras," she said. "I think they're dead."

It didn't take long for me to notice their blood soaked necks and the constant buzz of flies. My stomach rumbled. It had been a long time since I'd eaten. I needed food.

"Really? You actually have an appetite. Unreal." Shaking her head, she continued on to the first house to our left and stopped at the closed door as though dreading to go inside. "Do you think vampires killed them?"

"The tracks would indicate so," I answered, studying the mess of footprints tracking in and out of the pastures in frenzied paths and deep indentations. "They were running, whether to get away, to get the sheep, or perhaps both."

"Those poor sheep."

"Those poor *people*. Why do you hate barbarians so? They stopped raiding Port Valor decades ago."

"I have my reasons."

She took a deep breath and pushed open the door. I followed her inside. The logs of the houses, built from huge ebonwoods and other mountain trees, had to have come from the northern Eastwood Mountains of Hezral. With the faded, worm-eaten walls, it was likely they came from those earlier raids. Food, lumber, and cloth were once the top items on their list of things to plunder from our city. Luckily, King Damien had stepped up patrols and built catapults to throw flaming piles of dung on them when they entered our harbor. That put an end, albeit a smelly one, to barbarians raiding Port Valor.

Sunlight filtered through cracks in the mortar. Dust traveled along the yellow light, landing on a very large, low bed in one corner of the room. Its mattress sank so low in the middle, it almost touched the floor. A wide path streaked through the dust across the room, as though something or someone had been dragged, and ended at a tea-stained curtain. Behind that was a small storage room. The shelves were filled to the brim with food jars, cheeses, and smoked meats. Back in the great room, bowls of moldy, partially-eaten food sat on the table. A covered pot hung over cold ashes in the hearth. I went to it, opened the lid, and grimaced. Cabbage and ham soup, uneaten and rotten.

"It's like they were having dinner and then disappeared," Mira said. She lifted a towel off a basket of cold bread. A spider crawled across it, and she jumped back with a shudder.

"Or they were attacked." I pointed up above to the sleeping loft and the busted hole in the ceiling. Climbing the ladder to the loft, I picked up the smell of days-old blood on the mess of bedcovers strewn across the floor. "No one here, either."

A moan came from somewhere below. I didn't bother with the ladder, but leapt down over the edge of the loft and landed in a crouch at Mira's feet.

She yelped and backed away. "How did you do that? Are you hurt?"

"No." I knew I should have been more discreet, but time was of the essence. "Did you hear that?"

"Hear what?"

Standing dead still, I listened again, and there it was. Low and piteous. Desperate.

"Below us," Mira said. "There must be a cellar."

157

I searched the room, darting from hearth to sleeping area to table. Nothing. "Where is it?"

Frantic, I flew out the door and circled the house, but the foundation was solid. No cellar door anywhere. Only one thing crossed my mind—Mavelle. Was she locked up below ground somewhere being tortured?

"Lysander!" Mira yelled from inside the house. "In here!"

Rushing back inside, I thundered through the house until I almost collided with her. She put a finger to her lips and led me to the curtained-off storage room. She pulled the curtain back and pointed to the floor. A square outline was cut into the boards, with a round iron handle in the middle.

The hinges made a terrible squeak when I yanked it open.

"Lysander, wait—"

Ignoring Mira's hesitance, I plunged inside and landed on the soft dirt floor below. It took only a moment for my eyes to adjust. Dead rats lay at my feet, bloody and smashed, some decapitated. The whole place smelled of musty earth, mold, and death. The moan came again, louder now.

Mira hurried down the ladder, stopping on the last rung. "There's an aura—down that way." She pointed to the end of the cellar at the rear of the house. I hoped she was going to tell me it was Mavelle, alive. Maybe not well, but alive.

I started to take off, but Mira grabbed my sleeve.

"It's not human," she said.

The light from the floor above didn't reach far beyond us, but I caught movement in the dark. Something slow, but big. "Mira, get your daggers."

She slid the blades from their sheaths just as a fat hand with long nails smacked the dirt. The fingers curled and clawed, dragging the body behind them little by little. A mess of knotted brown hair followed, inching along with every desperate pull from the arms. The face turned upward. Blood-rimmed eyes locked on mine. Fleshy lips opened to reveal yellowed fangs. I backed up to keep myself between Mira and the vampire.

More of it came into view. Huge, impossibly huge. Barbarian, with the customary slit eyelids and symbols carved into her skin. But with a body three times larger than a healthy woman. Blood spattered her skin. Pus-filled ulcers broke open in a failed effort to hold her obese flesh in place. Had she been able to stand and walk, she'd have already been upon us, but all she could manage was a pitiful attempt at dragging herself to her potential prey—us.

She moaned a dry, wailing sound, swiping at me with her overgrown nails, but all she hit was air.

"Oh, goddess," Mira whispered. "She's starving."

I couldn't help but pity the creature. Clearly, she had already been afflicted with a disease that made her so obese. Turning her was beyond cruel. She must have subsisted on rats, catching those that had wandered in to eat their fallen kin. Her cheeks were sunken in—she'd not eaten nearly enough to maintain her girth.

"End her misery," I said.

After a long pause, Mira nodded and drew a dagger. Legs wide, with one foot forward in a lunge, she held the dagger palm down and blade flat. In one quick thrust, she released the weapon. It flew in a perfect line low to the ground and sank deep into the vampire's neck. The creature let out a blood-curdling wail and grabbed at the dagger handle, pulling it out and pushing herself up on her arms. Mira was ready to throw the other one when the vampire's arms shook. From the top of her head down, she turned to black ash, which fell to a massive *poof* on the cellar floor.

Mira escaped up the ladder. I held my breath, found her dagger in the carnage and shook off the ash. She was heading out the door to the courtyard when I emerged.

"Mira, wait!" But she kept going. I caught up with her easily, taking her hand before she could get any farther. "You did the right thing."

"That's not it," she said, hunching over like she could vomit.

"What is it then?"

"There are more. Many more. In cellars, under beds, anywhere out of the light. As soon as I killed her, I felt their energy buzzing in my head and in the pit of my stomach."

"Any signs of life?" I couldn't conceal the hope in my voice, even though I knew what she was going to say.

"No, not yet anyway."

I drew my sword—between her silver blades and mine, we could hopefully end this village's curse before sundown.

In the next house, we opened a door to a dark pantry and discovered an elderly couple who lay side by side on the floor. They slept the breathless sleep of the undead, oblivious to the living world. Soon as the light hit them, their eyes snapped open, hissing with fangs bared. I lifted my sword and brought it down through the old man's neck. Just a heartbeat later, I did the same with his wife. I had a feeling that these were the easy ones.

Across the courtyard, we entered a larger house. The common area reeked of forgotten food. Wooden dolls and toy wagons were scattered around, some of them smashed into splinters. Mira picked up a doll, which had a missing leg and arm.

A muffled cry came from below us. Slowly, Mira turned to me with intense dread in her eyes.

The cry came again, louder, more urgent. Hungry.

As with the first house, we found the cellar entrance in the pantry. I went first, with Mira close behind. On the damp brick floor, lined up perfectly as though posed for a funeral, were a man, woman, a teenage boy, two adolescent girls, and…

Mira's face went pale. "Goddess, no," she whispered, covering her mouth.

The baby was latched onto its mother's breast, but pulled away and cried, leaving two bloody holes over the nipple. Tiny fangs stuck out of bare gums. The father's eyes popped open. He sprang from the ground like he was catapulted and came straight at me howling, fangs bared. I braced myself, sword ready. His eyes widened, noticing the blade a moment too late. The force of his jump impaled him all the way to the hilt. One arm came up and swiped my face, leaving stinging scratches. Then he dissolved into a lump of black ashes.

The dust cleared. Mira stood over the children, her daggers dripping with black, sticky blood. She'd stabbed the boy and two girls, who turned to ash one after the other.

Tears streaked down her face. "The mother wasn't turned," she said. "She's dead. They all fed on her."

Coming closer, I could see what she meant. The mother's arms, neck, and bare calves were a mess of holes and blood. The skin on her exposed breast and the nipple, gnawed and mangled. She may have not been dead for more than a couple days, but it was long enough for the infant to be starved for blood. Again and again, it tried to suckle, only to pull away, ripping its mother's skin even more with every try. The child was too young to know what must sustain it, wanting milk, but needing blood. Neither one flowed from the dead mother.

Mira squatted down, sobbing. She held a shaking dagger with one hand and covered her mouth with the other. The baby saw her, crying out in a helpless, hissing scream.

"I c-can't," she cried, though there was only one way to end the child's suffering.

"Come." I helped her stand then led her to the ladder. "Go up and wait for me."

She took another look at the starving baby and clung to me for a moment, laying her head on my shoulder. I held her while she cried then gently nudged her to the ladder. She wiped her eyes with her sleeve and climbed out.

I did what had to be done.

Chapter Eighteen

~ Mirabelle ~

I couldn't stop crying. Outside, despite the severe cold, I gulped the frigid air to catch my breath. This place—this beautiful green island with cozy homes and gardens and livestock, had once been a village of families living normal lives. Happy, laughing children and proud parents, all gone. Hopes, dreams, stories passed down through generations now desecrated and destroyed because a necromancer took delight in it. If she wanted me, why didn't she just come for me instead of hurting all these people? I'd have gladly given myself up if I knew how or where, but no, she wanted to torture us first.

But, why that poor baby? I knew such evil existed, but it's one thing to know and another to see it. If I'd never been born, he would probably still be alive. So many things would be different. All the people I loved would be alive and happy. Loralee, Mom, Dad, Mavelle.

Lysander. I'd put him through so much heartache. I couldn't change the past. How was I supposed to change the future?

The house's log wall held me up while I leaned against it and wept until I couldn't breathe. Wiping my cheeks with cold, trembling fingers, I noticed a juniper bush by the front door. Fine green needles peeked out from the layer of snow that blanketed its flat, pruned top. Tiny gray-blue berries hung in bunches from the stems. This variety, I knew to be toxic, thanks to my studies at the temple.

Just a few would do the trick. It wouldn't be pleasant, but if I were dead, maybe this witch would get bored, let Mavelle go, and move on. I picked some of the berries and smashed them between my fingers. Sticky

162

purple pulp dripped from my knuckles.

The door opened, and Lysander stepped out. He looked around for a moment before finding me hunkered against the wall.

He went still, flicking his gaze between the potential death on my fingers and my face. "Mira...those are poisonous."

I held them close to my face. It would be so easy to lick my hand and be done with it. "I know."

"You know I won't let you die."

"Why not? Why do you care?"

"I've always cared." His voice was quiet, but thick with concern. "Why do you hate yourself so much?"

Before I could respond or take a fatal mouthful of berries, he sprang for me, grabbed my hands and wiped them forcefully on the front of his shirt. The warmth from his chest beneath the thin cloth warmed my hands and triggered more tears.

I let him take me into his arms. He stroked my hair and whispered, "It'll be all right, Mira."

His strength both supported and shamed me. All this power inside me, and still so useless, so weak. Yet another child I couldn't save. It wasn't fair.

"What monster could take such pleasure in hurting innocents?" I concentrated on his warmth and breathed in his musky scent—yet another thing about him I'd never forget. Being wrapped in his arms, if only for a moment, stemmed the tide of tears and helped me focus.

"Necromancers feed upon life, for they have lost their own souls. They long for the satisfaction of a beating heart, a loving touch, words of kindness they may have never experienced." He paused, holding me a little tighter. "The baby is at peace now. No one else was there to offer him mercy. We were able to give that to him, if nothing else."

I nodded against him and pulled back, glancing up at his eyes. They were green, beautiful and kind, just like him. In another world, I'd let myself get lost in them, but I couldn't risk such indulgence. Not now. Not ever.

Wind whipped across the cove, freezing the wetness on my cheeks. A burst of snow from oppressing clouds drifted onto our heads. I pulled my hood up and wrapped my cloak tighter. The sun disappeared into a dim, gray light. It wasn't night, but was it dark enough to wake the undead?

A door flew open on a house nearby.

Apparently, it *was* dark enough.

A grandmotherly vampire emerged; she sniffed the air then pinned us in her sights. She was on us in two seconds. Lysander drew his sword and made one smooth swipe through her neck. Her body ran past him while her head bounced along the ground, rolling in the opposite direction. It reminded me of a magic trick the clowns of the Traveling Opera might have performed. Except for the black blood and ash flying through the air as her body disintegrated.

One door after another burst open. So much for getting to all of them while they slept.

"I hope you're up for a fight," Lysander said, kicking off his boots.

"Looks like I don't have a choice….um, what the hell are you doing? You want to lose your feet?"

"No, I don't want to ruin another pair of boots."

"I take it this is a recurring symptom of your job?"

He laughed. "You could say that."

Unsheathing my daggers, I spun their hilts around my fingers in an unnecessarily theatrical performance. *Why not? I'm about to die. Might as well go out with some flair.*

"There's my girl."

Good thing we had the proper weaponry for vampire-killing. Like my daggers, his sword had been constructed of the finest silver from the dwarven mines of Minzck. Their production involved adding a super-secret acidic compound during the smelting process. Not only did it help keep the final product sharp, requiring less time at a whetstone, but it had the added effect of causing a complete breakdown of any undead tissue. That meant that if we could get in a good swipe or stab on a vampire, it should be enough to destroy them. Of course, that also meant we had to avoid their fangs and be quick enough to outmaneuver their incredible speed. As Dad once said, silver blades were only as powerful as the person who wielded them.

Widening his stance, elbow high, Lysander held his sword in front of him, across his chest. His green eyes sparkled with anticipation. His aura flared with black, orange, and red—like I'd seen with Leogard's paladins when they sparred. Intoxicated with battle, fueled by courage. Lysander, once my gentle, harmless promised one had become a warrior.

I didn't have time to swell up with pride. A young female vampire charged me. Blood matted her blonde hair and darkened her face and neck. Her eyes may have been blue at one time, but now they were a murderous shade of undead red. As soon as she entered my strike range, I sliced her arm and spun away. She recoiled. I jabbed the blade between her ribs. She shrieked and fell, dissolving into a pile of gray ash as she hit the ground.

The remaining vampires—I counted at least ten—lingered near their houses-turned-tombs. They shuffled around excitedly, like cats about to pounce on a mouse. Lysander nudged me toward the fertility shaft. One of the carved protrusions poked my back. Probably some ugly, wooden penis, but I didn't want to look.

Two male vampires charged next, one for each of us. One of them had a dreadlocked beard. A few feet away, he leapt, flying through the air at Lysander with a nasty hiss. Lysander dropped to a crouch. The sharp silver blade of his sword blurred as he slashed and lopped off the vampire's legs below the knee.

My guy had a short black beard and decided to imitate his friend, running and launching himself at me. I dropped to a crouch like Lysander did and slashed at the vampire's torso. Black blood sprayed my face. Not having the luxury of distance like a sword, my cheek took a hit from his claws.

I stumbled back, falling against the fertility shaft. The creature crashed into the scene of a woman riding a man. Its torso split open where I had gutted him, spilling entrails all over my acolyte robe, a moment before his body and insides turned to ash. A black cloud of it rained down on me.

I rubbed my eyes and coughed, gagging from the rotten stench. It felt like something dead had crawled into my lungs.

"Mira, you all right?" Lysander plunged his sword into a stout female vampire then swung his feet up and drop-kicked a skinny teenage boy with nasty-looking fangs.

That one slid across the cobblestones, then sprang to his feet.

Blinking past the ash that clung to my eyes, I lined up a dagger straight down my palm, index finger on the end of the hilt. I threw it like a spear, sinking the blade into his temple. He went down and joined the multiplying piles of ashes across the courtyard.

Six more.

Three of them—a man, woman, and young girl—moved forward. This trio must have decided we weren't invincible after all and required a group effort. They all charged at once. Lysander jumped in front of me. I scrambled to my feet, using a disproportionally large wooden penis to pull myself up. He swung his sword in a blur of motion, decapitating the man, disemboweling the woman then lopping off the starving vampire girl's arm. They disintegrated in a row of three ash piles.

Three more.

These were all men. A pair of twins with bald, tattooed heads and long mustaches, and a massive guy with blond hair in a ponytail and matching goatee. He would have been desirable with those stacks of muscles and handsome face, had he not been a mindless bloodsucker.

The big one sped toward us. Lysander impaled him. The vampire roared and spun wildly with the sword still stuck in his belly. He flung Lysander to the ground several feet away before going *poof* into a cloud of gray ash. Lysander rolled to his feet, swordless, leaving me wide open and down one dagger. The twins decided to join the fray and ran for us. Their long mustaches trailed behind them.

Lysander dove for his sword and exhumed it from the burly vampire's ashes. He sliced through one of the twins' ribs. The other twin flew straight at me. Palms sweating, I widened my stance and crossed my arms in front of me. In my right hand, I gripped the dagger handle as hard as I could, blade pointed out. If I could deflect him with my bare arm, I could cut this baldy enough to add him to the ash pile.

He dodged to the right. I imitated the move, but he switched directions before I could do the same. I'd fallen for his feint, an amateur mistake my dad had all but drilled out of me before I was ten years old. The vampire ash and blood had gotten to me, burning my skin, stinging my eyes, and choking the breath from my lungs. In a fight, distractions can be the downfall of even the most experienced fighters.

Baldy knocked the dagger from my hand. His iron-hard fingers clamped my throat. He bore yellowed fangs, revealing missing and decayed teeth in the rest of his mouth. His breath—oh dear goddess, his breath—it turned my stomach inside out. Everything would have come up, had he not been crushing my esophagus. With no effort at all, he lifted me off the ground then smashed my back against the fertility shaft. What little breath remained in my lungs came out in a wheeze.

So, I was going to die at the hand of a bald vampire with a flowing mustache and bad teeth. Of all the interesting ways I could perish—basilisk poison, choking on a hard-boiled egg, murdered by a deranged clown from the Traveling Opera—never once had this scenario crossed my mind.

Fangs fully extended, he dove for my neck, but stopped an inch from my skin. A growl rumbled behind him. The vampire flew backwards like someone had tied a horse to his waist and yelled, "Yah!" He let me go, and I fell to the ground in a heap. It could have been something worse come to kill me, but at least I could breathe again. Gasping for air, I coughed around the vomit stuck in my throat.

Movement a few yards away drew my eyes to the action. I expected to see Lysander chopping the vampire's head off. But it was someone else entirely who dragged the creature away by its flowing mustache.

Some*thing* else, actually. A cat?

Not just your typical four-legged mouser either. But a very big cat with short, dense black fur, subtle stripes a shade darker…but with clothes and a sword belt? The cat threw the vampire to its back on the cobblestones, stood over it and roared. Its fangs were much more imposing than any vampire's—a good two inches long on top and bottom. I backpedaled myself up against the fertility shaft and held to a smooth, round wooden breast like it could help me make sense of this vicious fight. The cat's limbs were structured like a man's. He stood on two feet and wore tattered pants and a shirt. It had clawed hands instead of paws and huge cat feet that looked capable of jumping to the roof of a house in one leap. He had the wide head and blunt ears of a tyger.

Where the hell was Lysander? Maybe another vampire had dragged him out of my sight, but what was this feline thing? Enemy or friend? I hoped for the latter, but didn't know whether to cheer it on or run.

Lying on the ground, the vampire blinked once with its red eyes,

167

looking every bit as confused as I was. The shock must have worn off in another blink. It sprang up. The cat man kicked him back down. It tried to spring again, but the cat kicked it down once more. The vampire must have decided that wouldn't work, because then it rolled away and tried to spring up from its belly.

The cat pounced on the vampire's back, knocking it flat again. Palming the creature's bald head, he dug his claws into its scalp.

"Where is she?" roared the cat man. His voice was raspy and hard to make out.

The vampire answered with a spitty hiss. It tried to reach back and grab its captor. The cat creature clawed its arms, drawing black blood and a shiver-inducing shriek.

Still gripping the vampire's scalp, Cat Man banged its head into the cobblestones. "I said, where is she?"

In a long, breathy scream, the vampire called out, "Mistressssssss!"

Leaning close to his ear, Cat Man growled, "Your mistress isn't here, but when I find her, she'll wish she'd never been born."

He banged the vampire's head into the cobblestones again. Once, twice, three times, turning its forehead into a bloody pulp. The stone beneath its skull cracked. Pulling a silver cord from a pouch on his belt, Cat Man forced both the vampire's hands behind its back and tied them together. Then he stood, picked up the apparently unconscious vampire with ease, and slung it over his shoulder.

He carried the vampire toward me. I scuttled away from the fertility shaft. Away from him, whatever he was. I tried to scream for Lysander, but my throat still hurt from the choking attempt and wouldn't make a peep. I felt blindly along the ground with my hand. There—one of my daggers. My fingers closed around the hilt. I whipped it out and pointed it at the cat-vampire combo, but my arm shook like a cowardly butcher.

Cat Man strode to the fertility shaft, hoisted the vampire over his head and hooked the creature's tied arms over the top of the shaft. Then he let go. The vampire slid down ungracefully, bumping on every genital protrusion along the way until its backside hit the ground. Its head lolled, mouth opened in a weak hiss. A broken fang tumbled out into its curled mustache.

Black-furred chest rising and falling, the cat man turned his head and looked at me with bright green, feline eyes. My hand still wobbled, but I held tight to the dagger, ready to throw it at him if he started for me. In reality, it would likely bounce off his nose and piss him off more. But...his clothes and that sword belt looked eerily familiar. Had I accidentally licked some of that juniper juice? Or had the basilisk venom and vampire blood turned my mind to mush?

His whiskered cheeks lifted, stretching his big kitty lips into a wide smile. "Are you really going to kill your best friend?"

"Lysander?" I had finally went insane or this thing had eaten him and took on his personality.

He rumbled a laugh and shook himself like a wet dog. Fur became skin from head to toe. The man I knew stood before me, with a shadow of a beard, no claws, and no fangs.

Had I been the fainting sort, I'd have been thankful to still be sitting on the ground. Instead, a million questions perched on my tongue. Only one took flight. "The Tyger...you're really *a* tyger, not just a local legend."

He nodded, walked over to me, and crouched at my side. "I told you we all have our secrets."

Chapter Nineteen

~ Lysander ~

Mira couldn't stop staring at me, not that I blamed her. But she could have scared the life out of any unfortunate mortal at that moment. With black vampire blood stringing from her hair and their ashes smudged across her face, she could blend in with the undead.

"You need a bath," I said, grinning as I sat on the ground beside her. "Want me to lick you clean?"

"Um, no, though I'm sure you're used to tongue baths." Mira searched in vain for a clean corner of her robe to wipe off her daggers and opted for a clean patch of grass instead. "Makes me wonder why you have that fancy bathroom in your house."

"I like nice things."

"But, how—what are you?" She kept extending and retracting her hand toward my cheek, never touching me, but her fingers twitched as though fighting against her restraint.

"Lysander Devlin, the Tyger, at your service. And what we have here is the vampire who took Mavelle from me and disappeared before I could catch him the first time. Now we have a lead or some bait, depending upon how much information this thing can give us."

"Oh, that's good, I guess." She glanced at him, then resumed her stare-down of me, avoiding my eyes as usual. "But you still didn't answer my question. Were you always like this?"

Her intense assessment brought a rush of warmth to my skin and a tightening need to my groin. Incredibly bad timing.

I got up and found my sword among the ashes, wiping the grime from the blade onto my pants. "Are you hurt?" She shook her head, but I could tell she was exhausted. Probably starving too. "Let's go get you cleaned up and get a bite to eat. We'll need our energy."

"Where?"

I shrugged. "Pick a house."

She shrank back. "I don't know, it seems wrong, like trespassing."

"We've surely killed every villager that was left. I doubt anyone will protest."

"What if more of them arrive from the other islands?"

"We'll keep turning them to ash. If we hole up in one of the houses, we might be better able to fend them off if they come for a visit."

After looking over herself, she grimaced then nodded. "Fine, but how did you become whatever it is you are?"

"We'll talk about that later."

I sheathed my sword and went back to her, holding my hand out to help her stand. She stared at it for a moment, then took it. Her grip was surprisingly strong. I held on for a few seconds, in case she felt dizzy from being nearly suffocated.

With a shy smile, she pulled her hand from mine. "I'm fine. Thanks."

Our vampire captive groaned, wiggling a bit from his seat at the fertility pole.

"What about *him*?" she asked.

"He's tied up with silver cord, which practically immobilizes vampires and other dead things if you can bind them with it. And that fertility pole is solid. I bet they buried it at least six feet and cemented it with mortar."

"What about the sun? Won't it cook him if the storm clears?"

"I don't think this snow will dissipate before nightfall." White flakes fell all around us. Two landed on Mira's filthy cheeks. I reached out and wiped them away, smearing the ash. A tiny smile flitted across her lips before she went still and ducked her head. Smelling fresh blood, I noticed nasty puncture wounds on her neck.

"Were you bitten?" I asked. Blood trickled from the wounds, not appearing to come from any major vessels.

"No," she answered. "Fingernails—he had me by the neck, but

would have bitten me had you not turned cat and beat him to a pulp. He was overdue for a manicure if you ask me."

Her humor dredged a laugh from me. It was one of the reasons I had loved her so much. But that was then; this was now. Laughing wasn't on the agenda. Clearing the emotion from my throat, I stared up at the sky, not that I needed to, but I had to focus on something other than Mira. Old stirrings warred with the here and now. I couldn't let myself go back to what might have been. I had to find my wife. I loved Mavelle, of that I was certain. But Mira had made me proud today. She had chosen to stay and fight, and she had fought well. Yet, I couldn't let that pride turn into something more.

"Come, let's go to the old couple's home. They looked old enough to step into the Great Void anyway. We can pretend they were long lost relatives who left us their cozy cottage. I can heat some water so we can wash up. No licking required."

My mind produced an image of me running my tongue across a few inconspicuous places on Mira's body. And there went my cock, rising to the occasion.

Damn it, focus!

A smile played on Mira's lips as though she were thinking the same thing. "All right. Meet you inside."

She went on ahead, while I tightened the cord around our vampire's wrists. I circled around to face him. He opened his eyes and made a lunge for me, but I didn't flinch, and the cord held tight.

Crouching down to his eye level, I asked, "Are you going to tell me where my wife is, or will I have to send you to the Great Void without your supper?"

He hissed, which looked rather pitiful with one of his fangs broken and the other hanging by a thread.

"Really? Well, fuck you too." I stood, kicked him in the head, and he was out cold again. The man may have been a joy in his mortal life, but any resemblance to goodness had been sapped away from him at a necromancer's whim. Not that I cared, because once a vampire, always a vampire until the final death. But this one knew where Mavelle was or at least where she had been. I'd never attempted any intelligent conversation with a vampire and didn't know if it was even possible.

Torture, though distasteful to my senses, could be the only useful way to get anything out of him.

Nothing like a little violence to ease an aching erection. But I wouldn't stay out here avoiding Mira all day. Those wounds of hers looked pretty bad.

Sniffing the air, I smelled nothing but blood, death, and rot, with the crisp scent of fresh spring grass in this idyllic island valley. Such a shame—it would have been a beautiful place to take Mavelle after the wedding.

I swallowed past the lump in my throat and the dread tightening my chest. Something bigger than a necromancer's entertainment was brewing, and we were right in the middle of it.

The wind picked up. My shredded shirt did little to provide warmth. For the first time in a long while, I felt the cold and shivered. I jogged into the little house, hoping to start a fire in the hearth, heat some water and clean up. Then I'd find some clothes and continue questioning the toothless bloodsucker outside. The great room had a big fire pit in the middle and a vented hole in the roof over top. Mira sat on a low stool near the pit, huddled up, all dirty and cold. She didn't acknowledge my presence, just stared into the cold ashes. I thought it best to leave her be for now, so she could sort out her thoughts and I could avoid her questions for a while longer. I wouldn't be able to hold off her inquisition forever. Surely she couldn't read my thoughts—had her powers advanced that much? If so, she would have seen some explicit tongue licking.

Luckily, she just sat there, expressionless and lost in whatever thoughts lingered in that incredible mind of hers.

I found plenty of kindling and logs stored by the wall and a striker hanging on a post by the fire pit. It didn't take long to get a decent fire going. By the door sat a large varnished barrel that held fresh water. Having no access to anything but seawater, the locals collected rainwater and snow, which they melted and added to their water supply.

A pitcher hung over the barrel. Using it, I dipped out the water and poured it into a large metal pot with a spout on one end. Then I set the filled pot on the ashes at the edge of the fire. It would take a few minutes to heat it up. Just long enough for me to face the questions hanging between us like the smoke from the fire.

"Does anyone else know?" she asked.

"What I am? No."

"Not even Mavelle?"

I stuck my finger in the tepid water and wished it would heat faster. "No. I don't think she would have loved me any less, but I couldn't risk anyone else knowing. Even with the old Shaman gone, old habits die hard. As do people like you and me if we're discovered."

"So your parents never knew either."

"No. I wanted to tell them, but the necromancer killed them before I got the chance."

"A necromancer? I thought it was a bandit attack."

"That's what I told everyone. I couldn't tell them anything else." I had almost reached my truth-telling limit. Soon as the water was warm enough, I'd announce bath time and hopefully avoid more questions for a while.

"How did you become…like that?"

"A tyger? You can say it."

Her cheeks turned rosy. "Right. A tyger."

It sounded entirely too good coming from those plump red lips. I dunked my finger in the water again. Still not hot. I scooted the jug closer to the fire with a poker. "Taking a while, huh?"

"You still didn't answer my question. Were you born like this?"

I let out a sigh and scratched an itch on my arm that didn't exist. "No. I was turned to one."

"By whom?"

"By a man who found me not long after you left." The memory sent a cold shiver through me, even though the heat of the fire curled my eyelashes. "I took off walking until I fell unconscious. He found me like that and…well, he was a mystic of sorts. He had this tyger skin that I put on to stay warm. It adhered to my body and changed me."

"That must have been terrifying."

"You could say that. But then, he trained me to hunt and kill. He became my mentor, sort of a father figure, since…" The words wouldn't leave my tongue. I breathed deep and blinked away a few tears.

"I'm so sorry I wasn't there for you when they died." Her voice wavered, and I didn't have the patience or courage to see her crying again.

"Well, I killed the bitch that murdered them. I eventually found my way back home, told everyone that bandits had attacked us, and poor Lysander the orphaned tyger became the center of attention. End of story."

"What happened to your mentor?"

I tested the water again. Plenty warm enough. Yanking up the water pot, I said, "Time to clean up and continue our search."

Mira followed me to the narrow ladder, where we climbed up to the loft. It was a single room with a low, double bed situated against the rail along the loft's edge. That position probably allowed a good deal of heat to rise from the fire pit below and keep them warm. Back when they were alive and needed to keep warm, that is. By one of the sloped walls that formed the ceiling, a small table with narrow legs held an empty washbasin. I wiped the dust from it and poured in most of the warm water from the pot. A quick search produced a few rags and towels, plus extra clothes from a trunk that would have to do until we could wash and mend our own.

"Wash up. I'll wash downstairs and scrounge up some food," I said, not waiting for Mira to answer before scurrying back down the ladder with the water pot.

The bottom floor consisted of only the great room with a kitchen area at the rear of the house and the small pantry where we'd found the old couple and removed their heads. Their ashes blew around in the drafty air coming through the chinks in the mortar. I pulled the curtain across the doorway, closing what had become their tomb so we didn't have to breathe and eat their remains.

I found a wooden bowl, poured the rest of the water in it, and set it on the kitchen table. I shrugged out of my shirt, deciding my pants were still intact enough to suffice. Then I quickly washed up. The skin on my chest burned as I ran the rag over it. There were a few bad scratches I hadn't noticed before. They'd be fine, healed completely within the hour thanks to enhanced tyger regeneration. But Mira's wounds would need some care.

The kitchen appeared to be stocked with big bunches of dried herbs that hung from the rafters, bottles of various extracts and oils, and small containers of salts and other minerals. Perhaps the woman who lived here had served as the village's healer. I bet Mira could use some of these things to make a poultice.

Noises came from upstairs. She was probably finished by now. I could ask her for a recipe and mix it up for her so it would be ready when she came down.

I climbed up the ladder, meaning to inquire about the ingredients without going all the way up. A flash of movement caught my attention. I stuck my head up over the floor of the loft.

That was my first mistake.

Mira stood only a couple yards away, naked and bathing, with her back facing me. I watched.

That was my second mistake.

How could I not? Her hair was still up in a messy Mira-style bun. She lowered a towel from her face now clean from all the vampire ick. She raised her arms and untied a ribbon from her hair. A pink ribbon. Surely it wasn't the one I'd given her, but it had that pie-wedge notch in both ends.

Had she kept it all these years? I couldn't help but smile while I imagined her holding it against her bare skin, touching herself while she fantasized about me. There went my cock, joining in on my inappropriate thoughts. You would think that would have been enough to make me stop watching. It wasn't.

Next, she slid two pins from where they were crisscrossed within that mess of locks. A curtain of mahogany escaped its confines and fell in tangled waves past her brown shoulders and to the middle of her back.

And her back—it was strong, well-muscled, tapering at her waist. Her hips rounded into petite, but perfect buttocks. She combed through her hair with her fingers and, as I suspected, her arms appeared just as strong as the rest of her. Mirabelle Hearton was not by any means a stout woman, but she hadn't spent the last ten years doing embroidery.

She took a rag from the washbasin and tilted her head to one side. In long, one-way strokes, she wiped the mess from her hair before moving on to her neck. In the tarnished mirror, I caught a glimpse of her breasts. Not ample, but firm and perfect, peaked with dark red nipples. As she rubbed the cloth along her wounds, she sucked in a breath. Perhaps I made a noise out of sympathy, because she plopped the rag back into the water and grabbed a towel. Covering her chest, she spun around and caught me playing voyeur.

"Lysander? Oh, um, I'll be done in a minute."

"Yeah, that's fine. I'll just …yeah, I'll just leave you to it."

Her eyes locked on my chest. "Wait—you're wounded."

"Am I?" I'd forgotten about the scratches already, as well as my name, occupation, what day it was…

I looked up again, startled. She had wrapped the towel around herself and knelt a few inches in front of me. A rare occasion, someone catching me off guard. My hair bristled on instinct. Mira focused on my wounds, tentatively reaching for them. I caught her wrist.

She flicked her gaze to mine then focused on my scratches. "You're hurt. I can make a poultice for it."

"You can?" *Right, herbs…and other things…kitchen.* Her smell overpowered my senses, and I couldn't form the words.

"Sure, I saw herbs in the kitchen. I can whip up something."

Good, she'd seen them. I didn't have to reveal my mental incapacity. "What about you?" I pointed at her neck.

"I'm fine. Go downstairs. I'll be right there."

"Only if you let me make you something to eat."

She smiled and shook her head. "If you must."

I made it back down the ladder, but stumbled on the last rung. What the hell was I doing? Mavelle needed me. Mavelle. My wife. And here I was ogling Mira, the woman I'd once loved. The woman who'd left me. Time to busy myself in the kitchen. Nothing like good old cooking to occupy the mind. I found hard-as-a-rock stale bread. That wouldn't do. I'd have to venture into the pantry.

Holding my breath so I wouldn't breathe in the ashes, I stepped through their curtain and tiptoed past the piles of what once were human beings.

"Sorry," I said, feeling the need to apologize for desecrating the old couple's last resting place.

Searching the dusty shelves, I wondered how long they'd been married, if they'd been happy. That's what I had envisioned with

Mavelle and with Mira long before that. Perhaps it was better to never get married at all.

I finally came across a block of moldy cheese and some dried meat and tiptoed back out, closing the curtain carefully behind me. The meat smelled like rabbit, but it didn't matter what it was, so long as I could satisfy my hunger pangs. I gnawed off a piece. Mira was there in the kitchen, busy with a mortar and pestle at the table. She wore a white, loose-necked blouse and a brown skirt that was about two sizes too big. She'd pinned the hem of the shirt to the waist of the skirt. I chuckled.

"What? It's not like I had much to choose from. This lady was a healthy-sized woman. Here's a shirt for you." She grabbed a lump of fabric on the table and tossed it to me. Just a plain beige linen shirt that buttoned in the front. I put it on, but the sleeves ended halfway up my forearms and squeezed my biceps like tourniquets. I tried to button it at the bottom, but it wouldn't stretch enough to allow it.

Mira laughed that time. "Fits perfectly! If you like a tight fit, that is."

"Yeah, yeah, I guess we're even."

Herbal aromas tickled my nose as she worked. She picked up a bottle of whale oil and added a few drops.

"Oh, hey, did you find some food?" She glanced at the pantry and gave a little shudder.

"Cheese and rabbit jerky." I found a knife hanging on the wall above the table, put the block of cheese down and carved off the mold. Then I sliced off a couple of nice chunks, took two plates from the shelf, and wiped the dust from them. On each plate, I added a chunk of cheese and a couple of pieces of the dried meat.

"Nice," Mira said, nodding at my plating skills. "Thanks."

She turned, bowl in hand, and scooped up some of her poultice with two fingers, aiming them at the slashes on my chest.

I shook my head. "No, not until you eat."

"Really, Lysander..."

"We had a deal." I picked up her slice of cheese and held it to her lips. She slowly parted them, taking me back to our last kiss on the dock and many before that. While I was caught up in reminiscing, she chomped off a bite and startled me.

"Haffy?" she said through her mouth full of cheese.

"Yes, now you may smear some of that green goo on me." I ate more jerky and a bite of cheese, trying to distract myself, because I didn't know what her touch might do to me. Would it help to envision my late grandmother's wrinkly face and arthritic hands?

She scooped up a glob of her poultice. "What happened to your mentor? Where is he?"

Damn that memory of hers. Should have known she wouldn't let it go.

"He's dead. He wanted me to murder...innocent people. I refused, and he tried to kill me, but I killed him first." Admitting that I had come within seconds of killing her parents didn't seem like good timing. Especially with her about to touch me and my heart picking up its pace in anticipation.

"That's terrible. But I'm glad you survived. It can't be easy doing what you do."

Soon as Mira's fingers made contact, my pectoral muscles flinched. "Does it hurt?"

"No, you're f-fine."

"No, I meant when you become The Tyger."

"Not anymore." With gentle strokes, she rubbed the poultice over each slash. It stung at first then tingled with a cool sensation like snow on my bare skin. I watched her as she worked. Her expression was calm, her fingers sure, like she'd done this a thousand times.

"What's in that?" I asked, my voice sounding a little more ragged than I expected.

"Turmeric for infection, sage for warding off bad energy, a little mustard seed to reduce swelling, and a few drops of whale oil to hold it all together. It's not magic, but it works."

Even without magic, the poultice provided immediate relief. The real magic was in Mira's touch, the way she traced gently over each bloody scratch, paying more attention to the deepest wounds. She could have just dabbed on the poultice in the no-nonsense method most healers employed. But, Mira lingered a little longer, rubbing along the wounds as she worked, doing more than just treating the condition. Her warm, gentle movements must have soothed anxiety and earned trust from her patients. It certainly worked on *this* patient.

"You're good at that," I whispered.

"Loralee taught me well." She blinked a few times, and I knew that look—the drawn corners of her mouth, the trembling lip. Mira missed her friend. Had she ever missed *me* that much?

"She was lucky to have known you."

She withdrew her hand from my chest, briefly met my eyes but averted them just as quickly. "Lucky? I betrayed her. Because of me, everything she worked for is now rotting in the catacombs under Leogard."

Taking her by the shoulders, I said, "Look at me."

"No. I can't."

"Of course you can."

She wrenched herself free and slammed the mortar and pestle on the table. "No, I can't. I can't look at anyone."

"I trust you."

"Why? You should be the last one to trust me."

"Does it matter why? I just do."

She planted both hands on the table and hung her head low. "Goddess, that's almost exactly what you said the night before I left, when I asked you why you loved me."

My arms trembled, aching to hold her, to ease her pain as she had mine. "It was true then, and I trust you now. Please look at me."

She shook her head. "No."

That was it. I couldn't keep myself from her anymore. In one stride, I grabbed her and spun her around to face me. If it hadn't been for the wounds on my chest and how hard she'd worked to mend them, I'd have held her against me. Instead, I held tight to her upper arms.

"Let me go!" She tried to pull away, thrashing like a Hezrali horse in a chute. She must have been mindful of my wounds, or she would have been pounding my chest.

"No. Stop blaming yourself for what happened to Loralee. Ivy forced you to do what you did. I trust you—you're stronger than this, Mira."

"I hurt people. I hurt *you*."

"You didn't mean to."

"Don't you understand? This…" She locked eyes with me and turned on her power. Rich brown swirls caught me in their rhythmic circles. Clamping her eyes shut, she broke the spell as quickly as it had begun. "…is what hurt you. It wasn't real. None of it was real."

"What wasn't?"

"Anything you felt for me."

"You're saying you made me love you?"

"Yes…oh, goddess, I don't know. If I did, I didn't do it on purpose. I didn't know what I was until about a year before I left. That was about the time you stopped putting fish guts in my boots and started bringing me flowers. I could have influenced you and didn't realize it."

"Is it that hard to believe that someone might *actually* love you?"

"How can I be sure that I haven't been influencing everyone from the day I was born?"

"Because I know what *I* felt, and it was real." She had relaxed under my hold, so I released her arms and lifted my hands to her face. Her cheeks were warm on my palms. A few tears escaped from the corners of her clamped-shut eyes. "You were more than my best friend. I wanted to spend my life with you long before I ever showed it. I just didn't know how until then."

Finally, she opened her eyes and allowed them to meet mine. They weren't swirling with power. They were simply brown and beautiful, like I'd always remembered. As pretty as they'd been that night on the dock when I kissed her for the last time before she left. Her lips were just as red and plump, but too weighed down with sadness. Fuck that.

I dove for her lips. Her sharp intake of breath meant I'd surprised her, but she responded quickly. Her fingers gripped my waist, making my breath hitch. Our kiss deepened, my tongue flicked against hers. Just a taste was all I wanted. To refill a little portion of the hole she'd left in my heart. But with Mira touching me like this, wanting me, responding instead of running…I wanted more.

Her blouse slid down on one side, offering up her bare, clean skin. With my hands tangled in her hair, my lips sought her neck. Her pulse knocked against my tongue, but I left its hypnotic rhythm and licked a trail from her collarbone to her shoulder. Mira's weight shifted as though her knees had given up hope of keeping her upright. Just as well, since I had no intentions of letting her remain on her feet.

Gently I gripped her buttocks and lifted her to sit on the edge of the table. She didn't resist. Instead, she wrapped a leg around my waist and pulled me closer. Her urgency sent a surge of desire to my cock. It pressed into her thigh, and she went still. Slowly, as though gauging my reaction, she brought her hand to it where it bulged inside my pants. One stroke, then two. Had we been naked, she could have wrapped her fingers around it, pumping me until I came all over her or fucked her until neither of us could see straight. But this slow seduction, barred with a thin layer of cloth, aggravated the tyger in me. A low growl rumbled from my chest, while I lifted her skirts and tracked my fingers up her thigh until I found the hot wet folds I wanted so badly to explore. Her legs parted, inviting me in.

"Mira..." I slid a finger inside, and holy fuck, she was hot and wet. She felt even more amazing than I'd ever imagined. I'd explode if I didn't get these pants off and let my cock take over.

She rocked her hips to meet me halfway. "Yes. Please, yes." Each word came out like a breathy incantation. I'd kill a thousand vampires to be the answer to her prayers.

While I worked her with one finger, then two, I got my pants unfastened with my other hand and was about to drop them at my feet.

Then someone screamed.

Chapter Twenty

~ Lysander ~

We froze, Mira looking stunned, and me so damn hard it hurt. My fingers were still inside her, slick with her wetness, but they might as well have been painted in guilt. I slid them out and stepped back, fastening my pants and breathing hard. What the hell had I just done? And who screamed?

"What was that?" I ran to the window and peered out to see nothing but an empty courtyard and our vampire prisoner slumped against the fertility pole.

"I don't know," Mira whispered. She slid off the table and smoothed out her clothes.

The scream came again, cutting through the heated silence. I knew that voice.

"Mavelle," I whispered.

I wasted no time with shoes or a shirt, but ran out the door, shifting to the Tyger as I did. Once my feet touched the cobblestones, I stopped to look around and take a sniff. Our vampire captive was still securely tied to the fertility pole. He thrashed about when he saw me, hissing through broken fangs.

Ignoring his show, I took in every odor imaginable from dead sheep to seawater and Mira's tempting scent on my skin. No trace of Mavelle, even on the breeze. Nothing moved but the injured vampire, the clouds overhead and a bird on wing, fighting to fly straight in the imminent blizzard. Night encroached. Ominous shadows crawled across the courtyard. My eyes adjusted, stinging as they transformed, turning the dim of night into the light of day.

"Mavelle!" The wind carried my animalistic voice to the edge of the village and into the upward slopes of the forested valley wall.

"*Hellllp meeeee!*" Her cry was weak, far away, and bounced around the walls of the cove. No matter which way I rotated my ears, I couldn't pinpoint the direction.

"I'm coming!" But I didn't know where to start.

Something shuffled behind me. I spun and swung at it, realizing it was Mira a second too late. But, she ducked with amazing speed. My claws only caught a few strands of her hair.

"Watch it! I'd rather not be bald, thank you." She looked up at me from her crouching position, holding one dagger above her forehead for protection. "Is that Mavelle? Where?"

"I don't know."

"You sound so weird like that. I'm not sure I'll ever get used to seeing you with cat whiskers and stripes. I'm going to stand up now. Can you keep your paws to yourself?"

I nodded, recalling how my 'paws' had been all over her just a couple minutes prior.

Mira stood up, backing away a safe distance, eyeing me like I might rip her throat out at any time. She wore her cloak, fastened at the neck, covering her over-sized clothing.

"Maybe we should split up," she said.

"No, not yet." I pulled my gaze safely away from Mira's temptation. It was hard enough to accept how close I'd come to bedding her. Harder still to accept her eagerness in rescuing my wife. Every evil thought I'd had about her over the past ten years was wrong. The Mira I had loved when we were sixteen was the same beautiful, amazing, brave woman I'd always known. Things would be easier had she been the selfish hag I had thought she was for the last ten years.

"Which way?" she asked, looking around, then back to me.

"I don't know." Winds shifted, coming from the wooded hillside beyond the village. Sniffing the air, I caught evergreen sap, dirt, moss, traces of deer, rabbit and other small creatures that must now be scarce due to the vampire infestation. No Mavelle.

But, her voice rode upon the wind again, torturing my ears.

"Lysander! Why didn't you protect me?"

This time, it seemed to come from the hillside behind the village.

"Where are you?" I sprinted across the courtyard, leapt over a fence, and ran across a pasture. Guilt pounded through my chest with every stride. Back cracking, my body bent forward, and I shifted to all fours. With the speed of a natural tyger, I covered a quarter mile to the hillside's gentle slope in a few seconds.

"Wait!" Mira called for me, but I'd put too much distance between us.

I couldn't wait for her. Snow stung my eyes and nose as I broke past the tree line and began the ascent. Claws extended for traction, I darted around rocks and leapt over logs, senses attuned to every movement, sound, and smell in the hopes of finding a trail. From what I knew of the place, at the very top of the rise, the island had broken from the mainland generations ago, leaving a steep, deadly cliff. I didn't have much island left to search.

Yet, I kept running. I knew I had heard Mavelle. My advanced hearing made that possible, but then again, what if grief had tricked my mind into thinking the whistling wind was her calling for me? Smells of sea, kelp and fish grew stronger the farther I climbed. It wouldn't be long before I reached the edge—the barrier between survival and a horrific death on the surf-battered rocks below.

A sudden gust of wind wafted sulfur into my nose. Fully engaging my claws to grip the cool, mossy earth, I slid to a stop at the top of the hill, a few yards from the cliff's edge. Thick black smoke spiraled at the edge. I'd seen this before.

A necromancer's portal. I shifted partially, unfolding myself to stand on two feet, reaching back to draw my sword.

Shit.

I was still barefoot and shirtless. My pants ripped at the seams from the full shift to tyger. And no sword. No weapons but teeth and claws. Would that be enough?

The last time I saw one of these had been the night I killed my first target. The night I killed a necromancer. I'd ripped that one's throat out back then so I wouldn't hesitate to tear into this bitch. But what if she brought another horde of vampires? I wouldn't stand a chance.

A boot, followed by a long leg emerged. Not female. The side profile of a man followed. Recognition dawned—I knew the hunched posture, the puny shoulder, the cheek, and the scar extending from the corner of his eye to his temple. The other half of him remained shrouded in the portal.

"Peekaboo," he said. "Looking for someone?"

"Harker." His name was poison on my tongue.

He opened his mouth wide and screamed in Mavelle's voice: *"Help, oh help me, tyger man. I want you to fuck me with your tyger dick!"*

My jaws nearly came unhinged with a throat-rendering roar.

Harker laughed. "Easy there, kitty."

"Where is she?" I had to keep my head. I couldn't pounce yet. Not before Mavelle was back and out of harm's way.

He shook his head and held up his index finger, ticking it from side to side. "Patience, boy. Don't ruin our reunion."

"I'm not here for a reunion. I want Mavelle back."

"You thought I was dead, didn't you? I thought I'd taught you a better than that, boy. Pity—if you'd have gone downstream a mile or so, you'd have found me clinging to life on the riverbank and you could have finished me off for good. Luckily, someone else found me instead."

"What's your point, Harker? What do you want?"

"We want Mirabelle."

I knew it would come to this. Before the wedding massacre and everything that had happened since, I would have probably captured Mira, wrapped her in pretty paper, and handed her over happily if it meant having Mavelle back in my arms again. But things were different now.

Perhaps I could appeal to his greedy side. "I'll give you everything I own. All my money, the gadgets, the house, everything."

"Really now? All that, huh?"

"Yes. Just hand over Mavelle."

Labored footsteps crunched through the leaves and rocks downhill. Mira was finally catching up to me. Hair bristled on my neck.

"Gladly." Harker's body swiveled toward me. The other half of him that had been hidden within the portal's cloud emerged. As did pair of small, bare legs that dangled from his arms. Then a petite body wearing a

186

torn and dirty wedding robe, a limp arm, and a pale face.

Mavelle.

No, please no.

Harker bent forward and dropped her. She rolled down the incline straight for me. I knelt and caught her at my feet. Lifeless eyes stared up at me.

"Mavelle?" I put my fingers to her neck and felt nothing. She hadn't been bitten or otherwise wounded from what I could tell. "Can you hear me?"

"She won't be hearing anyone again. Courtesy of my mistress."

Desperate to hear a breath, see a blink, feel a pulse, I leaned close, keeping my fingers on her neck. No, these fingers weren't mine. These were the fingers of a monster, grotesquely strong and clawed. Rage drew my lips into a snarl. She never knew. I'd kept what I was from her—the thing this monster of a man had turned me into. And now he'd returned to twist the knife.

"Where is your mistress?" The animal inside clawed at my veins, demanding blood.

"Somewhere. Everywhere. Nowhere." He lifted his hands and eyes to the heavens as though preaching to the gods themselves. "She brought me back from the precipice of nonexistence. She is the beginning and the end. The giver and taker of life. Seek her, and you shall find eternity."

Mira reached us, panting hard. "Lysander, what—?" She froze by a tree, leaning against it from fatigue and shock. "Oh, goddess."

The swirling black vortex pulsed as Harker laughed. "Ah, Mirabelle Hearton. Just the girl I was looking for. I remember you calling out to your deity one night in Leogard. I think I was her first. What fun! She's a really good fuck."

Slowly, I looked over my shoulder at Mira. She shrank back, chest heaving, eyes huge, and jaw trembling. I didn't want to piece together the implications. Not yet.

"What did you do to Mavelle?" Fur bristled along my back, my long tail swished back and forth like a whip. The Tyger couldn't be tamed this time.

"You mean I don't get all your money now? I handed her over like you asked." Harker put a hand to his chest, blinking innocently. "Quite the pretty thing, your wife. What is she—twenty or so? The mistress took what she wanted and instructed me to deliver her straight to you. I'm a bad boy though. I had a little fun with her first."

Images flashed through my mind—ones I would never be able to erase—while my heart worked overtime, pounding against my chest. This time, I'd make certain I killed him. Claws and teeth bared, jaws open to the point of unhinging, I sprang. I'd tear him apart and spit his miserable head into the sea.

He swiftly jumped back into the portal, where the black ether swallowed him completely. My claws managed to graze his flesh. Harker screeched. But the portal and everything in it dissipated into thin air before I could do any real damage. The ground disappeared beneath my feet, replaced with frothy sea and jagged rocks far below. I had leapt too hard and too far, right over the edge of the cliff. Flipping around, I clawed for solid ground, but found none.

"No!" Mira slid to a stop at the edge, belly down, and cast her arm out as far as she could.

I grabbed for her, made contact, and clamped down. She cried out; her body jerked forward from my weight. My feet found purchase on the cliff side so I didn't drag us both down to sure death. With my other clawed hand, I scratched around until I had grappled enough dirt and webbed roots to support me and relieve her of the burden. I let go of Mira's arm and scrambled up the side, shifting to human form at the top.

Mavelle still lay lifeless a few feet away. I ran to her and fell to my knees at her side. Her body, once so full of energy and constant movement, now so still. Her empty eyes, once so full of joy and love, stared up at nothing. Mira crawled over, checked her pulse and leaned close to Mavelle's face.

Seconds dragged by. Seconds that felt like ages, while I pictured every moment I had spent with Mavelle. Her sweet laughter, the way she'd jump onto my lap and throw her arms around my neck. Occasional curses she would let slip, then apologize for, even though such nasty words coming from her pretty mouth were incredibly adorable to me. She took such joy in the simplest of things—decorating our home, baking, knitting me lopsided socks that I endlessly praised. And in our bed, so much passion wrapped in such a petite package. Making love to her made me forget every dark moment of my life. Waking up to her sleepy smile and whispered, "I love you," meant more to me than every treasure on Tallenmere.

Slowly, Mira sat up, wiping tears from her cheeks.

Dread wrapped its icy fingers around my heart, leaving me dizzy and disoriented. For the first time in a long time, the freezing wind seeped through my flesh. From head to toe, a violent shiver rippled through me. I picked up Mavelle and sat there, rocking her in my arms. Her body was cold, her limbs rigid.

"Can we save her?"

A moment of agonizing silence followed.

Then Mira said, "I'm sorry, Lysander. She's gone."

~ Mirabelle ~

I braced myself for a keening wail, a deafening cry or roar. But Lysander remained quiet. He cradled Mavelle to his chest, whispered comforting words to her, and stroked her hair. Then he simply stood up with her in his arms and started back down the hillside toward the village.

The wind picked up, throwing snow at my face and freezing the tears on my cheeks. Lysander disappeared behind the trees. The portal was gone, but what if Harker came back to finish us off? All I could think about was that barbarian's icy fingers on my skin, the pain and fear, complete and total helplessness.

Stumbling to my feet, I drew my daggers, but a fiery hot spasm shot through my left arm. The daggers tumbled from my hands; I had to bite my tongue to hold back a scream. On my forearm, where the bloodgems waited to kill me, were puncture wounds. Lysander's claws must have stabbed me when he grabbed on. Blood streamed from the holes, dripping to the mossy ground. Two of the gems glowed brightly, pulsing in time with the scorching pain. If he damaged them, I wouldn't have weeks left. I'd be lucky to have days.

The fire in my blood rushed through my veins, straight to my heart. I clutched my chest. Crushing pressure, searing heat a thousand times worse than any indigestion brought me to my knees. It traveled to my stomach, convulsing my insides. I vomited what little food I had eaten onto one of the tyger tracks Lysander had left. It soon turned to dry heaving. My eyes watered like two faucets with me lurching on all fours, though I had nothing left in me to expel but blood and guts.

The chest pain subsided. Finally, my stomach settled enough for me to sit up on my knees.

I might be dead soon, but I have to go to Lysander now. Sucking in laborious breaths, I wiped my mouth with my sleeve and scratched along the ground until I found my daggers. Once I had them safely sheathed, I stumbled to my feet and followed him, one tortuous step at a time. Complete darkness had closed in. I had to feel my way down a rough slope on unfamiliar terrain. Rocks tripped me, trees came out of nowhere, bruising my shoulders and knees. Thorns snagged my clothes and tore at my skin. The barbarian monster could be lurking in the shadows, ready to inflict his brand of torture. Or there could be a vampire villager we had missed earlier. Or barbarians from warring clans on neighboring islands who had sailed over to find the source of all the commotion.

It didn't matter. I kept going, feeling my way, using the downward pull and the papery bark of evergreens to guide me. The symbols on my arm glowed red, still sending burning pulses through my veins, though the pain had lessened enough for me to deal with it. Pity they couldn't be bright enough to light my way. Up ahead—a mile, half-mile? I couldn't judge distances well—a light warmed the dark of night.

Finally, I stumbled from the trees, crossed the back pasture, and entered the village. The vampire we had captured hissed as I passed, but I didn't stop. In the neighboring pasture, Lysander knelt over Mavelle's body, stroking her pale cheek. He'd stuck a torch in the ground, and a shovel was sticking up next to it. I bent and stepped through the fence between two slats and stood there, listening to him weep. I wanted nothing more in that moment than to go to him, to hold him in my arms, and try to give him some measure of comfort. But, this situation and our past—both drew an invisible line between us I knew I shouldn't cross.

He lifted his head and took a shaky breath. "She was afraid of the dark. I can't bury her...I just can't."

Somehow, I pushed the words past my dry, trembling lips. "We should take her back home. I can prepare the body with herbs from the kitchens here. It will preserve her long enough to—"

Slowly, he turned his head and looked at me over his shoulder. "You will not touch my wife."

"But, I can—"

"I don't care what you can do. Go rot in hell."

His words hurt me more than poison gems ever could. "Lysander, why would you say that?"

He leapt to his feet and spun around, then stalked toward me. His eyes glowed yellow, dilating into large reflective circles. "Why? You have the gall to ask me that? You fucked Harker back in Leogard. And you want to know a dirty little secret? I saw what you did a few weeks later."

"W-what?" Tremors weakened my knees. I backed up against the fence, holding to a post to keep from falling.

"Going deaf now, oh miss acolyte, miss protector of life?" The question ended with a growl. He kept advancing. Fur burst forth from his skin, quickly covering his entire face. His nose elongated and widened, his mouth stretched into a strong cat's jaw. Sharp teeth replaced dull human ones. Round ears sprouted from the top of his head. "You were with child, and you got rid of it. I assumed you'd had a fling and didn't want to deal with the consequences. Women do that all the time, but…you fucked Harker? How many times did it take to make a baby with the man who took everything from me?"

"You d-don't understand."

His voice rumbled from deep in his chest. "No, I don't. I don't understand why any of this had to happen. But I know one thing. It should have been you instead, not her lying here." He lifted a dark-furred, clawed hand toward me. I couldn't back up any further. He was looking right at me. I could mind-bend him into leaving me alone. I could make him forget Mavelle and everything, run away with me, and never look back if I wanted to.

But I couldn't. He was right. It should have been me instead. I held to the fence, hoping he would rip out my throat and end this once and for all.

Instead, he withdrew his hand and took a step back. Then he roared,

"Go! Leave us alone!"

Tears blurred my vision, my lungs wanted air, but I couldn't draw enough breath without breaking into crippling sobs. I willed myself to turn and crawl back through the fence, where I fell onto the grass on the other side. Lysander picked up Mavelle, leapt easily over the fence, and walked up the road that led to the dock.

He'd probably sail away with Mavelle's body and leave me here to die. I rolled to my back and stared up at the night sky. Breaks in the clouds allowed glimpses of stars. Stray snowflakes drifted onto my cheeks, leaving a quick cold kiss before they melted and joined the water in my tears.

I'd thought I was doing the right thing when I left home, but instead, I'd left a wake of destruction that could rival any typhoon. I deserved to die and would gladly take Mavelle's place right now if I could. She may not have been related to me by blood, but she was my sister, and I loved her dearly. I wanted to kill her murderers as much as Lysander did.

But damn it, dying and giving up wouldn't solve anything, and I couldn't explain anything to Lysander with him so lost in grief. The necromancer was still out there, my dad and many more still missing. I had to do something. But what? Besides being skilled with a dagger, all I had was an ability to bend minds. Our enemies weren't likely to walk right up and let me do either of those things.

A few yards away, still bound to the fertility pole, the vampire thrashed about, twisting his body to try and dislodge the silver cord around his wrists.

There *was* one thing I could try. But, it scared the hell out of me.

Chapter Twenty-One

~ Mirabelle ~

Rolling to my side, I dried my face with my sleeves and eased myself to all fours, trying to summon enough strength to stand. Though wobbly, I finally stood upright. One foot in front of the other, dagger drawn, I slipped around behind the creature and held my breath. He didn't seem to notice me there, as he still fought with his restraints and kicked up dust with his flailing legs.

Lysander said all these vampires shared some connection with their creator—the necromancer. If this connection existed on a psychic level, there was a chance I could tap into it.

There was also a chance I could lose my sanity or worse.

Closing my eyes, I drew in a few shaky breaths. I almost lost my grip on the dagger, so I held it between my teeth and wiped my palms on my cloak. Frightened as I was about my upcoming death, having my consciousness trapped somewhere beyond my control was much more terrifying. But I had no choice. We had to finish what we'd started.

When the vampire paused in his escape efforts, I gripped the dagger tightly, darted around to the front of the pole and squatted in front of him. His red eyes widened as he flattened his back against the wood. The next moment, he bared his fangs, hissed, and lunged at me.

Pressing my dagger to his throat, I slapped my other hand to the side of his head and locked my eyes on his. His legs thrashed. He shrieked so loud it jarred my head and blurred my vision. His rancid breath almost made me break contact and start heaving again, but I held firm.

With as much concentration as I could, I relayed a command

through my eyes and into what I hoped remained of his mortal psyche. The sensation of a surface-level connection buzzed across my forehead.

Relax. Stay still. I'm not going to hurt you.

He slumped against the fertility pole. I pushed a little deeper, felt the tug inside my head, a sensation of heaviness that signaled when I'd made a stronger connection. Now the question was, could I gamble on him not breaking free? Inch by inch, I lowered the dagger from his throat while holding eye contact. He didn't budge, so I gently dropped the blade beside me on the ground, but not out of reach in case I needed it.

Adding my freed hand to the other side of his head, I held on firmly, steadied myself, and allowed my mind to push further, past the point of suggestion and into the realm of cognition. I'd only been to such depths once when I pulled Loralee from another vampire's influence. That experience had jarred me, but I swallowed down the fear and continued.

My vision gave way to the mind's eye, where my brain tried to make sense of what was happening by turning the psychic journey into physical-world images. I plunged into a blood-red sea, setting a course through the vitreous fluid. Vampire sickness tainted the waters, flowing past me in black currents like oily tar. Ahead, a soft yellow glow signaled the entrance to the optic nerve. I steered my consciousness straight into the blinding light. All it took was one further mental push. The nerve opened up, swallowing me into its highway. On it, I traveled fast as light down a long narrow tunnel. The walls sparked with energy like a blade to a blacksmith's grinding stone.

Just when I thought it would never end, my mind's eye slowed to a stop. A lobed, fleshy barrier rose high before me, like Leogard's grand white walls—the vampire's brain. Except these walls were infected. Black, tarry liquid crept along the crevices and dripped from one lobe to the next. It moved as if it had a mind of its own, changing direction, pausing, then speeding up again. This, I recalled, was the vampire's sickness, the undead energy that turned normal mortals into bloodthirsty beasts. There was no cure for this insidious disease, apart from destruction of the reanimated body.

Here, I hesitated. If I dove deeper, I could become trapped within the sticky confines like Loralee had been. But, unlike her experience, I had no one to pull me back out. Yet, I had to take the risk. Pushing

194

ahead, my mind's eye watched as the tarry sickness parted like a curtain before me. Was it welcoming me inside? Did some part of the vampire's mortal spirit still have control, in the hopes of being healed?

From the deepest reaches of my brain, near all the subconscious activity centers, I gathered the will and momentum to drive forward. My mind's eye plunged into the wet, fleshy walls and spit me out into a misshapen corridor. I ducked and dodged along the twists and turns where images flashed along the walls above, below, left, and right in four-dimensional glory. Most were too fast for me to decipher. Some slowed down as though the man might be pondering them as he smoked a pipe. These were common thoughts and intentions—plans for building a boat, fallow fields in need of a plow, a young woman's bright smile, flushed cheeks, and tussled hair as she lay on a pillow.

Further still flashed darker images and sounds. Villagers running, screaming for family members, sheep bleating, growls and shrieks, tearing flesh, slurping, limp and bloodless bodies scattered across a courtyard. And there in the middle of it all, from the man's viewpoint as he lay on the cobblestones, stood a naked, pale-skinned woman, her arms lifted to the heavens as she laughed. Blood splattered on her bare skin. She rubbed it onto herself, lingered on her breasts and moaned in orgasmic ecstasy. All around her, green wispy smoke closed in like ethereal spokes on a wheel, disappearing into her body until she screamed and fell to her knees panting. Her face, though blurred with smoke and hair, I recognized immediately.

Ivy. Traitorous high elf daughter of Leogard's high priestess, the woman who had exploited my powers to get back at her sister. Her evil had come full circle, turning her to this…monster.

Temptation had me reaching for my dagger to slit her throat and end this madness. But no, this was in the past, nothing but a memory. I had to steady myself and keep my anger in check. If all went as I hoped—doubtful, but miracles did happen—I would have the chance to make her suffer in reality.

Suddenly, the vampire's vision shrank to a pinpoint view and shot straight forward into Ivy's chest, plunging my mind's eye into darkness. I fought to keep down panic. On my body's side, my ankles wobbled and my teeth chattered. But I couldn't just roll away and be done with it. I had to break the mental connection first, or my consciousness would be trapped in there, while I would be left out here as little more than a breathing shell of a person like Princess Loola.

I tried to pull back my consciousness, but all around me, sticky webs closed in. My heart pounded, sweat poured down my back. The frigid wind froze it on my skin and chilled me to the bone. My eyes burned, desperate for a blink to wash away the ash blowing in from the courtyard. I wouldn't be able to remain in this position for much longer.

Focus! Just a little longer.

Light gradually returned. My mind's eye opened to a large almond-shaped window. A shutter opened and closed at regular intervals, briefly blocking out the light. It stayed open long enough for me to see a chamber with lit candles in sconces and on tables. Scrolls, tomes, and loose papers littered the space. A rat scurried behind a shelf where dusty jars of eyes and other unidentifiable disgusting things stared back at me.

The window turned, and a bed appeared. On it sat a naked man. It was Harker. He gestured toward the window, and it came toward him. That's when I realized—this window wasn't a window at all. I was seeing through the necromancer's eyes. Though Ivy's eyes. He lay back, and she climbed on top of him. She moved up and down while he groaned with pleasure.

She turned her head to look behind her. In came another man who slipped out of a robe and let it fall to the floor. His naked body was pale, thin, and shapeless. He had black hair in a ponytail and thick dark eyebrows over brown eyes. His black beard, which was trimmed very short along his jaw, ended in a long, oiled point. Where had I seen him before? He moved in close, giving Ivy a sloppy, tongue-flicking kiss. Then he bent down and kissed Harker where he lay on the bed.

Ugh. Being voyeur to this orgy sent burning bile up my throat, but I had no choice. I had to identify their location before I escaped from this mental hell.

The other man lay down beside them with a perverted grin and watched while Ivy rode Harker faster. He stroked his hard cock and panted, his wide, lustful eyes glued to the pelvises beside him. With head thrown back, he trembled and moaned then spent his seed onto Ivy and Harker.

Disgusting. I gagged, but swallowed past it. Stomach acid burned my tongue. But now I recognized him. Prince Halcyon. I would have never imagined he'd be involved in such depravity. I pulled my focus from the disgusting display on the bed and onto the space above his head. On one of the sconces, I caught an insignia of a golden lightning bolt with the initials D.M. carved on each side of it. Those letters stood for Hezral's king, Damien Mallex. My father, who had been in the castle to deliver rare catches of expensive crab, got on well with the servants. He'd come home and share secrets of the royal family with me. One thing he confided was that only furniture and other items in the castle itself could carry Damien's insignia. If found in anyone else's possession, it could result in prison or death.

But now I knew the location of Ivy and Harker's lair. They were in King Damien's castle, or more likely the dungeons beneath.

This whole thing disturbed me beyond a nightmare. Complicated didn't begin to explain it. Was the king even aware of this? Was he aware his son was involved? If he was, what did that mean for the future of Hezral?

I'd never get these images out of my head, but I had gotten what I came for. Now I had to get out of here.

I began to pull my mind's eye backwards, gently. Hopefully what I had seen wasn't too far in the past. If it was, they could have moved elsewhere since then. At least we had somewhere to start.

Finally, I turned my consciousness around, ready to plunge back the way I had come. Before me hung the dark curtain separating the vampire's mind from the necromancer's. It was the only way out. I dove for it, once again re-entering the vampire's scattered thoughts, speeding along the loops and folds until the sparks of the optic nerve came into view. All I had to do was zip through that, through his eyes, and I'd be free.

Yet as I reached the entrance to the nerve, a black, thick liquid seeped down, reaching for me. I had to hurry. Like getting a second wind in a race, I gave it one last, final burst. My mind's eye shot down the optic nerve.

I'd almost made it into the vampire's eye when a black, sticky web blocked my way. I'd put so much effort into a speedy escape, I couldn't slow down, but plowed straight into it. The webs wrapped around me, cocooning me inside.

Ivy's voice battered my senses. *"Naughty, naughty girl. Did you enjoy watching me? Why not stay a little longer?"*

"Fuck you!"

"Oh, you will. Soon. And you will beg me for more."

Crying out, I summoned all the strength I had and tore through the cocoon. I started to reel in my consciousness, back into my own head where it belonged. Yet, it felt like wading through a pool of thick syrup. Finally, I'd gathered enough of my thoughts to be fully aware of my physical surroundings. My hands still held the vampire's head in place. I was about to break eye contact when something jerked my body backwards.

I hit the ground. Terrible sounds came next: a roar, a shrill scream, ripping flesh and snapping bones. I tried to move, but couldn't will my limbs to do anything. My eyes couldn't focus well, but something bounced along the ground beside me. Like a ball with a...mustache?

"Mira!" Lysander's blurry, frantic face loomed over mine. "Oh gods, Mira, what have you done?"

"I know where they are," I whispered, but I couldn't hold my eyes open.

He lifted me off the ground, running with me in his arms. "I'm sorry. Please forgive me. I'm so sorry."

Ivy laughed inside my head. *"Oh, how sweet. But I'm not quite ready for you to find me yet. Since your lover disturbed the bloodgems, you may have a little over a week until my mother's handiwork melts your flesh from the inside out. So, let's play a while, shall we?"*

Like a criminal tied down with heavy blocks and tossed into the ocean, my mind sank into an abysmal sea of cold, dark memories.

Things I'd buried deep were unearthed one by one. Scenes flashed before me. I was back at a party at the palace in Leogard. I lingered by the buffet, feeling out of place as usual in a crowd of elven nobility and wealth, but mesmerized by the gorgeous dresses and perfectly choreographed dances. Loralee was very sweet to include me in these things, though no one approached me except Sir Francis, the handsome half-elf paladin every woman swooned over.

He bent in a graceful bow. *"Would you do the honor of allowing me to dance with you?"*

"Are you sure? Wouldn't you rather rescue Princess Leona from Lord Sivenya's terrible waltzing?"

"I would, but it seems you and I are both destined to be without our soulmates. Now, are you going to keep me in conversation for the evening, or shall we dance instead?"

If I'd have ever loved anyone besides Lysander, I could have easily fallen for Sir Francis. We didn't meet often, but when we did, we enjoyed each other's company. Maybe it was because neither one of us quite fit into elven society. Yet both our hearts were claimed, so we never progressed beyond friendship. It didn't keep him from being the most chivalrous of holy warriors when it came to asking lonely ladies for a dance.

We shared a dance then I sneaked out early. I needed to clear my head, to stop thinking about Lysander and stop wondering if he still thought about me. If I was right, my influence would have worn off by then, and he'd simply think of me as that funny girl he once knew.

That night, I was lost in thought, walking alone on the street.

Stupid, so stupid.

The memories flickered and opened again with me in a strange bed somewhere—maybe one of the ramshackle tavern inns by the docks. Someone moved on top of me, hot sweaty skin against mine. He spoke, and I'd never forget that raspy voice.

"You like that, huh? Want me to fuck you harder?" It was Harker— the man who had stepped from the portal. I knew his voice immediately when I came across him and Lysander at the cliff's edge, but that night I couldn't see his face.

What had he done to me? I couldn't move, but I could feel everything. The pain as he forced himself inside me, the bruising fingers on my arms and breasts. I could smell his sweat and the liquor on his breath. But it was pitch dark. I couldn't get a lock on his eyes to mind-bend him into killing his miserable self. All I could do was cry and pray that it would be over soon.

That memory faded, and a new one wobbled into focus. I was sitting in Ivy's private quarters in the Temple. Cold sweat dotted my forehead and palms, nausea came in waves, while I kept second-guessing my reason for calling upon her. She handed me the vial of liquid. It was frothy, green, and smelled like fermented seaweed. My stomach churned.

She pushed it into my palm and closed my fingers around it. *"Hold your nose while you swallow it. I have used it myself with no ill consequences."*

"I'm scared."

"Don't be. You have every right to choose whether or not you want to bear a child".

The memories rewound to the beginning, repeating themselves in an infinite loop, sometimes with added horrors like my parents as skinless zombies. Or Harker as a winged demon snatching me up with his talons as I tried to run away. And through them all came Ivy's hollow laughter, mocking me at every turn, toying with me like a cat who's not interested in killing the mouse. No matter how hard I tried to wake up and escape her nightmarish hold, I couldn't.

Not until she grew bored with the game or until I died, whichever came first.

Chapter Twenty-Two

~ Lysander ~

Port Valor, one week later

Tannah hesitated at the front door. "Are you sure you'll be all right? Could I get you anything else before I go?"

"No, thank you. I appreciate your help with everything."

Poor Tannah, though not quite thirty, looked a good ten years older. After her husband Silas and their newborn died, Tannah and Silas's other wife Flora were claimed by one of the Wharfmaster's younger sons, Rufus. He drank heavily and beat all six of his wives on a whim. Because Tannah and Flora were transplants from another household, his four original wives ganged up on them.

After a particularly bad beating, Flora hobbled to a dock one night and threw herself into the sea. Tannah persevered somehow, but had never had any more children. Rumor was she had been pregnant a couple times, but her four rivals would hold her down and kick her in the abdomen until she miscarried. Another rumor claimed Tannah started the terrible fire that claimed Rufus *and* those bitter wives. Whatever the truth, she hadn't been arrested and used her widow's stipend to buy a comfortable little home at the edge of town.

She looked sadly over to the ottoman where Mira lay unconscious. "It's the least I can do. Miss Hearton helped me give birth to my son, so I could at least hold him for a little while before…"

"I know. We'll see you soon."

Silence reigned once more when she left.

After everything we'd been through, we were back to where we started. My wife lay dead in our family's crypt. Mira had been out for a week, and thanks to Tannah, we had managed to keep her clean and hydrated. I sat beside her as another seizure began. Cold sweat dampened her face. Her muscles tensed from head to toe, and she shook like a compressed spring ready to break free.

During our voyage back home, I didn't think she'd make it, though I pushed the ship's engines to their limits. Darvis and the others who had gone to search for Mavelle were still gone. Luckily, his wives and some other neighbors—I couldn't recall who they were—helped me lay Mavelle to rest in the crypt and made Mira comfortable as possible when I didn't have the mind to do anything more than grieve.

"Keep breathing," I said, turning her to one side so she wouldn't swallow her tongue.

Whatever had hold of her mind wasn't letting go. She should have never tried to bend a vampire. Did I do the right thing in tearing his head from his shoulders? Or did I only manage to trap her in some undead mental hell? I knew why she did it—I'd blamed her for everything, and she wanted to make amends. If anyone deserved blame, it was me. I'd vowed to keep Mavelle safe, but didn't. I'd basked in the glory of being The Tyger, living for the praises of my neighbors instead of being content with the simple life. If I'd have been more thorough, less prideful of my abilities, I'd have made certain Harker was dead.

Mira relaxed, panting and sweating hard. I rolled her to her back, dipped a rag into a bucket of cold water and wrung it out. Slowly, gently, I wiped her face and neck, hoping it provided her some relief. I tried to keep my voice from breaking, but couldn't. "I've blamed you for everything for so long, I couldn't see how wrong I was."

She stirred, letting out a soft groan. I dropped the rag into the bucket and took her hand.

"Wake up, Mira. Fight it—you can do this."

Her lips moved, but nothing came out. Nearby, I kept a bowl of clean water that I'd been giving her when I could to prevent dehydration. Along with clear broth, it was the only thing I knew to do in order to keep her alive. I picked up the bowl, and with a clean napkin, dipped a corner in, and squeezed some water into her mouth.

She swallowed then parted her lips as though she wanted more. Did that mean she was coming around? I didn't want to get my hopes up, but I could only imagine how thirsty she must be. Hungry too. If she did wake up now, it would take some time to build up her strength.

"Here, drink." Quickly, I dipped the napkin into the bowl and squeezed more water between her lips, watching anxiously to see any more signs of her waking.

She sighed and went still again. I set the water bowl down, rested my elbows on my knees, and let my head hang low. What more could I do besides taking her to Leogard to ask or force the Priestess to remove the bloodgems? I could sneak inside the Temple easily enough. I might not have Mira's mind-bending ability, but if I played it right, I'd be able to nab the Priestess and coerce her into submission. Some might call it torture, but it usually worked.

That plan might not do anything to help Mira wake from this trance, but at least one danger would be eliminated. I'd kept an estimate of the time she had left. We should have a little over two weeks, just enough time to get to Leogard. Harker and the witch still posed a threat. They could show up at any time to finish us off, but my house was better fortified than any other place in the city. We stood a better chance in here. My quest to find *them* was off for now. Nothing mattered but taking care of Mira.

Grimacing as though in pain, she stirred again and whispered, "Let me go."

Was she dreaming or trying to tell me to give up on her? I kissed her cool forehead. "No, I won't let you go. Not again."

Guilt squeezed my chest. Saying such things felt like cheating on Mavelle. Her smell lingered in the house, wafting up at random times as I walked from room to room or opened a cabinet that housed her things. Her smell was strongest in our bedroom. I hadn't gotten the courage to step over the threshold yet. Memories crowded the space. We had shared our bodies, hearts, and souls in the most intimate way a man and woman could. No, I could never sleep in that room again. At least not in the foreseeable future. For now, what little sleep I did get was on a pallet on the floor beside Mira.

Something brushed my ear. Startled, I jerked my head up. Mira's weak smile greeted me. She lowered her hand. But I snatched it up again, scooting closer, a dam of emotions constricting my throat.

I swallowed hard and smiled. "Welcome back."

Her words came out in a dry, ragged whisper. "I'm starting to think you're bad luck."

With a sniff, I wiped the tears off my cheeks and scooted closer. "I thought...I thought I'd lost you."

"Mavelle?"

"She's gone."

She must have forgotten or thought it had all been part of her mental state. Saying it out loud, that Mavelle was gone...dead...it hurt too much. Damn it. I couldn't hold it back, and broke down in shoulder-jarring sobs. I turned away so she couldn't see me. So much for maintaining my composure.

Mira reached out and touched my arm, giving it a weak, but comforting squeeze. "I'm sorry."

"It's not your fault." The statement felt strangely cathartic, now that I'd accepted its truth.

She took a deep breath and averted her eyes, letting her hand drop beside her again.

"Are you in pain? Can I get you anything?"

"Water."

I snatched up the bowl and started to squeeze the rag into her mouth again. Mira cocked an eyebrow. "Really?"

"How else was I supposed to keep you hydrated?"

"You did good."

"Here, I'll help you sit up." Setting the bowl down, I grabbed some pillows from the floor and gently propped her up on the ottoman. Once she was upright enough, I held the bowl to her lips, tipped it and watched her suck up every last drop.

"More," she said, breathing deeply as she rested her head on the pillows.

"I'll bring you every drop of water on Tallenmere if that means you'll stay alive and well."

* * * *

Two glasses of water and a bowl of broth later, Mira was sitting up a little better.

"Are you in any pain?" I asked.

"My head hurts, that's all. Can you make me some tea?"

I sprang from my chair, eager to do whatever she needed. "Chamomile?"

She laughed quietly. "Easy there, Tyger. No—I'll take licorice and cat's claw tea if you have it."

"Odd combination."

She lifted one shoulder in a slight shrug. "It helps with weakness."

"You would know that, wouldn't you?"

"Of course."

Her smile made me want to leap for joy, but I was a professional assassin, not a giddy boy whose best friend had just woken up after a weeklong stupor. *Shit.* I couldn't keep the smile off my face.

"Can I get you anything else? Soup, bread, cheese?"

"No, but a hot bath would be wonderful." Those big brown eyes crinkled when she smiled. I'd always loved her smile.

Clearing my throat, I started toward the kitchen. "I could probably make that happen."

It took a few minutes, but after some digging around in the cabinets, I found both the licorice and cat's claw. Mavelle had stocked our kitchen well, taking great pains to label everything carefully in her small, neat handwriting. Everything here reminded me of her, and the nagging uncertainty of how I'd carry on without her reared its ugly head again. No—I couldn't go there yet, not with so much danger still lurking. Tea making and taking care of Mira would keep me occupied enough for now.

With a steaming cup of aromatic licorice and cat's claw tea, I sat down beside her and gently touched her forehead. "What happened in here while you were out?"

She shivered. "Have you ever had a nightmare?"

"Yeah." I handed her the tea.

"Imagine one that lasts a week without end." She took a sip, and closed her eyes as though appreciating the hot brew.

"That must have been terrible. What did you dream about?"

"It doesn't matter." Her teacup clanked against the saucer. She set them down on her lap. "Serves me right for taking a tour of a vampire's mind."

"Why did you do that?"

"I had to." She shrugged like her near-death and eternal nightmare aftereffects were nothing more than an everyday chore. "I had to know where they're hiding."

"And where is that?" Now that Mavelle couldn't be saved, my question sounded tired and apathetic. But Mira's dad and the others were still out there somewhere. Whether dead or alive, I knew she would want to find them.

"In the castle dungeons."

She must have not regained her senses quite yet. "That's impossible."

"Is it?"

"King Damien would never harbor a necromancer. He hates them—he had me kill one and steal the work of another. Why would he now keep one under his protection? Especially one who has hurt and killed many of his people? He came by personally one night while you were still out to offer his condolences."

"It's possible he doesn't know. I saw Prince Halcyon there, doing…things with them."

"Damien said the prince is headed to Leogard on some diplomatic trip."

"What I saw may have happened in the past, but I know what I saw, and if I learned anything at the Temple, it was to never assume people don't have ulterior motives. There are very few pure souls in existence. Most of them are babies."

She turned her face away, lip trembling. But her eyes were stern, her chin lifted in stubborn defiance. Mira may have been lying here, broken and battered, but her spirit remained strong. I'd always loved that about her.

"I know who the necromancer is," she said.

"Who?"

"Ivy. As horrible as she was in Leogard, I still didn't think she'd go this far."

I let my head fall back against the back of the chair. "This is so fucked up. So we have a potentially clueless king, a corrupted prince, a treasonous alliance with a Leogardian socialite turned necromancer, and Harker Stone, the insane bastard who turned me to a tyger and killed my wife. What are they after?"

"Me."

"Besides you. Something bigger is behind all this. We're a means to an end, but what end?"

"I don't know." Mira took a deep breath. "But I need to tell you something else."

"What is it?"

"Years ago, with Harker—"

"That's in the past. You slept with him, but you couldn't have known he was such a bastard."

She rubbed her temples and closed her eyes. "No, I didn't sleep with him, Lysander. He…forced himself on me."

Her words knocked the breath from my lungs. My fingers tightened on the arms of the chair. "When?"

"It was a few years ago, after a party. I left early, alone, at night. Not my smartest move, I know. The next thing I knew, I was in a dark room with someone…on me. I couldn't move. I couldn't get to my daggers. I couldn't even focus on his eyes so I could mind-bend him. But I was awake enough to know what was happening, and I could hear his voice and see his aura. I recognized it the night he appeared on the island. He may have drugged me or something, I don't know. But by the time it wore off, he was long gone, and I had no idea where to find him. A few weeks later, I discovered I was pregnant, so I went to Ivy for help."

"I'll fucking rip him apart." Every muscle in my body twitched. I squeezed the arms of the chair so hard, the wood cracked. The Tyger wanted out. He wanted blood.

"Soon, but not yet." Mira put her hand on my cheek and actually looked me in the eyes. They didn't swirl with her mind-bending powers. She finally trusted herself to not hurt me. Her courage soothed the beast enough for me to release my death grip on the chair.

She continued, "I got an expulsion potion from Ivy and took it back to my room, but before I could drink it, I changed my mind. I thought of that little baby the Shaman had murdered, how innocent he was. He couldn't help being born, much less being deformed, but he deserved a chance to live. So did my baby. I poured the potion out and decided to keep the child."

"You have a child?" The question felt so odd on my tongue, warring with everything I had accused her of for so long.

She shook her head. "No. A few weeks later, I had a miscarriage. But, I had come to accept the idea, had decided to love the baby no matter what. It just wasn't meant to be."

Why I hadn't considered that Harker might have raped her, I didn't know. Somewhere in my heart, I must have wanted to believe my mentor couldn't have been such a monster. But, he'd made that painfully clear. How blind could I be?

"Why didn't you tell me this before you bent the vampire's mind?" I asked.

Shaking her head, she sighed. "It's not exactly the kind of thing you blurt out, especially with all the horrors *you've* faced these last few days. You didn't need an added burden."

"I should have made sure he was dead. I won't make that mistake twice."

"Calm down, Tyger. Kill him for what he's done to you, not me. I moved on, and I'm all right. Well, as all right as I can be considering this." She held up the glowing symbols on her arm.

"I'm sorry, Mira. I should have been there in Leogard, protecting you, instead of thinking the worst."

"It's not your fault. I would have thought the same, had I been you. By the way, those tyger eyes are really growing on me."

I lowered my head, blinking rapidly, not realizing I had partially shifted. Even my tyger fangs had emerged.

"I'll be back." I took her empty cup back to the kitchen and remained there for a while, splashing water on myself to cool my head. Never before had I wanted to kill someone as much as I wanted to kill Harker Stone. He'd ruined my life—not just mine, but Mira's too. I'd find him as soon as we returned from Leogard with her curse removed. Then I'd make sure he died a horribly slow death. Once my eyes and teeth returned to normal and I didn't feel like ripping out a throat or two,

I returned to the great room.

"Do you think you can walk?" I asked.

"I don't know." She made a wobbly attempt at sitting up and swung her legs over the side of the ottoman. They dangled there, and she closed her eyes, catching her breath. She'd not be able to walk for a while until she'd regained her strength.

"Let's go." I scooped her up in my arms.

"What are you doing?" she flung weak arms around my neck, staring at me wide-eyed.

"You said you wanted a bath. I'm carrying you to the washroom."

I expected her to say no, but she exhaled and rested her head in sweet surrender against my chest.

* * * *

~ Mirabelle ~

Lysander set me down on a bench in his gigantic washroom and started filling the tub with steamy water. He took a couple bottles from the shelf and added a few drops of bath oils, followed by a sprinkle of bath salts from a ceramic jar. A melody of aromas filled the air—sweet talaberry blossoms, lavender, and cloves.

The tea was already working, making my pulse a beat or two faster. It didn't help that I sat on a stool in a thin linen gown, watching Lysander as he sat on the side of the tub. He tested the water with his fingers. His hands were strong and agile, capable of killing in an instant, but eager to be gentle and kind. The muscles in his arms flexed while he adjusted the faucets, fetched towels and a clean robe. Some of the boy I once knew came out in his soft expression, his lips twitching from side to side as he concentrated on getting things just right.

Goddess, how I loved him.

He'd taken such good care of me, when he could have left me for dead. For having been asleep for nearly a week, my teeth were clean, and I didn't smell half bad. Nor did I have any rashes or sores from lying in one spot. Thinking about him cleaning my body's most intimate parts sped my heart a couple beats more.

"D-did you take care of me this whole time?" I asked.

He drew his attention away from the filling tub and onto me. The corner of his mouth lifted in a half-smile. "Yes, but I had help. I made sure you had water and broth and didn't swallow your tongue during the seizures. Tannah Lurck took care of the more personal aspects."

"Oh."

He turned off the water, stood, and dried his hands. "Ready for your bath?"

"Very."

I took his outstretched hand and tried to stand, feeling the cool bricks beneath my feet. But, soon as I took a step, my knee buckled.

Lysander caught me before I hit the floor. "Let me help."

Supporting me with one arm, he walked slowly beside me as I limped to my waiting bath. He picked me up and set me on the warm brick edge of the tub, facing the steamy water. My legs sank knee deep. I sucked in a breath.

He was still behind me, holding to my waist to keep me from falling in. "Is it too hot? I can add more cold."

I shook my head. "It's nice. I'll get used to it."

With a few gentle tugs, he pulled my gown from under me where I sat on it. My heart thumped so loudly against my chest, he probably heard it.

"Y-you're not going to let Tannah do th-that?" I tried to still the quaver in my voice, but couldn't.

He went still, his hands still fisting the hem of my gown. "She's gone to sell eggs today. Would you rather wait for her to help you?"

I knew what the proper answer should be, but I'd never been a very proper girl. "No, you're doing fine."

Wordlessly, he lifted the gown over my head and took it off. He stood back a reasonable distance, enough so that he probably couldn't see anything but my bare back. Even so, I could feel his stare. Looking over my shoulder, I watched his aura shifting with colors: yellow, violet and orange. He was weighed down with worries, anxious for my safety, and grieving from loss. Submerged beneath those, a bright red aura pulsed as though it longed to emerge completely. Though I hadn't had the pleasure of experiencing it for myself, I knew what it was. Arousal. Passion. Excitement. Had it not been for our circumstances, he wouldn't have hesitated to bed me then and there. And I wouldn't have protested at all.

So I wouldn't prolong the torture of naked me in front of him, I held to the sides of the tub and slid collarbone deep, into the warm bath. The bath salts and oils had clouded the water enough to provide modesty. He watched me with a worried frown for a moment, probably making sure I wouldn't sink and drown. Then he turned to walk out.

Loneliness expanded like a hollow ball in my chest. I didn't want him to be out of my sight yet. "Lysander?"

He stood in the doorway with his back to me, turning his head slightly my way. "Need something?"

"Please don't go."

His shoulders rose and fell as though he need to catch his breath and weigh that decision. "All right."

He made his way to the stool and sat, leaning forward with his elbows resting on his knees. He kept his gaze on the floor, shoulders slumped. Dark circles under his eyes told me how tired he must have been. I should have encouraged him to sleep instead of staying with me, but I didn't want to be alone. All those horrible nightmares remained at the forefront of my thoughts.

"Thank you. I should have said it before. You've been...extraordinarily kind to me after everything I put you through," I said.

Sadness darkened his features. His gaze drifted to the side of the tub, but no further. "The past is in the past. What happened then wasn't your fault. We have no choice but to carry on and make the most of our time."

Carefully, so I didn't expose myself, I filled the small pitcher with warm water and poured it over my head. Once my hair was done, I picked up a sponge and set to work washing myself. The water felt heavenly warm and soft, so fragrant I feared I might fall asleep and drown if he weren't there to keep me awake.

Then another reality hit me. "I don't have a lot of time left."

The bloodgems in my arm flared, sending a burning streak upward as though they heard me discussing my demise and anticipated their role in it. I winced and rubbed my shoulder.

He said, "We're leaving for Leogard tomorrow. I've arranged the fastest transportation possible."

My heart sank. He didn't know the bloodgems were working faster than we expected.

I didn't have the courage to tell him that, so I'd have to be firm. "No."

"No?" This time, he lifted his head and directed an unyielding stare right at me. "We have no choice. I won't let you die."

Unfortunately for him, I'd always been more stubborn. "*I* have a choice. We were too late to save Mavelle, but we could still save Dad and the others."

"Your time is running out. No. The search is off for now."

"Like hell it is. My father is out there somewhere. Dead or alive, I don't know, but he deserves to be found. They all do. And Ivy must be brought down, or she'll continue on her path of destruction. As well as Harker."

"Yeah? Say we do storm the castle and find Harker and this bitch. What if they capture you?"

"We can't live on what ifs, Lysander. Besides, you'll be there to protect me."

"And what if I can't?" He shot up from the stool and paced the room. "I couldn't save my wife. I couldn't protect you from him back then. What makes you think I can protect you now?" His voice broke. "I can't lose you again, Mira."

Violet dominated his aura—so much sorrow, so much pain. My desire to go comfort him trumped any and every reason why I shouldn't. He went for the door, going somewhere to gather his senses, get some fresh air, whatever, but I couldn't let him walk out on me.

"Lysander, wait."

"I need some air. Stay put." He paused for a second then walked out, his heavy footsteps pounding down the hall to the great room.

I pushed myself from the water and perched on the edge of the tub. As quickly as I could, I held to the tub and eased one leg over the side, then the other. The robe was on the floor, so I picked it up and wrapped it around me. Though my knees shook, I was able to stand.

One step forward. So far so good.

Another step. Still wobbly, but I was making progress.

Another step and my knee gave out, pitching me forward. I hit the floor with a thud, palms smacking the bricks. The impact made me see double and sent a gush of incendiary blood from the poisoned gems through my veins and into my chest. I cried out in agony.

Lysander rushed back into the room, knelt down and scooped me up in his arms. His eyes instantly changed to the brilliant green of a tyger. His voice rumbled. "Mira, for creation's sake, why do you never listen to me?"

Gritting my teeth, I took a few breaths until the pain subsided enough to talk. "Because…you look so magnificent when you're angry."

He held me close, unblinking eyes full of power and longing. Behind his sorrowful violet aura, a brilliant red bloomed brighter. Love. This is what it felt like, being wrapped up in the arms of the man I adored. He had loved Mavelle and still grieved for her, but despite everything, I knew he still loved me.

His lips collided with mine. I wrapped my arms around his neck, drinking in his kiss as though it were a miracle cure. He carried me down the hall. To where, I didn't care, so long as I could feel him inside me.

Chapter Twenty-Three

~ Mirabelle ~

We ended up at the door to the room I had slept in the night before we set out on our first failed mission. Instead of adjusting my weight in his arms and turning the knob, however, he lifted his foot and kicked the door open. Wood splintered—the door swung wildly and hit the wall behind it, knocking a piece of pottery off a shelf with a crash.

His eyes flashed like he'd caught a prized deer. Had I driven him to full-on tyger, all instinct and no cuddle? A shiver ran through me as he reached the bed in two big strides. I wanted this. I wanted him, but...I didn't want pain. Just before I thought he would toss me on the bed and break me in half, he stopped and lowered me gently to the mattress.

He hovered over me, keeping his body weight off me with arms braced on either side of my head. A few silent seconds passed, as though he were trying to calm the beast inside. The muscles under his striped tattoo quivered. I ran my fingers over it, reading the words clearly for the first time: *Only through pain does one become strong.*

Maybe it was true. He'd survived so much, yet persevered, where other men may have ended their lives to escape such pain.

His eyes became human again. "I don't want to hurt you. We shouldn't do this. You should be resting."

"It's all right. Want me to help you?"

He looked aside, breathing hard. I knew he feared surrendering his mind to me.

"Just a little, just enough to keep the tyger at bay, but the choice is yours."

"All right, do it."

Soon as his eyes met mine, I made the connection and sent a telepathic message that I hoped would lead to the best day of my life. *Bring out a little of the Tyger, but keep the rest inside. No rage, no pain. Make love to me, but do it slowly, gently. Be my protector.*

I closed my eyes, breaking the spell. A growl rumbled in his chest, his eyes shifted to brilliant green, but that's where it stopped.

"Are you sure?" He lowered his eyes as the violet aura of his sorrow bloomed around us.

Not acceptable.

"Positive." I took his face in my hands and reeled him in for a kiss. And oh, what a kiss it was. Swift, hungry, with just enough restraint in the pressure to keep from hurting me.

He pulled away and asked, "Do you trust me?" The rumble had grown deeper, his eyes brighter, dilated with excitement that just bordered on animal instinct.

Blinking up at him, I swallowed down a rising fear before finally nodding my approval.

"Good, because I'd never hurt you, Mira. Not in a million years." He followed up his promise with a gentle kiss to my neck.

Then a lick across my collarbone. A warm, sandpapery lick. My breath hitched.

"If you don't like that, I can switch."

"No, don't."

He lingered there a moment, warm breath against my skin. His fingers found the edge of my robe where it divided my breasts. I closed my eyes. My heart raced. Tension squeezed my neck, but if I was going to let him do this, I had to let go. I had to surrender.

"Tell me where to touch you," he whispered, brushing his hot lips across my earlobe.

What did he say? My brain couldn't process language or form a coherent thought. All it wanted was him.

He raised his head and smiled. "Where do you want me to touch you? Tell me, Mira."

Only one answer made its way to my mouth. "Everywhere. Touch me everywhere."

Slowly, he pulled the robe aside. My nipple hardened to the point of near pain. He kissed my collarbone again, leading his lips on a leisurely course to the mound of my breast.

Would he? Wouldn't he? It felt like a game, a tortuously delightful game.

Then he licked, stroking his rough tongue across my breast, but not quite to the summit. Instead of climbing to the peak, he circled it. Licking, drawing closer with every lap. I shifted impatiently beneath him. His cock pressed against my inner thigh, hot and ready to go, but Lysander was master of this domain.

A gentle bite just under my nipple startled me. I sucked in a loud breath.

Lysander chuckled, using one finger to skim my areola in slow, deliberate circles. "Tell me what comes next."

Really? He wanted me to say it? Of course he knew what I wanted, how could he not? His request was pointless, maybe, but it empowered me. He didn't want me to feel dominated.

His selflessness drove me wild.

I whispered my command before I lost courage. "Suck my nipple."

He grinned while he lowered his lips to my breast. At first, he lightly teased, running those warm, wet lips across my flesh until I whined and arched against his mouth. So evil of him, playing with me like this.

He went really still, his lips just barely forming suction. Then he raised those tyger eyes and locked them on mine. I held my breath. With a quiet growl, he sucked up my nipple in one quick motion. I cried out in pleasure and surprise.

Though my only sexual encounter to this point had been a horrible thing I wanted to forget, I wasn't so jaded as to think people couldn't enjoy sex. Sure, the fear still lingered, but I was there with the man I loved more than anything, and I wouldn't let fear keep me from enjoying every moment with him. And dear goddess, was I ever enjoying it.

Slowly, he began to suckle, drawing it in then out. How much better could it get? I fisted the sheets in my hands, arching in wiggling excitement to give him as much as he could take. He sucked harder, pulling my nipple deep into his mouth and working it with glorious pressure. Hot wetness spread between my legs.

Yes, it could definitely get better.

Mr. Agile was able to shrug out of his shirt and slide out of his trousers while sucking my nipple like an erotic maestro. He slid back up against me, his cock hot and throbbing against my inner thigh, making me even wetter. His other hand didn't remain idle long—it joined in, cupping my other breast and kneading it until I moaned. He pinched that nipple between his thumb and forefinger, twisting it and pulling until I cried out.

He went still, his voice rumbling against my wet skin. "Do you want more? Or should I stop?"

"Yes, more. Please don't stop."

"As you wish." He drew my nipple between his lips again. His rough tyger tongue scratched against the tender skin, but it didn't hurt. The friction, combined with the heat and slickness of his mouth felt glorious. I brought my hands to his head and tangled my fingers in his black hair.

He paused and withdrew, blowing air across my nipple until it peaked to impossible heights in the cool breeze. "What do you want now, Mira? Tell me where to touch you."

If this is how he wanted to do it, I'd play along, so long as it ended with us both completely spent. "Rub me, put your fingers inside me."

He rested on one elbow, sliding his hand from my breast, down my abdomen, summoning gooseflesh along my skin. At the inmost corner of my thigh, he stroked slowly, gently, playing on the edge at my wet, impatient lips. I bucked my hips. His thumb answered the call, hitting exactly where I wanted it. Round and round he circled, rubbing that bundle of nerves until it swelled in response. Every movement brought stronger pulses of energy.

Close-my-eyes-and-buck-my-hips wonderful.

Then he slipped a finger inside. I gasped. Every muscle in my legs tensed.

He stroked slowly in then out, circled my lips, making me wetter. Then he dove in again. "Is this what you wanted?"

"Yes! More." Excitement built so much I wanted to see what he was doing to me. I raised myself up on my elbows so I could watch. "Another finger."

A lock of his messy black hair framed one of his green tyger eyes. Goddess, he was beautiful.

He did as I asked, plunging two fingers inside me. "Want more?"

I nodded, breathing hard, unable to look away from his muscled chest and arms, that strong sure hand, wet fingers extended, disappearing then reappearing. I clenched down on him as he sped the rhythm. Faster, deeper, stimulating all the right places. Pleasure streaked up my spine. Spun my head. Set my heart on fire.

He smiled, watching my reaction as he pinched my nipple with his free hand.

Crying out, I bucked my hips into his pumping hand, arched my back, and let the orgasm spill from my clenching sheath and radiate into all my limbs. The bloodgems burned slightly, but I didn't care. They could burst open and kill me now.

At least I'd die happy.

* * * *

~ Lysander ~

I pulled my slick fingers from Mira and licked them, savoring her unique taste. "Mmm, just as good as I'd always imagined."

Her eyes grew wide. Sweat dampened her forehead.

Concern overshadowed my desire for a moment. What if she had a setback or another seizure? I couldn't live with myself if I'd hurt her.

"Are you all right?" I slid up to lay beside her and kissed her tenderly.

She sighed and smiled. "I'm more than all right. I'm in heaven."

Thank the gods. Though my groin still ached for her, I took her hand in mine and threaded my fingers through hers. I couldn't help feeling guilty. Mavelle had been dead for only a week. Grief still sat like a lead ball in the pit of my stomach. And here I was, already fucking another woman.

Then again, Mira wasn't just another woman. She'd been my best friend, the girl I'd always wanted to share my life and bed with. And I would have, had things worked out differently. This was more than fucking. A lot more. Closure to a long separation and years of resentment. Like forgiveness.

Bringing her hand to my lips, I kissed it softly and searched her big brown eyes. "I'm sorry for all the things I said to you. I realize now that you left to protect me. All that matters now is keeping *you* safe."

"I've never felt safer," she said while stroking my cheek. "I should have said it a long time ago, and maybe it's not the right time now, but I love you, Lysander. I always have and always will."

Her words drew tears from my eyes. So much for being a god in the bedroom. I couldn't bring myself to return the sentiment out loud just yet, but I could show her. My erection heeded the call, and I moved to settle over her. I'd have been content to keep admiring her face and eyes for a while—amazing eyes that belonged to an even more amazing woman. But Mira opened her legs wide and wrapped them around my hips.

She pulled me in for a kiss, then whispered, "I want you inside me, Tyger."

"Are you sure?"

Mira nodded. "I trust you."

"But I don't know if I can trust myself." With Mira's taste and smell threatening to drive me mad, if her influence didn't hold, I could end up tearing her apart in blind desire. I'd never shifted even partly for Mavelle—she never knew that I was anything more than a celebrated assassin. And making love to her in total human form felt safe, easy. Mira knew everything. She accepted me for what I was, but that might not be enough to keep her in one piece.

"It's all right," she said, "trust me."

She lifted her hips, bucking them against my very ready cock.

Point taken. I arched my back and slid past the wet, gentle resistance of her lips. She closed her eyes and smiled. The head of my cock pulsed, needing to fully submerge itself into her. But I wanted to make sure she wasn't in pain.

She kissed me, flicking her tongue against mine, then pulled back and whispered. "What are you waiting for, Tyger?"

That's all it took. I slid inside her. Her head fell back, her eyes closed, and she let out a loud sigh. She bucked again. I withdrew slowly to the edge of her slit then slipped back in, a little harder, a little deeper.

She felt so good on my cock. Tight and wet. Perfect.

"Don't stop, please don't stop." Her nails scratched a light trail down my back.

"Mira." I growled her name and gripped her butt with one hand.

Slowly, I pulled out and drove in again.

She stiffened when I lowered my nose to her neck, inhaling her scent. I licked her ear with my rough tongue. She giggled.

Enough teasing. I plunged in deep, groaning as her sheath clenched and pulsed around me. I sped the rhythm. Her breath quickened. She dug her nails into my back. Such painful pleasure. My hips slammed into hers, faster with every thrust. Mira let go of me and fisted the sheets again.

Eyes squeezed tight, she arched her back spread her legs wide. "Goddess, yes!"

Her core squeezed down on me, growing tighter the harder I pumped. Pressure built until I couldn't hold it in any longer.

I started to pull out, but she grabbed my buttocks.

"Don't you dare," she said.

Oh hell yeah. If she wasn't worried about it, then neither would I. The prospect of having a child with Mira fed my desire even more.

Every muscle in my groin contracted. Head thrown back, I let out a roar that shook the house. My cock exploded inside her, spilling my seed as hard and fast as it could until it was spent. The Tyger subsided completely as well, leaving only me, sliding in and out of her until she relaxed and exhaled with a sigh.

I collapsed beside her onto the bed, pulling her onto my chest. She rested her head under my chin, catching her breath. "I never thought it could be so…wonderful."

"Well, I do aim to please."

She chuckled, rubbing her hand across my chest. "If I had known this is what I'd be missing, I might have never left."

"You certainly made it memorable, calling out the Tyger. Weren't you afraid?"

"A little, yes, but I don't have a lot of time left anyway."

Not expecting to be reminded of her impending death, I went still.

"Actually, you know what I feared most?" she asked.

"No, what?"

Mira propped herself up on one elbow, thick brown hair falling across her bare shoulders and onto my chest. Gorgeous. "I was afraid your penis would be covered with barbs, like a real cat."

"What if it had been?"

"Then I'd have called upon Lysander's magnificent cock. It's a win either way."

That made me laugh. I wrapped her up in my arms and kissed her deeply. "There's the Mira I fell in love with. Now, let me cook you something decent and then we'll get some sleep. We'll leave for Leogard at dawn."

She shrugged and flopped back down on the bed. "If you say so."

After a nice meal of seal steaks, potatoes, and bread, Mira and I curled up in the great room on my pallet by the hearth. In a few minutes, she was dozing peacefully. I stayed awake for a while, memorizing every line of her face, listening to her breath and heartbeat. No matter what it took, I had to save her. I could no longer imagine life without her. Without a doubt, I would have been perfectly happy with Mavelle. I loved her, still did, and she'd occupy a space in my heart that no one could fill. But Mira had owned the greater portion of my heart ever since I could remember. And I'd always been a one-woman man.

Spooning up against Mira as close as possible, I nuzzled up against her neck and whispered, "I love you."

Morning came too soon, the pink sunrise announced with a rooster's crow right outside the window. I reached over to shake Mira awake so we could hit the road, but all I found were blankets and furs.

"Mira?" Scrambling to my feet, I tried to stop panic rising. Had she gone and done something stupid without me? We had fallen asleep naked, but I didn't bother to cover up as I ran to the kitchen. Nothing. The washroom. Nothing. I took the stairs two at a time and burst into the guest room.

Mira stood there, facing me, with a dagger in each hand. She wore a clean acolyte robe, only she had altered it. The long flowing sleeves were slit to leave her forearms exposed. She'd cinched up a corset around it, drawing her waist in and accentuating her cleavage and hips. The skirt also had been slit, held together loosely from thigh to hip with leather

221

laces.

In an instant, my cock came to full attention. "Holy…shit."

Her head tilted to one side as her eyes settled on my erection. I took a step back. Maybe she had decided to capture me after all. Her lips curved up in a wicked smile. Color had returned to her cheeks, her eyes were no longer sunken in. Instead, they sparkled with excitement.

She spun both daggers around on her fingers. "I've given up tyger hunting. I'm going to catch a necromancer. Would you care to join me?"

How could I say no to that?

Chapter Twenty-Four

~ Mirabelle ~

Power surged through me—buzzing from head to toe in a current of little shivers. I could even hear it, like a quiet and tolerable ringing of my ears, except it came from everywhere, not just my head. How it had manifested, I didn't know. The energizing tea had never had that effect on any one that I knew of. Of course it could have just been the energetic second wind some people experience shortly before death.

Whatever it was, I didn't care. I felt good, really good, better than I had since before I left home a decade ago. Between the tea and overwhelming need to find Dad, not to mention Lysander's extraordinary lovemaking, I was ready to tackle anything.

"I'll…get dressed and pack some supplies." He started for the door, his body moving stiffly like he had to force his limbs to do his bidding.

"Wait," I said.

He spun around so fast, I almost laughed.

"We can't let you go out like that. Come on, let's get some relief."

Turning toward the bed, I leaned over the mattress and lifted my skirt over my hips. My undergarments were designed with a convenient opening to make relieving oneself in an acolyte robe easier. That left me wide open and ready, dripping wet in anticipation.

With a low growl, Lysander reached me in two strides, grabbed my waist with strong, trembling hands and plunged his cock in so deep, it almost hurt. He withdrew and dove deep again, fucking me hard and fast. His girth alone filled every inch. My sheath stretched to fit his frantic pace. The friction of his head slipping in and out between my lips drove

223

me to the breaking point. The orgasm began at my core as a small tremor and shook its way along my limbs into a full-body earthquake.

"Goddess, yes!" I never knew I could love him inside me so much.

His skin smacked against mine, his fingers dug into my hips, and his cock became stone stiff. He roared as he came, pumping his warm and wonderful seed into me until he finally slowed to a stop. He fell to the floor and let out a loud sigh. I stood up straight, still throbbing and exhilarated.

He was magnificent lying there on the bearskin rug, all flushed and spent. If we didn't have a bigger mission to complete, we probably wouldn't have seen the light of day for a week.

The future whispered its ugly truth as soon as I came down from the heights of ecstasy. Chances were I'd never get to make love to Lysander again. I silently thanked the goddess for finally being able to enjoy being with a man in such a heavenly way.

Lysander got to his feet, came over and wrapped me in his arms. "I really ought to drug you and take you to Leogard. This is madness."

"Maybe. But we've never lived the conventional life, have we?"

"No, we have not." He smiled, but it didn't reach his eyes. His sorrowful violet aura was back again too, overshadowing the others. Oh how I wanted to see his green, happy aura once more. And the passionate red, blooming like a brilliant rose around him as he made love to me.

In somber quiet, we dressed and left the house. He still thought we had time to complete our mission and get me back to Leogard. I couldn't tell him otherwise.

Instead of taking us to the main road that led out of Port Valor and to King Damien's castle, he brought us to Bearden's Fishhouse. The sign on the door, scribbled hastily with charcoal, read "CLOSED". With Darvis and Mavelle dead I didn't know if it would ever open again. Even the streets around us remained quiet. The few people we did see looked at us with varying expressions and auras—some accusing, some confused, but all of them frightened. Seeing Lysander and me together probably didn't help matters.

What bothered me most, however, wasn't people thinking badly of me. What bothered me was that a heartless evil had infected Port Valor. As muddy, smelly, and crude as this town and its people could be, it was still home to hardworking, loving families who would lend a hand to their neighbors without even being asked. It was home to Lysander, the man who I'd loved since before I knew what love was. And as hard as I had tried to forget it, to write this place off as a nasty excuse for a city, Port Valor was *my* home, too. I couldn't bear to abandon it again just to save my own skin. Chances were high that I could fail and die, but at least I would die trying to save my home and the innocent people within it.

"What are we doing here? Getting drinks for the road?" I asked.

"No, it's the easiest way to reach the castle unnoticed." He produced a lockpick from his belt pack and had the door open in two seconds. "Come on."

We hurried inside and shut the door behind us. With all the blinds shut and no living soul inside, the usually boisterous tavern was deathly quiet and too dark to see clearly. Make that too dark for *me* to see clearly. Lysander didn't hesitate, but disappeared into the dim interior. Unfortunately, that power surge hadn't given me super sight like his. In a few seconds, my eyes had adjusted enough for me to hone in on his aura and wind my way through the tables and chairs. Filtered sunlight slipped through the window slats and caught the dust we kicked up. Lysander was waiting for me by the door to the basement, grinning like the sly cat he was.

"Having trouble, Mira?" His smile disappeared, replaced with a concerned frown. "Are you all right? Perhaps you should stay here and let me scout ahead first."

I shook my head. "I may not have tyger eyes, but I'm seeing your aura just fine. It should be enough to guide me."

"Oh? And what does my aura say?" His voice was so soft and gentle, it reminded me of a purr. He stepped close and slipped his arms around my waist.

"It says you're missing our loved ones and that you're worried about me when you shouldn't be. It also says something else."

"What's that?"

"It's not for me to say." I put my head on his shoulder, hugging him tightly, feeling his strong heart beating against mine. "I'll let you tell me when you're ready. Until then, let's go hunting."

He pulled back, searching my eyes, which until recently I'd never allowed anyone to do unless I wanted to bend them. Lysander's were beautiful, green, flecked with brown. Love warmed their depths, and I could have stood there looking into them for hours. He leaned in and kissed me tenderly, reminding me of our last night on the dock ten years ago. Was this a goodbye-just-in-case kiss? I hoped not, but we weren't children anymore. We were realists.

He let me go and pointed to the door, whispering, "Keep watch when we're down there. I can see and smell pretty much everything, but I can't see auras like you can. Stay right behind me, hold my hand if you want."

"Of course I want." Smiling, I followed Lysander down the basement stairs. Or rather, I followed his aura because the dim light from the main floor only reached so far down.

We were afraid to light a torch or carry a lantern, fearing the light would give us away before anything else did. He could see perfectly in the dark anyway, and I could see well enough with the bright, shifting colors of his aura. And there were his eyes, occasionally glancing back to see if I was still there, now lit up into the brilliant green of a tyger's.

The basement, used for storing the tavern's enormous supply of libations, smelled of yeast, oak, soured fruit, and musty earth. We traversed a straight path over the uneven brick floor, down a narrow aisle, brushing past barrels of beer and ale. Lysander stopped at the rear of the room, bent down, and swept aside a heap of blankets and straw. Most likely used by Marlow and his twin wives. I shuddered. Death would be better than having been married to that large, smelly man.

Goddess rest his soul.

I knelt close so I could see a little better. Lysander had uncovered a wooden door in the floor like the ones we had found in the barbarian homes. Except this one had no apparent handle. The only thing adorning the bare wood was a round brass emblem with a pattern of little holes. I looked around us, thinking he might need a crowbar to pry it open, not that I could find one without fumbling around the basement.

He pulled off one of his big silver rings and held it upside down an inch above the emblem. To my surprise, the ring grew legs, sort of. Thin silver spikes had emerged from beneath the central gem, bent like joints in a spider's leg, and stuck their ends into the holes on the emblem. They and the emblem itself ticked and turned counter clockwise until something clanked like a lock being disengaged. The wood shuddered. One edge of the door lifted enough to allow Lysander to get his fingers under it. Hinges creaked as he opened it, and a gust of cold air wafted out. Lysander coughed and gagged.

Then I knew why. A horrid stench burned my nose. I held my sleeve over my face and backed away a few feet, coughing to clear the taste from my mouth and airways. The passage below didn't smell like mildew, earth, and stagnant water like one would expect from an underground tunnel. It smelled like decomposing flesh, old blood, and disease.

It smelled like death.

* * * *

~ Lysander ~

Once I could breathe without gagging, I climbed down the stairs and helped Mira down behind me. I'd been through this passage a thousand times, reporting to Harker back in the days before I knew he was a traitorous bastard. But this time, things were very different. This time, I was hunting, and not just any criminal but a foe that had managed to ruin my life within minutes. A foe that had turned an entire village into vampires and left them to starve and rot. A foe that had killed one woman I loved and had almost killed another.

With silent steps, I crept along, holding Mira's hand and keeping her behind me. Doubt weighed down my progress, like boulders tied to my feet. What were we doing, going into this nest of evil alone?

We should have gone to Leogard, gotten the bloodgems out of Mira's arm and rallied some paladins to come to our aid. I knew a few personally. Sir Robert, captain of the seventh unit and his friend Sir Francis had killed vampires and necromancers before. They had magic shielding to protect them. What did we have? I could turn into a kitty cat and had too damn sensitive of a nose. Mira could read auras and bend minds, the latter being useful only when she could look her target in the eyes, which was near-impossible when she couldn't see in the dark.

We'd come too far to turn back now, so we had to make the most of it.

So far to me, the passage didn't look any different. Same dripping wet stones, same straining timbers that shored up the narrow tunnel. They would hopefully last long enough to keep Port Valor from falling in on us.

"Do you see any auras?" I whispered.

"Not yet," she whispered back. She stopped and placed her hand on one of the walls. "But I *feel* them."

"How?"

"I don't know. Just a slight hum through my fingers and into my mind. Their thoughts are whispering to me. I can't make it out, but they're down here. Our friends, Dad…Ivy." She dropped her hand and turned her frightened face to mine. "She knows we're coming. I think she still has a connection to my conscious mind."

"Let's not keep her waiting then."

"She may be able to see and hear us, so don't tell me about anything before you do it."

"Fair enough."

This tunnel to King Damien's castle cut straight through town and up the hill to where the giant fortress sat on the cusp of Cavitel Valley. There were others as well, all of their entrances sealed like this one. Only the most trusted of the king's subjects, myself included, had the means to open them. They served not only as secret routes for his spies but also to give dignitaries from other provinces the means to meet with him in secret. It also provided a means of escape for the king and his court should the castle come under siege.

Perhaps they had served more nefarious purposes of which I hadn't been aware. I'd never distrusted Damien, nor his son Halcyon, nor had they given me reason to do so. They paid me well and genuinely seemed to care about Hezral, despite their reclusive lifestyles.

Then again, I had made the mistake of trusting Harker. What a fool I had been.

The putrid air became worse the farther we went. My stomach tried to crawl up my throat and expel everything in it. I stood still for a moment and swallowed it back into submission. Damn this nose of mine.

Mira, on the other hand, didn't seem bothered by the ever-decreasing air quality. As though she knew what I was thinking, she put a soft hand on my shoulder and smiled sympathetically. "I learned to get used to smells pretty quick working at the Temple. I could tell you stories that would be enough to make you lose your breakfast and then some."

Fist to my mouth to keep from heaving, I mumbled, "No thanks. I'll take your word for it. Any auras?"

"No, not yet. But the energy is stronger. Feels like a bee buzzing inside my head." She smiled and nudged my arm. "I should have packed some lichen cakes and ginger root. They're sooo delicious."

"Haha, very funny. I'll be fine."

She squeezed my hand, which prompted me to keep walking. "How far does this go?"

"A mile or so. It opens up to a cavern system from which most of Port Valor's fresh water is pumped."

We finally began our ascent to where the tunnel advanced up the hill with about a half mile to go.

"It's similar to the catacombs in Leogard," I told her, trying to sound as intelligent as possible. "But it's carved naturally by time and water instead of men. Once you reach the caves, you keep following a narrow path that traces the outer wall of the main cavern, high above an underground lake. It's said that the Great Sea Serpent seeks refuge there."

"Really? You mean we're drinking and bathing in a big fish's pee?"

I laughed. "Perhaps that's what gives Port Valor's beer such a distinctive flavor."

"I wouldn't know. I prefer wine."

Laughing again, I pulled her to me suddenly, causing her to yelp in surprise. "This is what I've missed most, Mira."

"What's that? Exploring smelly caves with me?"

"No. Just you and me, talking, joking, sharing a laugh together. You've always been my best friend."

"Don't get mushy on me now, Lysander." She rolled her eyes and shook her head, but then she planted a kiss on my lips. "But, yeah, I've missed that too. And so much more. Now let's go."

The sound of flowing water grew louder the higher we climbed. Whoever had dug this tunnel had the good mind to install some wide stones that served as stairs so we had less chance of slipping and rolling back down to where we started. Mira became winded a quarter mile from the top. I knew the climb had been difficult for her, having been weakened from the vampire mind-bending and resulting stupor.

Without a word, I scooped her up in my arms. "I should have made you stay behind."

"Since when have you been able to make me do anything?"

"Since never. I just had to be in love with a stubborn, beautiful girl, didn't I?"

She lay her head on my chest. "Are you?"

"Always have been. That's never changed." Guilt for admitting my feelings for Mira still constricted my chest into a tight, dense ball of emotion. But not as badly as before. Perhaps it was the polluted air getting to me, but I could almost imagine Mavelle cheering us on.

It's about time you two were together. Excuse my language, but go get that bitch and her minions and make her pay for what she's done.

Once we reached the top, the main cavern yawned wide before us. Stalactites of all sizes hung from the cave's ceiling high above. Water dripped from them like a steady rain. I set Mira on her feet.

"Is this where the lake is?" She squinted into the open space behind me, where the towering walls wept streams of fresh water into the deep lake far below.

"Yes, but be really careful. There's a hand rail, but not much of one. Hang on to me, all right?"

"You don't have to tell me twice," she said, holding my hand in a vise grip. "No visible auras in here yet, but the energy is getting stronger. Like a hummingbird darting around inside my head. There are people crying…I think one of them is Dad."

"Hopefully that means he's still alive, and it's not simply a ruse. I'm going to have a listen now, so be very still." Shifting my inner ears to tyger mode, I filtered past the sounds of rushing, dripping water and honed in on others. Voices, footsteps, chains rattling—all of it muffled and not very close. Had to be coming from the dungeons. A solid iron door marked its entrance at the far end of the narrow path.

"What do you hear?" Mira whispered.

"People, chains…close your eyes for a second."

She let out a sigh, but did as she was told.

I removed my headset, which was folded into a compact rectangle, from my belt pouch. Then I put it on, stuck the sound pieces in my ears and unfolded two round lenses from the band, flipping them down in front of my eyes. Next I pressed the clear gem on my ring. It glowed with a gentle light in a spectrum that only those of the feline persuasion like me could see. On my bracelet, I twisted the largest silver gear. Two clicks left, four right, six left. A matching clear gem popped up. I pulled the gem from the bracelet, and my six-legged clockwork spy came to life. It wiggled impatiently, wanting to explore.

Dropping to a squat, I adjusted the headset and placed the little guy on the ground. It ticked quietly as though waiting for instruction. I lowered my left hand, held my fingers down and wiggled them to imitate a crawling insect. My ring served as the transmitter, linking the headset to the tracker beetle. The little device scurried along the curving path to the dungeon door and disappeared easily under the crack. I stilled my fingers, waiting.

The clear lenses fogged into a messy static. It took a moment, but the image finally came into focus. I turned my hand left and right, which also turned the beetle and transmitted whatever it saw to me.

"Everything all right?" Mira whispered.

"Yes, and you?"

"I'm fine. Do I need to keep my eyes shut?"

"Yes, only for a few seconds more. Hold to the wall if you feel unsteady."

In the lenses came a vision of a wide, very long and dimly lit hall, with cells on each side. I didn't see anyone yet. But moans, whimpers, and cries echoed from everywhere, sending chills across my skin. Steadying my hand, I walked my fingers again, moving the tracker beetle a little further down the hall and along the edge of the wall until it reached the corner of the first cell on the right. Slowly, gently, I walked the beetle past the corner and turned my hand so I could have a look inside the cell.

Against one wall, a man was seated on the floor and chained, arms stretched out above him in shackles. His mouth hung open, emitting an almost-constant moan. Two figures stood over him, one clothed in a light blue robe like Mira's. I recognized the other one's boots and slender legs.

Harker.

"It's not working," he said. "Decomposition has barely slowed."

"This is a waste of time," a female answered in an ominous, airy tone. That had to be Ivy. "We have to find the lab."

"I need some fresh kills."

"We have no more young ones. Only the old are left, and I don't have the power to feed upon them yet."

"You will soon."

"I never imagined you would be so infatuated with corpses. But, I'm close enough to dead. Is that why you stay?"

"You know why I stay," he said.

He fisted her robe and tried to pull it up. She puffed a breath of air that resembled green smoke. Harker broke into a coughing fit.

"Not now, you fool."

I caught a glimpse of pale skin—not indigo. Not a dark elf. Angling the beetle's head up, blonde hair came into view. Moving the beetle around enough to see her face, I could tell it was Ivy, or had once been. She fit the description of the 'witch' who had taken Princess Loola's soul with those red-rimmed eyes and deathly white complexion.

I knew her from somewhere else too. The necromancer Syrilla, my first kill, had a high elf lover who disappeared into a portal before I moved in to attack. It was Ivy. I wondered if she knew it was Harker, and not me, who planned and ordered her lover's demise.

Damn, I wished I'd armed the tracker beetle with a poison dart when I designed it instead of deciding against it. If I could barge through the door, I could surprise and kill them both during their bickering. But the door was locked and heavily barred from the inside. I could probably kick in the door in full tyger form, but I couldn't do a sneak attack with that much racket. Not even the lock-picking talents of my beetle friend could help with the door barred shut.

Before I moved on with the tracker, I had a better look at the chained man, easing the beetle a few steps ahead. The man's bared teeth weren't bared at all. He had no lips, no skin, and no eyelids. Just muscle and sinew stretched and rotting over bones. But he wasn't dead. And he wasn't a stranger. He still had hair. It stuck up like a range of sharp, silver-streaked mountains all over his head.

"Oh dear gods," I whispered.

"What is it?" Mira whispered back.

"Darvis."

How was I supposed to tell Mira what I had just seen? Especially if her dad and the others had also been experimented on so cruelly.

"Lysander?" Her voice shook.

"Keep your eyes closed."

"I feel something."

"Hang on," I said, walking the tracker beetle back under the door and back to me. Then I took off the headset and put everything back as it was. "Open your eyes."

I looked up to see Mira staring wide-eyed toward the edge of the path. "Auras. Several of them. Climbing up the walls."

She had no more than spoken the words when an arm breached the edge, clawing at the rocky path. I drew my sword, backing up to guard Mira between the cliff edge and tunnel entrance. A head popped up next—a red-eyed, hissing female vampire. She scrambled to the top, ducking under the handrail. She crouched, teeth bared into a hungry grin. More followed all along the cliff edge.

They rushed me. I let the Tyger burst free, roared and swung my sword. "Mira, run!"

A vampire barreled into her from the tunnel's entrance and knocked her over the edge.

She screamed, disappearing into the dark depths.

"Mira!" I tried to dive over the edge, but they swarmed in and dragged me into the dungeon.

Chapter Twenty-Five

~ Mirabelle ~

Falling forever into darkness, I expected to hit water or rock or something soon, but empty space surrounded me. The only light came from Lysander's enraged aura and the gray sickly auras of the undead on the cliff above, growing fainter the farther I fell into the abyss. Maybe there was no lake down here, but a bottomless hole, a portal into the Great Void. What if I never really died, but existed in an eternity of nothingness? That frightened me more than death. I'd much rather smash my head on a rock and spill my brains, freeing my soul to fly to the heavens and be with the goddess. Because then at least I could still *be*.

That was my weakness, I realized. Control. Sure, I could control others, but I'd never felt in control over my own life. The only choice I had now was to accept my fate as a greasy smear on the rocks at the bottom or to accept my descent into nothing.

But I'd always been stubborn.

Water splashes grew louder. Cool mist wet my face. The lake—it had to be just below me. I flipped my body over like a cat ready to land on all fours, then straightened myself out, hands outstretched together overhead, chin down. A great shock of cold swallowed me as I cut through the dark surface of water and dove straight down.

Thank the goddess I knew how to swim. With fierce strokes, I turned back and finally breached the surface again, sucking in a giant breath. Above, where Lysander's and the vampires' auras had been, it was now completely dark. Light—I needed light.

Treading water, I searched in vain for the faintest glow, no matter what its source, no matter what horrors it might lead me to. Pitch-black darkness meant death, like the tiny baby who'd been sacrificed to the midnight sea. Like my baby who never drew a breath. Like the one who'd been turned into a helpless, starving vampire in the barbarian village. The babies I couldn't save.

I took a deep breath and swallowed down my regrets. Lysander and the others needed help. I wanted to cry out for him, but didn't want to draw attention unless I couldn't find a way to get to him. With a big kick, I started swimming. We were in a cave, and I'd fallen off a rock wall, so there should be a wall within reach before the cold sucked away my muscle control.

Finally, my hand brushed rock. I slapped around the hard, smooth surface, trying to find handholds, an opening, anything I could use to get me out of the water and avoid freezing to death. But I found nothing. Even the finger-wide cracks I tried to grapple weren't enough to cling to. Every time I tried to pull myself up, I slipped and fell back in with a frigid splash. I traversed around the wall, repeating the process until my knuckles were scraped raw. Finally, I stopped to catch my breath. I wasn't going to make it out going upward.

My teeth chattered. I'd soon lose consciousness. If I screamed, maybe the vampires would come drag me off to wherever they took Lysander. I could make a deal with them. Let him go in exchange for me. That's who she wanted, right? Ivy hadn't taken enough from me—she wanted it all.

But, I couldn't give up. Not yet.

Instead of looking up, I peered down into the water. Maybe I'd spot something that could help me? The Great Sea Serpent perhaps? Yeah, right. I could see nothing at first but darkness and more darkness. And then…a light. No, it couldn't be. My eyes were playing tricks on me. Nerve impulses damaged by cold and poison.

But it pulsated and moved. I could swear it. Maybe it was some sort of luminescent fish. Whatever it was, I had to swim for it. Without knowing the depth, though, I might not be able to hold my breath long enough.

The necklace! My frozen brain finally remembered the fish-shaped amulet King Sturgeos had given me. I'd never tested it, but I had made sure to put it on before I left. With numb fingers, I stuck the fish's tail in my mouth and breathed through it. It felt like I was just breathing through a water reed or something. But I'd breathed what felt like air in Ustamer while the mer-people swam in it. This device couldn't be any more unlikely, so I had to try it. The worst that could happen was getting a mouthful of water. I let myself sink beneath the surface and inhaled through my mouth. Lo and behold, I breathed in air, just as easily I had in Ustamer.

I didn't take time to ponder how it worked. I scanned the depths until I spotted the light again. It seemed to be getting closer, but still far away. Kicking hard as I could with nearly-numb legs, I swam down. Ten feet, twenty, thirty? The light grew brighter. The fish amulet worked perfectly, allowing me to breathe and not drown, though the pressure had intensified, pressing into my ears until they hurt. I could reach it. Just a little further.

But then my arms stopped working. And my legs—I couldn't feel them. Couldn't will them to propel me any farther. My mind drifted beyond reality, didn't register the cold, and didn't register anything much except that pretty light. Golden and pure, come to take me to the goddess. My lips lost their grip on the fish amulet. It floated out of my mouth and into the abyss.

Cold and darkness had won. I closed my eyes and succumbed.

* * * *

I woke to warmth. I remembered feeling warm once. How long ago was that? I remembered fires in Mom and Dad's hearth, summer days picnicking with Loralee in the Southern Plains, being wrapped up in Lysander's arms. My eyes opened to air, not water.

And light.

Still soaking wet, I lay on solid rock, while a mermaid hovered above me.

"Ladyfish?" I whispered.

She nodded, but put her finger to her lips and looked all around us but back to me. On her neck she wore an amulet similar to mine, with a warm golden glow. That must have been the light I followed.

"How did you find me?"

Pointing to her amulet, she said, "Neck lass. It sistur to dis one." She pointed to mine. "Leed to you."

Sister amulets? Is that what she meant? Had mine been meant for Loola?

"Where are we?" My body felt warmer by the second. A kelp blanket of sorts was wrapped around me. How it was heated, I had no idea, but it gradually thawed my muscles. I felt stronger by the second.

"Bad plass. King Dameen's cassul."

"Yes, it is a bad place." She must have come in through an underwater passage and brought me out that way.

"Lysanner wan saf my sistur and uthers. Less hap him."

"I want to help him. Do you know how to get to him?"

She nodded, then stood and held out her hand. "Too too oowie."

I unwrapped myself from the blanket, took her hand, and pulled myself up. "All right, let's go."

* * * *

~ Lysander ~

Two insanely strong vampires wrangled me onto a stone altar, then strapped me to it with three wide iron bands on hinges that came over me and locked into place on the other side. The dark, dank cell had sharp instruments and probes with jagged protrusions hanging from the walls. It didn't matter how much I struggled, even in tyger form. I couldn't break free, and if I did, their fangs would tear my throat out in an instant.

"Where did you hide the opening gem?" Ivy's airy voice rushed into this torture cell, or whatever it was, and brushed across my face in a sulfuric cloud.

I knew what she was talking about, even if I didn't know what it did, but the last people I'd seen with it were Mira's parents. They tried to tell me where they hid it once, but I didn't want to know, just in case a day like this came. Concentrating hard, I shifted back to human form and tried to grab at the fasteners, but the vampires tore through the skin on my forearms with their jagged nails and gnashed their teeth. It burned like hell.

Mira—I didn't care what happened to me, but could she still swim? What if she'd hit the rocks? I had to get to her. I thrashed around until the straps bruised me to the bone.

Ivy glided in and leered at me, inches from my face. "What's the matter, Tyger? Cat got your tongue?"

Had she been anything but a heartless monster with incredibly bloodshot eyes, I might have found her attractive. She was tall, very tall, with long platinum blonde hair and pointed ears. A high elf. Her eyes, the part that wasn't rimmed with red, were a surprising shade of pale blue. She had long lashes that curled seductively upward to perfectly sculpted eyebrows. Rounding out her features was a petite nose and flawless skin, and you'd never know she was anything but an impeccable specimen of the goddess Innessa's creation.

Except for those eyes.

"Who are you?" I already knew, but would she admit being the middle reject daughter of the great High Priestess of Leogard?

"I am called many things—White Witch, Soul Devourer…Death."

"How about Ivy Munroviel?"

Her eyelids fluttered as though that name were as foul as the sulfuric breath she exhaled. "She is no more. Tell me where to find the opening gem, and I'll let you and your lover go."

In the corner of the room, Harker lingered in the shadows. He shuffled and grunted, probably pissed about the deal she was trying to strike with me. I cut a wicked glare at him. He shrank back against the wall. Good. He *should* be scared of me. If I got the slightest chance, he would pray for a quick death.

Turning my attention back to Ivy, I asked, "Why do you want into your sister's abandoned laboratory so badly?"

"Why indeed? Could it be that I loved my exiled sister and long to continue her research?"

"Right, and I'm allergic to cats."

She laughed daintily, like she was truly amused and still a lady. "My plans are my own."

"You want to take over Hezral, to dethrone Damien and Halcyon."

She laughed again and shook her head. "Prince Halcyon can't see beyond what's between his legs. Your beloved King Damien is clueless, perhaps even more so than King Leopold. Damien believes you have the kingdom under control. Such blind trust. But no, who would want this cold, treeless void you call home? I am bound for a much warmer destination in the middle of the Southern Sea."

"Ironhaven—why am I not surprised?"

"You really are smart for a cat."

"What is Emperor Sarvonn promising you in exchange for all this? Why do you need Mira?"

"So curious, too. Harker, your transformation spell worked very well on this one."

"Too well," Harker muttered.

"Tell me where the opening gem is, and I'll let you go."

I kept struggling with my restraints with slow, silent pressure, biting back a rising panic so she wouldn't sense my fear. "If I knew where it was, I'd tell you. But I don't. If you let me go, I might be persuaded to hunt it down for you. I'm good at that."

"Oh I know what a good hunter you are." She touched my shoulder, sending a queasy jolt to my insides. My stomach clenched. Rage spiked. "Do you remember your first kill?"

I couldn't look into her eyes without retching, so I focused on her touch. With only a feather-light pressure, she skimmed her finger down my bicep. Behind that delicate contact, she blazed a trail of pinprick pain and a stripe of tyger fur that prickled from my skin. My teeth shifted, and I squeezed my eyes shut with a quiet growl.

"Yes," I answered.

"Good, and do you remember her name?"

"Syrilla."

"Excellent. Yes, your first kill was a beautiful indigo-skinned dark elf by the name of Syrilla. My friend, my mentor, and my lover. She taught me many things, but our work wasn't done. I still had much to learn, but alas, you came along and killed her."

"Good riddance." My voice rumbled. The further her touch traveled, the more the Tyger emerged. Rage threw my senses into a frenzy and clouded my reasoning, but I clung to the truth as I knew it for as long as possible. "But, I only followed orders. Harker wanted her gone so he could have you to himself."

The red in her eyes intensified; she threw a malevolent scowl on Harker.

"He's lying," Harker said, but his voice trembled like a scared little boy. "That little traitor turned against me."

When her trail of transformative touch reached my hand, all five of her fingers traced over mine, coaxing out fur, paw, and claws. *Shit*—she knew what she was doing, how uncontrollable I could be when completely consumed with the Tyger. I had to stall her, turn her against Harker. Unless Mira could miraculously appear and sink her daggers into the bitch's back, that's all I could do.

"Oh come on," I growled, "you don't believe that, do you? Harker lusted after you from the first moment he saw you with Syrilla. He doesn't like to share."

"Is that so?" Her body levitated off the floor in a sickly, sulfuric cloud. She floated above me, hair and robes billowing against whatever dark force held her aloft. "Tell me, Harker, how did it feel to bed Syrilla and me together?"

"Exquisite."

She reached down with one finger and traced a path from my temple to my jaw, bringing the Tyger to life on my face. "And how did it feel to see her alone with me?"

"Terrible."

"Is that why you brought the Tyger with you that day? To make her pay for bedding me without you?"

"Yes."

"If there is but one thing I have learned in all these years, it's that life is not fair. If we want something and do not act upon it, then it is our loss. Harker acted upon it. Syrilla wasn't prepared. Though I would rather have her with me than this filthy barbarian, it was *her* failure that led to her death, not his."

Harker chuckled quietly, unbothered by her assessment of him.

I'd counted on her being devastated by the truth. Instead, she wrote it off as natural. It reminded me of those days I trained with Harker.

Do you feel sorry for a turnip when you eat it? No, so don't feel sorry for your prey.

Ivy levitated inches above me, parted her lips, and brought them to mine. My mouth opened of its own accord. Her tongue darted in, exploring deep. Instead of rot, her kiss tasted as sweet as warm honeyed mead. Intoxicating, yet loathsome, like a drunkard who hates his addiction but can't live without it.

Her hand slipped inside my trousers and gripped my cock. I willed myself to hate her touch, but my body betrayed me. She held my lips captive, sucking on my tongue and stroking my cock until I couldn't take it anymore. I came in her hand, hating myself with every pump.

Worse still—Harker watched the whole damn thing. The bastard lurched from the shadows, jerking himself off while Ivy finished me.

She withdrew her hand and with her mouth still on mine, she inhaled deeply, drawing the breath from my lungs. My eyes watered and cheeks sank in, while my head and chest pushed up against the restraints.

She pulled away, smiling in satisfaction like she'd had a delectable morsel of candy. Then she exhaled, returning what she'd taken into my lungs, along with something that jolted my senses into full tilt. It expanded my ribcage, arched my back, and stiffened every limb. It forced out the mindless beast I'd kept dormant since the night I killed her lover.

Soon I'd lose all ability to speak, to think, to reason. I could only summon one word, and it came out in a guttural, earth-shaking roar.

"Mira!"

Chapter Twenty-Six

~ Mirabelle ~

Lysander's roar jarred my head and sent goose pimples across my skin. Poor Ladyfish's gills flapped like mad. She trembled all over, and I knew she wouldn't stand a chance out of the water with no weapons. We traversed up a spiral passageway. Ladyfish had retrieved my amulet, so now both of them provided enough soft light for us to find our way along the damp, dank tunnel. It seemed to go on forever, but considering how far I'd fallen, if it went all the way to dungeon level, it would have to be one long damn walk.

"Do you know how far this goes?" I asked her.

"Dis drain to lak, keep dungun dry. Not far naw."

That made sense. It was a drainage pipe, but it sounded like we were headed in the right direction.

Energy hummed in my head. Someone was close. I stopped and tried to sound brave. "Ladyfish, can you go find help? Get the mermen, and tell them to bring their tridents."

Her third eyelids blinked a few times, as though she were hesitant to leave me, but she finally nodded. At least those tridents had a chance of skewering a vampire and slowing them down, with those poisoned anemone spikes on the end. And Ladyfish would remain safe and happy with Randell.

She ran back down the passage, soon out of sight behind the spiraling walls. Unless her kin were waiting in the canal above, close to the castle, they'd never make it here in time. I couldn't stand around and wait. Lysander needed me.

Oh goddess, what is she doing to him?

My legs wobbled. Now was not the time to be weak. After a brief rest, I continued up the passage and held to the outer wall for support. The clammy stones buzzed with the growing energies of the undead.

Two sickly gray auras rounded the bend and rushed me. I pretended to be oblivious to their presence, slapping the wall with each step like a blind woman might do.

When they were a couple yards from me, I drew both daggers, palmed their handles and threw them like spears. They sank into both auras. Vampiric screams echoed through the passage. I crouched against the rock wall while they collapsed into a whoosh of ash that peppered my face. Coughing, I crawled ahead, trying not to recoil from the sticky mess of vampire blood and ash, and found my daggers in the carnage.

Ivy's voice skipped through my mind. *Good job, little mortal.*

Leaning on the wall, I gritted my teeth and squeezed my eyes shut. "Get out of my head!"

I will soon enough. But first you have to find me.

"You can count on that, Ivy. I won't let you control me again."

Don't speak too soon. She shrieked her way from my consciousness, sending horrific pain through my head. I pressed my palms to my temples, but smiled through the agony. I'd pissed her off. Good.

Once the migraine of a lifetime had passed, I started forward again. Up ahead, the passage brightened just a little with dim torchlight. Energies from several lifeforms vibrated through the wall and into my fingers. Training my eyes on the light, I could make out a few vague auras. Some were undead, others weak, but alive. Was Lysander among them?

Fear gripped me, tried to keep me frozen in place, tempted me to turn and run.

No—I would not give in, not while blood still coursed through my veins. The passage came to a dead end with a solid wall. Above me, maybe five feet up, a crisscross pattern of light shone down. Probably the grate for this drainage tunnel. A ladder made of iron rungs embedded in the wall led up to it.

Quietly as possible, I held a dagger between my teeth for quick use if needed and started climbing.

243

At the top, I drew in a deep, sulfur-ridden breath. Energies surged through the ladder rungs. Shifting emotions charged the air. Whispers brushed my past ears. I recognized some of them. People from our village, crying out in silent pleas.

Why are we here? What have we done?

My wife, my beautiful wife…

Kill me, please…

Those poor people—their pain squeezed tears from my eyes. I shook my head to clear their thoughts and concentrate. Though I probably couldn't save them at all, becoming a blubbering mess certainly wouldn't help.

I waited for a second, watching for movement. No one stirred nearby that I could tell. Gently, I pushed up on the grate, testing its resistance and hoping it wasn't sealed. Otherwise, I'd be trapped. To my relief, it lifted, making a slight scraping noise against the stone. I had to be careful and slow, though I wanted to burst out and save the day. There could very well be vampires or something worse just out of sight, waiting to grab me.

My teeth clamped down tightly on the dagger. With both hands, I reached up and curled my fingers around the iron slats of the grate. It was all I could do to lift the weight, but it cleared the floor stones. Then inch by inch, I scooted it to the side. It made some noise, but not much more than the constant roar of airflow and the water far below.

Like a gopher emerging from its burrow in spring, I poked my head up to eye level, rotating it to scan my surroundings. The smell of human waste and rotting flesh almost overpowered me. I had to hold tight to the ladder and suck in air through my teeth and past my dagger. Vertical bars stood on one end, with an open door. Straw and body fluids littered the floor, and on one of the walls, a man was chained.

I eased myself up until I'd cleared the drain and crawled toward him. Then I froze. Bare eyeballs in rotting sockets stared back at me. A full jaw of teeth hung wide open, and a low, tortuous moan came from his throat. This poor man was still alive. Could he feel anything? Was he aware of his surroundings? Then I noticed his hair—stiff gray spikes sticking up all over his head.

Darvis.

The dagger fell from my mouth, but I caught it with one hand and held back a scream with another. What should I do? I'd put him out of his misery if I thought he had any blood left. But it could backfire and torture him more.

"I'm sorry," I whispered. "I'm so sorry."

He moaned, and his head drooped to one side. What if everyone was like this? What if Dad...Lysander...?

I kept my hand clamped over my mouth, unable to hold back the tears.

Breathe, breathe, keep it together.

The cell door was open. Good. That meant I could go out there and continue my search. There was no way to know if everyone was dead or alive unless I found out for myself. I dried my cheeks with my sleeve and got to my feet. Keeping my eyes averted from Mavelle's poor tortured father, I held my dagger point-down next to my leg, where I could throw it or jab it if needed.

I crept out the cell door. Horrendous odors corrupted the air, burned my throat and my eyes. Urine, feces, blood, vomit, unwashed bodies. I covered my nose and mouth with my sleeve to lessen the impact. Poor Lysander. I could only imagine how atrocious such smells were to him. How could Ivy or anyone choose to dwell in this place?

Low-burning candles in sconces provided enough light to reveal a long corridor of cells to my right. Sounds echoed along the passage— moans, bangs, weeping. Auras shifted inside each cell, all of them dense with sorrow and sickness. They whispered in my head like a roomful of clamoring people.

I squeezed my eyes shut, pressed my fingers to my temples, and gave a mental push outward. *Quiet! Let me think.*

The flurry of voices died down do a manageable dull roar.

To my left stood a barred iron door. Maybe the one that led to the cavern? That could be our way out. I ran to it and tried to lift the thick wooden bar, but it was solid and heavy. Putting both hands under it, I squatted down and pushed up with my legs. It didn't want to budge at first, but I grit my teeth and pushed hard.

The bar surrendered, lifting to one side on its hinge with a quiet *clunk*. I didn't open the door, figuring the noise of rusty hinges and metal scraping stone would draw a lot more attention. Sweat dripped down my forehead. My legs and arms trembled. The effort had been too much. I had to reserve some strength.

A familiar voice drifted down the passage in a loud whisper. "Mira? Mira, can you hear me?"

"Dad!"

I strode down the corridor, looking from one side to the other. Some cells were empty, but others held prisoners. I searched the gaunt faces approaching me from behind the bars. The townsfolk—people I'd known all my life—were naked and emaciated. They reached for me as I passed, brushing my sleeves. Their eyes held silent pleas for me to let them out or end their suffering. If only I had the time to mind-bend them into peaceful slumber. I fought back tears, searching each desperate face to find my father.

One of the cells held Nadene, the flower lady. She must have attended Lysander's wedding. Mavelle had worn a pretty white floral headband, probably constructed of Nadene's snowflowers. I stopped at her cell door and pulled gently, testing it, but of course it was locked. I didn't see keys hanging anywhere. Ivy or Harker or some other minion must have had them. I held to the bars. She wrapped cold, wrinkled hands around mine.

"Mirabelle," she whispered. "Bless you, child."

"Do you know where the keys are kept?"

She shook her head. "I've seen that horrid man with them, when he comes to drag someone out."

"What is he doing with them?" I was afraid to ask, but had to.

"I don't know. All the young ones are gone. Darvis down on the end…I think he's been tortured. Did you find him?"

She must have not known just how bad his condition was. Lying would be the gentler option for now. "I couldn't really tell, his cell was too dark. Did you see Lysander? Do you know where they took him?"

"No, but they dragged some hairy beast through here. It scratched and bit at them the whole way. Not long after that…" Her hooded eyes widened a bit. "It sounded like it roared your name."

She held my gaze with a steady, shrewd one. Had she figured it out? I didn't have time to lie or explain. Oh, goddess, what had they done to him?

"Your father's right down there." Nadene let go of my hands and pointed to my right as though she understood my urgency.

"Thank you." I started to walk away, but stopped and whispered, "I'll do everything I can to set you all free."

"I know you will, child. Bless you."

The corridor looked as though it curved around at the other end, so it was hard to estimate this dungeon's size. Did it spiral all the way up a castle tower? Or was it as complicated as Leogard's catacombs? That could make for an impossible situation.

And finally, a few cells past where the passage began to curve, there he was, reaching out to me through the bars of his cell.

"Mira, thank the gods you're alive," he whispered. "I thought they had killed you."

"Dad." I grabbed his cold, bony hand, spilling tears as I looked upon his haggard, starving frame. This wasn't my father—the robust, barrel-chested fisherman I'd known since the day I first drew breath. Had it not been for his voice and beard, I wouldn't have recognized him. "Oh, Dad, what have they done to you?"

"It doesn't matter. You have to get out of here while you can."

"Not until I get you and Lysander and the others out. Have you seen him?"

He shook his head.

Of course he hadn't seen Lysander—he'd seen the Tyger, but didn't realize they were one and the same.

He gripped my hand with both of his. "I'm sorry, Mira. I don't think he made it. But listen, there's a beast down the way. That witch and her vampires could be anywhere. Please get out of here."

"No. I swear by the goddess, I will get you all out of here or die trying."

Could I keep such a lofty promise? Probability wasn't on my side. Especially with the incredibly heavy, nauseating aura closing in on me.

A figure glided around the bend of the corridor on a yellow sulfuric cloud. Her aura was black, the shade of evil, tinged with green jealousy and red anger. She still bore the light blue robe of an acolyte, somehow crisp and clean among all this filth. Everything about her was the same, except her eyes. They were like two red orbs with a pale blue center.

"So touching," Ivy said. Her voice, once so snippy and crisp, now had a deep, airy quality like the first time I'd heard her in the Grove. "I once loved my father as well, though he loved his precious Loralee even more. Ironic, since she was not his child. But, blood really means nothing when it comes to loyalty, does it?"

Teeth chattering, I let go of Dad, pressed my back against his cell, and drew both daggers.

Dad cupped my shoulders and gave a comforting squeeze. He leaned close to my ear and whispered, "Courage, Mira. Don't be afraid. You have much more power than you realize."

From the time my abilities first manifested, Dad had drilled into me the importance of not using them, not telling anyone. Now he had given me the go ahead, pushing me forward instead of holding me back. The world went topsy-turvy for a second, but once it leveled out, a rush of true courage fueled me.

Thanks, Dad.

I spun a dagger around my fingers, and held them in an X like a deathly crossbones in front of me. "I didn't come all this way to attend your middle child pity party. Where is Lysander?"

Ivy smiled, but it didn't hide the anger in her eyes. "You always were the straightforward type, Mirabelle Hearton. Now put those away before someone gets hurt."

She casually waved her hand. A swift wind, followed by an agonizing burn spread over my hands. I cried out and dropped my daggers. They clattered to the floor stones at my feet. My skin was bright red and blistered like I'd stuck my hands in scalding hot water.

"You fucking witch!" Dad said, wrapping his arms around me the best he could through the bars. "Leave her alone!"

I cradled my hands close to my chest and trembled all over from the pain. It rivaled what I'd already felt from the bloodgems. Ivy clearly had an incredible amount of power. Killing her with daggers would be nearly impossible unless I caught her off guard. Not a chance.

Ivy didn't bat an eye. "Let me be straightforward with you, Mirabelle—give me what I want, and I will release him."

My jaw quivered so much, I had to fight to keep my voice steady and strong. "And the others?"

"Perhaps."

She spoke with no emotion save greed and malice. I'd never been on good terms with her, but her life in Leogard was surely a million times better than this.

"What happened to you, Ivy?" I asked. "What turned your heart into such a dark, ugly thing?"

She tilted her head to one side and smiled sweetly. "Am I really all that ugly, or am I simply the embodiment of mortal thoughts? Have you ever had a bad thought, Mira? Have you ever, just for the tiniest of moments, thought about what it would be like to sink your dagger into your mother's or father's back? Or at the temple, did you never wonder, for a heartbeat of time, what it would be like to place a pillow over a patient's head and hold it until they went still?"

I swallowed hard, never expecting this sort of psychological warfare. I'd come prepared to fight, to slash her throat, castrate Harker and reduce more vampires to ash. Not to question my deepest, darkest impulses.

She floated closer, glanced down at my abdomen, and applied a syrupy smile once more. "We all have those thoughts, and sometimes we act upon them. You acted upon it once, remember? The life that lived inside you—innocent, unknowing of its creation—you couldn't bear the thought of giving it life outside your womb. There is something very empowering in having that control, isn't there? Destruction to balance creation. Elimination of the old to make way for the new. But so few mortals have the courage to follow through with their suppressed longings. I have come to free the world from those chains."

Crazy. She'd gone completely drunken eel crazy. But even with all that power, she still didn't know everything, and she certainly didn't understand love.

Shame rippled through me with Dad right there to hear it, but I had to admit my secret. "You're wrong, Ivy. I didn't take that expulsion potion. I decided to keep my baby, but miscarried."

Dad squeezed my shoulder, offering me silent support.

I continued, "Yes, mortals have terrible thoughts at times, but most of us have a conscience. So forgive me if I don't buy into that noble philosophy of yours, but you will let these people go, and you will let Lysander go, or I will act upon my impulse to destroy you."

She grinned, but her lips quivered. "How precious, but let's strike a deal, shall we? I want the opening gem to Loralee's laboratory."

I'd gotten to her, admitting my secrets while exposing her ignorance. Subtle manipulation might have a better chance than a direct attack.

Though the pain in my hands made my eyes water, I shrugged innocently. "Sorry, I don't have it."

"If neither you nor Lysander Devlin possesses it, then I am certain you know where it is." She paused, then slid her gaze to Dad. "Or you entrusted it to someone close to you."

My mouth became a desert. I swallowed past the sand in my throat and shook my head. "No, you're wrong."

"So obvious. Well, it appears as though we have a bargaining chip." Ivy snapped her fingers. "Soren, Mischa."

Two wispy auras appeared beside her and materialized into pale-skinned vampires. They bared their fangs, dripping with blood. Who had they just fed upon? *Please not Lysander...*

"Tell me where the opening gem is, Mr. Hearton, and I will let your daughter go."

I shook my head and whispered, "No, Dad, don't."

He squeezed my shoulders again, then let go and exhaled. "It's buried in a grave with a bare tombstone near the Moon Grove."

I knew which one he was talking about—I'd hidden behind it to watch Lysander and Mavelle's wedding. And now the gem would be in the hands of Loralee's worst enemy. I closed my eyes and sank back against the cell bars. All Loralee worked for and entrusted to me would be ransacked, maybe to be used in ungodly ways. I'd failed her again. There was but one strand of hope I held on to with silent desperation. They'd have to find her laboratory first. She had hidden it well. No one knew where it was except for me and Loralee. And I'd die before I ever gave up its location.

"Search the graves," Ivy said.

"As you wish, Mistress." They dematerialized as quickly as they had appeared.

"If you are lying, I will not be merciful." She lifted a hand and waved it at Dad. He flew backwards like someone had punched him, hit the rear wall of the cell, and slid down into a crumpled heap on the floor.

I gripped the bars, wishing I could get to him, but he sat up. "I'm fine, Mira. Go, get out of here."

Ivy laughed. "Patience, dear Dad. While we wait for my assistants to return, I have one more favor to ask of you, Mirabelle."

"I want to see Lysander. Show me he is all right."

"In due course, love. But I must insist. I'm hungry."

"Then fix yourself a fucking sandwich. Take me to Lysander!"

"I don't think you understand." She darted straight at me like a hummingbird, but I stood my ground. It wasn't easy, however, not with her bloodshot eyes turning pure black, and her pale face crisscrossed with tributaries of dark veins.

She didn't look me straight in the eye, though. She knew better. Like I'd done with Lysander, she focused on my forehead or cheeks, anywhere but my eyes. Even with all that dark, deadly power, she still feared what I could do. Maybe Dad was right. All I had to do was figure out how to call upon all that untapped power. With scalded hands, bloodgems on the verge of melting me from the inside out, and a body so weak I could barely stand, a little power sure would be handy right now.

"I need souls to survive," Ivy said. "But I haven't the power to extract them from the old, like your father. All of the young we took have been consumed."

"How do you expect me to help you do this? And why in the goddess's name do you think I'd ever help you do such a thing?"

"Oh, darling, like your dear father said, you're so much more powerful than you realize. There is far more you can do besides putting someone to sleep or diagnosing an ulcer. With your power, I can extract any soul from any creature and do with it as I please."

"I think you're mistaken. You see, even if I could do that, there's no way in hell I'd help you do such a thing." Lowering my blistered hands to my side, I stood up straight and tried to intercept her line of vision.

She easily averted her eyes so I couldn't get a lock on them. "I thought you might resist. Perhaps I can persuade you."

Two vampires emerged from the darkness of a cell farther down

251

where the wall began to curve. They walked backwards and pulled a large rectangular object with them on a dolly like sailors might use to haul crates around on a dock. The object looked like a big stone table, turned up vertically on one of the short ends. The vampires smiled, revealing sharp yellowed fangs. They circled around, rotating the table along with them. Someone was strapped to the other side. A low growl rolled through the dungeon.

"Lysander?" I whispered.

Chapter Twenty-Seven

~ Mirabelle ~

Black fur with stripes a shade lighter covered him. Muscles bulged beneath the hair. His sharp claws were fully extended, fingers spread wide as he twisted and bucked against the metal restraints. Feline lips curled back over sharp tyger teeth. Green eyes with fully dilated pupils glared with pure rage. Unlike before, when Lysander's personality shared space with the beast, this time the beast claimed the entire territory.

I tried to lock eyes with him, tried to make a connection. But every time I started to feel the familiar buzz, his mind rebuffed me like someone smacking me in the forehead. Was the Tyger strong enough to keep me out, or was Lysander still in there somewhere, afraid to let me in?

"Lysander, can you hear me?"

"Oh he can hear you," Ivy said as she floated around behind me. Her cold fingers slid down the back of my neck, sending a shudder down my spine. "He also wants to kill you and everything that moves."

She lifted both hands. Her gray aura surrounded me, constricting like a snake. I tried to wiggle free, but nothing below my neck would obey. Worse still, within the paralyzing aura, a sensation like hundreds of fingers probed every inch of my skin, driving panic to the surface in a cold sweat. It found places I'd only wanted Lysander to touch, which wet my core with unintended desire.

Closing my eyes, I tried to ignore the pleasure and focus on the disgust. And on Lysander. "Don't do this to him. Please."

"We have come to an impasse, my darling." She floated a few inches off the floor, flying around me in a swift circle. Her lips brushed my earlobe. "I will let him go, and your father too if you will do as I ask. I'll be *very* good to you."

Her nails scratched lightly over the exposed skin above my corset, sending goose pimples across my chest and breasts. My sheath pulsed, on the verge of orgasm. Nausea churned my stomach, sent bile to the back of my throat. I had to swallow it down and breathe deeply to keep from vomiting and climaxing at the same time.

She picked up my arm with her icy fingers and trailed a wet path with her tongue across the symbols. The bloodgems flared, sending a streak of fire to my heart. I cried out from the stabbing pain, still unable to move.

"I can even remove my mother's curse. Shall we also make her suffer? You controlled her before, remember? You can do it again, and more. Together, we could rule Leogard, Hezral, perhaps all of Tallenmere. I was always ambitious."

"I'd rather die."

Lysander roared. He gnashed his teeth and fought against the restraints. Was he trying to defend me or eager to tear out my throat?

Ivy shook her head and sucked lightly on one of my fingers. "You are no good to me dead. I could reanimate you easily or turn you into a bloodthirsty vampire, but then that incredible power locked within your mind could be lost for good. I cannot risk that, but I cannot force you to help me without better motivation."

She kept me in her disgustingly arousing aura, then looked down the corridor. Dad's cell door flew open. The two vampires who had brought Lysander out bound Dad's hands behind him and pulled him from his cell.

"What are you doing?" I asked.

One of the vampires kicked Dad's legs from under him. He fell to the floor. His head thumped against the stone surface. He cried out and lay there, shivering.

"I am giving you a choice, my darling. You can still die if you wish. Or will you save your father instead?"

Disappearing into clouds of wisps, the vampires breezed behind

Lysander. One by one, the metal bands holding him down unfastened and swung aside. The last one let him slide to the floor, and there he crouched.

His tyger-green eyes locked upon my father. His low growl intensified into a snarling promise to kill.

Ivy released me from her paralyzing aura and floated well behind me. "You may want these." She waved a hand. My daggers levitated off the floor and flew straight at me, handle first. I caught them in my sweaty palms, hands shaking so bad I doubt I could aim properly if I needed to use them.

No, I couldn't use them. I *wouldn't*.

But, my father lay helpless between me and Lysander.

"Look at me! Lysander, look at me!" I shouted.

One ear flicked my way, but that was the only indication of his awareness to my presence. He stalked toward Dad on all fours. Only a few feet separated them. I didn't have time to negotiate.

Lysander sprang. I flipped a dagger, caught it by the tip of the blade, and threw. It spun ahead in a perfect arc, with the perfect aim my father had taught me.

It made a ripping sound when it tore the flesh between Lysander's ribs. The other one followed a half second later, hitting him in the thigh. He fell to the ground, just inches from Dad. I don't know if the silver had anything to do with it or if the blood gushing from his wounds did it, but the Tyger fled back into the man I loved.

Lysander lay naked on the floor. I tried to run to him, but Ivy wrapped her paralyzing aura around me again.

"No! Let me go to him." I screamed through my sobs, unable to bear the pain of watching him die in front of me.

Ivy's menacing order whispered into my ear. "Do as I ask, and maybe, just maybe I'll let you help him."

She walked into an empty cell, and whatever invisible force connected her to this cocooning aura pulled me along with her. Before we passed through the cell door, Lysander lifted his head from the floor.

His eyes met mine. "Save them, Mira. Find a way."

"Not without you! Please don't die!"

Ivy swept me inside the cell and through a door that slid open in the rear wall. I couldn't see him anymore. Everything we had gone through congealed into a dense ball of agony in my chest.

I let it all out in one eternal, throat-rending scream.

They sat me down on a stool inside the same room I'd seen while mind-bending the vampire. The nasty shelf with jars of ghastly things was there in one corner. Gauzy drapes hung from the bed canopy and walls. Landscapes in vivid colors and anatomically-correct sculptures lined the walls. Except for the one stone wall that housed iron shackles, whips, and glass rods with rounded knobs that were probably designed for various orifices, one might think it was a nicely furnished guest room in Leogard. I wished for a moment that I could go back there, that I would have known to slit Ivy's throat before she ever turned into a monster and made me do unthinkable things.

Before I exiled my best friend.

Before I killed Lysander.

There were no tears left to cry. My throat stung so badly I couldn't swallow. Two vampire minions stood guard by the door, licking their lips and teeth. Imagining, I guessed, about how different my blood might taste compared to a regular human. Would they take the hint if I inclined my head and exposed my neck? I wouldn't struggle. But I didn't have that option, not while there was still a chance to save Lysander and the others. I had a promise to keep.

Save them, Lysander said. *Find a way.*

Ivy emerged naked from a curtained-off area and stood in front of me. She wore a large oval-shaped amulet on a long chain with a huge clear glass globe in the center. Though her body at first glance appeared flawless, her skin was chalky pale, much lighter than a healthy high elf's complexion. Dark veins webbed beneath her skin. The chamber door opened, and another of my worst nightmares walked in.

The Shaman.

He wore that same swath of black makeup around his eyes that I'd seen in countless dreams. His hair was stiffened into a tall, spiked stripe. A vest of black feathers covered his chest.

But, the voice that emerged from his mouth was one that existed in memories I'd tried so hard to forget.

"There's my girl," Harker said. He knelt before me, focused on my breasts, and frowned. "Oh, why the tears? Aren't you happy to see your baby's daddy?"

I couldn't say a word. My body still remembered the pain of that night. Every part of me he had bruised and ravaged now ached, not from want, but from dread.

"So quiet." He reached out and squeezed my breast. I squeezed my eyes shut. "I'd love to make you scream again. Make another baby or two. We could let my mistress join in this time. What do you say?"

"Enough talk, Harker." Ivy said.

"As you wish," he growled. He stood and strode out, then came back in with someone in chains.

Nadene.

She had an iron collar about her neck. Her hands were shackled. She buckled under the weight of the restraints and fell to her knees in front of me. They probably weighed more than she did.

Harker settled on a chair at a nearby table, glaring at me.

Ivy stood behind me, planted her hands on my shoulders and whispered in my ear, "Let us test our theory, shall we? Ever since you bent my vampire's mind, we've had a connection, you and I. We should be able to use that to our advantage. Now, make a connection to this old woman."

"No," I whispered. "I can't."

"Yes you can," Ivy said. "Lysander's out there, bleeding to death. Don't you want to save him?"

Weariness deepened every wrinkle on Nadene's face. "I've lived a long life. Do what you must to save the others."

"I'm sorry." My voice sounded just as weary as she looked.

Save them, Mira. Find a way.

Somehow a spark of hope still remained. Blind faith, maybe, but I knew it depended on me following along for now. I locked eyes with Nadene and instantly connected. I'd never bent an elderly person's mind before. Her consciousness resisted me more than younger people, though I could see her thoughts and memories swimming around, blurry and distorted as though looking through a two-inch layer of ice on a lake.

With a sudden push, I broke through. A wave of energy rushed past me. Like cold black fingers, sticky and webbed like the mass I'd fought through in the vampire's mind. It shot past Nadene's consciousness, going deeper, spreading throughout her body like a multi-branched lightning bolt.

Then it retracted, drawing backwards, coated with Nadene's aura. Her soul. Ivy had used my mind to capture it. Her grip tightened on my shoulders, fingernails digging into my skin. Before she'd been drained completely, a brief memory of Princess Loola came to me.

Princess Loola, with no soul, but not quite dead. Because her soul-eater had been interrupted.

I had no idea if this would work or if Ivy would be able to hear the plan in my head, but I reached out with my mind's eye and captured the tail end of Nadene's aura. I pictured shears, cutting it off, letting the rest zip through me and into Ivy. The tiny bit I'd pruned off, I pushed gently back into Nadene's mind, hoping it would settle where it needed to keep her barely alive.

The connection shattered, and I blinked. Nadene fell to the floor, seemingly lifeless and limp. And hopefully not dead. I couldn't check for a pulse or any other signs of life without giving myself away.

Ivy came back around, stretching her arms high overhead, sighing with pleasure. The dark veins beneath her skin lightened and withdrew, as whatever dark force she employed retreated into her corrupted soul. The amulet she wore wasn't clear anymore. Instead a multicolored aura bounced around inside it like a fly trying to escape a window pane.

"It worked," Ivy said. "Can you imagine how well he will reward us for this?"

She walked over to Harker, leaned in and kissed him.

"What about a little reward for me?" he asked, squeezing her breasts in both hands.

"Patience," she said, pushing his arms down. "We will celebrate soon in Ironhaven."

He grinned at me, crinkling up his slit barbarian eyes beneath the black makeup. "Can we take the mind bender?"

"Perhaps, if she performs well."

What was she talking about? Had she captured Nadene's soul in that amulet? If so, what would she use it for? I thought she consumed souls instead of storing them. Though maybe that's why she wanted to store them—to make a stockpile of souls to devour when she grew hungry. But that didn't explain why "he" would reward them well for it. Something bigger loomed in the background of all this horror. Lysander, me, and how many others were being used as a means to some unknown end?

Lysander…how long had it been? He might have bled out already. Not knowing for sure was torture.

"Please," I begged, "I did as you asked. Let me go to Lysander."

"Not just yet. Let's try a few more, shall we?"

* * * *

~ Lysander ~

I rolled to my back, groaning and cold. Mira's dagger stuck from my thigh like a pin in a pincushion. Her other dagger lay nearby, having filleted my side open. Gritting my teeth, I pulled the dagger from my thigh. Bad idea. Blood gushed from the wound. I pressed my palm hard onto it, keeping enough pressure to slow the bleed. Then I rolled to my uninjured side and pushed myself up to a sitting position.

She'd aimed to wound, not kill, and though my side burned like hell, the leg wound worried me. I hated playing dead and knew her heart must be breaking in two, thinking she had killed me. But her daggers had broken the spell. Playing dead seemed the best course of action to take in hopes I'd be left alone long enough to get my wits back. It seemed to have worked. I'd lain there dead still, listening to one cell after the other opening, until it finally got quiet.

Now I had to get up and find her. But first, I needed a tourniquet.

Unsure where to find one, I pressed both palms to the wound to slow the bleed. Dizziness made the corridor spin. Beside me in his cell, poor Abbott lay bound and unmoving. Had I hurt him or worse? All I could remember was charging at him, hungry for flesh. Ivy had released the primal beast within me, the one I had always feared. The last few minutes—or was it hours?—were a mish-mash of nightmarish memories. The vampires had dragged him back in there after Ivy stole away with Mira. They hadn't returned yet, and hopefully wouldn't for a while.

Listening carefully, I finally heard him breathing. Thank the gods.

Now, where was everyone else? I'd counted a total of ten prisoners, counting Abbott and Darvis. That didn't include the younger ones that Ivy had already consumed.

Holding to the torture table they'd left standing there, I pulled myself to my feet. Blood spurted from my leg wound. I pressed my palm onto it as hard as I could and had to clench my teeth to keep from crying out. Any noise could alert the vampires that I wasn't dead yet. They might waft in here any second and finish me off, but I wasn't going to just sit here and wait for them.

One step at a time. Keep pressure on it. Good. Find something...

All these prisoners had been stripped naked, with no clothing or blankets at all in their cells. There was nothing in their cells now but buckets filled with human waste.

A few laborious steps later, and I stood outside poor Darvis's open cell, where he was still shackled against the wall, turned to a sticky, skinless monstrosity. His lidless eyes stared at me. His exposed teeth parted in a low, horrible moan. He couldn't speak, but I knew what he was trying to say.

My throat tightened with emotions I couldn't give into right now. Darvis was Mavelle's dad. We had gotten along so well, I felt like his son. I'd failed them both. Though the smell and sight of him threatened to make me sick, I limped inside his cell and leaned close to the hole in the side of his head that once was his ear.

"I'm so sorry," I whispered, hoping he could hear and understand me. "I failed you, but I'll do what I can to avenge both you and Mavelle. Rest in peace...Dad."

Letting go of my leg, I grabbed his head and whipped it around. His neck snapped. His head slumped forward as the rest of his writhing body relaxed against the wall. Quickly, I pressed my hand to my wound again. My eyes locked on the white sinews exposed on his leg where muscle met kneecap.

I needed a tourniquet.

"Forgive me," I whispered.

With as much concentration as I could muster, I shifted my arm to tyger form, extended my claws, and ripped the flesh from Darvis's thigh. The tendon had to be isolated, so I sliced away at the flesh layer by layer and pulled it away, revealing more of the white ligament.

Slippery blood and pus made the job difficult. I wished I had thought to bring one of Mira's daggers with me, where they'd been left lying in a pool of my blood. But I feared bleeding to death if I tried to go back now.

Once I'd cleaned muscle from tendons, I tied the long cord of one sinew above my wound and knotted it tightly. The blood flow slowed to a trickle. Luckily, it was a clean, narrow cut. It must have missed a major artery, or I'd probably have bled out already. A little packing should help staunch the flow completely and allow a clot to form.

Cobwebs hung in the corners of the low-ceilinged chamber. I limped around and gathered enough to make a nice wad of packing material, pressed it to the wound, and tied another sinew around it just tight enough to hold the webs in place. I should be able to take the tourniquet off soon so I wouldn't lose all circulation.

My stomach clenched with hunger. It messed with my head, tempted the tyger to come out and play. But I didn't want to risk being a mindless beast again. I had to eat. That would tamp down the impulses and help me heal faster.

Food, however, was nowhere to be had unless I went searching and then I'd probably run into trouble. I sniffed the air. Combined with the putrid stink of the dungeon and Darvis's outer tissues was the aroma of fresh blood and meat. I picked up the flesh I'd torn from him. Beneath the rot lay bright red muscle. It didn't smell diseased or poisoned, though it was still risky. I gagged, but choked back the bile. I had no choice. Eat my wife's father or let us all die?

Mira needed me, these people needed me. Choice made.

I ate.

Chapter Twenty-Eight

~ Mirabelle ~

Bodies lay in a neat row near the wall of the chamber. Each one, if I'd succeeded in cutting off Ivy's feed at the right time, should still have basic bodily functions at the bare minimum state. Neither Ivy nor Harker had noticed anything, and I couldn't tell from where I sat.

Ivy was too turned on with all the soul gathering to bother with checking them. Her amulet was nearly full, however, swirling with dense auras, a mish-mash of colors now combined into a weird shade of brown. How I would reverse this process, I had no idea. Lysander wanted me to save them, but how could I?

I clung to the hope that he was still alive somehow, that I hadn't hit any vital organs or blood vessels. Maybe he had found a scrap of bread or something and had time to heal.

It wouldn't do any good, but I pleaded with Ivy. "Please, let me go to Lysander and see if I can help him."

"He's dead. You're too late," Harker said as he entered the room. He dragged a body by a chain along on the floor behind him. But it wasn't Lysander. It was Dad. "I just checked him. He's cold as a winter stone."

He let go of Dad, who fell on the floor in front of me, hands still shackled. Harker walked over to Ivy and whispered in her ear. She nodded, glanced at me, and whispered something back to him. Harker strode from the room, and the two vampire guards followed behind him.

"Oh, you poor dear," Ivy said, with a sickeningly sympathetic frown. She slithered up to my chair and wrapped an arm around my shoulders. Her lips brushed my ear. "I suppose you have nothing much to live for now. We might as well harvest another soul. It's the last one I'll need."

"You're lying. Dad, tell me she's lying."

He lay there, staring at me. He'd been gagged with some kind of dark, round thing.

I shook my head. "No, I won't do this."

"In case you're wondering about the item in his mouth, it's a pressurized globe filled with terribly sharp shards of metal. If you take it out the wrong way, or if you hit it just right, it explodes immediately. Harker has become quite the master of Leogardian spells over the years and would have no trouble setting it off from a distance. Therefore, you can make this easy or difficult. Drain your father's soul painlessly, or he dies a horrible death, and you suffer horrendous shrapnel wounds before the bloodgems turn you to liquid."

Ivy was good at one thing—getting what she wanted by manipulating the love people had for each other. She had to be lying about Lysander. She had to be. Truth was not in her vocabulary.

I didn't want to ask, but I had to know. My voice broke, "Dad, is he dead? Is Lysander dead?"

He nodded, and I lost my mind.

* * * *

~ Lysander ~

"Here, kitty, kitty!" Harker called, running his staff along the bars of the cells. "Mirabelle couldn't keep her hands off me. She likes the rough stuff. Likes to be choked. I think I went a little too far this time, though. She whispered your name with her last breath. Thought you might want to know that."

My tyger lips stretched into a smile. He was trying so hard to get to me. It wasn't any wonder he had shacked up with a necromancer.

He'd been walking back and forth by me for a while, dragging people away. During the long pause before he came back for Abbott, I had gotten up and did what was needed to recover. I had almost laughed when he turned tail and ran back to Ivy. Guilt crawled through me—if

I'd had any strength before now, I'd have stopped the prisoner harvest. But something in my gut told me to trust Mira.

This, however, was the chance I'd been waiting for since they'd taken Mavelle from me.

It must have been driving him mad that he couldn't see me. One of the perks of being a tyger shifter was good camouflage. I hid against the wall of Abbott's cell, blending perfectly against the wet, stained stones.

Be more than still. Be the tree, be the rock, be the cold, dead object that hides you. You are the master of every muscle in your body. Will it to be unmoving until you say so.

The wound in my side had all but healed. The leg didn't need a tourniquet anymore and had clotted up nicely. Harker had the end of his shaft lit, sweeping it from side to side down the corridor. Even with the swath of black paint across his eyes, the fear shone through as his gaze darted about, looking for me.

Harker Stone had created a monster, and now he had to face his creation.

Two vampire minions followed him. The trio skulked down the corridor until they reached Darvis's cell. Harker went still. He couldn't have missed the broken neck, torn flesh and blood. He motioned the two vampires to head back the way they had come. Back toward me.

"Come out, come out, wherever you are!" He shone his staff all around the small space.

The vampires sniffed outside Abbotts cell, where I hid. My chest rumbled with a quick, low growl. Their heads snapped around in my direction. They ran in, clawing at the opposite wall. Then they turned toward my hiding place and bared their fangs. I smiled, because I knew what they saw. Two silver daggers floating by the wall.

Mira's daggers.

I wasn't quite as good as she was at throwing them, so I let them charge me. I dropped to a low lunge as they closed in. The blades ripped through their torsos. Entrails spilled from their bodies, turning to ash as they hit the floor. They shrieked a moment before the rest of their undead carcasses followed suit.

I dropped the daggers, held camouflage and stepped outside the cell.

Harker stood at the other end, eyes wide and frantic. The end of his staff crackled and popped like mad as he swept it around in a desperate attempt to find me. He backed slowly toward the door to the cavern.

Silently, slowly, I crept closer. Heel to toe, heel to toe. The only real challenge was relaxing enough to maintain camouflage with the changing surroundings—the bars on the cells, the changing shadows of the long, dark corridor. Every time he pointed the staff directly at me, I froze, not moving one whisker until he backed up again.

He reached the door, grappled around behind him and found the handle. With a grunt, he pulled the heavy thing open. "I know you're here, Lysander. Come on out. Let's talk like the good old days. Just you and me, yeah?"

In the same breath, he pointed the staff toward me and set it off. Red lightning streaked toward me, but I ducked. It hit one of the cells and crackled harmlessly down the bars.

He backed over the threshold and onto the narrow pathway in the cavern. "Did I tell you what happened when King Damien took me in? In those years between boy and young man?"

The son of a bitch hadn't told me a lot of things. Was he expecting me to pull up a chair? I crept closer.

"You know why King Damien is so reclusive? It's because he's a twisted fuck, that's why."

He was a good storyteller. I had to give him that. He took a couple more steps back. If he went much further he'd fall over the rail and into the lake. I couldn't let that happen. I'd made that mistake already.

Harker continued the story. "Damien and Prince Halcyon loved the young ones, especially boys. They'd get one from Port Valor now and then, have their fun, dry the kid's tears and send him home with enough money to keep him quiet. But then what luck! They found me, little orphan barbarian boy washed up on shore. No family to come looking for him. No questions asked. They took turns with me for years. Fought over me sometimes."

I stopped for a moment. Perhaps his tale was true. I'd trusted both king and prince and Harker and paid for it dearly. We all had our secrets, after all. If his story was true, I felt sorry for him. Such a past would surely be enough to drive one insane. He might have been a good man had he not lost his parents.

265

He barked a bitter laugh. "I cried about it at first. Boohoo, poor little me. But you know what? I started to like it. It was either that or go jump in the sea, right? I didn't want to die like that. So why not embrace my role?"

One more step backwards, and his back hit the rail. *Shit*. I had to do something soon.

"Harker Stone," he cried, "man whore to the king! Sounds important, doesn't it? I took all of it, asked for it, and needed more than they could offer. So they let me venture out into the woods. I think they hoped I'd get lost or eaten by a snowbear so they could find another less-demanding man whore. Well, what I found was Syrilla. And let me tell you, she taught me more than they ever could. You know what it's like being with a woman, right? I had no idea until then. But you know what? She taught me other things too. Things that made me a real asset to the king. I'd grown too big for them to be any fun in their beds by then, but I could cast spells and make prophesies. Some of them were even accurate. I became the Shaman. I had real power, yeah? Just one little prophesy made the king squirm. Someday a special child would be born that would lead to Damien's demise. I had to kill a few babies and cripples now and then for show until the right one came along. You were supposed to be that prophesy, Lysander. You and me, together, bringing down Hezral and beyond."

His story made sense. His voice had turned smoother, deeper, and saner than I'd ever heard him before. He spoke the truth. But he'd never taken advantage of me like that. Perhaps somewhere deep inside him, he had cared about me enough to not hurt me like he had been hurt. I could be grateful to him for such mercy. But I couldn't let empathy get in the way of what had to be done.

He turned and leaned over the railing, staff first, sparks orbiting the glowing tip. I could so easily pounce on him and push him into the lake. But I wouldn't make the same mistake twice.

Still in tyger form, I came within a yard of him and let go of my camouflage. "No wonder you're insane."

He swung the staff around. I caught it just below the business end. A streak of energy shot from it, hitting the cave wall. Rocks pelted the floor and bounced off my back.

"Ah, there you are." He smiled innocently, but his jaw trembled. "We can still make this work, yeah? Mirabelle's fine. I'll be a good boy and leave her to you. Let's pick up where we left off and start over."

"Tempting, but no. It's time to end this. Once and for all."

"Oh come on, we've had our differences, but who doesn't? This mistress of mine had me under her spell. Let's go take her down together, yeah? Like old times. It'll be fun. We can—"

I still held his staff by one end, but he jerked the other end down at an angle. It hit my leg wound.

Roaring in agony, I let go of the staff. My knee buckled, pain knifed up my thigh as warm blood started pouring from it again. He shuffled away and aimed the staff right at my head.

"Idiot. Still distracted too easily. Didn't you learn anything when you were with me?"

Down on one knee, I was a trainee again, submitting to a harsh and twisted trainer. Clenching my teeth, I breathed deeply to accommodate the pain. "Yes, you taught me a very important lesson. Only through pain does one become strong."

Head hung low, I bared my teeth. Harker's staff brightened. A crackling burst of energy erupted from it. I dove forward, straight into his legs. Sparks streaked along my back, singeing my fur.

The flimsy railing splintered. Harker toppled off the ledge, screaming. I held on to his ankles, claws dug in to give him an extra dose of misery. Before I fell past the point of no return, I let go of one of his legs and caught one of the railing posts. Splinters dug into my fingers, my claws slipped, but they finally held tight like a good set of grappling hooks.

Harker's weight nearly pulled my shoulder from its socket, but I didn't let go. His staff fell down into the darkness, clacking against the rock wall and throwing sparks along the way.

Though he dangled upside down, with only my claws keeping him from tumbling into the abyss, he laughed. "Seems history is repeating itself, huh Lysander? I don't think I'll survive this fall though. Might as well let me go and be done with it, yeah?"

"I would but...you taught me better than that." I held tight to his ankle, swung him back, then forward, once, twice, harder each time like a pendulum gaining momentum.

"What are you doing? Stop—let me go!"

"As you wish." On a strong upswing, I let go, flipping him from upside down to right-side up. I caught him again by the neck, plunging my claws in deep. He gurgled and kicked, eyes shining with terror. "I don't make the same mistake twice."

I squeezed down, crushing his windpipe, until my claws circled his cervical vertebrae. With a hard shake and a twist, his neck broke in my fist.

I flung him off me. He tumbled into the darkness. Light emerged from far below. Three mermen with glowing tridents breached the surface. Harker's body landed in their midst. They stabbed him with their tridents over and over like they were tenderizing meat. One grabbed his arms, the other two took his legs. They swished their tails, launched backwards in the water, and tore Harker Stone apart.

"Try to come back from that, you sick fuck." I waved to the mermen. They'd expect even more tit-tat from me for that favor, but first I had to get to Mira. I'd tit-tat for them forever if I could get her back.

I clawed myself back up to the ledge. Splinters stung my hands. The dagger wounds were bleeding and incredibly painful. My shoulder ached from supporting Harker's weight. On all fours, I took a few breaths and rubbed a hand over my tattoo.

Only through pain does one become strong.

Using every bit of that strength, I took off down the corridor, hoping I wasn't too late. My body wanted to drop and sleep for an eternity. But not until I killed the bitch who killed my wife.

* * * *

~ Mirabelle ~

I squeezed my eyes shut and shook my head.

"Open your eyes!" Ivy said. "Do this now or I'll kill your father right here. Is that what you want? Is it?"

She'd reverted from powerful necromancer to her old personality of whiny brat. The worst thing you can do when a toddler is having a tantrum is to give in. Harker and her vampire minions hadn't returned. I hoped that meant Lysander had come back to life and torn their heads off. But that was impossible. Dad had confirmed his death.

So, I said nothing, just sat there with my eyes closed tight, gripping the seat of my stool. Her bare skin brushed past me. I shuddered. She slapped my cheek on one side, then the other. My cheekbones took the brunt of it. I'd have some nice bruises, but still I kept quiet and kept my eyes shut. If Lysander was really dead, I didn't care what she did to me. But she needed me alive. She needed another soul for this amulet of hers. She wouldn't kill Dad yet, not while his tempting aura was there for the taking, but just beyond her reach.

"Damn you, Mira! You'll pay for this dearly, I assure you." Her angry breaths steamed my face. She took my forearm, squeezing it hard until the bloodgems scraped against my bones. I gritted my teeth. A burst of poison seared its way through my veins. Doubling over, I cried out. Dad whimpered and shifted around on the floor.

Oh goddess, I might die right in front of him.

"Open your eyes, Mira!" Ivy screamed. "I've sped up the breakdown of your bloodgems. You have minutes to live…unless you do as I ask."

She'd gotten desperate. If I died, she'd kill Dad, and that would be the end of it. We'd fail, and she'd go on to wreak more havoc.

But I did not open my eyes. My teeth chattered, sweat poured from my brow, down my chest and back. It felt like a blacksmith's forge had been lit inside my chest. She let out a furious shriek, grabbed my face, and pried my eyelids apart. She was right there in front of me.

Big mistake.

I stopped resisting and let my eyes pop wide open. I caught her gaze immediately and connected. She tried to back away, but slumped to her knees instead.

Her red-rimmed eyes couldn't have gotten any wider. Fear flashed in them as I dove inside her mind. I imagined myself covered in armor, impervious to the horrid images she tried to put in my path. There was Lysander, dead and bleeding on the ground. Mom reaching for me, with her neck torn to bloody shreds. Loralee crying, sitting alone on a deserted beach. Harker with an evil smile, holding my tiny, bloody baby in one hand and a baby boy with deformed legs in the other.

I pushed past it all, dove into the places her conscious mind couldn't reach. Soon, I found myself in a round chamber, its lobed walls filled with hooks. A string wound around each hook like a kite spool. Stepping closer, I realized they weren't strings, but strands of pure auras—the essences of each person Ivy had sapped souls from. That's how she got her power. More souls, more carnage. Each one thrummed as I went by it, resonating with the little pieces of each person I had helped her drain. Some of them I recognized by their specific resonance.

One of them was Mom.

Oh, baby girl, why are you here?

"Mom, I'm so sorry." Her aura strand thrummed with violet sadness. It was wound around the hook tightly. Ivy must have completely absorbed her soul that night as the vampire fed on her. I reached my fingers toward the strand, surprised to find it solid beneath a buzzing layer of energy.

What if...? I found the end of it and began to unwind it. I came to the end, finally freed it from the hook, but held on. It felt like being in the same room with Mom—her comforting, slightly coddling, loving presence. It was all I had left of her.

My sweet girl, you can let me go now. I'll be all right. I'll be free. One day we'll be together again, but not yet. Save the others, Mira. I know you can. I'm so proud of you.

It took every bit of resolve I had left, but I released her aura. "Goodbye, Mom. Until we meet again...I love you."

She drifted up and away, her aura disappearing from Ivy's consciousness. There were others like Mom, too, tightly wound around the hooks that bound them, victims who were dead in body, imprisoned in spirit. I released them all. A tremor rocked the chamber. The atmosphere became foggy. Ivy was weakening now that I'd taken away some of the energy she had stored.

I came to one last aura I knew very well.

Mira! Oh, Mira, is Lysander all right? Mavelle, my sweet friend. Even in death, she put Lysander first.

"Yes," I said finally. "Lysander is fine. He...loved you with all his heart."

I know, and I love him still. So very much. Please take care of him,

Mira. He has always loved you, even when he loved me.

"I will." I unwound her aura and let it go. "Goodbye, my friend. Until we meet again."

Goodbye, Mira. I will miss you, sister. Briefly, her aura wrapped around me in a spiritual hug. She drifted away, and I hoped with all my heart she would be at peace and we could reunite on the other side.

The only ones left were those Ivy had taken through me. They were loosely bound, maybe because I hadn't allowed her to consume them completely. They were also connected to the amulet she wore, so their auras were very faint. This would be risky. Would releasing them allow their souls to reenter their bodies? Or would they be completely sucked into the amulet? Or would they float away to the other side, never to return?

Voices murmured all around me, as though the little pieces of them I had kept were urging me on. I came to the hook where Nadene's aura was captured.

Don't be afraid, she said. *You've done your best, child. Whether we remain on Tallenmere for a while longer or pass on to the other side, we will be fine.*

Encouraged by her unyielding faith in me, I unwound her aura. Close to the end, it spun from the hook like thread being pulled quickly from a spool. Then she was gone.

The poison from the bloodgems jarred me. Horrendous pain threatened to pull me out before the job was done. It seeped into the walls of this mental chamber, weeping down in glowing red rivulets. I was running out of time.

Quickly, I released the others, five in total, and finally came to Princess Loola. King Sturgeos would have his daughter back. I unwound her and let her loose.

Her aura swam around me, warm with loving pink and happy yellow. *Tank oo, Meera.*

She swam up and away, and that was all the strength I had left. I pulled myself from Ivy's mind and broke our connection. She toppled to her side. Panting for breath, her skin had lost the dark webbing of veins, her eyes had returned to the lovely blue they once were. But she looked like someone starved. Her complexion was deathly pale, her cheeks sunken in so much her cheekbones protruded sharply from her face. Her skin stretched over her skeleton like it could barely hold in her bones.

But by the wall, where the all-but-dead townsfolk had lain, life had returned. Nadene sat up first. One after the other, they came out of stasis. Auras flickered then flared with a mixture of healthy greens and sickly reds and oranges. They would be fine with some rest, good food and water.

Ivy stared at them, then at me, and picked up her empty amulet with trembling fingers. She waved her hand toward the wall farthest from me. A spiral of black smoke appeared. It expanded into a portal. She crawled for it, dragging her wobbly limbs along the floor. Pitiful. What I wouldn't have given for my daggers right then to put her out of her misery.

The door burst open, and a tyger ran in.

"Lysander." His name hadn't left my lips when the symbols on my arm flashed a bright red warning.

The bloodgems released their poison.

I fell from the chair beside Dad. Poor Dad, still hogtied and gagged with a deadly device. Silent tears poured from his eyes. The man who had never been helpless a day in his life couldn't do anything now but watch his daughter die.

Nadene gasped. Another woman wept. But, I'd saved them. For once in my life, I did something right.

I forced a smile, even as pure agony stretched my fingers to their limits. Hezrali basilisk venom turned the bones and flesh of my left forearm into lava. Blisters popped all over my skin. My hand melted like a candle left in the hot sun.

"Mira!" Lysander leapt over Dad and landed at my side, turning to his human form. His face was smeared with blood, but more grief-stricken than I'd ever seen him.

I didn't want to leave him with so much sorrow. I wanted to see him smile again. "W-we have to s-stop meeting like this."

It didn't work. "Tell me what to do, Mira. Tell me what to do!"

"I saw her, Lysander. I saw Mavelle. She's at peace, and she loves you."

He blinked back tears, and his voice shook. "Thank you, Mira. I'm

272

happy to hear that, but I have to help you. She'd want me to help you. But, you're the healer, not me. Tell me what to do!"

"Kill Ivy."

She had almost reached the portal, held on to a chair and looked fearfully over her shoulder at us. Lysander's jaw tightened as his eyes shifted to tyger green. He moved as if he would pounce and tear her apart.

The poison worked its way up my arm, liquefying my elbow. I no longer felt the pain. Just heat, like a rush of hot air from an open oven door. Mom's bread. I could taste it. She used to get so excited when it rose just right.

Can you smell it, Mira? Come over here and smell it.

I can smell it from here, Mom. I'll be there soon.

Ivy had made it to her feet and stumbled into the portal. Lysander tore his gaze from her with a tortuous groan as though both sides of him were at war over his need for vengeance and his love for me.

He scanned the room quickly, then focused on the area near the townspeople. "My sword, there on the table."

The butcher grabbed it and tossed it to him.

The poison had spread past my elbow, leaving a trail of molten arm on the floor. I hoped it would reach my heart before my head. I didn't want to feel my face dissolving. I had really nice eyes.

Lysander hoisted the sword over his head. Half of my upper arm had joined the puddle of me on the floor.

"W-what are you doing?"

"Forgive me, Mira."

He brought it down in a silver streak.

I screamed.

Chapter Twenty-Nine

~ Lysander ~

The blade sliced straight through Mira's arm just below her shoulder and met the stone floor with a clang. I rolled her away from the sizzling remains of her flesh. She groaned while her eyes fluttered closed.

Goddess, if you exist like Mira believes you do, help her now.

A white cloth of some sort—a handkerchief, napkin, or something—lay nearby. Blood poured from her stump, but the flesh didn't disintegrate any further. Hopefully, I'd cut it off just in time. I wrapped the rag around it. Now for a tourniquet. I'd tied the sinews loosely around my wrist when my wounds had closed. But they weren't there. They must have fallen into the bottomless lake along with Harker.

Shit, oh shit, what now?

Something pink in Mira's hair caught my eye. The ribbon I'd given her for a wedding present. I pulled it out and tied it around her arm. The butcher and flower lady, followed by the others, came over to us on shaky legs.

I pulled Mira to my chest, uncertain how they would react. They might decide to kill us both because we weren't quite human.

But they didn't. They set to work, pouring water, pulling clean sheets out of cabinets, scrounging up herbs and salves among Ivy's morbid collection of arcane materials. The butcher poured absinthe over the end of a fire poker and heated it in the fire that blazed in the hearth.

We laid Mira on Ivy's bed. Every person she had brought back from death used their talents to return the favor. Soon, what was left of Mira's arm was cleaned, cauterized, covered in healing salves, and bandaged with a clean cloth. Nadene heated more water for me to wash off the blood, sweat, and all the other foul things from my own skin.

Once I was clean and in fresh clothes—whether they were Harker's or Prince Halcyon's I didn't care—I lay beside Mira and slept.

Sometime later I woke, but we weren't in the dungeon in Ivy's lair anymore. We were at home, on a pallet of furs in front of my fireplace. Had it all been a dream? I propped myself up on my elbow and saw Mira there, still asleep. A white bandage with some red seeping through still covered the stump on her arm. Not a dream, but how did we get here?

Smells from the kitchen tickled my nose. Bacon—oh, I'd kill for some bacon. And coffee. And toast. And eggs. My stomach growled.

Tannah came in with a tray, smiling brightly. "I saw you stirring and thought you might want some breakfast."

"You thought right," I whispered, not wanting to wake Mira. Her face was more relaxed and peaceful than it had been in a long time. "But how—?"

"I think you were both so exhausted, neither of you woke when they carried you out. What happened to that horrid elven witch?"

"She got away." Fury nudged the beast within, but it would have to remain caged for now. Until I found her. And I wouldn't let her escape again. I didn't make the same mistakes twice.

Tannah set the tray down on the floor beside me and shrugged. "Well at least you got out alive."

"The others? How are they?"

"Weak, but no worse for wear than they were in the harsh winter we had a few years back. But I didn't doubt you'd bring them back to us. You're our Tyger, our hero."

"I'm not the hero." I looked down at Mira, surprised to see her beautiful brown eyes staring back at me. "She is."

Mira looked around, her brow wrinkled in confusion. "Where are we?"

"We're home."

"Home." She let out a sleepy sigh and smiled. "There's no place I'd rather be."

275

Epilogue

Humiliated and starving, I kneel before the emperor. All the power that had once raged through me seems nothing more than a dream. He is my last hope for a future. But I must keep my eyes at his feet. I must show deference that I do not really feel. What I want is revenge, and now. But patience must rule my actions until I am restored.

"Ivy Munroviel," he begins.

That name grates at my senses. "Please do not call me by my given name."

"What shall I call you then?"

A few names appropriate only for imaginary deities come to mind. Some of them Harker and Halcyon had called me in the midst of sexual ecstasy.

Except for one.

I had loved a man once before I became a devourer of souls. He had been privy to my unorthodox studies and took pleasure in a woman who was not like the rest. He was a paladin. We were perfect opposites—holy and unholy, perfect and corrupted. But it wasn't meant to be. Because of my sister and Mirabelle, he was tried for treason and executed. I barely escaped, but I will never forget him.

His name was Rayne. He had given me a name I had not shared with anyone else.

"Well?" Emperor Sarvonn is growing impatient. "What shall I call you? If you are to be my wife, I need to call you something other than woman."

"Devora," I answer. "Devora Rayne."

"Very well. Devora it is. Do you have the soul stones?"

The empty amulet dangles from around my neck. "No…but I have one." I unwrap the chain that is woven through my hair and hand him the one filled amulet. Young souls roil and tumble in it—those I did not need the mind bender to help me capture.

Sarvonn takes it from me and nods. "One is better than none. Do you have the opening gem?"

"Yes, but we have yet to find my sister's lab." The vampires who unburied it from its hiding place in the graveyard by Port Valor's Moon Grove linger behind me. One of them hands me the gem, and I pass it on to the emperor.

Sarvonn holds up both the soul and opening gems, inspecting them with curious eyes. I focus on his feet again before he notices me studying him. He is mildly handsome for a human, but his power is evident, not only in his unnaturally long life but in the energy surrounding him. Hunger has weakened me to the point of longing. I suddenly crave his touch. I want to kiss him long and hard, to devour a portion of his soul and fulfill the ache within.

As though he has read my thoughts, he lifts my chin with a gentle hand so that I can stare up at him and meet his eyes. They are green in natural color, but ringed with red like mine. The color of blood, of passion and death.

"Your task was not an easy one," he says. "I am impressed that you accomplished what you did and that you came to me so willingly." He rakes his gaze over my naked body, making me shiver. "Not only are you beautiful, but to have an elven woman at my side will be another wound to Leopold's ego."

He does not love me, and I do not care. Here in Ironhaven, I will never go hungry. I will be a queen. "Yes, my lord."

"We will find the rest of what we need in due time. Until then, you must gather your strength. I have something for you," he says, holding his hand out to help me stand.

Once I am on my feet, he points to his bed. Two young dark elven women are there. They sit serenely on the edge of the bed, naked and relaxed. Willing sacrifices.

I smile at my future husband. "Care to join me?"

His servants undress him, and we take our time, feasting on pleasure and souls. The future is ours. All of Tallenmere will bow before us. Once we have the dragons.

THE END

About the Author

Mysti Parker is a wife, mom, author, and shameless chocoholic. She is the author of the Tallenmere standalone fantasy romance series, including the award-winning Hearts in Exile. Her first award-winning historical romance, A Time for Everything, was published in July 2015. Mysti's other romantic tales include The Roche Hotel romantic comedy series and contemporary novellas co-written with author MJ Post. Her short writings have appeared in the anthologies Hearts of Tomorrow, Christmas Lites, Christmas Lites II, Christmas Lites IV, The Darwin Murders, Tasteful Murders and EveryDayFiction.

Other writing pursuits include serving as a class mentor in Writers Village University's seven-week online course, F2K. She has also published two children's books (Quentin's Problem & Fuzzy Buzzy's Treasure) under the name Misty Baker.

When she's not writing fiction, Mysti works as a freelance editor and copywriter. She also reviews books for SQ Magazine, an online specfic publication. She resides in Buckner, KY with her husband, three children and too many pets.

The Tallenmere Series:
A Ranger's Tale
Serenya's Song
Hearts in Exile

Tallenmere Unleashed:
No Place Like Home
The Menagerie (coming 2016)

Connect with Mysti:
www.melange-books.com/authors/mystiparker
www.mystiparker.com
Twitter: @MystiParker
www.facebook.com/Mysti-Parker-103786449704221
mystiparker@yahoo.com